Sons of Avalon

Sons of Avalon
Merlin's Prophecy

Dee Marie

Conceptual Images Publishing

SONS OF AVALON: MERLIN'S PROPHECY

Published by Conceptual Images Publishing
An Imprint of Conceptual Images
PO Box 115
Minetto, NY, 13115
www.conceptualimagespub.com

To continue your journey, visit the *Sons of Avalon* website:
www.sonsofavalon.com

All efforts have been made to ensure the accuracy of Internet information and links, however, neither the publisher, nor the author may be held responsible for any inaccuracies or unforeseen URL changes.

Cover Design and Interior Illustrations © 2008 D. M. Haskell
Interior Design—Adobe® Creative Suite® 3 Design Premium

ISBN 978-0-6151-5052-9

Library of Congress Control Number: 2007909969

Printed in the United States of America

Dedicated To
Sir Stephen
My Husband and Soul Mate
For His Continued Support
And Unconditional Love

ACKNOWLEDGEMENTS

Unlike an award show, where music plays just moments into acknowledging all the people behind an artistic project, I am grateful for this opportunity to thank all the amazing people responsible for bringing this book to fruition. Over the years, the following *lords and ladies* have been relentless with their gentle mantra of, "So, is the book finished yet?"

From infancy my parents and maternal grandparents immersed me in the Arthurian myths. At birth I was brought home to live in Avalon, atop a queen's hill, nestled near the ocean. My mother, grandmother and aunt nurtured my artistic side and allowed my imagination to soar, while my father passed along his love of words and reading.

I am grateful to my daughter Colleen, for her unshakable belief in me. Without her never-ending, good-natured pestering and verbal prodding, the book would still be locked within my imagination.

Throughout the *Sons of Avalon*, I have weaved my sister Pamela's love of horses into the novel, as well as her understanding and giving heart. To my *other* sisters, Nancy, Elzanna, and Jackie...I value their sisterhood and their excitement at the novel's completion—and to my niece Cynthia, for her love of books, and letters of encouragement. I am also thankful to my mother-in-law, Mary, for her interest in the project and her continued love and acceptance.

A special "thank you," also goes out to my Uncle Donald Vann, for his artistic talent, and his love of Prince Valiant and Camelot, which rubbed-off on me, even at a young age.

I would be remiss without thanking my editors: P. Sanders, D. Parham, and C.G. Glasgow. Especially for their suggestions and opinions in regards to storyline and plot inconsistencies. I am also grateful to my dear friends, Paula, Valeri and Lillian, for reading through various revisions and championing my artistic efforts. These ladies have taught me the true meaning of comradery.

To Managing Editor, Nick Sorbin, and the staff of Renderosity, I am indebted to them for allowing me to be a vital part of their publications over the years; and especially to CEO and President of Bondware Inc., Tim Choate, for his love of all things Arthurian.

I am forever beholden to Dr. M. Humphrey for keeping my body and mind healthy throughout my years of writing the *Sons of Avalon...* and for his continued encouragement—and, to my other favorite Doctor, Professor Thomas Loe, for installing a true understanding of the written language and how to dissect a novel for its hidden meanings.

My favorite author, Martin Millar, for evoking a belief in the mystical properties of fairies, as well as his remarkable turn of a sentence and passion for life. He is a true friend and his novels have been a constant inspiration.

Unbeknownst to her, a single question from Mindy, changed the original storyline—when reading the first rough draft, she shot me an email with the query, "What about Vortigern and the dragons?"

To Loreena McKennitt for the sweet Celtic songs of inspiration. From her lyrics, and lyrical musings, Merlin's story not only endured, it flourished.

The Time and Again Books and Tea writing group; especially to fellow writers Debbie and Steve, for their relentless critiques and continued friendship, which prepared me to take criticism with an open mind and thick skin. Through the group, I came to understand that writing is a serious business, and that once written and released to the world, I cease to have control over my words.

Last, but most importantly, I wish to thank my husband, Stephen, for his unending patience and unconditional belief in my vision. He provided me the opportunity to not only chase my dreams, but to catch them. He has, and shall always remain, my knight in shining armor.

PROLOGUE

The earth rumbled as a lightning bolt flashed in the predawn sky splitting a giant oak at the meadow's edge. An eerie silence followed, broken by a hawk's cry.

Nestled within the womb of the shattered tree a baby squirmed, arms reaching upward. The hawk circled tilting her head from side to side and slowly descended. Cooing emerged from the tree trunk as the merlin gracefully perched upon the still smoldering bark. From her beak, she squeezed the juice of a large blackberry into the newborn's mouth. Eagerly the child drank his first meal.

***

"Enid, are you alright?" The old man inquired of his wife as he did his best to steady the big bay mare pulling the applecart. The pungent odor of smoldering bark overwhelmed the scent of ripe apples from the nearby orchard.

His wife, sprawled in a tangle of empty baskets in the back, grabbed the side of the wagon. Slowly she raised herself just enough to peer into the nearby field. Trying to catch her breath she whispered, "Arden, what was that?"

"How in Hades should I know?"

Curiosity overruled fear as the old man helped his wife from the cart. As they approached the fallen oak its multi-hued leaves rustled, beckoning them to enter. With caution they stepped and stooped through the fallen debris. Squawking, the hawk flapped her wings wildly as they approached the still smoldering tree stump. The old man waved his arms with equal passion dislodging the bird from its perch. Reluctantly, the hawk circled overhead, not wishing to leave her charge.

As the old woman walked closer, her husband extended his arm blocking her passage. As always, Enid ignored his warnings. With a gentle touch, she moved his arm aside and peered into the charred remains of the giant oak's trunk.

"Leave whatever is in there be!" the old man growled.

"Arden, it's a baby—a human baby!" Her mind filled with questions as she viewed the miracle nestled within the scorched amber and russet leaves. Covered in a thin veil of mucus and soot, the baby appeared unharmed by the trauma of his birth. His dark golden hawk-like eyes gazed at her, bright and curious. A sudden warm breeze tousled his thick feathered hair; its mixture of gold, copper, and browns glimmering in the sun's first rays. Overcome by a mother's instinct, with trembling hands Enid reached for the baby.

"Are you mad?" The absurdity of the situation fell heavy upon the old man and he began to pace. Fallen limbs and crushed leaves crackled as he tramped about.

"Arden, we can't leave this newborn here to die." Ignoring her husband's wrath, she continued to count the baby's fingers and toes. Satisfied that all digits were present, she gave Arden a reassuring smile.

"If you don't put him back, *he* will be the death of *us*! There is evil about this place. No human child is born from the womb of Mother Earth, with a lightning bolt as a father." Gazing into the heavens for guidance, anxiety seized his soul as he spied the circling hawk.

Soaring downward on graceful wings the hawk came near once more. This time the farmer and his wife froze in mesmerized disbelief as the merlin hovered close to the baby. With a slow confident motion, the infant reached his long fingers to touch the hawk's talon. The hawk gently rubbed her beak upon the young one's fingers then took flight, chasing the moon from the morning.

"You may keep the child." Even an old knight knew when to concede defeat. He added with caution, "As long as no one hears of how we came upon him, especially Lionel. All we need is for King Bors' favorite son to be privy to this day's events. That boy never knows when to keep his mouth shut." Shaking his head in frustration, he turned and stomped away. "Do what you will, that is what you always do anyway," he sighed. "Let's just get the boy home for a proper first feeding."

The old woman nodded. Wrapping the newborn in her shawl she made her way back to the cart. "What shall we call you?" The child's dark golden eyes searched the old woman's faded blue ones. A smile formed on his lips as his fingers grasped at a fallen lock of her gray hair. "But of course, *Merlin* it shall be."

Arden looked back at the two as a sudden gust of cold air made his skin crawl. He couldn't get out of there fast enough.

***

Not far from the destroyed tree, at the edge of the forest, golden-eyes peered, watching every movement the old couple made. Leaning against a tree, the brown hooded cape gave the petite figure an illusion of invisibility. Clutching her stomach, she slid down the tree's trunk into a pile of bloody leaves as the tears streamed. Closing her eyes tightly she sent a message skyward, "Watch over him!" Hearing the hawk's loud reassuring cry she knew the guardian would never be far from her child's side.

1

"Enid, come outside and sit with me awhile. With the Samhain celebration tonight our days of basking in the sun will be numbered." Five-year old Merlin leaned in the doorway, inhaling the aroma of soul cakes cooling on the table inside.

Before Enid could answer, two riders came thundering down the road, stopping just short of the house. As Merlin ran toward them, one of the young men jumped from his horse. He picked Merlin up with a brotherly embrace and twirled him around.

"Sir Lionel, you came!"

Putting Merlin down, Lionel laughed. "In the past four years have I ever missed your birthday?"

"No," Merlin smiled, "of course not."

Seated upon a giant warhorse, a second rider watched in silence. Merlin walked closer looking upward. "Good day Sir. I do not think we have met?" Merlin just barely reached the underbelly of the magnificent black stallion, and although barefoot, he showed no fear of the horse's massive hooves.

"Sir Lot, Prince of the Orkney Isles." The voice was soft and deep; a mature voice with an accent unique to the North Country. Lot leaned forward in his saddle as he weighed, measured, and evaluated the child. Outwardly the boy looked like any young Celt. Perhaps a bit smaller than most, with features far too beautiful to be wasted on a male.

Merlin held his ground assessing the prince. The tanned high cheekbones sported a fresh battle scar just below his left eye. His shiny, long, black hair was pulled back with a strap of leather.

A handsome young man, dressed totally in black. He made a regal yet ominous figure. "Sir, you are the first man I have ever seen with eyes as black as sea-coal. Is that the normal coloring from the Northlands?"

"No more than hawk-eyes are of Wales."

Merlin watched as Lot dismounted and stood next to Lionel. He pondered silently what an odd pair the two young men made. The redheaded, freckled-faced Lionel looked even younger than his fourteen years; short, lean, pubescent with an awkwardness that gave no hint to his royal parentage. In comparison, there was no mistaking Lot's lineage, although he appeared to be only a year older; Lot looked, spoke, and emanated royalty.

Nodding to Merlin, Lot gave Lionel a questioning stare.

"It is general knowledge among the townspeople, that although Merlin has the outward appearance of a child, he possesses the mind of the ancients." Lionel placed his hand near his mouth as he spoke, doing his best to conceal a grin. Although fully aware of Lot's cocksure ego, Lionel could not help but delight in the fact that for once, *he* had information that Lot was unaware of.

Lot was about to ask Lionel to expound on the meaning of his statement when Enid emerged from the house. He observed with caution as the old woman welcomed Lionel with a huge smile and open arms. Quickly, Lot took several steps back toward his horse as Enid hugged Lionel tightly, causing his companion's leathers to be covered with a dusting of flour from her apron.

"It is so good to see you. I hope you can stay awhile. Arden is out gathering the last of the apples from the orchard." Enid did her best to brush off Lionel's tunic, which only resulted in more flour being dispersed on his clothing.

Merlin took note of Lot's retreat; greatly amused that the young prince was doing his best to avoid both the flour and the affection.

"My dear Lady Enid, of course we can wait." Lionel kissed the old woman on the cheek. "We were just headed into the village for the celebration, but I wanted to give Merlin his birthday gift first. Oh, where are my manners? Lady Enid this is Sir Lot, one of King Vortigern's youngest and most honored knights."

Lot respectfully bowed his head in Enid's direction.

At the sight of Lot and the mention of the High King, Enid suddenly felt weak and grabbed Lionel's arm. Merlin rushed to his foster mother's side, and with Lionel's help, guided her into the house.

Smirking, Lot slowly removed his gloves of the finest black leather, lingering a moment in the doorway before following them in. He surveyed the room as he entered, similar to a raptor searching the ground for its prey.

"What is this? Having a celebration without me?" Arden's coarse, strong voice startled the group as he entered on soft footsteps.

Merlin watched with amusement as even the composed Sir Lot flinched.

"Arden!" Lionel smiled broadly. "You have arrived just in time..." Lionel caught Enid's gaze, as she shook her head, no, ever so slightly. Understanding that she did not wish for him to reveal her weakened state to her husband, Lionel quickly changed course, "...I was about to give Merlin his gift." Lionel slapped Merlin on the back and both ran outside.

Lot melted in the shadows of the room, leaning casually on the wall, arms folded.

"Enid, are you ok?"

The old woman smiled weakly causing the lines around her eyes to deepen. Reassuringly, she patted her husband's hand. "I am fine." She grabbed hold of his arm, bringing his ear next to her trembling, withered lips. "Lionel brought someone with him," she whispered, unaware that Lot was standing nearby. "He is Sir Lot, one of Vortigern's men."

Through wisps of Enid's graying hair, Arden slowly peered at Lot. As their eyes locked, the same sick, sinking feeling he had felt the day of Merlin's birth passed within him.

"Arden, look what Sir Lionel brought me." Merlin was more dragging than carrying a magnificent sword. Standing before his foster father, he could barely contain his excitement. With great effort, Merlin righted the sword and managed to drive the blade into the dirt floor—the bejeweled hilt blocking his vision.

Frowning, Arden turned his anger and frustration on Lionel. "What is a mere babe going to do with a sword that is bigger than him?"

Lionel laughed, ignoring Arden's sudden temper. After all these years he was accustomed to the old man's moodiness, to the point of being disappointed when it did not come. Arden, after all, had once been a great knight in the service of his father. From a very early age, everything that Lionel had learned about swordplay, about being a knight, about life, had come from Arden. Lionel remembered the day the old man left his father's castle in Brittany, and ventured across the sea to settle in the Welsh countryside. When Lionel had asked his father why Arden had turned his warhorse into a plow horse…the king wearily shook his head and said, 'Old knights often grow weary of battle and seek a more peaceful way of life.'

"Sir Arden…" Lionel began.

"Don't call me that." Arden gave a quick glance to Lot and back to Lionel.

Lionel smiled mischievously. "One day your Merlin will grow into his sword. When he does, I promise to be there to teach him everything about swordsmanship that you taught me."

"May the gods help us all when that day arrives." Arden plucked the sword from the dirt, feeling the weight and admiring the craftsmanship. He then leaned it casually near the door. After an uncomfortable pause, Arden looked to Lot and asked, "What brings you to our village?"

Before Lot could get a word in, Lionel spoke up, "We are headed to the celebration. To enjoy the bonfire, good ale, and if we are lucky, a lady's good company." Lionel winked in Lot's direction.

Showing no outward annoyance at Lionel's rude enthusiasm, Lot affirmed their plans with a single nod, but otherwise stood expressionless.

Arden grumbled under his breath, rolling his eyes at Lionel.

"May I have your permission to take Merlin with us? I promise to keep a close watch on him, and we can meet later by the bonfire…" he ruffled Merlin's hair, "…before the *real* fun of the evening begins."

Arden looked into Enid's frightened eyes, but he could not think of a logical reason to refuse Lionel's request. "Fine, leave the sword, take the boy, and swear to meet us before dusk at the bonfire."

Lionel picked Merlin up, tossed him over his shoulder and headed out the door. Lot bowed with reverence to the old couple. As he stood, once more Lot's eyes locked with Arden's. Abruptly, Lot turned and followed Lionel to the horses. Within moments they were no more than a dust cloud on the horizon.

"Oh, Arden, I wish you would not have let him go." Tears slowly followed the crevices of Enid's face.

"Have faith, Enid. The gods hold his fate tonight, and perhaps ours." Searching the heavens for Merlin's hawk, Arden viewed an empty sky.

2

"Sit still," Lionel pleaded. The chestnut mare tossed back her head as Lionel jerked on the reins, while attempting to secure a better hold around Merlin's waist. "Enid will have my hide if I accidentally drop you."

It was mid-day, and the celebration had already begun as they rode unnoticed into the village. The excitement in the air assaulted Merlin's senses. Restlessly, he sat wide-eyed in front of Lionel. The harvest had been exceptionally abundant over the past five years and the local farmers' carts overflowed with a rich variety of fruits and vegetables. Make-shift peddlers' booths, decorated with colorful ribbons, lined the dusty streets. From a nearby bakery the aroma of soul cakes whiffed through the open window, causing Merlin to inhale deeply and think of Enid.

Appearing out of nowhere, a masked man, dressed in bright costume, tugged at Merlin's toes, and as quickly, retreated into the crowd. Merlin laughed, recognizing the man as one of the mummers and travelers who flocked to the village; each with their own band of entertainers. Dancing through the streets, they beckoned all to come to their particular display of theatrics. They playfully fought in mock competition to see who could outdo the other; each group knowing that this would be the last celebration, the last chance for income, until the winter solstice.

Vessels of mead and ale magically appeared everywhere, as the sweet sounds of Celtic music intermixed with the rowdy bellows of those who had started their celebration early. In the center of the village a giant mound of dried cornstalks, wood, and leaves, stood ready to brighten the night sky—offering the twilight's portal to guide the dead from the Otherworld to dance among the living.

Above the village, on a grassy knoll; lambs, goats, and a giant bull were tethered ready for the evening's sacrifice. Near the livestock clustered a group of white-cloaked Druids, chanting softly under a giant oak tree. As their voices carried down the hillside the tiny hairs stood on the back of Merlin's neck. *Oh, yes*, he thought, *Samhain is indeed the best holiday of the year.*

Lionel noticed Merlin shivering. "Are you cold?"

"No, just excited."

Lot took the lead as they continued their ride to the far edge of town. Nearing the Dark Horse Inn, he turned in his saddle and gave Lionel a crooked smile. "I have some business to attend to. I'll take the horses from here. You and the boy can go back and start celebrating. I'll catch up with you later."

"Don't be too long, you'll miss all the fun," Lionel quipped with a mixture of concern and playfulness.

"It is the king's business, so it cannot wait. Go on. I'll be as quick as possible."

Merlin was puzzled by what business the High King could have in his tiny village, and was about to ask when Lionel swept him from the horse. Still perplexed and curious, Merlin reluctantly let Lionel drag him toward the food carts. Looking back Merlin noticed Lot talking to several young men, also dressed in black.

"Lionel, do you think we should see if we can help Sir Lot?" He tried to loosen his grip, which only made Lionel hold on tighter.

"No, let Lot do what he needs to. We are here to have fun. Now tell me, where do you want to go first?"

Back to the inn, Merlin thought, but he could see that was not an option. "Let's get something to eat and then find a bard. I am ready to listen to a good tale."

"A wonderful plan."

***

Lot and his group of men disappeared behind the inn, away from the revelry. Lot was the youngest of the six, yet the oldest was just seventeen, only two years his senior. Although they appeared to stand casually grouped, Lot had no doubt that they were all *his* men, loyal beyond reason, devoted to a fault *...his* men!

"Did you find what we came for?" The question was asked dispassionately, neither accusing nor inquisitive by the oldest member of the Young Royal Guard.

"Yes, Faustus, we move tonight."

As Lot unsheathed his sword, his men circled closer. In the dirt he mapped out the interior of Merlin's home. Silently, he marked areas; pointing his sword to each man as he assigned specific tasks. He then looked to each and held their stare; reassuring that they *knew* their duties.

"Remember, drink little or none. If we do not keep our heads tonight, we could possibly lose them by morning. Best to mingle in the crowd for now, but do not do it as a group. We do not want to draw any suspicion. Especially stay away from Lionel and the boy. We'll meet at the inn just before they light the bonfire." The group nodded in unison, and one by one vanished into the throngs of villagers.

***

Lot easily found Lionel; with his tousled, red hair, he was not hard to locate even in a crowd. Quietly, he stood beside him. "So, where is the boy? Did you misplace him already?"

Startled, Lionel laughed. He was about to playfully punch Lot in the shoulder, but stopped short when he remembered how Lot hated to be touched. "You found *us*, and just in time to hear a story from one of the greatest bards."

"I found *you*." Lot answered flatly, becoming quickly annoyed with Lionel's way of skirting questions. *Long live King Bors and his eldest son,* he thought.

Lionel gave Lot a smug smile, "No, you found us both."

As harp strings softly began to play, the villagers gathered together, hushing each other. A silence fell, broken only by the soft chanting of the Druids drifting down from the hillside. Then, a beautiful haunting young boy's voice rang out. He started with a ballad of the Roman invasion. Both women and men wept as Merlin sang of the death and destruction they brought with them. They cheered loudly as he sang of the Roman retreat and how the land once more belonged to its rightful owners.

"More! More!" the crowd urged Merlin on as he finished the last note.

Respectfully, Merlin handed the harp back to the old bard who sat at his side. "Thank you sir, for allowing me the pleasure of your time and the use of your instrument."

"I can see you have been practicing on the harp I gave you last year. Are you sure you do not wish to give the people one last song?"

"No. I am very sure. It is your turn now—no one can weave musical magic like you, and magic is what the crowds have come for today." Merlin bowed to the bard, then to the crowd, and made his way back to Lionel, surprised to see Lot.

Lionel gave Merlin an enthusiastic hug. "I could listen to you all day."

Merlin felt his face burn from embarrassment. "Music, like so much of life, is a gift from the gods. It would be disrespectful to not appreciate what the gods deem important."

Lot groaned loudly. He had taken about all that he could today and was overeager for night to fall.

"Do you not believe in the revenge of the gods, Sir Lot?"

"I believe in one thing—me."

Merlin could tell from Lot's tone that it was not a statement of pride, but merely of fact. Yet, he could not help but try to push some emotion out of him. "If you have no fear of the gods, who do you fear?"

"Fear is a useless emotion, and has no place within a knight."

"So, you do not fear anything. Not even the High King?"

"Especially *not* the High King."

"Hmmm…" Merlin quickly filed that statement away, "…not even death?"

"A knight going into battle cannot afford to fear death. Death is an honor."

"Do you wish to die?"

Lot's eyebrows narrowed, a slight twitch formed on his lips, and his breathing became ever so labored. For the first time Merlin saw that Lot could be provoked, could outwardly show emotion, he *was* vulnerable after all.

Lionel quickly put his hand over Merlin's mouth. Reaching into his pocket with his free hand, he pulled out a coin. "Merlin, why don't you go buy Lady Enid something nice from one of the peddlers."

With a childlike grin, Merlin took the bribe and skipped off.

"Forgive him, Sir Lot. Even though he is wise beyond his years, he is after all, just a boy."

Lot shrugged. Instantly regaining his composure, he thought of how much he was going to enjoy tonight's adventure.

3

Lot peered at the lone hawk gliding in the dusky sky, engulfed in the splendor of the rising moon, the *Hunter's Moon*, full, bright, with a pale blood-red tint. *A good omen,* he thought.

"So, you do appreciate beauty," Merlin shouted as he was pushed into Lot's leg by a jubilant merrymaker. Instantly, he felt Lot tense, trying to move away, but trapped by the crowd, both boy and knight awkwardly pinned against each other.

"Not another game of questions?"

"No, no more questions." Offering Lot a warm meat and veggie pasty he added, "I did bring you something."

Lot was about to rebuff the gesture, but his growling stomach reminded him that he had not eaten all day. He accepted the pie, nodded and began eating.

The ever-vigilant Lionel stood behind Merlin and squeezed his shoulders. "I think I saw Enid and Arden. Shall we try to find them?"

Merlin looked up to Lionel with weary eyes and sighed. The celebration had been fun, but now that the sun was setting he was starting to feel the cold. He was tired, and his belly ached from just a little too much ale and a whole lot of food.

"When you've taken the boy to safekeeping, meet me at the inn," Lot shouted over the crowd.

Picking up Merlin, Lionel shouted back, "I will not be long, save some ale for me."

Lot tossed the remains of the pie on the ground. Wiping his hands together, he fought his way through the crowd to the inn. Instinctively, he knew that one-by-one his men would follow his lead.

***

Enid and Arden were at the far outer edge of the still unlit bonfire. Lionel arrived with Merlin, handing him over to Enid, who was sitting on a tree stump. "I am afraid we wore him out today." Merlin cuddled into his foster mother's arms, glad to be out of the crowd.

"So, how much trouble did you boys get into?" Enid teased.

"A bundle, but nothing we couldn't get out of," Lionel joked back.

Merlin cringed as he watched Lionel reach over to once more ruffle his hair.

"You look tired Merlin, are you ready to go home?" Enid whispered in Merlin's ear. "We don't have to wait for the lighting of the fire?" she added louder as a question to her husband.

"If the boy has had enough fun for one day, we can go. I have seen enough bonfires to last me a lifetime."

Enid agreed, handing the sleepy boy over to Arden. "Let's go now."

"Do you want me to carry him to the cart for you?" Lionel asked.

"No, we can manage. Go enjoy yourself. I am not such an old man that I don't remember…" Arden's voice trailed off, lost in memory as he glanced lovingly to Enid.

"As you wish. I will see you in the morning on our way back." Lionel turned and eagerly swam through a sea of people to get to the inn.

The old couple made their way to their cart. Arden laid Merlin in the back on a bed of straw and helped his wife climb in next to the boy. Enid covered them both with her shawl. Contently, she smiled to her husband. "This reminds me of the day we brought him home."

Arden did not share his wife's joyous mood. Samhain had never been his favorite celebration. Evil forces were everywhere, and he felt eyes watching, waiting to steal his soul. Looking around he thought he saw silver-blue eyes glowing, but when he looked again he saw nothing and tried to brush off the feeling. Yet, the sudden cold chill would not leave. Even an old knight never forgets the feeling of being watched, and someone was out there, this he was certain.

The full moon rose, giving a pale pink tint to the early evening sky. Clicking loudly, Arden snapped the reins as they hurried down the dirt road. He was thankful when he saw the small hawk soaring in front of the mare, guiding them safely home.

Nearby, a lone figure dressed in black slinked in the shadows. When he was certain the wagon was well down the road he dashed back to meet the others, avoiding bumping into Lionel at the inn's door by mere footsteps.

Oblivious, Lionel entered the building and was not surprised to see a nearly empty room, as the majority of the villagers were gathering outside.

"Over here, Lionel, come join us." Lot motioned from the far corner. He was in an uncharacteristically jovial mood; surrounded by his men and several lovely serving wenches. Numerous half empty tankards, and pitchers overflowing with ale, covered the table.

Lionel could barely contain his excitement as he hurried over. He knew that tonight would be the turning point. Tonight, Lot had promised to transform him from a mere boy into a real man, and Lionel was more than ready.

"I hope you saved me some..." he looked over the ladies, "...of everything."

This brought a loud round of laughter from the table as he squeezed in between Dodinel and Nentres. Nicknamed the Boar and the Dove; as Dodinel's nature was as savage, as Nentres' was gentle. Dodinel was slow witted, yet powerful, while Nentres was quick of body and mind.

Lionel had spent the summer training for knighthood under Sir Lot at King Vortigern's new stronghold at Mount Erith. From an early age, Lot had shown an incredible fearless courage in battle. As a reward for Lot's grand deeds, he was given this small group of young knights, dubbed *The Young Royal Guard*, who were never far from Lot's side. Lionel was honored to be within such good company and friendly faces, and hoped one day to also be a member of the guard.

Directly across from Lionel sat Lot, and as usual on his left was Sir Faustus, a giant of a man and the eldest of the group. He was rumored to be Vortigern's bastard son by his own daughter. It had always baffled Lionel how Faustus treated Lot with respect instead of resentment, as it was very obvious who had the High King's favor.

On a nearby bench another of the High King's illegitimate sons, Sir Brydw, was in deep conversation with two serving girls. All the ladies loved Sir Brydw. Although he was ruggedly handsome, his rude and vulgar manner made him Lionel's least favorite.

"Where is Meleagant?" Lionel thought it very odd that the young prince was not at Lot's right side. Lot was exceptionally fond of Meleagant, who was often referred to as Lot's shadow. Their birthdays were separated by only a month, Meleagant being the older. Next to Lot, at only fifteen, he was the youngest of the Young Royal Guard, and by far the most inexperienced. Both young men, like Lionel, had been sent in their early teens to the High King's court from distant lands to be schooled in the ways of battle. While others struggled in the foreign, formal, and often brutal environment, Lot was the only one who truly flourished.

"Meleagant will be back soon." Lot gave Lionel a reassuring grin, and called out to one of the girls draped around Brydw's neck, "Keep our good friend Lionel's blackjack filled, he has a lot of drinking to catch up on." As if under Lot's command, the redheaded beauty quickly left Brydw and grabbed a full pitcher. Bending her ample breasted body near Lionel's face, she filled a tall leather tankard with their strongest ale. Lionel could feel both his face and loins begin to warm.

***

The last of Lot's men lingered in the doorway. Meleagant's silver-blue eyes fixed upon Lot's ebony ones, and he gave Lot a quick nod. *The Plan* had commenced.

4

Enid sat up in bed half asleep as Merlin's screams shattered the night. Throwing the covers from her frail body, she swung her bare feet to meet the cool dirt floor. In the darkness she felt Arden's callused hand grab her arm.

"Leave the boy! You baby him too much. He will never grow to be strong if you keep running to his side whenever his dreams turn to nightmares."

She patted his hand, and he let her go, knowing there was nothing else he could do, nor say, to stop her. He rolled away, pulling the covers over his head and fell back into a deep sleep.

Sighing, she shuffled in the dark to Merlin's small bed at the far corner of the main room. Since he was born, he had woken this way; screaming out in the middle of the night, holding his head in agony.

She sat down, cradling the young boy tightly in her arms. His hair and bedclothes were drenched in sweat. "Wake up, my little bird. You are just having a bad dream." Merlin shivered in her arms with both hands pressed hard against his temples.

Kissing his forehead ever so softly, Enid began singing as she rocked him gently. Immediately, a peaceful calm set upon Merlin, and she could feel him relax, knowing it would only be moments before he fell back to sleep. Smiling she gazed out the nearby window watching the now familiar silhouette of the hawk dancing in the bright light of the pink full moon.

Merlin was nearly asleep in Enid's arms when five men crashed through the front door. The old woman shrieked as the child was torn from her arms. Without hesitation Brydw, backhanded Enid across the face, watching dispassionately as she clutched her chest and fell hard to the floor.

Merlin fought his captors like a wild animal—kicking, clawing, biting. It took both Brydw and Dodinel to hold him still, while Nentres securely cocooned the boy in a woolen cape. Even then, Merlin continued to squirm and bite.

"Quickly, bind the boy's eyes, and get him to the horse!" A familiar voice shouted from just outside the door.

Nentres pulled a long thin piece of dark cloth from his pouch and wrapped it around the boy's head, making sure his eyes were tightly covered.

Like a restrained bird of prey, Merlin instantly stopped struggling. Accepting his fate, he gave himself over to the gentle arms that held him. A gust of cold air hit his face as he was carried outside. A horse snorted, as Merlin felt himself being lifted upward into the arms of his new captor.

Arden awoke, still dazed from his slumber. Hearing the commotion in the other room, without hesitation he charged into the middle of the fray just as Dodinel and Nentres were leaving. In the darkness he searched the room, first for Enid and secondly for the boy. When in the moonlight he saw his wife's bloody body on the floor and Merlin's bed empty, he turned manic.

Brydw and Faustus came together to block the old knight from charging outside to rescue Merlin, pushing him back into the room. Arden managed a hard blow to Faustus' face before Brydw was able to knock the old man to the floor, pinning his shoulders to the ground. Faustus wiped a trickle of blood from his mouth, and in a frenzy he repeatedly kicked Arden in the ribs.

"What now?" A quivering voice cried out in the shadows, his innocent eyes stared from one man to the next.

"You know *The Plan*," barked Faustus.

The bystander stood frozen as Faustus pushed past him, retrieving Merlin's sword leaning near the doorway, exactly where Lot had said it would be. Shoving the hilt into the reluctant young knight's hand, Faustus hissed, "Keep to *The Plan*—we leave no witnesses." Faustus returned to Arden and sat on the old man's knees to help Brydw hold him down.

The young knight begrudgingly approached. Standing over Arden with tears in his silver-blue eyes, he hesitated.

Instinctively, Ardent knew those were the same eyes that had been watching him in the village.

"Forgive me," Meleagant whispered, as he drove the sword deeply into the old man's heart.

"Cowards!" were Arden's last words.

Covered in a splatter of blood, Meleagant crumbled onto the floor. He had killed men in battle, but he never envisioned murdering an unarmed old man. He scrambled from the house like a rat, throwing himself on the ground, retching violently.

"To The Gods Be Dammed—Hurry!" Lot bellowed as his horse turned skittish.

Seeing that Merlin was secure in Lot's arms, Dodinel and Nentres ran back into the house. At that moment Enid moaned, and all eyes went from her to the eldest of the group.

"Leave," Faustus growled.

Upon hearing his command, Dodinel, Nentres, and Brydw, turned in unison, obeying willingly.

"Hurry!" Lot's voice broke with exasperation.

In a state of hysteria a terrified Enid swallowed hard, choking on the blood that trickled into her mouth from her battered lips and broken nose. Her panic set in anew as she felt the lone invader nestle next to her body. She trembled uncontrollably as the stranger's abrasive fingers gently brushed a wisp of hair from her face. Her tears streamed, as his sticky, wet lips kissed her cheek.

"I am sorry, but it is part of *The Plan*," Faustus whispered in Enid's ear, as his hands tightened around her neck. He could feel her pulse race, thumping rapidly. He counted the beats, until the rhythm stopped and he knew her life-blood would run no more. Huddled beside her for what seemed like an eternity, he was startled back from his nightmarish dream-world by Lot's voice screaming through the darkness.

"*We Must Go Now!*" Lot's patience was strained, and he realized that if he did not get the situation under control immediately, all could be lost. "Everyone to your horses. If you do not get mounted right now, I swear I will kill and bury each and every one of you myself."

There was such an evil pitch to Lot's voice that each man knew he would make-good his words. Nentres helped Meleagant on his horse, as Faustus staggered from the house. Soon all knights were mounted and galloping down the path. Just out of sight, a lone observer sat in a nearby treetop. Yet, no one but Merlin heard his hawk's cry echoing in the darkness.

***

Lionel woke at the first cock's crow, more by habit than by necessity. His head felt like a busy blacksmith had moved in. He was about to roll over and lose his stomach contents from the previous day, when he realized his right arm was trapped and painfully numb. "God, grant me the wisdom of hindsight. If this is what it takes to become a man I wish to stay a boy for a lifetime," he mumbled as he slowly opened his eyes to have his vision blocked by a mass of red curls.

Closing his eyes tightly, he tried to piece together what had happened last night, before falling into the abyss. His last clear memory was having a lovely girl, with hair of fire, sit on his lap, continually feeding him pitcher after pitcher of ale. *Yes, that was the good part of the evening.* In a cloud he vaguely remembered Nentres and Dodinel dragging him upstairs, stripping him of his clothes, and tossing him in the bed. Then, nothing.

He opened his eyes fully as he gave a quick tug, which released his arm from captive. Landing with a thud, naked on the floor, he shook his arm as painful imaginary needles grabbed each movement. He searched the room for his clothes. Finding them neatly folded on a nearby bench gave proof that Nentres had, without doubt, been there. The young girl did not move, and he worried that she may be dead, until he heard her moan softly in her sleep.

As quiet as possible, Lionel dressed and left to seek the others. Reaching the bottom of the stairs, he was disappointed to find the inn nearly empty. No sign of his companions, only the innkeeper's wife, and two maidens who were helping clean the clutter from the previous night's celebration.

Out of nowhere, a young boy tugged on his tunic. "You the one they call Lionel?"

"Yes." *It hurt to speak.*

"I have a message for you from Sir Lot."

"Can you talk a little softer?" *It hurt to listen.*

The young boy jumped on a nearby bench, standing on his tiptoes he whispered into Lionel's ear. "Sir Lot said that he was not able to wake you and that he had to return to Mount Erith immediately per the High King's urgent request."

"Was that the whole message?"

"No, there was something else."

"Which was?"

"Let me think. The man's voice was funny and I had a hard time understanding everything he said."

"Please think." Lionel urged the boy's memory with a toss of a coin.

"Oh yes, I remember now. He said for you not to hurry back to the fortress and that he hoped you enjoy the dawn of this new morning."

"And that was it?"

The young boy nodded and jumped off the bench.

I have no idea how I am suppose to enjoy this day when every part of my body is in pain. He walked over to the innkeeper's wife and asked if he owed her anything for the night's stay.

"A very handsome young man gave us more than enough to cover your room and board for the night. He also paid to have your horse ready at first dawn. You are indeed blessed to have such a good friend."

As Lionel walked outside he was thankful that he woke up early when the sun was still lingering low in the sky. With great difficulty he managed to mount his horse, and walked her at a slow pace down the dirt road back to the old couple's house. He was not sure if the lingering smell of Lady Enid's baking would settle his stomach, but he knew that it would be comforting to be within her company. He loved the old woman like a second mother, and he had faith that she could concoct a potion to cure what ailed him.

Halfway to his destination, the morning fog changed into a dreary drizzle, and then into a torrential downpour, turning the old dirt road into a muddy bog. The harder it rained, the more urgent he felt the need to find shelter, to get to the house. Looking skyward he shouted, "Enough already!"

"Finally," Lionel moaned as he reached the familiar path leading to the old couple's home. The door was swung open, and although he thought it a bit odd with the heavy rain, he eagerly dismounted and ran inside.

Mixed with the sweet scent of yesterday's baked goods, there was an odor that he could not at first place. He had flashes of hunting with his father, and it came to him that the other scent was that of a fresh kill.

Before his eyes could fully adjust to the darkness, he tripped over something on the floor. Reaching out to steady himself from falling, his hand came to grip with a jeweled sword hilt. He looked down into the dead eyes of his mentor, Sir Arden. He tried to scream, but nothing would come out. His feet slipped in blood and he lost his balance once more. With a sickening, sucking-pop, the sword freed itself from the old knight's body. Lionel found himself falling in slow motion with the sword in his hand.

Landing next to the once lovely Lady Enid, Lionel's gaze went to the bed above her body. Merlin's bed was empty. Again, Lionel tried to scream, tried to move, as Enid's empty eyes—demanding, questioning, accusing eyes—peered into his. Releasing his grip on the sword, it made a loud clang as it tumbled under the boy's bed hitting the stone wall. Finding his legs, Lionel scrambled backwards crablike out the door into the muck of the yard.

Pounding his fists into the mud, he began to weep uncontrollably with the heavens. Putting back his head he screamed Merlin's name, and he knew by the gods that both Merlin and his captors felt his vengeance.

***

Far away, Lot smiled to himself, it had been a grueling ride but they were almost to the fortress. In the end *The Plan* had gone well, and his mission accomplished. He thought of Lionel, and knew that this day his boyhood would be robbed from him forever—Lot never went back on a promise.

5

During the long journey Merlin relaxed, giving the illusion of slipping into a deep slumber. The mystery rider held Merlin so tight, that he could feel the man's varying heartbeats. But, it was the horse's hoof beats that he was most interested in, and he memorized each beat, mentally mapping his way home.

On their infrequent stops to water and rest the horses, Merlin feigned unconsciousness in hopes of gathering information as to his captors' identities, as to their destination. Although the men spoke in hushed cryptic tones, of a fallen castle and an urgent king; no names or specific places were disclosed.

***

After many hours the horse's labored breathing changed to short gasps as the loping turned into a pounding walk. Yet, it wasn't until the horse's hooves echoed upon the wooden drawbridge that Merlin became fully alert that he had arrived at the journey's end.

"You have done well." The words gave off a hollow sound as the Druid approached the rider.

The horse halted abruptly. Merlin felt himself being lowered into hands so icy that they penetrated the heavy wool cape, causing him to shiver uncontrollably. He forced himself to stop shaking; to take in all the sounds around him. His one-and-only objective—to get home.

First he focused on relocating the horses and their riders. Merlin could hear several men dismount, causing a loud shuffle of horses' hooves and riders' boots. The sounds quickly vanishing in the distance with not a word uttered from any of the men. Merlin was hoping to hear a name; just one name was all he needed.

"Come alive, child, your destiny awaits you." Removing the cloak cocooning Merlin's body, the Druid steadied the boy, who now stood on wobbly legs. Old bony fingers struggled to untie the scarf that covered Merlin's eyes. With exasperation, the Druid cursed aloud the man who created the knots.

As the cloth fell Merlin stood hawk-still, his eyes slowly adjusting to the light. Surrounding him; rubble of fallen stones encasing a partially built castle. As always, he searched the heavens for his hawk, and felt reassured when he saw her soaring above, barely visible. The clouds were so dark that his senses became muddled and he had no idea if it was dawn or dusk. Not that it mattered, he was a captive of this decay and he knew he would remain so if he did not clear his head and put his emotions aside.

The Druid handed the cloak and scarf to a nearby page, then quickly turned his attentions back to the boy.

"Your castle is in much need of repair," Merlin spoke softly.

Shocked to hear a calm demeanor in the inflection of the young boy's voice, the Druid looked down into Merlin's face expecting to see fear, instead he saw a child's innocent sweet smile. With his nerves momentarily shaken, the Druid gripped Merlin's hand, pulling him into the castle down a long hallway which led to the great hall.

Still dressed in his nightclothes Merlin padded along barefoot, his tiny tanned fingers gently encased inside his guide's skeletal ivory hand. Soft torchlight illuminated the way as they entered the great hall. Merlin's eyes danced with curiosity as he recorded the debris surrounding him. The room was immense, and its emptiness made it even more so. Upon the crumbling walls giant tapestries hung askew, attempting to disguise the decomposition. He walked cautiously upon the floor trying his best to not stub a toe upon the stones, which he felt jetting haphazardly with each footstep.

It was not until they reached the end of the long room that Merlin noticed the massive wooden throne—upon it sat an old man dressed in a long flowing purple robe—his beard neatly trimmed, his hair graying. Upon his head sat an ornately jeweled crown. Weak, faded, gray eyes stared from a gaunt face.

"So, this is the boy I have been seeking?" The king's crackled voice echoed within the desolate room.

"Yes, my lord," the Druid answered as he bowed deeply.

Merlin's eyes burned into the king; reading his mind as well as his heart. Vortigern had to look away, unable to withstand the boy's gaze.

"Take him to the tower and keep him under guard. Tomorrow is soon enough to deal with these matters." Vortigern waved his hand dismissively.

"King Vortigern, why wait for tomorrow for what we can settle now?" The words fell powerfully from Merlin's lips in a mysterious dramatic baritone timbre.

Startled, the king surveyed the room, searching for the source of the ancient voice. Squinting to view along the dark fallen walls, thinking the words must be coming from someone hidden within the shadows. Beads of fear and foreboding formed on his brow, dripping from the crown into his eyes.

"You request my advice, sir?" Merlin slipped his hand from the Druid's weak grip and slowly walked to the king, stopping only a footstep away.

"Not your advice, but your body," the king hissed.

"That is not what I have come to understand. On my long ride to your *fair* castle…" Merlin paused a moment and studied the decay surrounding the king, "…I overheard your *brave* knights discussing your dilemma. If I am to understand the problem correctly—each morning your men work throughout the day at a rapid pace to construct your castle—and by dawn's first light the previous day's work topples into stone fragments."

The king leaned forward until he was only a nose length from Merlin's face. "If you had truly listened to my men, you would have known that the only solution to my problem is your life's blood given in sacrifice to the gods. But how can anyone expect a mere infant to understand the words of grown men? A fatherless child, and if the rumor be true a motherless one as well. Surely you must be slow of wit as well as young of body."

Suddenly the king relaxed, realizing the foolishness in this. *How could a mere boy rattle him, the High King of Britain?* As Vortigern sank into his throne, he threw back his head letting out a roar of laughter.

"Sir, you would be wise not to dismiss me because of my youthful appearance. My life was meant for better things than to be sacrificed so that your castle can stand." Merlin's eyes glowed as his hands motioned around the ruins, and his head began to ache as he spoke, "For if the truth be told, beneath your hill fortress is a cavern with a bottomless pool." Lowering his voice to a whisper, he continued, "Within this pool sleep two dragons: one red, one white. Each morning they awake anew and start their struggle for power, for escape, causing the walls of your newly built castle to crumble."

The king leaned forward once more. He had only heard of dragons, and although he had never seen one, he was sure they existed. More curious now than ever, he hung on each word that flowed from the boy's mouth.

"I shall make you a pact, *dear King*. If my words are not true you may have my body to do with as you please. However, if I am right, you will allow me to return unharmed to my homeland—so that I may watch over the burial proceedings of my foster parents."

With each word Merlin uttered, the king felt an invisible hand grab his heart and squeeze tightly.

"Call your men and have them start to dig so that the dragons will be freed at the first light of a new day." Merlin turned his back on the king and walked to the Druid. Pressing his hand to his forehead, in a child's voice he pleaded, "Please take me to my bedchambers as I am over-tired from this day and wish to rest."

They silently walked from the hall, leaving Vortigern alone and lost in his thoughts. The Druid led Merlin to a small room, latching the door as he left, dashing all hopes for a quick escape. Exhausted Merlin crawled into the straw filled bed and sank into a deep sleep.

***

The latch scraping, mixed with the giant door's creaking, startled Merlin from his world of dreams.

"Get up boy, the king commands an audience with you immediately," as the guard spoke, he yanked back the bedcovers. Grabbing Merlin's arm, the guard jerked him from the bed, pushing him through the open door and into the dark hallway.

In a stupor, Merlin tried to find his footing as the guard maneuvered him through the castle. Nonchalantly he rubbed the sleepy-dust from his eyes with one hand, as the guard pulled him along with his other. Exerting a loud relaxing yawn, Merlin paid little attention to his final destination, until coming to a sudden stop, as he bumped into Vortigern's leg.

"Good morning young Merlin, I hope you slept well." Impervious to Merlin's intrusive gesture, Vortigern stood stoically on the stone walkway overlooking the castle. As the old king spoke, his eyes remained transfixed on the workmen digging deeply into the hillside directly under the fortress.

"I slept like a king," Merlin grinned as he continued to stretch his arms and yawn. Impishly he glanced sideways for the king's reaction.

Vortigern snatched the scruff of Merlin's nightshirt and jerked him upward, depositing him on the walkway's stone ledge. Momentarily teetering, Merlin regained his balance and his composure, as he came once more, eye-to-eye with the notorious High King.

Slowly Merlin ran his fingers down the king's robe, quickly gripping a handful of cloth as a menacing smile formed on his lips. "Dear King Vortigern, there is one more matter that I feel obligated to reveal, before you release me to journey back to my home."

Unsuccessfully, the great king tried to step back, tried to undo the child's death-grip, tried not to listen to the words that he feared would come next.

"Your men are close to uncovering the hidden dragons' lair, and when they do, the dragons will take flight." Under his clinched fist, Merlin felt Vortigern's heart pounding.

The king stood frozen as the boy's prophecy continued to flow.

"Heed my words old man…" Merlin taunted, "…the dragons are not just the downfall of your castle. They also foretell the downfall of your reign as king." The earth quaked, as the workers broke through the side of the fortress. Rocks crumbled, tumbling down the hillside, followed by a cascade of water.

Merlin could feel the king begin to tremble as he continued to foretell the future, "Look into the heavens. Do you see the smaller white dragon?"

Vortigern strained his eyes, searching the sky. Merlin's words were hypnotic, and as the old king looked upward he did indeed see the vision of a small white dragon illuminated by the early morning sun.

"The white dragon represents the evil Saxon army that you have allowed to overrun our lands…" Merlin paused to let the vision solidify, "…now, see the red dragon?"

The king nodded without taking his eyes from the sky.

"She is Britain. She is what you have given away. What you have nearly killed."

The king shaded his eyes as the bloodied white dragon cried out in triumph, and the red one plummeted from the heavens. Briefly the king turned his gaze from the dragons to Merlin, his eyes full of questions.

Merlin continued, "Do not feel content in the outcome of your conspiring with the enemy. This very day..." Merlin snarled, "...a mighty force moves upon you. It shall be here before the next new moon sets. Watch for the banner of the red dragon. The brothers—the true owners of the crown you wear—will devour you with their breath of fire and take back what is rightfully theirs. The evil you have inflicted upon this land, their birthright, their Britain, will no longer go unnoticed. Nor, unpunished! Enjoy your castle, my lord, for its life shall now be longer than yours."

Quivering, the king peered into the heavens once more, but instead of dragons, he saw a dove, blood red from a fresh kill, falling at his feet. Circling the sky a lone hawk cried out with victorious anger. Turning back to Merlin, the boy had vanished.

***

Holding his hands to his temples to stop the pain, Merlin staggered down the old Roman road, hurrying as fast as his short legs would go. Hearing horse hooves behind him, his heart raced with panic. Peace replaced fear as he heard the gentle chime of fairy bells. Looking over his shoulder he saw a snow-white pony. As the rider pulled next to him, he noticed the bells were woven into the mare's mane.

As the pony came to a stop, Merlin looked upward to see a forgotten, but familiar face. The rider's hand extended downward in open invitation. Gently, she pulled Merlin onto her lap encircling him in her arms; he melted into the folds of her cloak. He swam in her familiar scent, tilting his head back to view her face, their perfectly matched golden-eyes locked. Without a word she flicked the reins urging the pony homeward.

"I knew you would find me, Mother."

6

They traveled all of the day and into the night. Bathed in the light of the moon's glow, Merlin's eyes grew heavy. Listening to the fairy bells blended with the steady rhythm of the pony's gate, he was lulled into a world of sweet dreams.

The warm sun and cool waters rushing upon his bare feet slowly brought Merlin back from his slumber. He squirmed in his mother's arms as tiny fish nibbled at his wiggling toes. Opening his eyes, he watched the waters rise to cover their legs, as the fairy pony swam with ease across a misty lake.

Merlin whispered, "Mother, in my travels to King Vortigern's fortress I don't recall riding across deep waters. Do we not travel to oversee the burial of my foster parents?"

"No my son, they are already safe within the arms of Mother Earth."

"Where then does our journey take us?"

"Here, home to Avalon."

Merlin gasped as the morning fog lifted and the first visions of Avalon filled his senses. There, rising before him, an emerald green island. The crystal blue-green waters of the lake lapped gently upon the sparkling, white, sandy shores.

A large conglomerated mass of crystals sprouted from the top of the island's lone tor, taking on the form of a small transparent castle. The early morning sunrays wove magically through the prisms, creating tiny waterfalls of shimmering rainbows. They danced within the dewy leaves of the apple orchard that crowned the hillside's base. Even though late in the season, the twisted tree branches were still laden heavy with red ripe apples; their sweet familiar scent filling the air.

"We truly are home." Merlin turned in the saddle and kissed his mother softly on the cheek.

As they reached the shore, Merlin eagerly slipped from his mother's arms sinking his bare feet into the silky sand. Without asking permission, he bolted up the hillside toward the orchard, laughing with childlike delight.

Near the edge of the orchard his mother dismounted and removed the pony's tack. Swatting the mare on the backside, the pony galloped into the shade of the trees.

Jumping to a low tree limb, Merlin grabbed two apples. Losing his balance he tumbled down the hill. He landed at his mother's feet, which caused them both to fall softly onto the mossy grass near the sandy water's edge. There they lay bathed in sunlight for the remainder of the morning.

***

Suddenly Merlin bolted upright, "Mother?"

"Yes, my love?"

"I have enjoyed our time together, but I wish to avenge the deaths of my foster parents. Every moment that is wasted is precious time lost."

"Revenge is the same as hatred, and hatred is a useless emotion."

"I can remember someone advising me on how fear was a useless emotion." He stood, wiping a mixture of sand and apple juices from his hands as he stared across the lake to the mainland.

"Fear can be a healthy emotion, but hatred will kill you from the inside out. It causes the living to walk as if they were dead." She sat up, pulling her knees into her chest wiggling her toes in the sand.

"So, what happened to them was *right*?" He refused to look at her as tears pooled in his eyes.

"No…" she sighed, "…it was neither right nor wrong. It was just *their time*."

"Their time?" He turned to face her, his nostrils flaring, tears streaming down his dirty face. "How can you sit there and so casually say *it was just their time*?"

"The gods and goddesses work in ways that are mysterious to— mere mortals."

He walked to her and fell to his knees, "It does not take a mortal, nor a goddess, to see that it was no mystery that they were murdered because of me." Collapsing onto her lap, he began to sob.

"Their paths were sealed when they were born. Mortals are not allowed to change their destiny." She calmly stroked his hair as she spoke.

He looked up at her, wiping his nose on the sleeve of his nightshirt. "What of me, Mother? Am I a mere mortal? Is my destiny sealed?"

"Your destiny is written, but *not* sealed."

"Your words are soothing, yet far too confusing for me to understand." Merlin sighed, rubbed the tears from his eyes and rolled on his back, content for the moment to watch the clouds create pictures in the heavens. "This is truly a place of peace."

With a warning lilt to her voice, she cautioned, "It is also a place like no other you will ever visit. The apple isle has mystical properties."

His mother's words brought him from his daydreams, sitting up he grimaced, "Magical properties?"

"Mystical properties," she corrected. "Time folds in peculiar ways within our sacred realm. Some stay for years and when they leave they are no older than the day they arrived. Others age ten mortal years for every day they linger here—while still a chosen few seem totally unaffected by the mystical force of our fairyland."

"So, Mother, you are telling me that fairy blood runs though our bodies...my body?"

She neither confirmed nor denied the query of his lineage. "All living beings, be they animal, mortal, *or fairy*, are given special gifts at birth. Some choose to embrace the gifts, while others do their best to live in denial."

Merlin flashed back to his conversation about denying the gods that he had with Sir Lot on the day of the harvest celebration. Anger rose inside him with the sudden realization that the familiar voice of the rider who held him captive; the voice he could not quite place, was indeed Lot's.

His mother gently put her hand on Merlin's forehead. "Let your hatred go, little one. He was only following orders, fulfilling his destiny, as you must fulfill yours. Men are often forced to do bad things for what they perceive are good reasons."

Merlin looked at his mother wide-eyed. "How is it that you can read my thoughts?"

"Your thoughts are easy to read, as you are a part of me, as I am of you."

"What *is* my destiny, and in what way will your island weave its magic into it?"

"At the moment of birth, each mother must make a sacrifice to the gods and goddesses. Mine was to give your soul back to the land onto which you were born. Your spirit belongs to Britain. For all the days that you walk upon, or lie under her soil and or seas, you shall be forever known to the world as Britain's guardian."

"That is a big burden that you have placed upon these small shoulders, Mother." He skipped a stone across the lake, intently watching the ripples dissipate.

"Yes, you are right. The burden is always ten-fold the blessing."

"So, Mother, what is the twist of fate? How can my destiny be written, but not sealed?"

"At the instant of your birth, as the goddess placed upon you my soul's blessing, the gods intervened and slipped their own blessing into your heart. So that both heart and soul may at times be at odds. Thus, unlike other men, you carry within you the ability to see into the future, with the capability to change, not only your fate, but, the fates of those around you. I caution you to use this gift wisely, as it is never prudent to tamper with destiny. To anger gods and goddesses is to make your bed with the demons."

Merlin looked at her with a heavy heart as her words bathed his brain and drenched him to his core.

"As to what part the island will play, remember the mystical properties?" she continued.

Merlin nodded, eagerly awaiting his mother's explanation.

"Britain is in urgent need of your help, her future is in your hands, thus, your destiny demands that the island fold your years forward in time. Soon, you shall fall into a deep state of slumber, and when you awake you will find growth to both your body and mind."

"How is that possible?"

"Last summer, do you remember Lady Enid showing you how a water-worm magically transformed into a dragonfly?"

Merlin did not question how his mother knew of these things. He thought back on his summer with Enid. How she had explained the cycle of life through the morphing of a slimy creature that could only live in water, and how it magically turned into a dragonfly that could only survive in air. "She said dragonflies were fairies with wings and heart but no head." He chuckled, picking up a handful of sand and letting it slowly pour through his fingers.

His mother laughed softly, "Perhaps they are."

"Will my forward journey in time be painful? Will it make my head ache?"

"With all blessing comes burden. Do not worry. The pain will be short-lived and nothing that you are not able to tolerate." Retrieving a pouch she wore on a leather cord around her neck, she untied it, pouring a white powder into her palm.

Merlin's eyes went wild and his heart began to beat violently as she placed her hand under his nose. He wanted to run; he wanted to wake from this dream; he wanted to be anywhere but here.

"Relax, my little one, it will be over soon. Now, breathe in deeply."

Reluctantly he obeyed, inhaling the white powder into his nose, into his brain, into his very soul. He instantly felt himself rise above the world and he watched as an observer, as his body below grew from child to young man. He could feel his mind being filled with the wonders of the world as time flashed before him in rapid succession: hours instantly turned to days, days to months, months to years. He watched until he could watch no longer, and he felt himself plummet to earth—*hard*!

7

An early morning mist lay wet and heavy on Merlin's naked body as he woke from the nightmare. His mouth tasted like wool and he yearned for something to drink. When he tried to sit up his head ached so badly that he fell back immediately, pressing palms hard against his temples. He rolled from side to side in great agony.

"Mother!" he bellowed. "What have you done?" His words fell dead against the heavy curtain of fog, refusing them entrance to cross the great lake. No one answered. No tender hands came to cool his heated brow. No soft lips were there to kiss away the pain. No loving voice to lull him back to sleep with songs of Celtic lullabies. He was alone on a rocky coastline, the sweet smell of apples replaced by the pungent odor of decaying fish. Without a moment of hesitation he knew that he was no longer on the shores of Avalon, and he doubted if the fairy island actually existed, except perhaps in the fragments of his twisted memories.

He pulled himself into a fetal position, shivering as the ice-cold waters lapped upon him relentlessly, giving him a feeling of being both dead and reborn. Despite the pain, the cold, and the fear, he wanted to just lie motionless, to stay in this one position forever.

From behind him, the familiar sound of a horse snorting brought Merlin slowly back to his senses. Suddenly a large velvet nose pushed hard against his neck rolling his face into the water. Coughing and spitting he jumped to his feet to come face to face with wide-set black eyes. In the fog, the mare's misty gray coat gave her a transparent ghost-like appearance. He reached out to touch her, half expecting his hand to flow through her body, as a hand would pass through thick fog. He was taken-back when he realized she was as solid as him.

"Whoa, girl." He grabbed her bridle, and reaching up with the other hand, he dug his fingers firmly behind her ear and scratched vigorously. With another loud snort, the small gray mare nuzzled into him, rubbing her head up and down against his chest.

Letting the reins drop, he circled her slowly. "You are so beautiful." Merlin tangled his hands in her long thick mane and buried his head deeply, soaking in her scent and absorbing her warmth.

When he came up for air, he noticed a package neatly wrapped in deerskin tied to the saddle. Trembling fingers eagerly opened the bundle in hopes of finding anything to cover his body from the cold. "Thank you, Mother," he whispered as he pulled out dry riding clothes and boots—especially welcomed, a woolen hooded cloak, a perfect color-match to the mare. He wasted no time dressing, not giving a second thought as to the size of the clothing.

Magically the mist lifted giving way to an exceptionally clear autumn day, with a bright blue sky and brisk nip to the air. Still thirsty, he made his way to the water's edge, cupping his hands to drink. As he squatted on the shoreline he looked down and saw the reflection of a young man, he guessed near the ages of Lionel and Lot. Startled he jumped up and twirled around, searching for the stranger. Only the mare stood casually behind him, pulling leaves off a nearby tree.

Ever so slowly he walked back to the lake, peering once more into its mirror, only to find the same reflection staring back. Simultaneously, both young men traced their facial outlines, fingers gently exploring forehead, cheekbones, lips, and chin. His heart raced when he realized he and the water-creature were one in the same.

"Mother," he screamed with anger across the lake, "how long did you keep me a prisoner of your heathen realm?" His temples throbbed, the pain nearly unbearable. He vaguely remembered those lost years, but his memories were clouded and confused.

"You thief!" He raised his arms and waved his fists. "You witch! You have robbed me of what childhood I had left!" He paused, waiting for a reply to come across the lake, an explanation, an apology, but nothing, only the echoes of his own words. Dropping to his knees, hands cupping his face he whimpered, "You took my dreams, and stripped me of my boyhood, adding memories that have not yet existed." Softly crying he whispered, "I swear by Hades, I hate you."

Looking into the sky, he tried to find his guide, his guardian, but there was no sight of the hawk. He felt totally abandoned, lost, and lonely. His head began to ache again, and it was all that he could do to pull himself on the mare's back. He slumped over, letting the reins rest upon her mane. His trust shattered, yet, he could do no more than put his trust in her, hoping that the gray knew the way home, wherever home was now.

8

The mare took to the woods rather than the road. The ache in his bruised body soon matched the pain within his head. Tree branches continually slapped upon his legs and arms. Finally, as the sun began to set, the woods opened into a clearing.

Curious, he sat up in the saddle as he rode past an old charred tree stump. Pulling the horse to a stop he smiled sadly. "I know this place." Dismounting, he examined the location of his birth. Ever so gently he ran his fingertips across the tops of the fairy ring of mushrooms that danced around the fallen tree's base, the guardians of his sacred shrine.

"We are almost there." He rubbed the mare's nose and she snorted, nodding as if she understood.

The mare's eyes suddenly filled with fear, and it was all Merlin could do to keep her from bolting back into the woods. He felt a breeze overhead and a sharp pain in his right shoulder. Turning his head slowly he feared the worst and was pleasantly surprised to see the predator's eyes he was looking into were the eyes of his lady hawk.

"So, you did not abandon me after all?"

The hawk gently rubbed her beak against his ear, playfully nibbled his earlobe and took flight.

Perhaps this night will be the beginning of new things. Merlin mounted the now calm mare, his spirits lifted by the hawk's return. He urged the gray to a full gallop and they raced down the old dirt road past the apple orchard to his foster parent's home.

As the little cottage became visible, he pulled up short. His heartbeat quickened, as he first smelled, then saw smoke bellowing from the chimney. *Could his memories have been wrong, was it all a bad dream?*

Were his foster parents still alive, or, after all these years did new people occupy his home? Proceeding with caution he dismounted, hesitating momentarily, he knocked on the door.

The door opened a crack and a familiar voice spoke, "I thought I heard someone."

Merlin's legs started to buckle as he looked into Lionel's face. His old friend appeared to have not changed a day from the last time he saw him at the harvest celebration. Same height, build, and voice, yet when Merlin looked into his eyes the loss of innocence was readily apparent. *Was it his imagination, or had Lionel remained forever young?*

"I have traveled far…" Merlin paused not sure what to say next, not sure if his foster parents were alive or dead, not sure of reality, "…to visit the Lady Enid and Sir Arden."

"Please come inside. Any friend of the old couple is a friend of mine. You look tired and hungry. I was about to eat, and there is more than enough food for two." Lionel swung the door open, inviting the stranger inside.

"Thank you for your kindness. Would it be possible to water and feed my mare as well?"

"But of course." Lionel took a lantern from the nearby table to light their way. As they walked to the barn, in the flame's glow, Merlin could see that Lionel's eyes were red, his face puffy and swollen. There was no youthful spring to his step, no boyish grin, no attempts of hair ruffling.

After settling the horse in for the night they walked back to the house, Lionel paused before entering. "Did you know the old couple well?"

Merlin's heart sank as he heard Lionel speak of his foster parent's in the past tense. "I knew them in my youth; they were like parents to me."

Lionel lifted the light higher to illuminate the stranger's face. With a questioning gaze he examined the boy closely. His hair was rather matted and hung to his shoulders, yet his high sunken cheekbones and thin but perfect nose gave his ancestry away. He was a pure Celt, perhaps of nobility. Although slight of build he guessed the young man's age to be around his own. His face lightly tanned, and the eyes, Lionel knew those eyes—they were Merlin's eyes. *How odd*, he thought

"Hmm…" Suspiciously, Lionel stood in the open doorway blocking Merlin's entrance. "Since the old couple moved to this village, I only know of one son that they fostered."

Merlin stood in the doorway, bathed in the lantern's light, tears welling in his eyes. His mind ached and he felt defeated. He could think of no plausible explanation to tell Lionel, so he merely shrugged and said nothing.

Lionel could see that the visitor, although a mystery, was no threat. He moved from the doorway and, with a friendly gesture, once more welcomed him into the room.

Merlin paused, taking in the familiar environment. From the glow within the fireplace hung a big black kettle, the wonderful aroma of lamb stew filled the air. He closed his eyes and breathed deeply as pleasant memories of his childhood played within his head.

"Sit and warm yourself, I will get us something to eat."

Merlin unclasped the fairy forged broach at his neck, placing his cloak upon a nearby bench he surveyed the room. Except for the absence of his foster parents, nothing had changed. He looked sideways at the bed that once held him securely as a child. The bedding was still rumpled. It took every bit of inner strength to push the memories of that ill-fated night out of his consciousness.

Two crude but comfortable chairs were situated before the blazing fire. Merlin sank into the one that had once held Arden. He watched as Lionel busied himself ladling two bowls to the brim of steaming stew. A sad smile passed between them as Lionel handed Merlin a bowl. Sitting down next to him, in what once was Enid's chair, both young men stared silently into the fire as they sipped from their wooden spoons.

"So, how long have you lived here?" Merlin mumbled between bites.

"Less then a week," Lionel sighed deeply, letting his spoon drop into the bowl. Turning to look at Merlin he choked out the words, "I am sorry to bring you such dreadful news. The old couple died recently."

"Recently?" Merlin's hand froze in mid-air. *Was it possible that his visions were wrong. Could the couple have lived all these years?* A heavy guilt fell upon him as he thought of the anguish they must have gone through wondering what had happened to him.

"I moved in right after the tragedy."

"The tragedy?"

Lionel put his bowl on the floor, rubbed his eyes with both hands and continued. "It was the morning after Samhain. I had spent the night in the village and was on my way back to the cottage when I found them…" Lionel turned his face toward the fireplace in an attempt to conceal his tear-filled eyes from the visitor, "…dead, murdered, and the boy gone."

"How long ago was this?"

"Six days ago. Six long endless days," Lionel paused. "At first I thought I would go mad, and indeed there were moments that I thought I had."

"Just six days ago?" Thinking that it would be improbable for Vortigern to try and steal a second child, Merlin asked softly. "What was the name of the child who could not be found?"

"Merlin, his name was Merlin, it was his fifth birthday."

A flash of cold foreboding dashed through Merlin's body and he sat in silence as Lionel finished his tale.

"After I buried Lady Enid and Sir Arden, I managed to come to my senses long enough to ride into the village. Everyone searched for days, but the heavy rains had washed away all traces and dashed all hope of tracking the evil that took the boy. It was as if he had vanished, as if the living dead had taken him to the Underworld." Lionel could no longer contain his emotion, lowering his head into his hands, he wept openly.

Merlin's head began to ache again, as logic gave way to reality. *Was it possible? Had he only been gone a week, not ten years? This can't be happening.* The room began to blur, he tried to say something, anything, but his voice was broken. In the distance he heard the bowl thump to the floor as it fell from his hand. His body went limp as he slipped into an inky darkness.

Lionel, tears still flowing, quickly grabbed for the falling boy before he could hit the floor. Picking the sagging figure up, he carried him to the empty bed, the child's bed.

"I hope you are just tired from a long journey and not ill, I could not endure to bury another so soon," Lionel spoke to the motionless body, as he tugged at the boy's muddy boots and covered the stranger with the gray cloak.

He sat on a bench watching over the slumbering figure for several hours. The more he studied the face, the more he was amazed at the resemblance to young Merlin. Perhaps he was a long lost relative, as the stranger bore an uncanny resemblance to the child he loved so much.

***

The combination of sunshine drifting through the window and the shrill cry of his hawk brought Merlin back to consciousness. He opened his eyes and felt comforted by the familiar surroundings. It was only a nightmare after all. Here he was, waking in his bed, in his home. All was back to how it should be. Closing his eyes he smiled.

Opening them once more he began to shiver as a man's hand brushed a stray hair from his head, and he realized that the hand was his. The reality sunk in, it was true, the magic of Avalon had aged him, but not the world he had returned to. It had stayed the same. The horrors of that night were real. In an odd twist, it comforted him to come to grips with his situation.

Now, how do I explain all of this to Lionel? he thought as he sat up swinging his long, lanky legs over the side of the bed. Reaching for his boots, his hand slid to the hilt of the sword that Lionel had given him for his birthday. He pulled it from under the bed, dropping it immediately as he saw the dried blood that covered the blade. His mother's words rang out in his head, '*Let go of your hatred.*' Although he despised her, he still found himself valuing her wisdom. Slowly he picked up the sword once more and leaned it against the wall.

Still dressed in his traveling clothes, he walked to the door, leaning casually on the doorframe as he had done so many times as a child. Closing his eyes, he bathed in the warmth of the morning sun.

"Good, you are awake!" Lionel shouted from across the yard.

"Yes, thanks to you, and your hospitality, I am feeling more myself today, than I have in a long while."

Walking nearer, Lionel dropped the bucket of goat's milk when he viewed the stranger in full light for the first time. He was shorter than most boys his age, and his long legs gave Merlin the appearance of a young colt just getting his feet under him. In the early morning light the golden-copper streaks within his hair danced in the sunrays. His face was undeniably beautiful with uniquely feminine features. When he opened those hawk-like eyes, there was not a trace of doubt in Lionel's mind, that standing before him in the doorway was a full-grown version of Merlin. The boy he had been searching for had found his way home—as a young man! Lionel's mouth fell open, and for the first time in his life he could think of nothing to say.

Merlin smiled sympathetically, "Come inside, Lionel, I have much to tell you."

9

"I still can't believe it." Lionel gave Merlin a silly grin.

"I am glad that *you do believe*." Over the eight days of riding, Lionel's youthful chatter had returned. As long as he kept from ruffling Merlin's hair, he was happy to see Lionel's depression lifting.

"Like I said before, I am still having some problems wrapping my mind around the story of your birth, and all the tales you underwent in the short week you were gone. Especially those revolving around your rapid age growth…" he pulled his horse short and looked Merlin intently in the eyes, "…but, you know that I have and will always believe *in* you!"

Merlin had no doubt of Lionel's unconditional loyalty. He was someone who could be trusted. "Do you see any signs that tell us we are headed in the right direction?" Merlin quickly changed the subject. Lionel's recall of the Cornish countryside, along with the hawk's guidance had gotten them this far, and he did not wish to get lost now due to idle conversation.

"We have already entered Bodmin Moor. See that old beech tree on the knoll?" Lionel pointed to a lone gnarled and knotted tree sitting like a sentinel upon the hill's top. "It is only a half-day's ride from there. It would be good to rest the horses for the night, and get a fresh start at the first rays of daylight."

Although Merlin urgently wanted to push on, he agreed with Lionel that they should stop. The waning moon and heavy fog were making it more difficult for the pair to travel by night's light. Tomorrow would be soon enough. Upon reaching their evening's sanctuary both dismounted. "I'll water the horses in the nearby stream, while you collect wood for the fire."

Merlin gathered the reins from their two mounts, and the rope from his foster parent's old bay mare that they used as a packhorse. It had been Lionel's idea to bring enough food and extra clothing for their trip. While Merlin argued that the additional horse would slow them down, Lionel had reasoned that it would be a long journey over the moors. He further stated that it would be foolhardy to travel without supplies, which included Merlin's harp. '*A bard's music is food for the hungry soul*,' Lionel had stated emphatically.

In the end, Merlin was glad that he listened to Lionel. Patience was not a virtue that Merlin wanted to court, yet in his short span of years on this earth, and on Avalon, he had found out the hard way that even life's little lessons often came with costly consequences.

***

With the horses bedded down for the night, food in their bellies, and a roaring fire, the two began their nightly routine. Lionel always insisted that Merlin play him a ballad, followed by a game of questions and answers.

"What do you want to hear tonight?"

Lionel put more branches on the fire as he stalled for time. He knew that he would only get one ballad and he wanted it to be the perfect one. "I know! It is one of my favorites, and I believe one of yours. Sing us the tale of Alexander the Great."

With an approving nod, Merlin unbundled himself from his woolen cloak and plucked at the harp strings. The story of the Macedonian boy king was indeed one of his favorites. It was always the first ballad *he* requested from the traveling bards who visited his village during holidays.

Sitting on a log, Lionel listened intently, glad that Merlin's singing voice had not changed; it was still sweet, clear, and spellbinding. Lionel hung on each word, as Merlin sang of the life of the young victorious king who never lost a battle. He began the ballad with Alexander as a boy; taming the magnificent black stallion Bucephalus. He ended the tale playing softly as he sang of Alexander's demise, following his childhood friend Hephaestion into death. For it was not a war wound that killed Alexander, but love sickness from a broken heart.

"Beautifully done," Lionel sighed as he looked into the star filled heavens. "I do believe that Alexander and Hephaestion are smiling upon you whenever you sing their tale."

Merlin wrapped the harp in its cloth, leaning it next to the tree with the other items that Lionel insisted they pack. Blowing on his fingers to keep them warm, he waited for Lionel to ask the first question of many.

"Do you think we forgot anything back at the cottage? Anything that we would need to return for?" Lionel poked at the fire with a long stick, causing the sparks to dance skyward.

"Lionel, you ask the same questions each night." Merlin leaned against the old tree's trunk, knees pulled to his chest, wrapping his cloak tightly around his body, tugging the hood down as far as it would go to keep his nose, cheeks, and forehead from the biting winds. The seasons were changing rapidly, and even with the warmth of the fire the evening winds blew hard and cut knifelike through his leathers.

"What do you think happened to Lot and the rest of his knights? I hope they were not too disappointed that I did not join them. I really should have sent a messenger to King Vortigern's stronghold, to let him know what happened that fateful night." Lionel stopped short, cursing his words as he remembered that it was Vortigern who had orchestrated the cowardly deed. "Forgive me Merlin, I did not mean to bring up the High King's name."

In Merlin's retelling of the days of his disappearance, it had been difficult to explain the High King's involvement. Vortigern had been a man whom Lionel had apprenticed with, whom Lionel had looked-up to, and ultimately had been the man behind the deaths of the old couple whom they both loved so much.

"No harm Lionel. I am sure that the knights heard rumors of what happened."

"That is something else that I do not understand. I know that if Sir Lot was at the fortress, he had to have seen you. I know he would have been the first to come to your rescue."

Merlin just shrugged. In his tales of the horrendous night, Merlin had left out Lot's involvement in the abduction. It would have destroyed Lionel to know that his friend, the knight he aspired to emulate, was also the leader of the gruesome pack. All he had told Lionel of that night was that several men had blindfolded him and took him captive. Some truths were best left half-told.

"I wish you would not have taken the sword." Lionel continued his fire-play.

"We have gone over that before as well. It was the hands of the sword holder that killed Arden. You cannot blame *the sword* for doing the treacherous deed."

"Yet, I cannot help but feel that the sword is now cursed by association."

"What better reason to keep it? Safe by my side, stained with Arden's blood, as a constant reminder of what we fight for."

"And, again, what exactly is it that we are fighting for?"

"We fight for a free Britain. We fight for a land where innocent families will never know the fear that my foster parents must have felt that night." He dug his fingers into the soft ground, coming up with a handful of rich dirt. "We fight to defend Britain's soil, at any cost!"

"Tonight the only thing I am fighting is sleep." Tossing the last of the small fallen tree branches on the fire, Lionel sat next to Merlin. Mimicking his cloak cover, he nudged Merlin gently. "Tonight we shall surrender ourselves to slumber, and at tomorrow's first light, I pledge to continue our quest to protect this land that you so passionately love."

***

True to his word, when Merlin woke at dawn, Lionel had all three horses ready for travel. A small breakfast fire was built, with just enough heat to boil a pot of porridge, which they both eagerly devoured. When finished, Lionel doused the fire, cleaned the cooking utensils, and packed their remaining gear.

"Merlin, there is another thing that I am concerned about," Lionel queried as he swung onto his horse. "Before we started our journey, you asked me for the name of the most trusted knight I knew, and added that you were going to ask him to keep safe something of great importance to Britain's future. Why did you pick Sir Ector, who lives in a villa near Britain's southern coast over my father, a king, who lives across the sea in Brittany, in a mighty fortified castle?"

"Lionel, you know that my trust in you is unconditional." Merlin gently urged his gray mare forward, as they walked along slowly, enjoying the crisp air of the new day. "Unfortunately, those who would wish to steal the treasure that I seek also know how much I trust you. Your father's castle is the first place they would look."

"Wait, did you say the treasure you *are seeking*?" Lionel's voice became high-pitched as it often did when he was excited or, as in this rare case, aggravated. "You mean we have traveled all this way, and you do not even have in your possession what we are about to ask Sir Ector to keep safe?"

"Oh, better yet…" Merlin gave Lionel his most wicked grin, "… what we seek has not yet been created." Merlin pressed his knees hard into his gray and they raced ahead, with Lionel following him at a full gallop, packhorse in tow.

10

"That's the entrance to the Forest Sauvage that leads to Sir Ector's villa." As they slowed their horses from a trot to a walk, Lionel pointed to a narrow road leading into a grove of trees.

"Are you sure? It looks like the road ends where the forest begins." Merlin pulled his horse to a stop.

"Yes, I'm very sure. You wanted somewhere secluded to hide this mysterious treasure that you do not have." Lionel grinned. "This is it." At the first grouping of trees, the road became a path, which soon narrowed into a lane that a horse and rider could only traverse single-file.

"Hand me the bay's rope. Since you know where you are going, it would be best if you lead the way." Entering the forest, Merlin fell behind Lionel, content to marvel at the mystical place. Like Avalon even this late in the season the trees were still heavy with leaves. The canopy was so thick that if the occasional sunbeam had not filtered through, they would have needed a lantern to find their way in the musky darkness.

The twisting lane, combined with lack of the sky's visibility played tricks even on Merlin's senses. He was unsure of the direction; if they were going forward or back to the main road. Finally the forest parted letting the daylight burst through. So abruptly was the change from darkness to light that it momentarily blinded the young riders.

"Lionel," Merlin's eyes still trying to focus, trotted his horse forward, "This is the perfect place to protect our treasure."

"Halt, who goes there?"

The gray snorted loudly and pranced about. Merlin glanced to Lionel, and they exchanged grins. Dismounting, Merlin respectfully bowed to the guard. "My name is Merlin, and this is Sir Lionel."

"State your business!"

Merlin sank to one knee, which put him at eye-level with their young inquisitor, whom Merlin guessed was between four and five years old. The boy was dressed in leathers and brandished about a wooden sword. "We have come to seek council with Sir Ector on matters of the utmost importance."

The child guard stood his ground, glaring from Merlin, and then to Lionel. "You do not look like men with important business. You look like dirty beggars."

Standing, Merlin motioned towards Lionel, "We have traveled a long distance. Please excuse our appearance." Peering into the child's eyes, Merlin put his right hand upon the boy's shoulder. Visions flooded his forward memories, and he saw the boy grow: from child, to young man, to an aged knight. He saw him fighting alongside a fair-haired fearless boy-king. Finally, he saw the aged knight tossing a sword into a lake. Within this child he saw the right hand of destiny.

"Sir Bedivere!" Merlin whispered, the premonition causing his head to throb and his knees to buckle.

Lionel jumped from his horse, catching Merlin as he began to stagger.

"Who is he? How did he know my name?" Bedivere turned and was about to run as Lionel caught him by the sword belt with his free hand.

"Enough of these games. Take us to Sir Ector. *Now!*" Lionel had never imagined growling, especially to a child, and felt a tinge of remorse as he turned the boy around and looked into his frightened eyes. "If I let you go, will you please take us to Sir Ector?"

The boy nodded in agreement, regaining his composure as he adjusted his clothing. Picking up his wooden sword, he announced calmly, "Follow me."

"Do you think you can ride?" Lionel inquired of Merlin.

"Yes, if you can help me up." Merlin winced with each movement as Lionel lifted him onto the gray's back.

Tying the packhorse's rope to Merlin's saddle, Lionel walked behind Bedivere, leading both his horse and Merlin's.

Walking parade-style through the dusty long villa courtyard they quickly drew a crowd of onlookers. Villagers and knights-in-training, men and woman, young and old, all stopped what they were doing to gawk at the strangers. Just as they neared the main house the door flung open.

"What is going on out here?" There in the doorway stood Sir Ector, a short, plump, middle-aged man with a face that revealed an even-temperament. His eyes danced merrily with wonder at the sight before him.

Bedivere stood at attention, sword held high, bellowing in his loudest voice, "Sir Ector, I bring to you, Sir Lionel, and..." he paused with a puzzled look, searching his mind for the right word, "...and his wizard, Merlin!"

Lionel rolled his eyes, dropped the reins and walked forward. "Sir Ector, it is an honor to see you again."

Ector put both hands on Lionel's shoulders as he held him out for scrutinizing. He quickly searched his mind for a glimpse of recognition. "King Bors' Lionel?" He pulled Lionel into his chest and embraced him with a hug. It was not until Lionel began to gasp for air that Ector released him. "You were just a boy, only a few years older than Bedivere when I last saw you. How is your father?"

"I have had recent word that my father is in good health."

"And what is this, you ride with your own wizard? Is he ill?" Ector walked to the slumped over Merlin.

"No, not ill, he is just very tired. We have ridden hard for several days and are in need of your generous hospitality. Food and a night's lodging would be greatly appreciated." *Among other things*, Lionel mumbled under his breath.

Lionel helped Merlin from the mare, as Sir Ector motioned to a stable boy standing in the crowd. "Take their horses, and make sure they are well cared for." Turning his attention once more to Merlin and Lionel, he added, "Come in lads, there is food and drink inside." As he spoke, he brushed the dust off Lionel's back, "...and, you can get cleaned up."

Bedivere tried to follow, but was abruptly halted by the strong hand of the Master-of-Arms grabbing his tunic. A good whack on the boy's rear end from the broadside of a real sword's blade sent Bedivere scampering back to his guard duties.

"My lady, we have company. King Bors' son has come to visit." Ector shouted as he entered, followed by Lionel supporting Merlin.

The room was filled with a buzz of giggling serving girls who scattered in all directions as Sir Ector's wife entered. "Could it be? Is that the wee Prince Lionel, all grown?" She smiled brightly.

"Yes, my lady, it is so good to see you again." Lionel tried to bow, but doing so would have put both him and Merlin headfirst at her feet.

"Your young friend looks in need of a bed, and you both could use a good washing." She clapped her hands loudly and the eldest of the young maidens re-appeared. "Take these two young men to the guest room, bring warm water, and find them some clean clothing."

"Thank you, my lady," Merlin managed weakly just before he slipped into unconsciousness.

Sir Ector grabbed Merlin before he tumbled to the floor, easily picking him up. He carried Merlin upstairs, with Lionel following closely behind. "Your friend should be comfortable here," Sir Ector said with concern, as he laid Merlin atop a big feather bed. "The girls will be here soon, come down for something to eat when you are ready."

"Thank you, Sir Ector." Before Lionel could shut the door, two maidens appeared one on each side of a large wooden tub. Soon a parade of young boys ran up and down the stairs filling the tub from smaller buckets of warm herb-scented water. Fresh cloths for washing and drying were placed on a bench.

"Prince Lionel." A maiden entered with an armful of clean clothing. "My lady said that these should fit. She also requested; that after you are washed, you and your companion should join them for the mid-day meal." Without asking, she moved to Merlin's bedside. Dipping a cloth into the warm, scented water she tenderly washed the road filth from his face, neck, and hands. Next, she gently removed his boots and unbuckled his sword belt, handing the sword and scabbard to Lionel. "My lord, is there anything else I can get, or do, for you, or your friend?"

"No, dear lady, we have all we need."

"It was my pleasure to help my lord." She curtsied and smiled.

"Please thank your lady for her kindness, and let her know I shall be down as soon as possible." The maiden curtsied again and left the room, shutting the door quietly behind her.

Waiting a few moments to make sure the procession had ended, Lionel stripped off his clothing; washing several days of road grime from his body. The clothes that Sir Ector's wife had provided were not only clean, but also of the finest material. For the first time in over a year, he felt of royal blood. Before leaving the room, he placed his hand on Merlin's chest to make sure he was still breathing. Satisfied his friend was among the living, Lionel ventured downstairs.

"Follow me, my lord," the young maiden addressed Lionel as he descended the staircase.

"You clean up nicely, boy," Ector joked as the prince entered the dining room.

Lionel's stomach began to growl as he sat at the table opposite of Sir Ector. Brushing against his shoulder a young lady filled Lionel's goblet with mead. "Is your quiet friend ailing? Does he need food brought to him?" she inquired.

"No, he will be fine." Without thinking, he added, "He is prone to horrific headaches, brought on by the second-sight." As soon as the words fell from his mouth, Lionel realized what he had done, the secret he had betrayed. He wished he could retrieve his words, but he knew that only Merlin had the power to twist time. Instead he yanked off a large piece of bread and stuffed it in his mouth, hoping it would plug his thoughts from leaking out.

Sir Ector did not press Lionel for the meaning of his statement. Instead, he leisurely sipped upon his mead, inwardly amused at watching King Bors' youngest son devouring his guilty conscious with bread.

"What news do you bring from the realm?" Sir Ector's wife broke the silence.

This time Lionel weighed his words carefully before speaking. "I regret to bring bad news in such good company, but alas, there is much upheaval in both the north and the southeast." Pausing to gather his thoughts he neatly tore meat from the goose breast.

"Being secluded in Cornwall has its advantages, yet, it is good to be enlightened on current events," Sir Ector's words flowed easily, "what news of the High King?"

"Recent events have placed the High King's crown in jeopardy. The lower kings of the southeast struggle each day to hold back the Saxon forces that land upon their soil. Foreign invaders that came, by Vortigern's invitation, and now refuse to leave, claiming the High King willed the land to them."

"And the lower kings of the North Country?" With a greater hunger for information than food, Sir Ector pressed on, "How does the fighting go near the great wall?"

"The fighting continues. Picts constantly attack, especially near Hadrian's Wall." Lionel took a long swallow of mead and continued, "The Irish invade from the West, with the exception of your villa there appears to be no peace in any part of our homeland."

"And the kings of Brittany? How do they fair?" Sir Ector asked, sincerely concerned for the boy's family. "We have heard rumor of the young princes—Sir Ambrosius and Sir Uther. Do you know of any truth to *those* rumors?"

"At the moment Brittany remains a safe haven, at least from the Picts, Saxons, and Irish." Pausing once more Lionel relayed all the information he had concerning Ambrosius and Uther. "I was not there when the brothers landed upon Britain's shores, but I have heard from sound sources that the young princes have taken up residence within the city walls of Londinium. They fly the banner of the Red Dragon, and seek to dethrone King Vortigern. To take back their rightful station of birth. It is said that their armies are small in number, but growing in support each day."

"Yes, those are the tales that have reached us as well," Ector also took a long swig of his mead, ordering the maid to refill all of their goblets.

"I remember them as children, on our rare visits to Brittany," Sir Ector's wife chimed in. "The boys made an invincible and inseparable pair. Even as a toddler, Uther's swordplay was superior to any of the older children. And Ambrosius," she smiled broadly in recall of happier days, "what a beautiful child. He could always be found in the library. His mind was in a constant state of discovery."

"Not much has changed I suspect since they were children," Sir Ector reached over and patted his wife's hand.

"With age comes wisdom, one can only hope." She smiled with concern into her husband's eyes.

***

Upstairs Merlin sank deeply into the dark recesses of his mind, scrolling from one futuristic dream to the next. Once again, Bedivere filled his visions. As a youth, Bedivere stood near a sword imbedded in a stone as another boy struggled to pull it from its resting place.

Pressing forward in time, he saw the silhouette of Bedivere standing on Britain's shores, watching a young man lean from a small boat into the calm waters surrounding Avalon, plucking a sword from the fair hands of a water fairy.

Journeying even further into the future, he relived the vision of an elderly Bedivere tossing the sword back into the water, into the loving hands of the same fairy maiden.

Abruptly, he felt the curious, but pleasant aspirations turn into a present-day nightmare. His chest tightened. He began to panic as his body became paralyzed. His mind struggled to gain a semblance of reasoning, as he heard a voice cry out in pain, smelled flesh burning, and felt the heat from the flames that consumed Vortigern. Then, Merlin began to fall rapidly into a terrifying sinister chasm.

**

"Merlin, Merlin, are you alright?" Lionel shook Merlin violently. Frantically his eyes searched the room for anything that he could use to raise his near dead friend from the Otherworld.

Suddenly, Merlin sat upright with a start, gasping for air, heart beating wildly. It was dark outside and he began to shiver with fear at not knowing which realm he had landed. *Have I returned to human form, or am I still a spirit?* he speculated with apprehension.

"Merlin, it is me, Lionel. You are in Sir Ector's home." Familiar with the glazed look in Merlin's eyes, Lionel knew the words to bring him back to reality. "Listen. Hear your lady hawk cry out for you?"

Merlin's mind quieted and his breathing came under control as he listened intently to the far off hawk's cry.

"Lionel!" Grabbing Lionel's arm tightly, Merlin was about to tell him of his amazing new powers, but stopped short, knowing that Lionel *already* had enough secrets to keep.

"Yes Merlin?" He reached for a cloth, dipping it in the cool waters of the nearby bucket. Gently he wiped Merlin's brow. "You frightened me this time. I could not wake you. I thought you would never return from your private land of dreams." *Your private trip to Hades*, he inwardly sighed.

"I have had visions of Bedivere, and he is a vital part of future events." He looked into Lionel's face, thankful that he no longer asked questions in matters of prescience. "This place is his safe haven, and I beseech you to keep it so." His hand upon Lionel's arm tightened.

"I promise." Lionel was about to cry out in pain, when Merlin released his grip.

"I leave tonight. Before I go, I will add to the enchantment that already encircles the forest surrounding this villa. Any person with malice in their soul will become lost within the woods. They will become disoriented and ride or walk around in circles, eventually finding themselves where they began their journey, with no recollection of their travels."

"Well, that does seem like a grand plan." Lionel continued to wipe Merlin's brow. "If anyone can do such a deed, I am sure you are the one." He really wanted to believe. Oh, how he wanted to believe.

"Come, help me get ready for my journey."

"*Our* journey you mean?"

"No, Lionel, I must go on the next phase of this quest alone. The goddess calls me away to set the course for greater things to come. The destiny of Britain and her people depend on me leaving as soon as possible."

"What shall I tell Sir Ector? How will I explain your disappearance? While you are weaving your magic on the forest, why not put a spell of forgetfulness on the villagers, *and* on me?" Lionel lashed his words out in anger. "What do you wish me to tell Sir Ector of the secret treasure he is to keep for you? Once you create it that is!"

"It matters not what you tell Sir Ector of my leaving." Merlin began pulling on his boots. "When the time is right, I will send for you. As to Sir Ector, he is a wise man, an understanding man. Prepare him slowly for what will come."

"Prepare him for what?" The veins in Lionel's temples began to throb. "By the gods, how can I tell him what to prepare for when I do not even know?"

"Lionel, I have no time for this."

"All you have is time! You are a mere child masquerading in a man's body!" Again Lionel wished he could take back his words, yet he added, "And, who will be there when you become ill, who will be there to catch you when you fall?"

"I trust you, Lionel. Please, even if you do not believe, at least trust me. Now, come with me to the stables, I have learned a great deal tonight. The High King is about to fall, and the future of Britain depends on me being there when he does." Searching the room he found the sword and scabbard and strapped its belt to his waist.

"I would like to go with you. I too, as much as you, wish to see the High King fall."

"You are needed here. You must teach young Bedivere everything that Sir Arden taught you about swordsmanship, about loyalties, about unconditional love."

"I made a promise to Sir Arden to teach *you* all those things. Now, you leave, and my promise leaves with you."

Merlin sighed, "My training is now in the hands of the goddess. *Your* training of Bedivere…*" and the one to come*, "…is a crucial part of our goal. *Our goal!* Like it or not, you are a part of this, and staying here, for now, is the part you must play."

"I will not disappoint you, but you must promise that you will not forget me, and that you will send for me as soon as possible."

"It is a promise. Never forget, that you hold an important part of Britain's future within your keeping. I am just the foreteller of the treasure that is to come. Your deeds here, one day will make a boy into a king, and a king into Britain's liberator." He smiled inspiritingly, "Now, come help me saddle the gray—destiny awaits."

11

Merlin was thankful for the fairy-blood that ran within his horse, for her endurance was endless. What would normally have taken a fortnight, he was able to travel in half that time. He was thankful also for Lionel's gift of bread, cheese, and apples. He was most thankful for his hawk guiding him to the edge of his visions. Emerging from the woodlands, he heard the merlin's warning cry. Before him a lone rider galloped with lightning speed north-eastwardly on the old Roman road leading to Londinium.

Merlin tugged on the hood of his gray cloak to cover his face, pressing his knees into his mare he whispered, "Follow suit." Soon she matched the lead horse's rhythm. In the dust and mist Merlin appeared as the rider's shadow.

As they rode, rider and shadow, into Londinium, the people in the sparsely congested streets parted. Merlin felt the underlying tension within the massive city, and for an instant felt the fear of being trapped. He forced himself to keep his head down, concentrating only on the lone rider; to match his every move.

Deep within the walled city, through the courtyard of the once great Roman Forum, with its now empty shops, the messenger rode—coming to a sudden stop at the decaying entrance of the basilica. The rider dismounted tossing his reins to a waiting squire. On feathered footsteps Merlin mirrored the man's actions. He followed the messenger, through the courtyard's long walk to the great halls, through giant doors and into the main council room. He went unnoticed by the guards who assumed he was also a courier.

Abruptly the messenger went to one knee, bowing his head, he handed a vellum scroll upward. Merlin fell to his knee as well, head still down, hood still covering his face, his heart pounding so hard that he was sure its beats were echoing within the room.

"My liege, a message from your brother."

"And, who is your companion?"

"Sire?"

"There, behind you."

With a puzzled expression, the young messenger, still kneeling, awkwardly turned to face the statuesque gray-cloaked figure. "The Gods Be Dammed!" Scrambling to his feet, he screamed, "I know not of who this creature is." Instinctively, he reached for his dagger, about to pull back the spirit's hood and place blade to throat.

Merlin recognized the voice, and it was all he could do to maintain his composure and his silence.

"Stay your hand, Sir Lot!" the older man bellowed.

Lot froze, "As you wish, my liege." Not taking his eyes from the mysterious figure he calmly added, "Do you wish a reply to be sent?" He could hear the seal to the scroll break and the rustle of the vellum as Ambrosius read the message.

"Leave us for now. By the time you get something to eat, and saddle a fresh horse, I will have a return dispatch ready."

Reluctantly, Lot sheathed his dagger and departed, closing the giant doors behind him.

Merlin tried to slow his heartbeat, as he heard footsteps approach. As the soft clicking upon the marbled floor stopped, he felt his hood slowly being lifted, revealing his face. Opening his eyes, Merlin knew instantly that he was in the presence of greatness.

A strong yet un-callused hand reached out and touched Merlin under the chin tilting his head back, "Your name and your business?"

"My lord, I am called Merlin."

The hand tilted the boy's head back further to reveal a young man's face covered with the dirt of a long travel, "Not *the Merlin* who predicted the downfall of Vortigern's reign?"

Nervously he replied, "Yes, my lord, I am *that Merlin*."

"How can that be? The men who witnessed the scene said that the oracle was but a mere child. Are you wizard, knight, or madman?"

As Merlin stared into the eyes of his inquisitor his voice deepened, "My lord, I can feel your wisdom. Do you not agree that the truth always grows and twists with each retelling? I am neither a wizard, nor a knight. I pledge to you my life, that the one who stood before Vortigern and the one who kneels before you now, *are* one in the same."

The man looked into Merlin's face, seeking the truth, and finding it within his eyes, those unmistakable mystical eyes that he had heard so much of.

Merlin's stomached turned as he watched the hand swiftly drop from his chin and un-sheath a magnificent sword. His head started to ache with doubt and confusion. *There had been no visions of his death coming from a beheading. Was all to be lost here?* Franticly, he was about to plead for his life, when the majestic figure spoke.

"For your courageous deeds, as well as your passion and devotion to this land, and to its protectors, I, Ambrosius Aurelianus, bestow upon you the title of knight." The broadside of the blade tapped firmly from right shoulder to left. "Arise, Sir Merlin."

In a trance, Merlin obeyed, as he came face-to-chest with a giant of a man. Looking upward he peered into Ambrosius' clean-shaven face. His fair, flawless, chiseled masculine features gave him the appearance of a marble statue. His long, light reddish-blonde hair streaked with golden highlights fell like a lion's mane around his shoulders. The intellectual, yet kind eyes were a haunting blue-green, and they reminded him of the waters surrounding Avalon. He was dressed in a long white gown, around his waist a plain leather sword belt. The now sheathed sword concealed by a flowing purple robe embroidered in gold. Merlin guessed his age to be mid-twenties.

"Do not look so surprised of being knighted."

I am more surprised at not being beheaded, Merlin thought.

Ambrosius smiled warmly. "Sir Merlin, you have filled my thoughts since I was still lodged in my mother's womb—and you but a star in the heavens to wish upon. My dreams have been flooded with visions of a hawk morphing into a child, and the child into a young man who possesses the mind, heart, and soul of the ancients. You are the key that will open the way to our victories against the invaders. The gods have foretold that through you Britain's protector will rise."

"Prophecy, loyalty, my life, all I give to you freely," Merlin pledged. He had never experienced such feelings toward another human. Within Ambrosius he saw, felt, knew, that he was in the presence of perfection. Ambrosius was the vessel that he sought, the man who would give life to Britain's savior.

Ambrosius gazed back at Merlin with a mirrored look of admiration. "I do not wish to cut our time short, but it is urgent that I compose a reply to my younger brother." He walked behind a long writing table, where scrolls of maps, documents, and stacks of vellum overflowed. Dipping the reed pen into ink he began writing as he continued to speak, "Thanks to his military genius he has temporarily squashed the invasion of the Saxons on our southeastern shores. More important, tomorrow, we are to meet and journey to the High King's post-wedding feast— as uninvited guests." Pausing for a moment he looked up and smiled mischievously to Merlin, "Do you wish to join us?"

Merlin held out soiled hands for Ambrosius to examine, "Invitation or not, I fear that I am in no condition to join in on the festivities."

"You *are* rather clad in dirt." Ambrosius walked to the doors and had the guard summon a page. "Follow this young lad. He will take you to my private baths in the Governor's Palace. When finished, you will dine with me tonight and we shall talk at length of worldly and unworldly matters."

"I look forward to the night's conversation." Bowing, Merlin pulled the hood back over his face, turned and followed the page down a side corridor.

Moments later Lot emerged from the shadows, his boots clicking as he sauntered down the main hallway. "My lord, I have returned, and await your reply."

Ambrosius anticipated Lot's presence, as he always seemed to be crawling out of the darkness when least expected. Handing the sealed scroll over, he asked with authority, "Do my brother's troops leave the Saxon battleground this day?"

"Yes, my liege, they only await my return, for affirmation of your next destination of meeting."

"Go with speed then."

Lot bowed deeply, and hurried out the front entrance.

Ambrosius watched Lot until he was consumed by the darkness of the long corridor. Shaking his head he remembered how, at the first signs of Ambrosius' dragon banner, the young Prince Lot had squirmed his way into his brother's favor by turning against Vortigern. His betrayal had provided Ambrosius and his brother, Uther, with invaluable knowledge of the High King and his strongholds. Yet, for all of his priceless information, Ambrosius could not stomach anyone who was not unconditionally loyal to a cause. As much as Uther prized Lot, Ambrosius despised him. Of all of his brother's men, he put no trust in Lot and thought him to be treacherous. Yet, out of respect for Uther, Ambrosius tolerated him—at least for now.

***

With his long hair still damp from the baths, Merlin followed the young page through the halls in the magnificent Governor's Palace. Being clean was a pleasant experience, but wearing the flowing gown made him feel uncomfortable, and when approached with sandals instead of boots, he had insisted on going barefoot.

"Sire, I promise that your clothes, including your boots, will be cleaned and returned to you by morning." The page kept reassuring Merlin as they walked along.

"And my sword?"

"It too shall be returned to you before you leave in the morning. There will be no need for swordplay at our prince's table tonight."

Upon entering the library, the sudden sensation of heat rising from the floor made Merlin's toes dance. He was thankful that he had refused the sandals to have the opportunity to experience this marvel. Looking down he was enthralled at the artwork under his feet. Kneeling, his fingers traced the intricate mosaic of a young boy fighting a lion tiled into the floor.

Before the page could announce him, Ambrosius called out, "Welcome again, Merlin. I hope you do not mind eating in the library. The dining room is much too formal. I find that being surrounded by the writings of the Greeks and Romans most relaxing."

Standing up, Merlin lingered a moment as he surveyed the room. Sir Ector's villa had been impressive, but nothing could match the grandeur of the sight before him. Sheer white silks hung from the ceiling, casually cascading over long benches, which were also covered with exotic animal skins. The sweet scent of incense caused his nostrils to flare, and his eyes to water. Over a hundred lit candles were scattered about, sitting on small tables of varying heights. Their flickering gave an air of mystery, of magic, of intimacy to the space.

Ambrosius sat behind a large ornately carved writing table, once again surrounded by stacks of papyrus and vellum. On the wall behind him, and on the wall to his left, hung shelves that extended from floor to ceiling. Nestled within them were numerous scrolls, neatly tied with jewel-toned ribbons.

But, it was the remaining two walls that caught both Merlin's attention and his imagination. Upon those walls were giant frescos. To one side was the depiction of Achilles leading men into battle against the Trojans. On the other; Alexander the Great, upon his magnificent black stallion, rushing Persia's King Darius III at the battle of Gaugamela. Merlin had only heard of these men, these gods, ballads sung by the bards. He was mesmerized to see the stories come to life. As Merlin reached out to touch the image of Alexander, the soft voice of Ambrosius replaced his visions of ancient battles.

"Do you know of these heroes?"

"Oh yes, the paintings are unmistakable. They are depiction of the tales of Achilles, and of Alexander the Great."

"I am impressed. Most Britons are ignorant of the Greeks."

Still admiring the artwork, Merlin replied, "Most Britons are only interested in surviving from day to day. They have no need for foreign heroes, only for hope of a future when their land will not be overrun from invaders."

"My brother and I hope to change that."

Merlin turned from the battle scenes and studied Ambrosius. "So, you and your brother hope to become heroes?"

"No. Not heroes. We do not wish to be worshiped, only to restore this land to its rightful owners. We seek to drive out the savage, invading armies that land upon our shores in great numbers each day," Ambrosius' tone turned harsh.

Merlin simply nodded and awkwardly sat on a cushioned bench of beautifully carved wood. He adjusted the many pillows as he watched Ambrosius finish the last of his writings.

"My lord your meal is ready." The page bowed, as he motioned to the door. Several young boys brought in trays of food and vessels of wine.

Ambrosius left his paperwork and joined Merlin, reclining gracefully on a matching lectus opposite him. On a long thin table between them, pages laid out a feast of fruits, meats, cheeses, and breads.

A page handed each man a silver goblet, half-filling it with fine Roman, amber-colored wine. Another page filled the remainder of the goblet with water. Merlin cocked his head to one side and smiled, "For someone who despises foreigners, you seem to have embraced their way of living."

"For someone who knows well of Greek mythology, I am surprised that you are ignorant of Britain's recent history."

"I mean no disrespect. It was merely a question, not a slander of your heritage."

"Hmmm, my heritage, as I assume you must know, is the same as most present-day Britons. My brothers and I have both Roman and British blood. Our mother was pure Celt, and although our father was born in Britain, he is a direct descendant of a Roman emperor, and was a valiant honorable High King of Britain."

Riveted to each word, Merlin neither ate nor drank as Ambrosius spoke. True, he had heard, even sang the ballads—the tales of the great former High King and his three sons; of their struggle to power; and the king and his eldest son's ultimate demise. Yet, the story took on new meaning as it flowed from the lips of one who lived the tale.

Between bites of cheese Ambrosius continued, "When first our father, then our beloved older brother, were murdered by the villainous traitor Vortigern, we were sent to live with our uncle, King Budic, in Brittany. There, we were raised and educated in the ways of both Roman and Britain society. Immersed in the traditions of the Romans and Celts, our education instilled a great love of antiquity and a respect for both cultures."

"So, in your mind, you see the Romans as part of Britain, rather than her invaders?"

Ambrosius moved uncomfortably, giving great thought to Merlin's question before answering. "I cannot deny that Rome invaded Britain. That is a fact of history. At the same time, I cannot deny that I have Roman blood flowing within my veins." He pulled up the sleeves of his gown and robe to expose the underside of his arm, the reddish-blue veins pulsing, barely visible under his silky white skin. "Yet, I also cannot deny my Celtic blood that surges like a river where two bodies meet."

Leaning toward Merlin, without malice in his voice, he cautioned, "Never doubt my allegiance to my birth land. Nor forget that both my brother and I are native Britons. Our hearts and souls belong to this island and to its people. We shall die protecting what is ours."

Ambrosius paused to observe Merlin. Although attentive, the young man was wiggling about, doing his best to get comfortable. Merlin looked so misplaced, so out of his element, so much so that Ambrosius could not help but laugh aloud. "Merlin, you are the only person that I know of who can upset the balance of Prince Lot. Yet, you sit in front of me, with the inner-spirit of a raging bull, and the outward appearance of a young buck caught in a hunter's bow sight." *You remind me of my brother.* Ambrosius paused, taking a long drink of his wine.

It was Merlin's turn to feel uncomfortable. "My lord, although I know of worldly things, does not mean that *I am* worldly." He did his best to imitate Ambrosius in an attempt to casually lounge on the lectus, which resulted in an inelegant sprawl. Frustrated, Merlin continued, "I was raised in the country, and have never experienced the lavish lifestyle that you were, are, privy to."

"Each man is born into his place, his purpose, and his position in life. Yet, I truly believe that each man also has within him the ability to rise, *or fall*, from whence he was born." Ambrosius walked over to Merlin, adjusting the pillows behind him. "There, is that better?"

"Yes, thank you." Merlin felt his face redden. He neither knew nor cared if it was from the wine or from embarrassment.

"If you can wield a sword as well as you parry with words, you will make an excellent knight on the battlefield."

Merlin sat quietly sipping his wine, its sweet fruitiness set nicely upon his tongue, and with each sip he began to relax, feeling his inhibitions crumble.

Ambrosius returned to his bench, continuing to silently study the man-child in front of him. If only his brother could be here tonight, meet Merlin, and see things through his eyes. With the arrival of Merlin, he hoped that their lives would now have balance. Since they were children growing up in Brittany, Ambrosius had filled his brother's head with tales of the boy prophet. Now that his visions had turned to reality, he worried how his logical brother would react. Those thoughts he would hide away, until tomorrow, when they would journey to meet Uther. Tonight—tonight belonged to the dreamers.

12

Atop a grassy knoll, Merlin pointed into the sky. Both Ambrosius and Merlin watched the hawk's descending dance as she gracefully spiraled towards them. Three days earlier they had started out in a westerly direction from Londinium at daybreak. It had been a grueling journey to get to the agreed meeting place by mid-morning of the third day.

"Halt!" Extending his arm high into the air Ambrosius' command echoed backwards through his troops of cavalry. Removing his helmet he added to his generals, "We will wait here."

Merlin's mare was over-anxious. It was all he could do to get her under control. The gray sidestepped into Ambrosius' stallion. The giant white warhorse turned with mouth wide-open barely missing Merlin's leg. "Sorry, my lord, my mare is not usually this excited."

Ambrosius smiled knowingly in Merlin's direction. "Horses are like people. Even the most composed can become uncharacteristically unpredictable in a heartbeat."

"What of your brother, my lord?" Merlin inquired with innocence. "Is he horse-like?" With trepidation he quickly studied Ambrosius' expression. Over their travels the two had talked late each night. Ambrosius spoke non-stop about his future plans for Britain, and his brother's many victories over the Saxons. How Uther was a brilliant strategist as well as a courageous warrior. How his brother's men would follow Uther into the depths of Hades and back. The pride and love Ambrosius held for Uther was beyond reproach, and Merlin hoped Ambrosius would not find his question offensive.

"Is my brother horse-like?" Ambrosius laughed. "I refuse to answer that question. As a warning, I would also advise you against posing *that* question to Uther." Raising an eyebrow and shaking his head, he laughed again. Turning serious he added, "I am eager for you to meet him Merlin. Uther is truly a man of greatness."

"Like you, my lord?" Merlin sheltered his eyes from the bright sunlight shimmering off Ambrosius' polished bronze breastplate. Although dressed in an eclectic mixture of Celtic and Roman battleground leftovers, in Merlin's eyes, Ambrosius appeared godlike.

Ambrosius paused, searching for the words, searching for the truth in his answer. "No, Merlin, I am not, nor shall I ever be a man of true greatness. I am but a diplomat, a statesmen, a peacemaker with words. Now, my brother, on the other hand, holds an uncanny knack of knowing how a battle will rise and fall before it begins. His intuitive military logic, strategy, and fearlessness makes him a hero on the battlefield, and nearly invincible off of it."

"Nearly invincible?"

"You have heard the bards sing of the ancient gods. I fear my brother has his Achilles' heel, as do we all."

Boldly, Merlin was about to ask Ambrosius if he would share his brother's weakness with him, when the ground began to quake. There, just visible on the horizon thundered a multitude of horsemen. Following closely behind were well over four hundred foot-soldiers marching in perfect unison. Suddenly a rider broke formation and at a hard gallop raced up the tor. The horse's giant hooves dug deep into the soil, covering the hillside with clumps of scattered sod.

"It's about time you got your lazy arse out of that city and joined us on the battlefield," the rider shouted, removing his helmet as he approached.

Merlin gave Ambrosius a frightened glance.

"Brother, I would trade you positions any day."

As Merlin scrutinized each man, he doubted the sincerity in Ambrosius' words. Although the rider had the same eyes and was the same build as Ambrosius, the similarity between the two stopped there.

"Who is this young pup who rides beside you?"

"Little brother, this is Sir Merlin."

"*Sir* Merlin? Rather young and far too pretty for a knight isn't he?"

Watching Merlin squirm uncomfortably, Ambrosius smiled

sympathetically towards him. "He is old beyond his years," he laughed. "Merlin, this is my brother, the infamous Sir Uther."

Merlin bowed as deeply as he could from the back of his mount. "It is a pleasure to meet you, Sir Uther. Your brother has told me many tales of your victories against the invading Saxons."

Uther shot Merlin a dagger glare. "Those are not mere tales boy, but factual events!"

Unsettled by the warrior knight, Merlin sat quietly sulking as the two brothers fell into deep battle strategy. There was nothing about Uther that would convince Merlin he was Ambrosius' younger brother. Indeed, Merlin found it hard to believe that Uther was only in his early twenties. His face was tanned and weathered giving an aged appearance; his manner crude and brisk; his hair dark short and Romanesque; his beard neatly trimmed. There was nothing Celtic about Uther, nothing civilized, and most assuredly nothing noble.

It was not long before Uther's army surrounded the base of the hill. The armored horses danced restlessly, as their riders awaited further orders. It appeared to Merlin as if the countryside had become a human wave, as one by one the massive sea of foot soldiers dropped to a kneeling position, in efforts to conserve energy.

On Uther's signal four of his riders, on smaller swifter horses, ventured up the hill. Only Ambrosius noticed Merlin nonchalantly pulling his hood over his head, concealing his face as they approached.

"Ambros, let me introduce you to the newest members of our alliance: Sir Nentres, Sir Dodinel, and Prince Meleagant. They, like Sir Lot here, were trained under Vortigern, and have been invaluable as both swordsmen and informants."

Studying the men under sheltered eyes, Merlin noticed the only one who winced at the word *informant*, was Nentres. Lot and Dodinel sat impassively, while Prince Meleagant fidgeted nervously with his reins.

All eyes focused on Merlin as Ambrosius loudly announced, "I too have news to share brother. Sir Merlin has come to court as our advisor."

"Merlin?" Lot whispered as he strained to get a better view of the man under the hood. His face turning ashen as he realized that his shadow-rider—Ambrosius' newly appointed advisor—was the young man mounted before them.

Uther whacked Lot on the back, nearly knocking him off his horse. "Compose yourself boy, you look like you just saw a ghost." Looking into Lot's eyes, for the first time Uther saw a glimmer of fear.

Merlin's hand slipped to his side, moving his cloak back ever so slightly to reveal the hilt of his sword. Every muscle in his body twitched, and his breathing became labored as he spoke, "Sir Lot and *his friends* are old acquaintances of my family." Merlin spat out the words; more a challenge to battle than an affable greeting.

Lot dug his heels into his horse and started toward Merlin, with Dodinel and Meleagant following suit.

Instantly, Uther drove his big black stallion to bar his men from attacking, while Ambrosius as swiftly did the same to protect Merlin. Both brothers' knees were pinned against each other as their horses pawed the ground.

Uther shouted, "I care not what the quarrel is between you. I order it to stop now! There is no time for infighting." Turning to his brother, their burning eyes clashing, he added, "Keep your pup on a short rope, I have no patience for anyone inciting disorder among my troops."

Although Ambrosius' eyes showed his emotions, outwardly he remained calm. Leaning into his brother Ambrosius put his lips to Uther's ear, and spoke so softly that only his brother could hear. "Send your mongrels back to your camp, before *I* sic *my dog* on *them.*"

The anger in Uther's eyes vanished, as he slapped his brother on the thigh squeezing tightly, letting out a loud roar of laughter. "Well done, brother, come join us when…" sneering at Merlin he added, "…you get your pretty boy advisor under control." He turned to the four riders and motioned them down the hill.

Ambrosius could feel Merlin's mare pressing hard against the side of his stallion. "Brother, my troops will be at your disposal before you can raise your men to their feet."

Uther saluted his brother, put his helmet on, and galloped after his knights.

***

Upon reaching his troops, Uther began giving orders to move-out. He searched for his four young knights, finding them, as always, hovered together away from the others.

As Uther approached, Meleagant, muttered to his companions, "Did you see the sword?" His face turned pallid as he leaned over his horse and dry-heaved.

"Will the young prince be able to ride, let alone fight?" Uther's words bit hard, with disdain overriding concern.

"Yes, my lord." Lot moved his horse to meet Uther face to face. "We all have our unique ways of preparing for battle. Unfortunately this is just Meleagant's way. He will be fine now that his stomach is emptied."

Under the watchful eyes of Uther and Lot, without a word, Meleagant forced himself to sit upright. Nonchalantly, he wiped his mouth on the back of his hand, bowed his head to Uther, and then to Lot in acknowledgment that he was ready to ride.

Satisfied, Uther turned his attention once more to Lot. "I need you and…" he looked about the ragtag group of boys, "…*your men*, to go ahead of us and scout the borders surrounding Nether Wallop. Especially the hillsides near the Wallop Brook for any signs of Vortigern. Once you have located the old king, send word back to me with…" Again he surveyed the new recruits—besides Lot, there was only one he truly trusted, "…with Nentres."

"Yes, my liege, we shall set out right away." Lot would much rather give orders than take them. Although he admired and respected his new commander, he was anxious to get out from under Uther's wing and watchful eyes.

Uther could sense the tension in the young knights, but he had no time to address the underlying problems. In the end he was forced to put his faith in Lot's proven ability to rise to any task that he handed him.

As Uther road off to join his troops, Lot quickly addressed his men, "Heed my words, the gray cloaked stranger with Ambrosius, *is not*, *cannot*, be the same child that we took to Vortigern's fortress less than a full moon ago. Reason dictates that this Merlin is but a commoner, a mere mortal with the same uncommon name."

Lot stared into each man's eyes to read their reactions, their thoughts. As expected, the always-calm Nentres accepted Lot's logic as truth. Dodinel, a man of pagan beliefs, appeared apprehensive, but Lot knew he would go along with the wisdom, at least until something proved otherwise. It was Meleagant whom Lot was most concerned. Since the night of Merlin's abduction, the young prince had not eaten a bite, sustaining himself only on ale or wine. Lot was worried as he watched his friend's health fade rapidly. His face was drawn; dark circles surrounded his red swollen eyes. The most disturbing thing to Lot was how Meleagant was constantly, physically and mentally, fidgeting, never being able to get a moments peace.

Pulling the reins tightly, Lot kicked his stallion hard, causing the animal to rear, the front legs of the beautiful beast lashing out. He looked to the others and grinned. As his horse's hooves thumped to the ground he raced southward, never looking back, yet he knew that the three followed his lead without hesitation.

***

Still on the hilltop, holding his cavalry until his brother's troops moved, Ambrosius turned his attentions to Merlin. "So, do you wish to tell me about your hostility towards Lot?"

"Forgive me, my lord, but there really is nothing to tell."

"Nothing *to* tell—or nothing that you *wish to* tell?"

"All I can tell you about Lot, is never trust a man whose only loyalties are solely to himself."

"You are not telling me anything that I do not already know."

"Thus, my lord, I repeat, there is really nothing *to* tell."

Ambrosius leaned into Merlin, looking deeply into his eyes, and speaking in a fatherly tone, "I back my brother on all military matters. Internal strife cannot, and will not be tolerated. Period!" Putting on his helmet he added, "I fully understand a man's need to keep parts of his life private. Every man has his secrets. Just remember that, by your pledge to me when you were knighted, you are under service to Britain; which is service to me, and also my brother. We are two-halves of a whole."

"I will not renege my pledge to you, my lord. I am in your service."

"And to my brother?" Ambrosius' eyes searched the base of the hill as he leisurely raised his arm letting it swiftly fall forward. He moved his horse slowly down the hillside, Merlin riding close by his side, with the cavalry following in a rhythmic meter.

Merlin gave his answer much thought, "My pledge of fidelity has belonged to Britain since before birth. As to your brother; my oath of loyalty was given to you unconditionally. If to serve you, I must also serve Sir Uther, so be it."

Satisfied with Merlin's answer, and without reining in his stallion Ambrosius turned in his saddle, "Have you fought in many battles Merlin?"

"No, my lord, I fear that the knight, you so hastily dubbed, is in reality a virgin of war."

Ambrosius smiled sadly, "The prophets say, to take an untried knight into his first battle brings victory to his commanders. If there be truth to the prophecies, within two rising moons, we shall see."

13

At twilight the scouting party arrived near the outer edges of Nether Wallop, making camp under a giant beech tree, sheltered from behind by a thick forest. The air rapidly turned bitter cold. The winds blew hard, occasionally parting the thick cloud cover to reveal a sliver of moon.

"Only a small fire." Lot sat watching Dodinel doing his best to start a campfire despite a sporadic drizzle. "We do not want to give ourselves away to Vortigern's scouts."

Dodinel grumbled, as he continued to blow on the smoldering twigs and leaves until he succeeded in producing a steady flame.

Limbs cracked behind them announcing footsteps within the forest. "Did you hear that?" Meleagant was on his feet, sword unsheathed.

"It is ok, Meleagant." Lot reached up and pulled the prince by his tunic, causing Meleagant to sit abruptly on the log between himself and Nentres. From the edge of the forest came a single, short, sharp whistle. Lot turned and signaled back with four low-pitched owl hoots.

Within moments two men emerged from the woods. "We thought you would never get here." Even in the shadows, Faustus large frame and gravely voice made him easily recognizable.

"It has been far too long since we were last in your company." Dodinel jumped up, ran to the men, giving both Faustus and Brydw bear hugs.

Nentres sat quietly. He glanced to Meleagant to gauge his reaction of their old companions' arrival; watching with concern as Meleagant's fingers twitched on the hilt of his still unsheathed sword. Nentres caught Lot's glance and in silent understanding casually swung his arm around Meleagant's shoulder to keep him from bolting.

Lot motioned to Faustus and Brydw to sit, as he immediately began his interrogation. "So, what news do you have of Vortigern's wedding feast?"

The two brothers sat across the fire from Lot, as Dodinel searched his pack for a wineskin that Lot had asked him to stow away for their reunion. Upon finding it, Dodinel plopped himself next to Brydw, handing him the skin. After taking a long swig, Brydw, passed the wineskin to Faustus.

"Dodinel, you dog. When did you turn from Celtic ale to Roman wine?" Brydw wiped his mouth with the back of hand and started to laugh.

Impatiently Lot broke in, repeating his request, "What news?"

"The High King took his new Saxon wife a fortnight ago." Faustus took another long swig of the wine, smacking his lips at its sticky sweetness. "All went well until right after the wedding ceremony, when word came that Uther had arrived on Britain's southern shores with his armies. Needless to say, the bride's family quickly departed. No Saxon ever wished to be left out of a good fight."

"And Vortigern? Did he follow them?"

"Our dear father? Join in the battle?" Brydw chuckled.

Faustus shot Brydw a hard elbow to the side, causing him to bump into Dodinel. "Show respect, brother! There was a time when Vortigern would have been the first to lead the battle cry." He reached over giving Brydw a helping hand to right himself.

"Respect? What respect has that old man ever given either of us?"

Instead of answering, Faustus took another long swallow from the wineskin. When he was done, he handed the skin to Lot.

"How many Saxons were left behind to guard the current High Queen?" Refusing the goatskin, Lot continued, "How many of Vortigern's original army still fight for him?"

Handing the wineskin to Brydw, Faustus answered. "Only a small army of Saxons remained with the bride, I would say no more then forty. As to Vortigern's original army, each day the numbers dwindle, and they are scattered throughout Britain." Faustus stretched his long muscular legs. "If you are asking how many of his original army are still at the hill fortress, around seven hundred well-trained foot soldiers. No cavalry, with the exception of Brydw and myself."

Angrily Brydw added, "The king's legitimate son refused to come to the wedding. He refused to sit at a Saxon table. He preferred to engage in battle near Hadrian's Wall, which put him as far from Vortigern and his new wife as possible." Brydw slapped his half-brother on the back. "Yet, we the bastard brothers go where we are needed, loyal to a cause, unbeknownst to the king, it is not his." This brought a roar of laughter from all, even Nentres and Lot. All that is, except for Meleagant who sat stoically, tapping his sword absentmindedly in the dirt.

"What else can you tell us of the king's stronghold? Is he expecting a visit from Uther?" He was about to mention Ambrosius, yet, he was uncertain of the brothers' allegiance and wanted to hold back some elements of surprise.

"Your hotheaded, young rebel leader, whom you all swear fidelity, would be wise not to underestimate the High King. True, he is old, but with age comes experience and wisdom. Vortigern knows Uther's armies are out there, and he has his own scouts that are unconditionally loyal to *their* king." Faustus smirked as he studied Lot, hoping to push a reaction, yet disappointed to see that Lot, as usual, listened impassively. "Tell Uther that it would be to his advantage to strike soon, while the king's attentions still surround conquering his lust for his young bride, instead of quenching his thirst for masterminding the perfect battle plan."

Lot sat silently, pondering Faustus' words. "How many non-military are within the fortress?"

Faustus looked to Brydw and shrugged. "Including merchants, farmers, servants, women and children..." he shrugged again, "...all together, maybe a hundred, maybe less. None a threat in battle." Brydw nodded in agreement.

"And of the fortress, can you draw its parameters?" Lot stood, snatched the sword from Meleagant's hand, and walked to Faustus, handing him the steel to use as a map indicator in the dirt.

Nentres whispered in a low calm voice, "Be still young Prince," as he tightened his grip on Meleagant's shoulder.

Again, Faustus looked to his brother for assistance as he began to map out an outline of the fort, marking the armies' quarters; the king's living quarters, and the usual placement of lookouts. When finished he turned to Brydw and asked, "Have I forgotten any areas that would be of importance to victory, brother?"

Grabbing the sword Brydw sketched out additional details, including all entrances and exits, not forgetting the underground escape tunnel to the north of the fortress. "There are no catapults within the walls, yet, there are a great many of Vortigern's men, as you already know, who are expert archers."

"And the buildings, are they constructed of stone or wood?"

"It's an old pre-Roman fortress, mainly wood, very little stone. But, it is situated on a hill surrounded by a low lying forest, making it impossible to approach without being noticed, and it has stood for centuries." Brydw smiled, as he took another long drag from the wineskin, once again an offer to drink was made to Lot, who, once again refused.

"You both know that I do not drink, nor encourage my men to drink, until *after* the battle is fought, and won."

The brothers nodded and Faustus reached for the skin, "So, I see that we are officially no longer considered your men?"

A hush fell over the group, as Lot gave the brothers his best reassuring grin. "Faustus, you know that I have always had the utmost admiration for both you and your brother. Do I not show my respect, even now, by consorting with you on battle plans, against my former king, against your father?" He motioned for Dodinel to sit by Meleagant, and for Nentres to join him in reviewing the map.

Nentres squatted close to the ground, putting each line, each mark, each placement to memory. When finished he looked to Lot, "They've done well. It appears to be a detailed depiction."

"See there brothers, we all appreciate your input to this grand battle we are about to fight," Lot smiled casually as he spoke. "Sit, drink, and enjoy the rest of the evening with us. Enough talk of strategy, we have more engaging conversation to share. So, what have you two been up to since we last parted company?"

Nentres stood, and nonchalantly rubbed the map back to dust with the toe of his boot, never taking his eyes from Faustus and Brydw. When he was assured they were once again deep in good-humored conversation, he slowly blended into the darkness of the night. Mounting his stallion, he stealthily set off to meet with Uther, leaving the brothers drunk and oblivious to his departure.

"The mist is setting in heavy tonight," Faustus mumbled just before the world around him began to spin uncontrollably. He tried to stand, but his knees would not allow it. He felt the weight of his brother upon his shoulder and was unable to right him. "What madness is this?" he tried to shout to Lot, but it came out as a whimper, strings of spittle spewing from his mouth.

"It's all part of *The Plan!*" Meleagant screamed from across the fire. Breaking from Dodinel's grip, he danced about wildly. Throwing back his head, he gave out a loud possessed laughter that echoed throughout the forest.

"Control him!" Lot shouted to Dodinel.

Not sure how to control a raging lunatic, Dodinel did the only thing he knew. He laid a heavy fisted blow to the boy's chin, knocking him out cold.

Lot pressed his palms to his eyes and rubbed hard, listening to each sound the night made. When he was satisfied that all was quiet, and no one was immediately coming to the brothers' rescue, he lowered his hands and opened his eyes, surveying the damage, and calculating the cleanup.

Faustus lay convulsing over Brydw's motionless body. Both men's faces were ashen. Brydw's once handsome features were unrecognizably twisted, his wide-opened eyes once young and sensual, now empty, reflecting only a death dance with each flicker of the campfire.

Dodinel cradled the unconscious Meleagant, dabbing the blood off the prince's face with the edge of his cloak. He looked up to Lot for instructions as to what to do next.

"Leave him be, Dodinel. I need your help."

Gently resting Meleagant's head on the ground, grudgingly Dodinel obeyed Lot's orders. As he rose, he opened his mouth to speak.

Lot, anticipating what was to come next, picked up Meleagant's sword and pointed it with a swift thrust. "Not a word," Lot spoke softly. "Not a word," he repeated. "We were all in agreement that any man who plots the defeat of his own kin cannot be trusted."

Dodinel nodded.

"With all the noise, this camp is no longer safe. Help me drag the bodies to the woods, we'll cover them with leaves and come back later to bury them properly."

With clinched teeth Dodinel hissed, "They were once our companions. They fought along side us in many battles. They trusted us." He took in a deep breath, "We owe them a proper burial. We owe it to us, or we shall forever be haunted by the watch dogs of Hades."

"All men die, it is part of the worldly plan. It was not my plan, but that of the gods to take these men, this day." Lowering the sword, Lot bent down, and pushed Faustus off Brydw, watching his chest heave in labored breathing, eyelids flickering wildly, yet the only sounds that came from Faustus' lips were gurgled moaning.

Dodinel's massive frame easily lifted Brydw's lean body, tossing him over his right shoulder. With his left hand he grabbed one of Faustus' legs, as Lot grabbed the other. They pulled and carried the dead and half-dead men deep into the woods.

"This far enough?" Dodinel asked as he dropped Brydw's body into a pile of newly fallen leaves.

"Yes, this will do."

They worked quickly, first covering Brydw with leaves and fallen tree limbs, and then covering Faustus.

"You know he is not dead. Do you wish me to end his suffering?"

"No need, the poison will do its job soon enough. We have to get back to Meleagant, ready our horses, and return to Uther without delay."

Ripping the sleeve from his shirt, Dodinel tied it to a nearby sapling. "The least we can do is leave a mark."

"Dodinel, we will come back." Lot paused for a moment to gather his thoughts, "In the confusion of the battle tomorrow, we will come back and place the bodies near the fortress. No one will be the wiser of how they died, and they will be assured of a proper burial."

"The brothers' entrance into the Otherworld is on your head," Dodinel growled.

"As are many before them," Lot sighed, "and, I am certain, many will be in the future."

14

The early morning mist hung thick around Merlin's legs. He felt like a child as he uncomfortably stood next to the armor supply wagon, allowing Ambrosius to ready him for battle. "Is this all necessary?"

"Your life is in my hands. You *will be* protected," Ambrosius said flatly.

Tugging at the chain mail shirt under the leather breastplate, Merlin tried his best not to writhe. He was just getting used to wearing his new body, and now this.

As Ambrosius tightened the last of the breastplate straps, Uther approached on horseback, with Nentres riding at his side. "Brother, when you finish dressing your boy..." Uther sneered at Merlin, "... come join the field commanders, we are in urgent need of your expertise in matters of great importance."

"I will be with you right away, Uther." Ambrosius rummaged through the wagon and found Merlin a helmet that he thought would fit. He was not concerned with the urgency in Uther's voice. Nentres entered camp late last night. They had gone over everything, into the early morning hours, ad nauseam, in regards to Nentres' information concerning Vortigern's current military status and the fortress layout.

"Ambros, *that* can wait." Impatiently, Uther pointed to Merlin. He then gestured toward the distant woods surrounding the hill fort. "*This* cannot!"

Reluctantly, Ambrosius handed Merlin the helmet, smiled patiently to his brother, elegantly mounted his stallion, and rode off to the council meeting.

Tying the helmet to his mare's saddle, Merlin mumbled under his breath, "How can that pompous creature be a great leader of men?" Grabbing his cloak, he hurriedly clasped the fairy broach causing it to prick his finger. He was about to send a curse skyward, when from behind him a playful voice broke through the morning haze.

"I wouldn't let Sir Uther hear you say that."

Merlin turned quickly, coming face to face with Lot, who was also dressing for battle. Behind him Dodinel searched through the wagon's rubble for suitable armor for himself and Meleagant. Leaning next to the wagon, Meleagant teetered on the brink of collapse. His nose and lips bloodied, his cheek swollen from Dodinel's hard right jab that had been strategically placed the night before. The Prince's vibrant silver-blue eyes were now dark and empty.

"So, who are you anyway?" Lot asked, pressing into Merlin. "Better yet, who are you pretending to be, and why?"

Meleagant moaned. Both men looked in his direction. Slowly the prince began to slip to the ground. Merlin instinctively attempted to move to his rescue, only to be blocked by Lot.

"Do not touch him." Lot sidestepped Merlin, steadying the Prince. "He is not your concern."

Merlin stood frozen for a moment. "As you wish," he spat. Clinching his fists under his cloak, he abruptly turned, pushing his way through the mass of soldiers to the council tent.

***

Upon Merlin's approach, without hesitation, the guard opened the tent's door flap. Merlin eased quietly into the company of Ambrosius, Uther, and their top generals. At one end, Nentres stood deep in conversation next to Uther's left, as he pointed to different sections of the map marked in the dirt floor.

Ambrosius motioned Merlin to his side. "Don't mind my brother. He is always on edge the morning of battle," he whispered as he casually put his arm around Merlin, pulling him near.

Merlin stood in the winged comfort of his protector as he gazed at the map. In the middle of the floor a mound of dirt, on top, stones tactically positioned in places of importance. Twigs, representing the forest, surrounded the base of the miniature tor.

"Sir Arrok," Uther pointed to a thick piece of bark at the east side of the mound. "You are in charge of the first group of foot soldiers. You will storm the main gate with the battering ram on the eastern side of the hill." Running the tip of a spear up the hill's side, he turned to his old friend, King Pellinore. "Pelly, you and your son, Aglovale, will follow Arrok, with the archers." Looking around the room he snarled, "Where is Lot?"

"I am here, my liege." Lot lifted the flap to the tent and took his place at Uther's right.

"Lot, you, Nentres, Meleagant, and Dodinel will go with me, and half the cavalry, around the northern side." Looking across the map to Ambrosius, "Brother, you, Uriens, Carados, Brastias, and Ulfius will take the other half of the cavalry around the southern side. We will meet and enter the fortress at the west gateway."

Pellinore, knees creaking, knelt close to the map, scrutinizing the east entrance to the Danebury hill fort. "Uther, is that a second wall inside the first? Are there two main gates to breach?"

"Yes, my lord, your assumptions are correct," Nentres answered for Uther.

"If your scouts are right," Pellinore glanced to Lot and Nentres as he spoke, "the long corridor to the inner main gate enclosed within the second wall looks like a deathtrap. Are you sure we will be able to penetrate it?"

"You still have good eyesight and good senses old man," Uther said lightheartedly.

Nervous laughter broke out among the men.

"As in all battles, good men, brave men, indispensable men, will die! But, you, Pelly, along with Arrok, and your son, only need to hold off the advancements of Vortigern's defenses until Ambrosius and our cavalry break through the west gate. You will not have to hold them back long. I pledge that we will have the hill surrounded before your men break through the outer entrance."

Pellinore put his hands together, offering up a prayer, "Uther..." he paused and looked to the other side of the tent, "...and Ambrosius, we, your loyal kings and princes put our trust, our kingdoms, our lives in your hands."

"Trust me Pelly, when I say that we value the lives of each man, be he nobleman or foot soldier. Each man who has joined with us, who follows us into battle this day, is no less a brother than my own brother." Staring across the improvised map into Ambrosius' eyes, he continued, "As I would willingly give my life for my own brother, so would I lay down my life to protect each of you."

Ambrosius mirrored his brother's words with a single reassuring nod; first to Uther, then to Pellinore.

Satisfied that his words reflected his motives, Uther eagerly concluded his pre-battle strategy. "Lot, you will lead a section of cavalry behind me. When we get to the northern underground passageway, you will stay with Nentres to guard the entrance. Spread your troops along the perimeter of the tree line to the western gate. Uther jabbed his spear into the bottom of the tor, at its northern center's edge. "My gut tells me that before the sun sets on this day, Vortigern will be slithering out of the old Roman escape tunnel like a snake."

"If he tries, my liege, you can count on us to drive him back to his nest," Lot grinned as he spoke.

Once more an uneasy laughter burst out among the men.

Ambrosius leaned into Merlin, and loudly asked, "Now, Merlin, tell us, do you see victory for our cause today?"

Before him, the earth-map began to come alive. "I see…" Merlin glanced to Ambrosius for reassurance before he spoke. "I see Saxons fighting alongside Britons, Saxons fighting Britons, and the worst image of all—Britons fighting Britons. Warriors' axes and swords clash. Body parts litter the blood soaked battlefield." Putting his palms to his temples he continued, "Fire fills the fortress; horses and men cry out in agony, tortured women and children scream in terror—and then silence." Before collapsing, he looked to Ambrosius, "Out of the blackened skies, I see the red dragon banner flowing triumphantly."

Ambrosius supported Merlin, as Uther ran to his side, his feet crushing the makeshift battlefield. The brothers mirrored a knowing smile as Uther lifted the young prophet, gently depositing him into a pile of pillows.

"Well Ambros, it appears that you no longer need me to fight your battles, when you already have the answer to their outcome before we step foot on the battlefield," Uther smirked.

"Come now brother, you know that without you and our brave men, there could be no victory to prophesize."

Uther turned to his squire. "Bring me the physician. We need to get this boy-knight to his feet." Looking to Ambrosius, he continued, "I am sure the little sage would wish to see his predictions realized. It will be good for him to endure first hand what he has only experienced through his visions. It can only make him a better prophet, a better servant to our cause."

"My lords, your horses are ready," Ambrosius' squire stood near the tent's entrance as he made the announcement.

"Will you join us, Ambrosius, or have you taken up the role of nursemaid?" Uther inquired with concern mixed with irritation.

"Not to worry, brother. As soon as the physician arrives I will be at your side."

Abruptly, Uther turned and silently stalked out of the tent.

Pellinore stood, waving his hands in the air, and announced, "Come men, we have a tyrant to slay, a kingdom to win back, and a new High King to crown!" A loud roar rang out from inside the tent, which soon extended to the troops outside.

15

"Ambros, this day we liberate Britain, as well as regain our heritage. This day we fulfill our father's destiny," Uther mused, sitting at the hill's base upon his black stallion. Absentmindedly, he focused on the red dragon banner, fluttering above the line of infantry spread out in front of him, in perfect formation.

"I concur, brother." Ambrosius, eyes closed, listened to the heavy breathing of his warhorse; the stallion's ribcage rapidly contracting and expanding under his legs, emulating his own nervous excitement. "This will be our defining battle, it has been foretold." Opening his eyes, Ambrosius glanced left, to Merlin, sitting in quiet meditation upon the tiny gray mare dwarfed by the surrounding warhorses.

Leaning into Ambrosius, Uther implored, "Brother, are you sure you do not want me to oversee Merlin? Or, better yet, leave him behind with the pages. I am having second thoughts about him joining our forces today. I fear that you will become careless from trying to watch his back."

"Merlin is under my charge. I pledge to you that I will not be reckless with his life, nor my own."

"As you wish," Uther grumbled. In anger, he tugged on his reins, causing the stallion's head to flail. Nearby, loud retching further aggravated his growing frustration. Positioned to Uther's right—Lot and his men. The Young Royal Guard had replaced their swift stallions with powerful chargers, and they stood at restless attention. Scowling, Uther glared in Lot's direction.

Shrugging, Lot shook his head, letting out an exasperated sigh as he reached over and gently patted Meleagant's back.

Behind them, over three hundred cavalry; their steeds' nostrils snorting steam from the frigid morning air. The riders doing their best to put their mounts to ease; as beasts and horsemen waited in agitated anticipation of the forthcoming battle charge.

On Uther's signal, the foot soldiers and archers, under the command of Pellinore, Aglovale, and Arrok, rushed up the twisted path, through its surrounding forest. Reaching the hill fort, they began assaulting the outer of the two eastern gates.

Uther and Ambrosius separated. Half the troops following Uther and the Young Royal Guard, while the other one hundred fifty followed Ambrosius and his generals, with Merlin riding close to Ambrosius' side. Both sets of cavalry ran in tight formation close to the tree line's lower edge that surrounded the base of the tor, their view hidden from the hill fort above.

East

As Arrok and his men reached the gate a loud battle cry rang out from inside Vortigern's fortress. A lone sentry's cry mixed with the first sounds of the primitive battering ram as it crashed against the wooden gate.

Aglovale's infantry formed a line in front of his father's men. At his command, his troops raised and locked their shields, giving shelter to Pellinore's archers from Vortigern's anticipated arrow shower.

"Draw, Archers!" Pellinore yelled to his shooting line. His archers' nocked their arrows, pulling their bows taut, awaiting the signal to shoot—and nothing. No more shouts from the enemy, no arrows from beyond the fortress walls, no infantry pushing against them, just the steady pounding of the battering ram against the wooden gate.

"Stand Fast!" Pellinore commanded. The archers let down their arrows, lowering their bows.

A loud roar from Arrok's men filled the air as they crashed through the first gate. "Hold!" Arrok cried out, as he peered down the long empty passageway leading to the enormous inner gate adorned with metal. Arrok made his way back through the infantry lines to confer with Aglovale.

At the same time Aglovale was advancing to Arrok's side. "It smells like a trap." Aglovale said, as they stood in the wooden rubble and stared towards the second gate.

"Do we advance or regroup?" Arrok asked nervously.

"Hold steady, I sent a messenger back to Pellinore, we await his reply."

Within moments a young runner came bursting through the lines. "My lord, I bring you word from Sir Pellinore." He bent over to catch his breath. Through gasps he continued, "Sir Aglovale, you are to divide your shield line. Half will advance to the gate, followed by Sir Arrok's troops with the battering ram, and the rest will wait behind to cover Sir Pellinore's archers."

Aglovale looked to Arrok, both men nodded in agreement, sending the messenger back to Pellinore, requesting that he send word to Uther that they were on the advance.

West

Ambrosius' cavalry and generals spread out behind him, hugging the hill fort's lower line of trees, as he reached the west gate moments ahead of Uther.

"Do we wait or attack now?" Merlin's heart raced as he pulled his sword from its sheath.

"We wait," Ambrosius whispered as he searched the horizon for signs of his brother.

***

Uther and his men were about to reach the west gate, when he twisted in his saddle and motioned a command to Lot, who instantly pulled his stallion sharply to the right, spreading his men along the northeastern hillside, as he headed back to the northern entrance. Uther then continued to the west wall.

***

"You are late," Ambrosius quipped.

Uther just grinned as he approached. "We were detained by a messenger from Pellinore. It seems Vortigern has some tricks left that he wishes to teach us on battle strategy."

"Brother, I think it is about time we became the teachers."

Uther laughed loudly, turned, and galloped up the west side of the hill through a narrow path within the trees, with Ambrosius in hot pursuit, followed by Merlin and fifty riders.

North

Leaving their troops safely within the lower tree line, Lot and Nentres nearly collided as they raced toward the entrance to the northern escape tunnel. Both men dismounted, as they began their frantic search for the hidden hatch.

"Here, Lot, right where Brydw said it would be," Nentres whispered, as he was about to pull at the large moss covered metal ring partially concealed in the grass.

"Wait!" Lot rushed to stay Nentres' hand. "We wait for them to come to us."

"Wait?" Nentres cocked his head, with a look of exasperation. "Do we not want the advantage of a surprise attack? We can enter the tunnel and be inside the fortress before Uther and Ambrosius reach the back entrance."

"Those are not our orders," Lot sneered. More than anything he hated his judgment to be questioned.

Nentres saw the anger in Lot's expression and backed off the confrontation.

"Ride back to Dodinel, tell him and Meleagant to stagger their men along the upper side of the tree line. Make sure they understand that they must, at least for now, stay veiled within the trees."

East

On the east gate Arrok and his troops advanced cautiously, their shields held in the infamous Roman turtle formation. The men crept more than marched, intertwining through the narrow passageway. Upon reaching the inner gate, Aglovale motioned for Arrok to tunnel his men with the battering ram under the shield formation that snaked from one gate to the next. Close behind at the outer gate entrance, a second line of shields formed, with the archers close behind, awaiting Pellinore's orders.

As the sharpened tip of the log hit its first blow against the metal gate a rain of arrows fell from the fortress above. Men screamed in agony as arrow after arrow slipped between the shields below, embedding within the thighs and feet of the approaching infantry.

"Draw, Archers!" Pellinore yelled to his shooting line once more.

Again his archer's nocked their arrows, pulling their bows taut, awaiting the signal.

"Loose!" Pellinore bellowed.

Hundreds of arrows flew with great accuracy. The shield lines directly below the wall quickly scattered. Some not moving fast enough as great numbers of Vortigern's archers fell like death stones from the wall, crushing those below. Regrouping, the shield lines continued their assault against the impenetrable door.

West

On the other side of the hill, Uther and Ambrosius astride their mounts watched as two men tossed roped wall hooks upward to scale the west outer gate. Upon reaching the top, the scouts surveyed the inner wall and scurried back down.

One of the men ran to Ambrosius. "My lord, the back entrance is blocked by debris. It will take a half day to remove all the wood, rocks, and carts that are pushed against it."

With exasperation Ambrosius quizzed, "Are there any signs of Vortigern's men? Any signs of Saxons?"

"No, my lord, there is no one."

From the north, a rider galloped to Uther. "My liege, I bring a message from Sir Pellinore. Our men have broken through the first gate, but have been unsuccessful in penetrating the second one."

"Any word from Lot?" Uther's stallion danced under him as he spoke.

"Yes, my liege. Lot found the escape tunnel's hatch."

Uther looked to Ambrosius, "This has been far too easy."

Ambrosius nodded in agreement. "We have them. Now we have to decide if we wait for them to surrender. Or, we try to breech the wall and go in fighting."

"You know as well as I that Vortigern will never surrender." Uther looked toward the heavens, as a murder of ravens flew cloud-like above the fortress. Looking back to the messenger, he barked, "Tell Lot to ready his archers, if we set fire to the outer barrier it will give us easy access to the inner wall, and perhaps smoke the old man out through the secret passageway. Let Pellinore know that Lot will be setting the outer wall aflame, and that he needs to pull his men back, well outside the first gate." The messenger set off to the north, as Uther looked to his brother, nodding to Merlin.

"Merlin," Ambrosius commanded, "Your horse is as swift as any messenger's, we need you to ride to the south and let the commanders know of the current situation. Tell them to advance to the inner side of the forest. They must hold their positions and ready their men. Under no circumstances are they to allow anyone to escape the fortress walls. Next, ride the perimeter of the hill, and bring us a status report of our troops."

South

Merlin raced off, disappearing within the grove of trees toward the southern edge of the hill. Upon reaching each of the generals, he conveyed Ambrosius' message. When done, he pushed his gray hard toward the east gate.

East

"Pull Back! Pull Back! Arrok shouted, his men dragging the dead and maimed from within the passageway as they retreated.

"Stand Fast!" Pellinore ordered his archers, as they slowly backed into the protection of the forest's edge.

Merlin reined his horse hard as he turned the corner to the east gate, just as Aglovale raised his hand to the shield line. Merlin watched in horror as he felt a lone arrow swoosh in front of his face. Gulping down bile, he watched as the arrow's shaft pierced the fleshy gap of Aglovale's neck just between helmet and breastplate. A command gurgled from the dying man's lips, and Merlin saw the hunger in Aglovale's eyes for his last earthly vision to be that of his father.

"Aglovale!" Arrok shouted above the din of battle. He pushed his way past Merlin into the cluster of troops, sliding to the ground, grabbing the young prince in his arms. But, it was too late. Aglovale was bathed in blood, eyes frozen searching towards the woods, mouth opened to words that would never be heard. Picking up the lifeless body, Arrok worked his way back to the forest's edge, walking closely behind Merlin.

Pellinore grabbed the reins of Merlin's horse, "Get word to Uther and Ambrosius that we have pulled our men back from the wall." Confused he looked into Merlin's tear-filled eyes.

"My lord, I am so sorry," Merlin sobbed.

The old king knew that this was Merlin's first battle and took pity on him with words of reassurance, "Sorry? It is not your fault that we sounded the retreat." Giving him a fatherly smile, Pellinore patted the toe of Merlin's boot.

"No, my lord, it is not our retreat that I am sorry for, but, instead for your loss." As Merlin spoke, Arrok approached the old king, pressing hard into him. Arrok looked down to the man limp in his arms.

For moments, Pellinore stood dumbfounded as he searched for life in the pale face of his eldest son. "It cannot be," the words fell softly. The archers and shield lines went quiet as he repeated the words in a deep mournful wail, "It Can Not Be!" All eyes went to the old king as he wrenched the boy from Arrok's arms. Falling to his knees he cradled Aglovale tightly.

Merlin turned to Arrok, "I am supposed to get a status report from Sir Pellinore, to bring back to Ambrosius, but..." he looked down and sighed deeply.

Arrok, growled, "Use your eyes fool." He pointed to the broken gate, to his broken troops, and lastly to the old king covered in his son's blood. "There is your status report."

With a red face and wet eyes, Merlin nodded in a silent understanding, yanking on his mare's reins, he set off at a hard gallop to the north.

North

Nentres raced to the north entrance, as Lot was organizing the troops. "Pour oil in the firepot," Lot yelled to one of the men. Turning to face the rest of the mounted archers he shouted, "Wrap your arrows, we are going to light up the noon sky!"

Nentres pulled Lot aside, "We have a problem."

"What now?"

"Meleagant has vanished."

"What?" A dazed and confused Lot searched Nentres' face.

"When I rode back through the lines to give the order to nock arrows, Meleagant was not with his men. When I queried Dodinel, he said he had not seen the prince since daybreak."

Looking skyward, Lot screamed, "Aaaaaaaaah, we have no time for this! No time!" Turning, he stormed to his horse, grabbing a handful of mane, he swung onto the stallion's back.

"Do you go to look for him?"

"No!" Lot waved his arm toward his cavalry waiting at the forest's edge, and then toward the fortress. "I cannot."

"I instructed Dodinel to manage his troops and Meleagant's."

"That is all that can be done." Lot reined in his stallion.

Northeast

It was just mid-day and Merlin had already had his fill of war. Trotting his mare close to the inner side of the tree line, he came upon Dodinel and Meleagant's cavalry. The riders sat at attention, with bows, lances, and swords lowered, but ready in an instant for a command from their leaders.

Dodinel grunted as Merlin approached.

"Sir Dodinel, I am to get a report from you and Sir Meleagant as to your status, to send to Ambrosius."

"I report to Lot or to Uther, not to Ambrosius, and especially not to you, his toy soldier," Dodinel smirked.

Merlin casually rode his gray alongside Dodinel's warhorse and reached snakelike under Dodinel's helmet, grabbing his throat, squeezing his larynx tightly. Pulling him downward, Merlin snarled, "Don't mess with me, you coward. I have just seen a man die in front of my eyes; a brave knight, an honorable man, a firstborn son. If possible, I would it have been you, instead of Pellinore's eldest." As he released his grip he commanded, "Give me your status report—*Now!*"

Dodinel's hands clutched his throat as he gasped deeply for breath. He gazed wildly at Merlin in disbelief that this small boy wielded such strength. "We…" he croaked out the words, "…we have seen no one on the wall yet, the troops are ready for the command to fight." Bending over, he coughed loudly and spit phlegm.

"Where is Meleagant? Does he not lead his cavalry?"

Looking Merlin in the eyes Dodinel coughed his reply, "Meleagant is with Lot."

"It matters not, where Meleagant, truly is." Merlin glared back. Instinctively he knew Dodinel lied. "Uther and Ambrosius command that you conceal your men on the verge of the inner circle of the forest, and keep as you are, in readiness for battle." He kicked his mare, racing toward the northern tunnel entrance.

North

Merlin arrived to the north just as Lot and Nentres' archers approached a flaming vat of oil. Their horses sidestepped and whinnied loudly as they rode near the fire. One by one the archers dipped their grease-cloth arrowheads into the pot, setting the arrows aflame. On Lot's command fifty arrows flew into the sky hitting their target. Within seconds the wooden outer wall of the fortress caught in a raging inferno that raced from east to west. With only a sidelong glance to Lot, Merlin continued his ride circling the fortress, racing the flames to Ambrosius' side.

West

Merlin found his place between Ambrosius and Uther just as the west gate engulfed in flames. They watched as the outer wooden walls and gate began to crumble, sending sparks and black soot into the heavens. The ravens cawed franticly as they scattered, racing into the forest's treetops, yet refusing to leave, knowing they would be well fed by evening.

"On the south side, the men stand ready, but have seen no movement," Merlin spoke quickly, wanting to get the words out before their status changed. "The northeastern side is the same. No, movement on the walls, and Dodinel awaits your commend to strike. As you can see, Lot and Nentres have ignited the fire ring."

"And of the east gate?" Uther kept his eyes on the wall as he spoke.

"Regretful news from the east gate. They have endured many casualties, the worst being the death of Sir Aglovale." He paused to let the words sink in, and was taken aback by Uther and Ambrosius' reactions to the news: no tears, no anger, no comments. Merlin looked from one man to the next, both sat upon their horses staring into the flames.

"What now, brother?" Ambrosius asked.

"We wait."

North

Lot and Nentres pulled back their archers into the woods—the firepots still glowed near the perimeter of the trees, the wooden wall smoldered on the edge of collapse. Black smoke filled the air, causing their eyes and throats to burn. Branches broke from deep within the forest as they heard a rider pushing through the undergrowth. Suddenly Meleagant burst through a cloud of smoke, dragging something behind his horse and waving a small white strip of cloth.

"I have him! I have him!" Meleagant screamed; eyes white, pupils dilated.

Nentres pushed his stallion into Meleagant, lunging for the crazed rider's reins. At the same time, Lot yanked the rope from the prince's bloody hand. On the other end of the line was the bloated body of Brydw, the rope knotted haphazardly around his ankles.

Meleagant giggled like a maiden as he put a finger to his lips and whispered to Lot, "He was alone."

Lot looked to Nentres with panic, and then back to Meleagant.

"What do you mean, he was alone?" he asked as he slid off his horse, struggling to untie the ropes from around the dead man's boots.

Meleagant leisurely dismounted, squatting next to the body, his fingers busily picked at the knots. "What I mean is exactly what I said." He looked to Lot with an amused expression. "There was only one body, one dead man, one brother to bring back."

Lot struck out in a crazed fit of anger pushing Meleagant to the ground, arm raised, fist about to strike.

Nentres jumped from his horse grabbing Lot's arm. "Get a hold of yourself!"

Lot stood, and began to pace about. He was thankful that the smoke was thick, and hoped it had covered the events from his troops. He peered into the trees to catch a glimpse of any of the cavalry who may have broken formation out of curiosity. All seemed quiet—too quiet.

Panic set in anew as he twisted to look back to the opened tunnel's hatch. "Nentres!" He grabbed Nentres' shoulder and pointed to the escape entrance and the small group of emerging Saxon warriors. Suddenly Lot felt a sharp pain in his left shoulder and he knew that the real battle was about to commence.

West

Through the dark cloud and burnt embers of the west gate another group of Saxon warriors manically charged; axes and short swords held high, shouting a horrific battle cry. They were followed closely by over two hundred of Vortigern's best fighting men.

"Attack!" Uther shouted. The cavalry forced forward, crashing into the human wall.

Merlin's frightened mare turned in circles and he clung tightly to her mane to stay mounted. He franticly looked to Ambrosius for assistance, only to catch a glimpse of the backside of the white stallion, as brother followed brother into combat. Unsheathing his sword, Merlin pulled the reins hard to the left, and he too entered the fray.

Swords, axes, and lances came from every direction. Chain mail chimed from the Saxon's deadly blows. Merlin closed his mouth to avoid the taste of Saxon and British blood as it sprayed upon his face, body, and horse. The stench of the dead and dying was overwhelming, and he did his best to breathe shallow, or not breathe at all. He swallowed hard to avoid retching, as his morning meal ebbed and flowed within his throat. With eyes tightly closed, he intuitively struck out, his sword accurately finding its target time and time again.

Instinctively, Merlin's fingers seized his sword in a death grip the instant he experienced a sharp blow to his back. Unhorsed, gasping for breath, he looked up in time to view a giant mace plummet downward. Shutting his eyes from his inevitable demise, a warm shower bathed his face. Upon the realization that he was not dead, Merlin cautiously opened his eyes. The mace, with detached hand, twitched sardonically next to his shoulder. No longer able to hold down his breakfast, turning his head to the ground, he heaved violently, his vomit mixed with the blood of the dead man's forearm.

"Get back on your horse. Now!"

Merlin looked up to see Uther, holding a sword dripping with blood in one hand, and the reins to the gray in the other. Somehow he managed to get his body to obey. On shaky legs he stood. Grabbing a handful of mane, Merlin swung onto his mare; the horse now covered from ears to tail in sticky burgundy. Once more Merlin fell into a battle-frenzy, clashing out with wild abandonment.

"Merlin! Merlin!"

Somewhere in a distant realm Merlin heard his name.

Their swords clashed, as Ambrosius cried out once more, "Merlin! It is Ambrosius!"

Through glassy eyes and wielded sword Ambrosius' face came into focus. "Sire?"

"Merlin, I need you to take a message to the south side. Uriens and Carados' cavalry need to join our efforts on the west gate. Brastias and Ulfius need to spread their troops out along the south wall, making sure they do not allow anyone to escape." Ambrosius continued to parry and thrust his sword as he yelled his orders to Merlin. "Do you understand?"

"Yes, my lord."

Merlin thrashed his way through the fight, jumping his mare over the fallen bodies as he raced to deliver Ambrosius' message.

South

Uriens was the first to view the wild apparition approaching, a red rider, upon a fiery charger. Drawing his sword, he was about to attack, stopping only upon hearing Merlin's voice.

"To the west gate!" Merlin screamed.

Without hesitation Uriens motioned to his men and sprinted to the rescue.

"To the west gate!" Merlin repeated as he galloped past Carados and his men.

Carados mimicked Uriens' actions, leading his men into the thick of battle.

Ulfius saw the cavalry move and advanced to Brastias' side as Merlin approached.

"Spread out, but stay to the southern tree line. No one is to be allowed to escape the fortress." Merlin then pulled hard on his mare's reins, racing after Uriens and Carados in a desperate attempt to rejoin Ambrosius.

East

The east wall was still ablaze, as Pellinore and Arrok's men regrouped, readying themselves for a second attack. Their vision impaired by the smoke, they heard the giant inner gates creak long before they saw them open. Battle cries from both sides ensued as the men rushed each other over and through the burning outer gate.

North

On the northern side, Lot slowly regained consciousness, finding himself near the open hatch. He tried to push himself up, but his left arm was useless. Through hazy vision, he looked to his shoulder in disbelieve as he grasped the shaft of the arrowhead protruding through his breastplate. With shaky hands he reached up, breaking the shaft near his body. Reaching to his back he groaned as he felt the arrow's feathers nestle close to his leathers.

"Lot," the voice could barely be heard over the war cries from the forest. Nentres lay nearby, an arrow jutting from his side.

"Nentres, be still. Do not move. I will come back for you. I swear." Lot searched the area for Meleagant, but he was nowhere to be found. Closing his eyes, he listened carefully to his surroundings. In the distant woods, swords clashed, men screamed; from above arrows whistled, making their way from the fortress' inner wall. Finally the sound he was waiting for, the rustle of someone emerging from the tunnel. Smiling, he slowly reached for his dagger, rolling from his side to his belly; he began slithering to the tunnel's doorway.

"It appears clear," Vortigern's unmistakable raspy voice wafted softly as he crawled from the escape route. Turning, he reached down to give Rowena a helping hand up.

Lot buried his head in the sod, pondering his next move. If it had just been the old king, he would not have hesitated, but now Vortigern's bride was in the mix. His orders were to let no one escape. Logically, he knew she was a Saxon. For an instant he contemplated the cost of having the blood of another innocent woman marked on his soul.

"Die you bastard! Die you Saxon whore!" The voice sang out from the forest.

Lot felt the thunder of horse hooves, approaching fast, beating on the ground, signaling disaster. Looking up he saw Meleagant on a full gallop racing toward the hatch, followed closely by Dodinel and his cavalry. In Meleagant's hand a lance held high over his head, the tip wrapped in cloth and set a flame. Before Lot could blink, yell, or move, Meleagant tossed the projectile.

"Burn in Hades, old man!" Meleagant shouted.

Vortigern stared in disbelief as the lance pierced his heart, setting his clothing on fire, and sending him spiraling downward into the tunnel on top of his young bride. Within moments a loud roar rang out as hungry flames licked and sucked the tunnel's wooden interior. From within the fortress, the timber keep exploded into a giant inferno.

West

From the west entrance Merlin froze as he watched the fortress become a bonfire. For an instant he was transported to happier days of the Samhain celebration. He was pulled from his daydreams by Ambrosius and Uther's loud shouts to retreat behind the tree line.

Through clouds of bellowing smoke men scurried about the battlefield, leaving the dead, and doing their best to retrieve the dying— all the time moving toward the protective edge of the forest. Merlin dismounted, threw off his helmet, fell to his knees, his hands pressing hard to his ears, trying to block out the screams emerging from inside the hill fort.

South

Shrouded by a rolling cloud of black smoke, hundreds of figures darted ghostlike, as a section of the southern inner wall gave way. The cavalry, who had sat silently awaiting battle all day, finally got their chance to enter the action.

"Charge!" Came the orders in unison from Ulfius and Brastias. Swords pulled, arrows nocked, they led their men in pursuit of the enemy. As per Merlin's orders, no one escaped. The first group gave no resistance to their attack. It was not until the second line of well-trained infantry emerged from the flaming hill fort's inner walls that they had the first suspicions of those they had slaughtered.

East

On the east gate, Pellinore and Arrok's men were suddenly attacked by a new kind of monster. Pushing through the gates, demons with axes and swords held high, bodies aflame raced—some screaming, others were beyond screams.

"Retreat to the woods!" Pellinore shouted as he watched the fortress turn into a funeral pyre. "The lords of Hades fight the battle for us now."

16

Into the early evening the troops waited and watched the hill structure turn from inferno to ash. The physicians were called to care for the injured as tents appeared along the upper tree line of the eastern and northern hillsides. Still covered in blood and soot, Uther, Ambrosius, Merlin, and the remaining generals entered the once regal fortress to assess the damage. The structure was burned to the ground with only wood fragments and charred bodies remaining.

As they walked past the collapsed southern wall and down the hillside, Merlin's hawk descended from the heavens, scattering the ravens from their feast. Squawking they flew from the trampled and burnt bodies of the slaughtered men, women, and children.

"We had no idea." Brastias sighed, as he stood next to Ambrosius.

"We were only following Merlin's orders." Ulfius sneered.

"My orders," Ambrosius corrected. "No one could have known that Vortigern would use unarmed defenseless servants, woman and children as a shield line for his infantry."

"I would have known, if anyone would have bothered to ask," Dodinel spat a mouthful of slimy, black secretion on the ground.

"What is done—is done!" Uther bellowed.

"Victory at any price?" Merlin murmured.

To the surprise of everyone, Ambrosius pulled Merlin into him. Dry-eyed Britain's new young High King held Merlin tightly, as the boy prophet wept uncontrollably in his arms.

In anger and disgust, Uther stomped back through the fortress debris, mounted his stallion and headed north to check on Lot and Nentres.

***

Before entering the northern physician's tent, Uther inspected the death tunnel, wishing to see for himself the evidence of Vortigern's remains. Next to the hatch's opening, the king's crown sparkled in the moon's glow. Uther smiled as he picked it up, absentmindedly rubbing the embedded jewels with his thumb.

Peering into the darkness of the tunnel's hole, he saw Vortigern's body, burnt beyond recognition, yet the king's sword remained near his side. Retrieving the weapon, Uther inspected it in the moonlight. He knew from the inscription upon the blade that it was the same sword that Vortigern had taken from the body of his murdered father twenty years prior. Grasping the hilt, for the first time today a rush of victory flowed through his body.

He plunged the sword into the soil within the circle of the crown. Uther was about to close the hatch, when he heard a whimper from under the king, near where the new queen had fallen. Jumping into the ashen rubble and pushing the scorched remains aside, he reached into a hollow within the side of the collapsing dirt wall. There, within Rowena's charred hand, wiggled a soot covered Scottish Deerhound puppy.

"So, we do have a survivor." Uther removed his helmet, gently placing the puppy inside as he exited the death trap. Retrieving the crown and sword he tied both to his saddle. Walking alongside his stallion he headed once more to the infirmary tent, his helmet tucked safely under his arm.

***

The guards bowed as Uther approached, pulling back the entrance flap. Shadows danced ghostlike upon the walls, eerily elongated by the candles' flickering lights. Caked with dry blood, Uther visibly shivered watching the pages run from one man to the next. The moans emanating from the injured assaulted his senses, causing his mood to turn dark.

"My lord, are you injured?" The physician asked franticly.

"No, I am fine." Uther's eyes searched for his young fallen knights.

"My lord, I have warm water and clean clothing available."

"No! I am fine," pushing the physician aside, he grumbled, "Where is Lot?"

"In the far corner, my lord."

Uther bent down and spoke to each of his injured men as he slowly made his way to the young knights. He sighed when he first saw Lot sitting on the ground with his back leaning against the tent's corner post. On one side lay Nentres, on the other Meleagant. Although both Lot and Nentres wore cloaks, they were stripped to the waist, blood seeping through their bandages.

"My liege," Lot tried to stand, but his left arm was still immobilized and his right hand was locked in a death grip within Meleagant's fingers.

"There is no need to rise." Uther dropped to his knees in front of Lot and reached inside his helmet, placing the squirming puppy on Meleagant's chest.

For the first time in weeks Meleagant's eyes opened, focused and unglazed. He smiled brightly as the furry ball nuzzled into his neck and began sucking on his earlobe. "Oh, my liege, your puppy is beautiful."

"Your pup," Uther corrected.

"Thank you so much." Grinning, Meleagant looked to Lot, released his hand, and held the puppy close.

"I bring you good news, boy; I have sent a messenger to your father. As soon as you feel able to ride, an escort will take you home. The battlefield has seen enough of you for now, as I know you have of it."

Lost within the puppy, Meleagant paid little attention to Uther's words.

"Thank you, my liege, for your kindness to the Prince," Lot spoke softly. "How is Nentres?"

"The physician gave him something to help him sleep, and said he will be fine, it will just take time for him to heal completely. The arrow passed through his side, but it appears to have only gone through flesh. We just need to make sure infection does not set in."

"And Meleagant?" Uther looked to the boy cuddling the puppy.

"He is unhurt physically," Lot sighed deeply, "yet, his mind comes and goes." He closed his eyes tightly, fighting back the tears, refusing to let Uther see him cry.

"And you?"

"Oh, I am fine. It is only a minor wound, nothing to worry about."

Uther smiled. As always, he was impressed with Lot's courage.

"Your Majesty." A young page stood beside Uther, holding a tray and trying not to spill the vessels as he bowed.

Uther took both tankards of ale, offering Lot one, as he drank from the other. "Go find us something to eat, boy," he commanded the page.

The warm liquid flowed down Lot's throat washing away the day's sins. Before he took a second swig, he inquired, "What of Britain now? Now that Vortigern is dead, will you be our next High King?"

"No. That honor shall pass to my brother. I have no desire to become king. No desire to be stuck in Londinium—and, certainly no desire to spend my days sitting behind a writing table."

"You would make a good king."

"Ambrosius will make a better one."

"In that case; long live the new High King." Lot raised his tankard.

"Long live my brother, the High King!" Uther took a long drink from his tankard and raised it as well.

"And what of us?" Lot motioned his head from one fallen companion to the next.

"Ah, yes, the Young Royal Guard." Uther acknowledged their formal title. "When Nentres and Meleagant are able to ride, you and Dodinel will escort the young prince to his home. The kingdom of Gorre will be a good place to spend the fast approaching winter. With the arrival of Beltane, you, Nentres, and Dodinel can either meet me in Londinium, or make your way back home to your fathers' kingdoms. You have all been away from home far to long."

Lot closed his eyes again tightly and took a long drink of ale. "Are we not to be present at the crowning ceremony?"

"Winter is fast upon us, we will postpone the official crowning until Beltane."

"With your permission, I will return as soon as possible."

"As you wish, but I assure you that Londinium will be a boring place in winter."

"Let us be bored together then." Lot raised his tankard to meet Uther's.

17

"Uther, it has been over a month since our conflict with Vortigern, yet, you pace about as if you are ready to jump into battle at a moment's notice. Enjoy the peace while it is here brother. You know it will not last," without looking up, Ambrosius spoke as he bent over mounds of paperwork at his writing table in the library at the old Governor's Palace.

"As long as the Saxons are on our eastern shores, and Vortigern's son and sole heir, resides to the north, there shall be no peace." Uther threw himself into a stack of pillows strewn on the floor, his boots scattering dirt clumps across the mosaic tiles.

"Word has it that Vortimer, had already broken ties with his father, long before the obliteration of the Danebury hill fort," Pellinore chimed in as he rummaged through the stacks of scrolls within the wall shelves. "Plus, our scouts have reported back each day, with no new sightings of Saxon ships arriving upon our shores."

"Granted, we have made a momentary truce with Vortigern's kinsmen. His legitimate son may have abandoned his father, but as you know, a bloodline is never truly severed. Let us hope Vortimer's promised allegiance to my brother—his new and rightful king—holds true." Uther grabbed an apple from a nearby tray and sank his teeth in deeply. With the sleeve of his shirt, he casually wiped the juices that ran into his neatly trimmed beard. "It is the Saxons' sudden retreat that worries me. Mark my words. As soon as Hengist gets news of Rowena's death, he *will* seek revenge."

"Why a Saxon warlord would allow that vile old man to marry his sweet young daughter is beyond all reason," Pellinore sighed, as he grabbed an old parchment and reclined on a lectus near Uther.

"Through royal marriages, treaties are made," Ambrosius inserted impassionedly, trying to keep up with the conversation while sorting through documents.

"A mutual agreement of love is heaven on earth," the old king smiled with a twinkle in his eyes. Chuckling, he added, "and a one-sided political marriage turns life into a living hell."

"If we could all be as blessed as you Pellinore, and marry for love," Ambrosius put down his pen and stretched. "Yet, from childhood we were taught that in marriage, alliances prevail over matters of the heart."

"It is not a woman's heart I am interested in…" Uther grinned, putting his index finger to his temple he tapped lightly "…it is her mind."

A nearby page covered his mouth, doing his best to stifle a giggle.

"Perhaps one day love shall come to us brother. At least for tomorrow, we can put aside our thoughts of war as the winter solstice approaches."

"Ambros, there is not a day, a moment, a heartbeat that we can afford to set aside thoughts of war." Uther took another bite of the apple and tossed the core to a page. "Bring us some of my brother's best white wine."

The page scampered out of the room. Bumping into Merlin, the apple core tumbled out of his hand. "I am sorry, my lord."

Pausing in the doorway Merlin entered cautiously, his white gown flowing gracefully, sandals clicking softly.

"Come in, Merlin." Deep into his correspondence, absentmindedly, Ambrosius motioned the boy prophet into the room.

"Where have you been keeping yourself?" Pellinore inquired.

Uther gave a sideways grin to the old king, "Where all pretty boys keep themselves, Pelly, in the Roman baths."

Ignoring Uther's taunts, Merlin acknowledged Pellinore with a quick nod. Walking around the large table he stood behind Ambrosius. Leaning over his shoulder, Merlin examined the writings. "Your Majesty, as you requested, I have been working on the preparations for the winter solstice feast."

"So, Ambros, you are training our young oracle to become a cook? Well done, brother."

"Uther, do you not have men to train?" Ambrosius sighed.

"No, brother, I have given my men the afternoon off as well, so that they too can prepare for tomorrow's celebration," Uther smirked.

Merlin glared at Uther from behind his brother's back. Unconsciously he clutched his hands, driving his fingers claw-like into Ambrosius' shoulder.

Amused, Uther watched Ambrosius do his best not to wince, as he gently patted Merlin's hand in an attempt to dislodge the human talons from his flesh.

"Merlin, why don't you join Uther and Pellinore? I am almost finished here and will be with you all momentarily."

Releasing his grip on Ambrosius, Merlin was about to take a seat on the bench opposite Pellinore, when Uther reached up and tugged on his gown, causing Merlin to sprawl awkwardly on the pillows.

Uther reached over and ruffled Merlin's hair, "Come now boy, do you not enjoy my company as well as my brother's?"

Merlin jerked his head from under Uther's hand. Scooting over to the edge of the pillows, he sat frigid, refusing to speak to his tormentor.

As one page came back with a tray filled with wine, water, and goblets, another page stood in the doorway. "My lord," the boy cleared his throat. Before he could continue, two young men pushed past him.

"Lot, Dodinel, you are here a day early. Good to see you both." Uther pushed Merlin aside to make room for the two knights. Both men were dusty from travel and their boots, like Uther's, left crumbs of dirt on the floor.

"The weather was changing quickly, so we pushed through the night. Not wishing to freeze under the stars when we could be warm under your roof." Lot smiled as he tossed his cloak to one of the pages.

"Your Majesty," both Dodinel and Lot addressed Ambrosius in unison.

Looking up Ambrosius nodded, acknowledging their presence and went back to work.

"Come sit, lads. Wine is about to be served. The new king will remove his nose from his paperwork and join us shortly," Uther tapped the pillows next to him as he spoke.

Merlin quickly got up and sat next to Pellinore, as Lot and Dodinel took their places on either side of Uther.

"What are you reading, Sir Pellinore?" Merlin inquired of the old king.

"I found a story of Homer's."

"Tales of Troy?"

"No, this one is a silly altercation; *The Battle of Frogs and Mice*."

"Ah, the story of trust, betrayal, and war," Merlin ran his fingers across the parchment.

As one page poured the wine, another page brought in additional goblets.

"It seems Merlin has learned all lessons of war from the works of Homer." Uther raised his glass to be filled, took a long swig, and leaned back into the pillows.

Pellinore patted Merlin on the back, "There are worse ways to learn of war."

Merlin was about to interject that he too had fought alongside the rest in the recent bloodbath.

"So, Lot, what of Nentres?" Uther quickly changed the subject, not wishing to get into a theological discussion with Pellinore, nor hear Merlin's complaints.

"His wounds have still not healed." Lot reclined next to Uther as he sipped from his goblet.

"But, the old Roman baths are good therapy; at least that is what Meleagant's father says," Dodinel intervened, as he sat crossed-leg in an attempt to get comfortable. "Do you have any ale? I can no longer stand the taste of wine."

"Bring us some ale," Uther commanded.

Lot stiffened ever so slightly at Dodinel's comment, yet his voice remained calm as he added, "Nentres said to tell you that he will be back to court at the first scent of apple blossoms."

"And, what of Meleagant?"

"He is better, my liege," Lot reached behind himself to adjust the pillows. "His mind is mending, largely due to the care and feeding of his new charge. The puppy is huge—he eats as much as Dodinel."

Smiling mischievously, Dodinel leaned back in the pillows, rubbed his belly and let out a loud belch.

Sitting with a full goblet of wine, even Merlin could not suppress laughter.

"Merlin, you are not drinking either?" Uther nudged Merlin with the toe of his boot. "Would you also prefer ale to wine?"

Merlin moved his foot just beyond Uther's reach, and said nothing.

"I am talking to you, little bird."

"Don't call me that."

Uther sat up, grinning wickedly. "Why, you little bastard. How dare you talk to the High King's brother so disrespectfully?"

Without thinking, Merlin tossed his wine into Uther's face. Letting the goblet drop to the floor, it rolled under the table, landing at Ambrosius' feet.

Uther lunged catlike at Merlin, pulling him from the bench. Pinned on his back, the warmth from the floor tiles surged through Merlin's thin robe.

"Not a wise move, little bird," Uther hissed.

Merlin's heart raced as Uther's eyes dared him to fight back.

"Enough," Ambrosius spoke firm but softly as he picked up the goblet handing it to the page to be refilled. "There shall be no fighting within our new home."

Uther pushed Merlin aside. Smirking to his brother, he wiped his face with his sleeve. "What a waste of good wine." He picked up his goblet and took a long swig.

The page returned with more drinks. "My lord, another?" he looked wide-eyed at Merlin who lay chest heaving, eyes glaring at Uther.

Reaching for the goblet, Merlin grabbed the vessel, and once more flung its contents into Uther's face. "Don't ever touch me again," he snarled.

All eyes went to Merlin. Lot attempted to rise; Uther shook his head in a silent command for him to stay his ground. Simultaneously, Ambrosius jumped up and ran from behind the table. Grabbing Merlin's arm he lifted him up and twirled him around, standing between his protégé and his brother.

Uther put back his head and let out a loud roar of laughter. Licking his lips he quickly stripped his clothing from the waist up, wiped his face, and tossed his shirt and tunic to a page, "What a waste of good wine *and* clean clothing."

Ambrosius relaxed and smiled softly, shook his head, and watched as the giggling pages ran from the library.

Merlin was the only one not amused. He adjusted his gown and addressed Ambrosius, "With your permission, my lord, I wish to retire for the night."

"And, what if he refuses permission?" Uther continued his taunting.

"Will you stay like a man, or go running to the Druid house like a pup with its tail between its legs?"

Merlin forced himself to relax, forced his fingers to unclench, forced his words to stay locked within.

Pellinore looked up from his scroll and asked, "Are you leaving, Merlin? Will you not stay a little longer?" With six sons and a child on the way, boys wrestling in the house were an everyday occurrence to the old king.

"No, Sir Pellinore. I have had enough conversation for one night."

"I grant you permission to leave." Ambrosius gave Merlin a paternal smile. "We will break fast tomorrow morning together." Looking to Uther, and back to Merlin he added, "Just the two of us."

Merlin bowed deeply, turned and walked elegantly from the room.

"Brother, why do you harass the boy so?" Ambrosius took a seat on the lectus opposite of Pellinore, and sipped his wine.

"Because, it is fun."

Both Dodinel and Lot broke out in shrouded laughter.

"Fun?" Ambrosius glared at the two young knights, instantaneously halting their merriment.

"Well," Uther let out an embarrassing laugh, "fun for me."

"It is not fun for him." Ambrosius set his goblet down and leaned into Uther, "Mind my words, brother. I warn you that Merlin is not someone to physically nor verbally torture, even if only done in jest; for your own amusement."

"As always Ambros, I will take your advice…" with a sweeping movement Uther placed his hand on his chest, "…to heart!" He chuckled and emptied his goblet.

"Brother, you are incorrigible."

"I know." Uther shrugged his shoulders and winked.

18

Persistent knocking brought the Arch Druid to the guesthouse entryway. Opening the door, he was surprised to see Ambrosius. "Your Majesty, it is an honor. What brings you to the temple yard this early in the morning?"

"I have come for Merlin." The words came out more abruptly than Ambrosius had intended. He rubbed his hands together; even gloved, his fingers were frozen.

"Would you like to wait inside? You can warm yourself by the fire?"

"No, I will wait here. Just tell him to hurry." Since boyhood, the Druids, with their mystical powers, had always unnerved Ambrosius. Yet, Merlin was different. Like Apollo before him—Merlin was *his* Delphi Oracle.

"He shall be out posthaste." The Arch Druid turned and smiled. The fact that the new king had refused his hospitality, had refused to even dismount, and had been knocking on the door with the toe of his boot was a great source of amusement.

Ambrosius watched the white-cloaked figure disappear into the tunneled archway, the shadows of his flowing gown danced on the torch flickering walls. Although it was six in the morning, the moon still hung heavy in the sky, blocking the sun from her entrance. "Never-ending nights, full moons, and Druids," Ambrosius said aloud as he shivered.

Footsteps sprinted upon the mosaic tiles as Merlin rushed into sight. "Your Majesty, I am sorry to have kept you waiting." Out of breath, Merlin adjusted his white cloak.

"I thought you had forgotten our meeting," Ambrosius smiled.

"No, not forgotten, just late—I beg your forgiveness."

The sound of horse hooves on gravel echoed in the courtyard, as the livery boy ran toward Merlin, the gray trotting close behind. "It is a cold morning for a ride," Elivri laughed softly as he stroked the mare's muzzle. Normally he would never initiate conversation with one of the cloaked-ones, but Merlin was not like the rest, and over the past month they had struck up a friendship—of sorts.

"Thank you, Elivri, for getting up so early."

"I am always here for you." Elivri cupped his hands to assist Merlin in mounting.

Upon returning victorious from the battle at Vortigern's Danebury fortress, the Druids and their followers had looked upon Merlin with renewed admiration. In their eyes, he was no longer a mere boy. He had earned the title of the High King's Advisor. This delighted Ambrosius greatly, much to the distain of his brother.

"Do they rise before dawn every morning?" Ambrosius turned to quiz Merlin as they rode through the courtyard, candlelight illuminating within one of the twin temples.

"Druids require little sleep," Merlin replied nonchalantly, "their search for knowledge is never ending."

"And you? Have you taken up their ways?"

"If you believe that a quest for knowledge is exclusive to Druids, then, yes I have." Merlin pulled his hood over his face as a gust of frigid air swirled.

"It is not *your* never-ending quest for knowledge that I am concerned about, but their *other* ways."

"Ah, you mean their pursuit of nature's secrets; their desire to understand and harness the unknown."

Ambrosius fell into a silence and did not speak again until they approached the bridge leading to the city.

"I wish you would reconsider your current place of residence. Uther and I both feel that it is inappropriate for you to live across the river." He tightened his legs and grabbed his stallion's mane as the giant horse slid on the icy bridge.

"No disrespect, Your Majesty, but I suspect that Uther would wish me to live as far from him, and you, as possible." Merlin's tiny mare stepped surefooted upon the frozen timbers.

Ignoring Merlin's presumptions, Ambrosius continued, "Even if you do not wish to live in the palace, at least move back within the city walls."

He let out a curse as his horse slipped again. "I hate having to cross this bridge every time I seek your advice or merely wish to be within your company."

"There is no need for you to personally fetch me. You know I shall come to your side the instant you summon." Merlin leaned forward, as the biting wind pierced through his clothing. He hated winter, and although he was not eager to enter the gates of Londinium, he too was overeager to reach the other side of the bridge.

"That is not the point!" Reluctantly, Ambrosius slowed his horse to a measured walk, "I need you nearer. I do not wish to go looking for you, nor send a boy in search. You are the King's Advisor! You need to be at my side, or within moments of being so."

"As you wish, I shall move into one of the palace's guest rooms before nightfall." Merlin was glad that his hood covered his face, concealing his deepening frown. Since becoming High King, Ambrosius had been more on edge with each passing day.

Once again they rode silently as they entered the city walls, consumed by their own agendas; both wishing the other would understand, yet, neither wishing to compromise. With heads down, they rode past the road to the palace, and past the forum. It was not until they had ridden past the amphitheater, and turned toward the auxiliary fort, that Merlin uttered further concerns.

"I thought we were to share the morning meal together—alone!" Merlin's voice broke childlike, revealing his disappointment as they entered the military stronghold.

"Have you ever known me to go back on my word?" Ambrosius admonished.

"No." Bewildered Merlin sulked. He was not accustomed to Ambrosius being anything but straightforward. He disliked being caught in a web of deception, even if it was only perceived deceit.

Running out to greet the riders, Ambrosius' young squire shouted over the roar of the wind, "Your Majesty, the table awaits—as well as a roaring fire."

Entering the officer's quarters for the first time, Merlin found the room crude, unadorned, and uncivilized. He had become accustomed to walking on heated mosaic tiles. With each step upon the harden soil floor, ice spikes coursed through the thin soles of his boots.

The walls were barren except for the flickering torches—no works of art, no tapestries. He coughed as his nostrils were assaulted by whiffs of musk mixed with soot and smoke. Yet his need to ward off the cold overruled his instinct to leave. He walked quickly to Ambrosius' side near the large open fireplace.

"Winter is setting in fast and hard." Ambrosius handed his gloves and cloak to a page, and turned to the fire rubbing his hands vigorously.

"Your garments, my lord," the page inquired of Merlin.

Shaking his head, Merlin pulled his cloak tighter, refusing to give up its warmth and protection. He wished to be anywhere but here, within Uther's domain, trapped within the walls of the enemy.

"Come, Merlin. Let us warm ourselves from within: good food, good drink, and good conversation." Ambrosius took his place at the long wooden table.

Eager to get the morning over with, Merlin sat on the bench opposite Ambrosius. With the prospect of spending time alone with the king, coupled with the warmth of the fire massaging his back, he soon found himself slipping into an unexpected state of contentment.

"Mead, my lord?" Ambrosius' squire asked.

"As long as it is for drinking and not tossing," Ambrosius looked at Merlin and smiled.

Merlin's face turned red as his fingers tightened around his empty goblet.

Puzzled by Merlin's reaction, the squire filled both vessels.

Silently, Merlin sipped from his goblet, the taste of honey-wine lingered on his lips as he pondered the king's intentions of this specific meeting place. Outside was filled with the sounds of soldiers awaking; mounted troops thundered through the narrow streets of the garrison.

"Do the men always train before dawn's first light?" Merlin asked as he reached for a slice of warm bread. "I am surprised that Uther is drilling the troops on the morning of the winter solstice celebration. He stated last night that they had the day off."

"My brother has a set routine. He runs his men through their formations at the same time each day, no matter what the sun's position may be, or the moon's for that matter." Ambrosius drank deeply, nodding for a refill.

"There appears to be more soldiers entering the city each day,"

Merlin stated casually as he popped a fig into his mouth sucking on its sweetness.

"With the first breath of Beltane we expect both the fort and the city to be overflowing with military, townspeople, and royalty." Ambrosius leaned forward. "That is why I need you close. As of today, we shall be training alongside the new recruits in preparation for the anticipated battles at winter's end."

At that announcement Merlin stiffened. Swallowing hard, he glared at Ambrosius.

"Come now, Merlin, you didn't think that you would be spending the entire winter deep in the clutches of the Druids?"

Better than being in the clutches of your brother, Merlin thought—but did not voice.

"So, what have you learned in your short stay with the wise ones? Have they initiated you into their realm so soon? Is that the reason you are so unwilling to join us in the everyday reality of life?"

"With each day your words reflect those of your brother," Merlin also leaned forward, elbows on the table.

"We are one in the same."

"No. You may be two sides of one coin. However, each side is distinct." Merlin clasped his hands together, intertwining his fingers. "That is the beauty of you. Even though you are part of the whole, you are extraordinarily unique."

"Never forget that each coin is perfectly balanced, and that each side cannot exist without the other." Ambrosius sighed, "I am nothing without him."

Merlin shrugged and reached for another fig.

"So, do they officially call you Druid?" Ambrosius picked at the slice of bread before him.

"As you know, the title of Druid is not taken lightly, and is only given after years of study. However, they have on occasion referred to me as an Ovate."

"I am aware of your adeptness for mind-travel, but was unaware of your healing powers." Ambrosius studied Merlin with renewed curiosity.

"There is much of what I am, or can be, that I too am unaware of, my lord." He wrapped his long delicate fingers once more around the stem of his goblet.

Standing, Ambrosius changed course, "I wish to address the need for you and my brother to get along. I do not expect the two of you to become friends, although that would bring me great joy. I do insist that you both be civil to one another." Walking to the fireplace Ambrosius looked into the flames, pausing to gather his thoughts. Turning, he leaned on its stone wall and added, "I have spoken to Uther and he has agreed that his treatment of you has been harsh and very unlike him."

"If it is unlike him, why does he persist in his verbal abuse?" Merlin turned on the bench to face Ambrosius, his back leaning on the table.

"His reasons are within him." Ambrosius took another long swig of mead and handed the goblet to the page. "As you grow older, you will come to appreciate the need for alliances. Think of my request as a learning experience, rather than a punishment."

Merlin was about to speak when the outer door burst open, a gust of cold air preceded Uther, followed closely by Pellinore.

"I swear that all of Brittany has far warmer winters than Londinium," Uther laughed as he stomped his boots on the hard-packed dirt floor.

"You can swear all you want, but it will not make the sun come from its hiding place within the clouds for several full moons from now." With his head down and his frozen hands covering his face, the old king nearly collided into Uther as they entered.

"Ambrosius, it is good to see you out from behind your writing table. A king's place is with his men." Uther pulled off a glove and reached for Merlin's half-filled goblet, drinking the contents down with one gulp. "It is too cold to walk around in wet clothing," he added, slapping Merlin on the back.

"Well, well, it is grand to have the two of you pay us a visit," Pellinore smiled, his eyes quickly becoming transfixed on the table filled with breads and fruits. Turning to a page he instructed, "Bring me a warm wine, my bones are cold from the inside out." With the anticipation of a full stomach, he began to gleefully rub his hands together.

Pulling a chair to the head of the table, Uther reached across Merlin. Filling a plate with an assortment of fruits and breads, he leaned back, propping his boots on the table.

"Brother, you are quickly turning into a barbarian; training, eating, and sleeping with your men. I formally request that you move back into the palace, at least from dusk until the morning training of your troops," Ambrosius pressed his back into the fireplace stones as he spoke.

"You realize that this is entirely your fault?" Uther grumbled good-naturedly to Merlin. "What do you think, Pelly? Should we spend our winter nights within the comforts of my brother's palace?"

"Oh, to sleep in a soft bed and place my bare feet upon a warm floor in the morning would be a welcome gift from the goddess for these old bones," Pellinore mumbled through bites of food.

"As you have so unselfishly agreed to join us on the training field, Ambros, on behalf of Pelly and myself, we accept your invitation of hospitality." Slowly Uther placed his feet on the floor, giving his brother a sheepish grin. It was against his nature to not stay with his men, but Ambrosius was no longer just his brother, and he respected the request of Britain's new High King.

"Sir Uther, do your men look forward to tonight's celebration?" Merlin was doing his best to keep his voice even and his manner civil as he sat with his hands folded, tucked safely under the table on his lap.

Looking to Ambrosius before speaking, Uther chose his words carefully, "Tonight's revelry will be a welcome diversion to the men's daily routine, a mere distraction until Beltane and the official crowning of Ambros. Now, *that* will be a day worthy of celebration!"

19

"Long Live The King! Long Live Ambrosius!"

"They have been chanting like that all morning," standing on tiptoes, Merlin shouted, leaning into Ambrosius' ear as the two stood outside Londinium's amphitheatre entrance.

"They have waited all winter to officially celebrate their new leader," Ambrosius replied; his eyes riveted on the half dozen Druids surrounding his stallion. "I wish they would leave him alone. I can understand why they must dress me in white, but why drape my stallion in silks and flowers?"

"It is their tradition, my lord," A young squire spoke up, as he draped a white cloak embroidered with golden threads around Ambrosius' shoulders.

"I know he must feel as I do," he sighed, "and can hardly wait for the ceremony to be over." Ambrosius watched as two of the Druids did their best to braid apple blossoms into the mane of the magnificent white beast as he swung his head from side to side.

"Your crowning and the Beltane celebration will be a welcomed change, especially after such a long restless winter." Merlin smiled as he gently extracted Ambrosius' long hair from under the cloak. This was the first time he had seen the young king nervous, let alone in a truly foul mood.

"Quit fidgeting with me," Ambrosius growled, stomping off to his horse and grabbing the reins. "Quit fidgeting with my stallion." Grasping a handful of mane, he swung onto the warhorse's back, only to slip off the other side, falling into the arms of a surprised Druid.

"Brother, this is no way to start your reign as king," Uther good naturedly taunted, as he galloped to Ambrosius side.

"It is about time you arrived, Uther." Ambrosius shook himself from the Druid's arms, brushing the dust from his white britches.

Leaning on his horse's withers, Uther smirked, "Today, I am glad I am not you."

"That makes two of us, brother. Today, I wish I was not me either." He turned to the Arch Druid, "Silk will not do! If my stallion must also be dressed in white, bring me a deerskin to sit upon." The Druid motioned to another, who ran off toward the stables.

"Well, brother, nearly late as always." Ambrosius reached up for his brother's hand, his white deerskin glove enclosing Uther's black leather one.

"I am, as always, on time." Uther grinned as the horns trumpeted for the first time inside the amphitheatre.

"Just barely on time," Merlin whispered as he walked to his mare.

Kicking his black stallion, Uther moved quickly to block Merlin's path. "Do you have something to say to me, little bird?"

"Let it be Uther, this day is unnerving enough, I do not wish to play peacemaker between the two of you." Ambrosius returned to his horse as the Arch Druid placed a white deerskin upon the saddle.

As Merlin moved around the black stallion's head, Uther nonchalantly bumped his horse into him. "We will finish this later, boy," he muttered.

"Gladly," Merlin parried, as he ran to his mare's side.

Uther had kept his promise to Ambrosius. Throughout winter he had been civil to Merlin. *Tomorrow*, he thought, *it would be time to renegotiate their brotherly agreement.*

"Ambros, I have good news," Uther bellowed over the second trumpeting of horns.

"Good news is welcomed today," Ambrosius shouted, this time swinging gracefully upon his stallion.

Uther beamed as he motioned three riders forward. "Look who has rejoined our troops."

Peering past his brother, Ambrosius smiled, "Nentres! It is good to have you back among us. Have your wounds healed?"

"It is a pleasure to be here on your day of coronation, Your Majesty, and yes, I am of good health. Thank you for asking," Nentres bowed from his saddle as he spoke.

"Ambros, it appears that we are being summoned," Uther said with urgency, as the horns trumpeted for a third time.

Before parting, Nentres added, "Your Majesty, you will make our people proud."

"Thank you, Nentres, it is good to have you here on this auspicious day." Ambrosius took a deep breath, the scent of apple blossoms woven into his stallion's mane filled his nostrils and he instantly relaxed.

Uther rode his horse to his brother's side and grabbed his arm, holding tightly he looked deeply into Ambrosius eyes and smiled. "Our father would be proud of you on this day, brother."

"His pride would be for both of us, Uther."

"Today is your day in the sun, Ambros. I am but a shadow of your greatness." As Uther spoke his eyes glowed with admiration and a brother's love. Releasing his hold, he turned to the riders directly behind him. Lot confidently held the red dragon banner, on his left Dodinel, and on his right Nentres. Behind them two hundred of Uther's best cavalry dressed in black, sitting upon black warhorses. "Move out!" he commanded.

Slowly, Lot moved in front of Uther as they entered the darkened tunnel leading to the amphitheatre's entrance. "Now, sire?" Lot looked to Uther for reassurance.

"Now!" Uther bellowed.

The crowds' chanting rose as Lot galloped into the arena, the red dragon banner fluttering majestically. The spectators roared even louder as Uther charged close behind. Within the center of the arena the Druids had placed a large circle of crystals, and the ring shimmered brightly as the men approached. Upon reaching the arena's center, both men came to an abrupt stop, their horses snorted, flailing their heads, hooves pawing the dirt.

Looking back, Uther nodded to Nentres and Dodinel as they approached the entrance. Behind them the cavalry divided into two groups of single file riders. Upon Uther's signal, the young knights led their men around the arena hugging close to the interior walls: Nentres turning to the left, Dodinel to the right. The cavalry spread out as they rode, until the inner ring of the amphitheatre appeared to be one moving mass of black.

As they met on the opposite side of the arena, a pale-faced Dodinel screamed to Nentres, "I saw him."

"Saw who?' Nentres yelled back as they passed, the cavalry weaving within each other as they continued to encircle the arena.

When Nentres and Dodinel met once more on either side of the main entrance, slowly one by one the cavalry halted behind them, completing a circle of man upon beast along the arena's walls. In unison the cavalry turned their horses to face Uther—both riders and horses bowing deeply to their commander.

Uther raced his stallion back to the main entrance; turned and galloped around the amphitheatre in front of his men. As he acknowledged each of his knights, they righted their steeds. Upon once more reaching the entrance, Uther raced his lathered stallion to Lot's side, positioning himself proudly under the flickering banner of the red dragon.

As the crowd continued to loudly rejoice, Nentres cupped his hands and shouted over to Dodinel, "Saw who?"

"Faustus!" Dodinel mouthed as he pointed to the spectators sitting on the south benches.

"Impossible, he is dead!" Nentres frowned as he squinted to look into the crowd, his vision impaired by the crystals and the noon sun.

"What do we do?" Dodinel screamed above the din of the crowd.

Shaking his head, Nentres also turned pale as he shrugged his shoulders. So intent was he on searching for their ghostly companion that he nearly fell off his horse as the heralds brushed by him to once more sound the trumpets.

***

Watching from within the tunnel, mounted and ready to ride into the arena, Ambrosius turned to Merlin, "What a wonderful display of horsemanship from my brother's cavalry, wouldn't you agree, Merlin?"

"You mean, *your* cavalry?" Absentmindedly, Merlin reached down to brush a speck of dust from Ambrosius' white deerskin boot.

As Ambrosius spoke, his eyes remained fixed on his brother in the center of the arena. "Today, I will officially become Britain's High King, but the military is, and shall continue to be under my brother's command. Although I wear the crown, never doubt that both Uther and I rule this land as one."

Merlin gave Ambrosius a crooked smiled and shook his head.

"It is time, Merlin," Ambrosius pulled back on the reins, as persistent trumpeting caused his stallion to stomp and paw the ground.

Two of Ambrosius' squires dropped franticly to the ground as a hawk swooped in, perching upon Merlin's shoulder.

"It is alright, she means no harm," Merlin assured them.

Laughing, Ambrosius motioned for the squires to rise. "You are full of surprises today Merlin, I am glad your hawk will be joining us. Her sign of strength will balance the doves' sign of peace," as he spoke the court's falconer approached.

"Now, Your Majesty?" The falconer asked as he darted to a large box.

"Yes," replied Ambrosius.

The bird handler unlatched the lid to the box, releasing a hundred white doves into the arena.

Six thousand spectators' voices pierced the air as Merlin entered the amphitheatre, hawk on shoulder, doves flying overhead. "Be still, my friend," Merlin whispered, as he felt the hawk quiver, eager to take flight. Slowly he rode to the center of the coliseum taking his place opposite Uther and Lot.

Next, on foot, ran two squires. Upon reaching the center of the arena they positioned themselves statuesque on either side of Uther's stallion.

The crowd hushed at the first sight of Ambrosius; horse and rider dressed in white, the new king's hair flowing. The golden threads woven into Ambrosius' cape glistened in the sun giving him a godlike appearance. Above the entrance maidens tossed apple blossom petals which wafted gently in the breeze, creating a floral mist around his horse's legs.

In unison the crowd broke their silence with screams of, "Long Live The King! Long Live Ambrosius!" The giant stallion reared tossing its massive hooves into the air, as Ambrosius got him under control by leaning forward and stroking the warhorse's neck, making soothing, hushing sounds. The stallion pawed the ground and danced sideways into the arena as the crowd continued to chant their new king's name.

Ambrosius waved to the onlookers as he made his way to the center of the coliseum. The newly renovated amphitheatre was packed with cheering Britons, all dressed in their finest attire. Kings and queens from every region of Britain, as well as their representatives and their servants had come for this joyous day. For many, this was the first sight they had of their new High King. Above the royalty sat the remainder of Uther's army, and above them the laborers and townspeople.

"Long Live The King! Long Live Ambrosius!" The crowd shouted for what seemed to Merlin like an eternity. The chanting became so intense that the first trumpet of the horns heralding the entrance of the royal witnesses went nearly unnoticed.

"Your Majesty, may I take your horse?" The boys spoke in unison as Ambrosius' squire reached for the king's horse's reins, and Uther's squire reached for his stallion's bridle.

Uther was the first to dismount, walking to Ambrosius as his brother's feet touched the dusty ground. "Your Majesty!" Uther bowed deeply, raising his head slightly, he grinned playfully and winked.

Merlin was confused, until he noticed Ambrosius smiling back to his brother with an equally cocky grin. Then the reality hit him. These infamous men standing before him were not gods at all, but mere mischievous brothers, boys dressed in regal attire, and the fate of Britain would soon be upon their shoulders! His head began to ache as he swayed in his saddle.

"Hear Ye! Hear Ye! Welcome the royal witnesses."

The herald's announcement rescued Merlin from a headlong dive into a futuristic daydream. Momentarily his inner visions miraculously were replaced by the march of nobility.

"King Pellinore of Listinoise!"

Through the side entrance an ornately decorated door opened and out walked the old king with a renewed spring to his step. His face could not conceal a fatherly pride as he made his way to the center of the arena.

"King Leodegrance of Cameliard!"

Merlin shivered with foreboding at the sight of this new face. A flash of future events dashed into his forward memories. He saw King Leodegrance's daughter, a beautiful young girl with long golden hair, dancing in a field of white roses. Twirling about she pricked her finger on a brier—the rose bed turned red, drenched in blood. Merlin pressed his hand hard upon his forehead to deaden the illusion as he softly spoke her name, "Guinevere."

"King Uriens of Rheged!"

Merlin had talked to the brave knight many times since they first met on the hill top battlefield, yet, this day he squinted his eyes as he saw the king in a new light.

"Beware the sisters, beware the kings' wives." Merlin flinched as his mother's voice whispered in the wind. Through frantic eyes he looked first at King Uriens and then to Lot and shivered uncontrollably.

"King Mark of Cornwall!"

Momentarily lost in the past memory of Sir Ector's Villa, Merlin closed his eyes. Smiling he envisioned the Cornish countryside with its rolling moors and purple grasses, and the night of friendship spent under a gnarled beech tree.

Abruptly, Merlin opened his eyes as his hawk dug her claws in deeply. Instinctively, he moved his gloved hand under her breast. Silently, she flapped her wings. Merlin held his breath as he watched her take flight over the heads of the approaching kings.

"Prince Lionel, son of King Bors of Gannes!" The herald ducked as he cried out the last name.

The crowd cheered as Merlin's hawk gently soared downward, landing gracefully upon Lionel's outstretched gloved hand. The merlin rushed up the Prince's arm and began rubbing her beak tenderly on his earlobe.

Upon seeing Lionel, Merlin's headache vanished. With great amusement he turned his attention to Lot. Grinning, he watched Uther's favorite knight turn pale at the announcement of the young prince. Stealthily, Merlin sidestepped his mare next to Lot: who stood staring at the boy and the hawk, with mouth open and eyes wide.

"He has grown in both body and spirit since you abandoned him." Merlin leaned into Lot and taunted, "I look forward to being present at the reunion."

Lot turned quickly, glared at Merlin and instinctively reached for his dagger. At the same time Uther's squire came between the two riders. "His majesty requests that you both dismount."

Grumbling under his breath, Lot handed the banner to the squire as he slid from his warhorse. He then took his place between Uriens and Pellinore, as the four kings and two princes formed a semi-circle of royalty around Uther and Ambrosius.

Merlin dismounted, feeling out of place, he stood with the squires behind the royals, clinging to his horse. Looking into the heavens he felt a deep sence of abandonment as he watched the hawk circumnavigate the arena and disappear from view.

A soft steady beat of drums began to pulse as Uther and Ambrosius raised their hands to quiet the crowd. From the main entrance hypnotic chanting emerged as the first of seven white-cloaked figures appeared.

"With this limb from the sacred orchard of Avalon, I purify the ground on which *The Worthy* stands." The Druid sang as he struck the staff of the silver tree branch into the dirt, causing tiny dust storms to rise. "With these blessed bells I ward off malevolent spirits," he continued as the music from the tiny fairy bells entwined around the bark floated skyward. Reaching the inner crystal circle he bowed deeply to Ambrosius, struck the staff a final time, and took his place next to King Pellinore, extending the royal circle.

"May the waters from the well where history has no beginning, bring *The Worthy* eternal wisdom," the second man chanted. In the palms of his outstretched hands he balanced two small glass vials; one contained a ruby-tinted liquid, the other a milky-white fluid. Reaching the circle's center, he offered them to Ambrosius.

Drinking from each, the new king felt a surge of energy as he became the mystical springs' new vessel.

"Cloaked in this silken robe, *The Worthy* will transform from mere mortal into legend," the third prophesized.

As the Druid approached, Uther removed his brother's white cloak, allowing the Druid to drape the red silken robe upon Ambrosius' shoulders.

Peeking through the circle of kings, Merlin squinted as the midday rays danced upon the shimmering burgundy garment.

"We carry the circles of glory, acknowledging *The Worthy's* power above all men who walk upon this earth," the fourth and fifth Druid voiced. They each carried a white pillow; resting on one a simple gold crown, on the other a golden torque and a ruby ring. Bowing before Ambrosius they each took a step to the side, leaving room for the last two figures to approach—completing the royal circle with a balance of mystical power.

All eyes turned to the entrance as the drummers stopped and a flutist played his first sweet notes. The sixth Druid entered the arena holding an earth-toned cushion. To his right the last cloaked figure glided, hands grasping a sword by its hilt, the blade pointing to the sun. They both had their heads down, faces concealed under hooded cloaks.

Upon reaching the center, the pillow was placed at the sword holder's feet, golden eyes peered from beneath the hood as a delicate finger pointed downward.

Obeying the command, Ambrosius knelt. A collective gasp from the kings broke the silence as a feminine voice loudly declared, "With the acceptance of the gods and goddesses, I pronounce you, Ambrosius Aurelianus, son of King Constantine, the new High King of Britain!"

Uther grinned, and the crowd cheered wildly when the lady thrust their father's recovered sword towards the heavens. Doing so, her hood slipped from her head revealing a mass of long amber curls and a face of stunning beauty.

Merlin roused from his piteous meditation at the first words that flowed from the lady's lips. Pushing Lot aside, he entered the sacred circle just as the woman placed the sword gently on Ambrosius' right shoulder. "Mother," he gasped.

Instantaneously, Lot grabbed Merlin by the cloak, shoving him backwards into a heap at the mare's hooves. Dazed, Merlin lay in the dust, peering around polished boots as his mother moved the sword to Ambrosius' left shoulder.

The Druid handed the lady the crown. Holding the thin gold circlet high she continued, "By accepting this crown, do you swear to be Britain's protector, safeguarding her shores from all invaders?"

"I do so swear," Ambrosius replied, as the simple circle of gold came down snug upon his head.

Next, the Druid handed her the golden ring. The ring's perfect red ruby shined brightly as she placed it on the heart-line finger of Ambrosius' left hand, "This day you merge in marriage to Britain and her people." With a smile she bent down and spoke softly into his ear, "The goddess blesses this union, and if you wish, may one day also grant you a second bride of flesh and blood."

"Britain shall always be my first and only true love," Ambrosius whispered back, becoming intoxicated by the lady's sweet voice and even sweeter scent.

Lastly, the Druid handed her the golden torque. "This dragon ring represents your bond of loyalty to the people of Britain, your children, whom you have sworn to protect. From this day forth it shall be your constant companion, an endless reminder of your responsibility, and Britain's unconditional love." Bending down she opened the necklace that was forged with a dragon's head continually chasing its tail. As she gently placed it around Ambrosius' neck, she felt the heat from his cheek as her lips brushed softly upon him.

"Arise, Your Majesty," proclaimed Uther, squeezing his brother's shoulders tightly.

Merlin scrambled to his feet as Ambrosius rose and the circle of kings merged in to congratulate him.

"Long Live King Ambrosius!" The crowd exploded as they rose to their feet, "Long Live Uther!"

"See brother, they love you as well," Ambrosius said as he hugged Uther.

"Never doubt, Ambros, that *we* love you more." Uther embraced his brother tightly as the throng of kings flocked upon the brothers.

Lionel turned to greet Merlin and was crushed to find his friend and the gray had vanished. When he spun around in hopes of obtaining information from Lot, he too was gone.

20

"I swear it is true," Dodinel was doing his best to convince Nentres and Lot that the man he had seen earlier was indeed Faustus.

"Dead men do not celebrate coronations." Lot turned to his horse and pretended to adjust the saddle's girth. He glanced to Nentres with a questioning stare.

Nentres shook his head *no*, indicating that he had not told anyone about Meleagant discovering only one body in the woods.

"I warned you that this would happen," Dodinel hissed.

"Enough!" Lot turned swiftly, lips snarled, eyes glaring.

"I told you that if the brothers did not get a proper burial that they would come back to haunt us. This living nightmare is on your shoulders Lot."

"I Said, Enough!"

"Be reasonable, Boar. Did you not see both men die?" Nentres stepped in between the two. He had not used Dodinel's nickname for a long time, and he hoped it would jar the giant of a man back to his senses.

"I saw both men die, but did not see both men dead!" Dodinel glared at Lot as he spoke.

Nentres looked from Lot to Dodinel with questioning eyes.

"There is no time for this foolishness," Lot spoke with his best voice of authority, as he mounted his stallion. "We still have the High King's business to attend."

"We have spent a lifetime attending a High King's business, and never has it led to anything but tragedy," Dodinel grumbled.

"Tonight our business is to continue our celebration." Nentres slapped his friend on the back and softly whispered, "We will continue this conversation in the morning."

Dodinel mounted his horse, nodding to Nentres before riding to Lot's right side.

Swinging onto his stallion Nentres rode to Lot's left, "There is one more matter of true urgency that we need to discuss…" Nentres paused to make sure that he had Lot's full attention, "…what do we tell the boy?"

"What boy?" Lot pulled on the reins to steady his mount.

Dodinel leaned his horse into Lot's and shouted, "Lionel?"

"Yes, Lionel, now hush!" Nentres rolled his eyes and continued to speak, as he too brought his stallion closer to Lot's side, "What do we tell the young prince of our whereabouts *that* night?"

"Tell him the truth. We rode straight to Mount Erith. Once there, we went into training, we did not see what happened to his childhood friend."

"A partial truth," Dodinel chimed.

"It is *the truth* none the less." Lot shot Dodinel a contemptuous stare that could be clearly seen even at dusk. "Do not add anything! I assure you that the young prince is as gullible as ever, some things never change. Now, enough questions, our services are required." He squeezed from between the two companions and trotted to the amphitheatre's outer entrance.

***

The arena was overcrowded with merrymakers; commoners mingled with aristocrats, women wore their flower adorned hair down. Many of the men dressed casually in Roman togas in hopes of making easy access to the night's anticipated entertainment. Most were walking about haphazardly catching up on idle conversation. Even more had already taken their places at the four rows of long makeshift tables that lined the inner walls of the amphitheatre's floor. All had access to the wine, mead, and ale that flowed freely.

In the middle of the arena, the ceremonial crystals were divided into two large rings, which stood ready for the sun to fully set, and the nine sacred woods to be brought forth as homage to the gods and goddesses. Three willow chairs were strategically placed between the dancing stone rings.

Upon the middle chair sat Ambrosius, dressed in a cloak of winter ivy, his gold crown replaced by a circlet of deer antlers. Dressed in black, Uther sat to his brother's left. Merlin, costumed in full white Druid garb, occupied the seat on Ambrosius' right.

"Ambros, do you know how ridiculous you look with your crown of antlers?" Uther taunted. They had been drinking all afternoon and both brothers were in good-humor.

"It is not the crown that you are jealous of brother, but the lady who placed it upon my head." Ambrosius raised his goblet and raised an eyebrow knowingly in Uther's direction. In his current joyous state and slightly drunken stupor, even the Druid celebration was a welcomed source of amusement.

"It matters not if the crown is of gold, bone or greenery, the man whose head it is placed upon, is still the High King," Merlin added sarcastically.

Giving Merlin a snarl, Uther turned his attention to the amphitheatre's main gate, where the three original members of the Young Royal Guard waited for orders to enter the arena. As a young squire handed each an unlit oil-tipped lance, Nentres grimaced watching Lot's hand shake as he reached for the spear's shaft—their eyes locked as visions of Vortigern's death danced between them.

"To Kings, Past and Present!" Lot shouted. Smirking he gripped the lance tightly, raising it in the air.

"To Kings, Past and Present!" echoed Nentres and Dodinel, who both mimicked Lot's actions.

"Am I late?"

The familiar voice was deeper than Lot had remembered. No longer the voice of a silly boy, but that of a young man. Perhaps, people do change.

"Lionel!" Dodinel pulled his horse closer to the prince and slapped him on the shoulder.

"It is good to have you back among us," Nentres' spoke softly, his words wrapped in sincerity.

"It is good to be back among old friends. I have missed your companionship," as Lionel spoke he seized the last lance with authority. Smiling, he took his place between Lot and Nentres. Dressed in black sitting upon an exceptionally beautiful black mare, he silently made it known that he too was now considered a permanent member of the Young Royal Guard.

Lot was the only one remaining quiet. Looking skyward, he mouthed, *Will this day of surprises never end?*

Without notice, a deafening gong rang out, causing the horses to whinny and prance—calming as the drums began to beat their hypnotic rhythm. The announcement sent everyone within the amphitheatre scurrying to their seats.

Five Druids entered the arena; heads down, hoods pulled over their faces. Nine carts, pulled by eighteen perfectly matched white riderless horses followed. Next to *each* cart ran four men, each clad from head to toe in red clay. The procession halted as they approached the passageway between the two crystal rings.

"Your Majesty, I bring forth the nine sacred woods," The Arch Druid, with his face concealed, bowed deeply to Ambrosius, Uther and then to Merlin. As he spoke, the remaining Druids reached into each wagon, lifting limbs toward the heavens, chanting in unison:

"For the continued energy of the goddess, we sacrifice the Birch!
For the continued energy of the gods, we sacrifice the Oak!
For the continued quest for knowledge, we sacrifice the Hazel!
For the continued long life of our King, we sacrifice the Rowan!
For the continued belief in the mystic, we sacrifice the Hawthorne!
For the continued protection of the Underworld, we sacrifice the Willow!
For the continued bliss of birth and rebirth, we sacrifice the Fir!
For the continued pursuit of love and family, we sacrifice the Apple!
For the continued search of joy and happiness, we sacrifice the Vine!"

As the Druids spoke, the Red Men quickly divided the nine wagons' contents, standing the limbs within the two crystal rings. Dancing sunwise they wrapped the standing branches with the vines. When the two mighty gatherings of sacred woods stood ready to surrender their lives for the evening's celebration, six of the Red Men squatted behind the Druids and tugged on their cloaks. One by one the white garments fell, revealing the nearly naked Druids, drenched in fresh woad paint from head to toe, transforming them into mystical Blue Men.

With the discarded cloak in hand, one of the Red Men addressed the head Druid. From a pocket within the robe, the Druid withdrew a leather pouch removing a miniature bow, a wooden drill, and a small rectangular board. Placing them on the ground near Ambrosius' feet, he then pulled a second pouch from within the first and extracted a handful of tinder.

Presenting each object to Ambrosius, the Druid uttered, "From the water, we sacrifice the withered grass of the sea. From the land, we sacrifice the dried husk of the lady's thistle. From the air, we sacrifice the down of the hawk and dove. From the heavens, we ask that the mighty sun god bless us with his eternal spark of light, and the mother goddess bless us with abundance."

A silence fell as Ambrosius stood. "In honor of this day…" Ambrosius bellowed, lifting his silver goblet to the setting sun, "… this day celebrating the beginnings of a new season of growth. Growth of both crops and freedom to our much-loved Britain—I declare the Beltane Neid Fire be created."

As the king's words echoed throughout the amphitheatre, the Druid crunched the tinder into a ball and kneeled in front of Ambrosius. Placing one foot on the hearth board he picked up the tiny bow, rotating the drill against its leather string, increasing its motion until the first flicker of fire appeared. Skillfully, he moved the ball of tinder into the sparks, creating the birth of the Neid Fire. Dipping an oil soaked arrow into the fire, he handed the flaming shaft to the new king.

Majestically, Ambrosius sauntered to the outer edge of the waiting bonfires, the flaming arrow held high, as the knights from the Young Royal Guard slowly approached in a single file. Lot bowed to the new king as he lit the tip of his lance into the flame, and turned his horse back to the arena's entrance: closely followed by a joyful Lionel, a somber Dodinel, and a reverent Nentres. Each knight dipping their lances into the fire and returning to opposite sides of the entrance. With the lances lit, the king handed the flaming arrow back to the Druid.

Another hush descended the crowd as the drummers quieted their beating to a slow tapping. The waiting torchbearers touched their flame tipped lances, creating a fire arch in front of the entrance as the procession began anew. From within the entrance the May Queen rode, her silken white gown flowed to the ground covering her pony's legs and backside. A crown of apple blossoms sat neatly upon her veiled head. Her long hair, woven with strands of gold and silver shimmered as it cascaded in soft waves down her back.

The familiar chimes of the fairy bells woven into the mane of the ivory pony could be heard over the soft rolling of the drums, causing Merlin to lean forward nervously in his chair. He had managed to avoid his mother during the light of day. With the rising of the full blue moon it was inevitable that he could no longer evade her presence.

"What's the matter, little bird? Nervous at the sight of a beautiful woman?" Uther laughed—wishing his chair was closer to the boy, so that he could give him a nudge.

Not wanting to reveal that his life began escaping the womb of the *Virgin* May Queen, Merlin sat quietly. He rubbed his eyes, willing the pain in his head to vanish. At the same time unable and unwilling to look away from his mother, as she rode in surrounded by four equally beautiful white clad lady warriors.

Ambrosius stood transfixed as the lady and her handmaidens rode beneath the fire arch. Although only spending a few moments earlier with the Lady of Avalon, his heart leapt at the sight of her transformation from Priestess to May Queen. Neither caring if it was love nor lust, he eagerly anticipated the rising of the moon and the prospects of her silken touch.

"Now!" Lot shouted to his men as the last of the ladies passed.

Lionel and Nentres held their lances high as they turned their mounts in opposite directions racing along the arena, pressing between the walls and the tables filled with onlookers. Coming together at the far side they abruptly halted.

Next to the main entrance the processional drummers savagely attacked their stretched hides, the beat growing louder and faster with each downward blow. It was all Lot could do to keep control of his horse as each beat of the pagan drums pulsed through the ground, through his stallion, through his body. With twilight fast approaching, Lot strained to follow the fire as he watched his men make their way around the stadium. When the distant flames turned into two steady flickers against the far wall Lot waved his lance and nodded to Dodinel.

A roar rang out from the crowd, as the pairs of riders converged upon one another, galloping around the arena in opposite directions, setting their flames to the torches lining the interior walls. Within moments, night once more became day as the amphitheatre danced in the firelight's glow. Upon meeting each other, the pairs of knights trotted in unison to the middle of the still unlit bonfires, taking their places behind Uther and Merlin. Uther turned in his chair and smiled proudly to his young knights.

Silently Merlin slumped into his seat, ignoring the Young Royal Guard, not realizing that Lionel was now among Uther's elite cavalry.

"Your Majesty," Merlin's mother softly spoke as she dismounted. Walking to the young king, she knelt at his feet.

"My lady," Ambrosius' voice trembled, "please rise." He wished to reach out to her, caress her face, hold her in his arms, but feared to even come within touching distance.

"Brother, if you will not help the lady up, I shall." Uther jumped from his chair, dashing forward and extended his gloved hand.

"Tradition, Uther," Ambrosius growled under his breath.

"To Hades with tradition, brother. The eve of Beltane was created to break with tradition. Wouldn't you agree, my lady?" Uther's hand cradled the lady's gently, as if she was a dove about to take flight.

"You are both correct," the May Queen's voice was soft yet commanding. "Beltane is a time for bending tradition, as well as upholding ancient beliefs and customs." Her golden hawk-eyes—Merlin's eyes— pierced through the thin gauze covering her face, burning deeply into Uther's soul.

"My apologies, my lady," Uther released her hand, bowed and stepped back, taking his place at his brother's side.

"My lord, your youthful exuberance shall be all the apology I require," she smiled sweetly. Motioning to her ladies, they rose, taking their places at her side.

With great amusement, Merlin watched the scantly clad Blue Men dance about, leading the royal group widdershins around the amphitheatre towards the northern tables of revelers. He had never seen this side of the Druids, and he quickly clamped both hands over his mouth, stifling the laughter. Turning in his chair to get a better glimpse of the parade, his heart pounded as his mother approached. Once more she was gracefully astride the white fairy pony. Her beauty had not diminished. He closed his eyes and drank in her unique scent of incense and apple blossoms as she passed. If she recognized him, she did not let on.

On the queen's right, proudly walked Britain's newly crowned High King. Merlin was awestruck—even with the foolish antler crown, dressed in green, wearing the cloak of leaves, Ambrosius once more posed a divine figure. The king's long, golden-streaked mane and his clean-shaven face only accented his youth and beauty.

In contrast, to the May Queen's left, walked a somber Uther. He was dressed in his usual black, his beard neatly trimmed. Although

Merlin noticed Uther's hair was beginning to show signs of growth, it was still worn shorter than his brother's and in a Romanesque manner. Even though Merlin knew that Uther was a year younger than his brother—Uther's outward appearance and stoic manner never ceased to amaze him that Ambrosius, now twenty-five, was the eldest of the two.

Following the May Queen—her court of warrior maidens. Their silver laced gowns shimmered in the glow of the torchlight. As they walked by Merlin's chair, a lovely young woman with red hair caught his attention. Merlin found himself flushed and jittery when she smiled in his direction. Looking away as Lot and his men dismounted and joined the group, their lances lighting the way for the May Queen and her ladies.

"Merlin," Lionel whispered. He frantically tried to get his friend's attention. At the same time he tried not to annoy Lot; the drummers drowning out his words before they could find their intended target.

"This is not the time, nor place," Lot barked. "Keep your mind on your duties."

Lionel scowled, but obeyed the orders. Lot was, after all, not only his friend, but also his commander.

Merlin's attention once more focused on the procession as one of the Red Men ran playfully behind the copper-haired maiden, tugging on her dress, causing her to giggle as she swatted his hand. The girl gazed in Merlin's direction, smiled enchantingly, and vanished into the darkness, engulfed by the remaining dancing Red Men.

***

Turning in his chair Merlin sighed, *alone again*. In the distance he could hear the laughter of the crowd mingled with the steady beating of the drums as the procession made its way around the arena. Looking into the heavens, he marveled at the rising full moon bathing the earth with its silver-blue glow. The silhouette of two hawks danced in the moonlight and filled him with sadness. *Even my lady hawk has abandoned me for another.*

"Excuse me, my lord, but I must beg you to rise. The Royals are returning, and we must remove the chairs." The young page gently tugged on Merlin's chair as he spoke.

Relinquishing his seat, Merlin stood with folded arms, as he watched the Red Men approach. They moved their bodies in a wild and bawdy manner, gently pulling at the White Warriors' clothing, taunting them with lewd words and exotic dancing. Until the lady warriors could take the abuse no longer, and they lashed out, using their mystical powers to calm and seduce. Each of the four reached forward and effortlessly pushed the savage beasts to the ground, until the stadium's dirt floor was covered with a blanket of Red Men.

As Merlin and the crowd cheered the mock battle, Ambrosius reached for the May Queen, lifting her from the pony, lingering just a little too long as he held her in his arms. The crowd collectively gasped in shock as the warrior maidens rushed to the High King. They pulled the queen from his arms, seizing the horned crowned from his head, yanking the cloak from his back. The maidens pranced about, tossing the cloak into one awaiting bonfire, and the stag horned crown into the other.

Seductively, the May Queen and her ladies danced around the king. Their hands caressing his body as he stood frozen. Ambrosius' heart beat in rhythm with the drums, his eyes transfixed, never leaving the Fairy Queen. Slowly his body began to move and he joined the ladies in an exotic dance of passion. When the drums suddenly stopped, the king was drenched in sweat, blood surging through his veins, his breathing labored.

"Well done, brother, well done!" Clapping his hands Uther broke the silence, as the crowd once more erupted into an ear-shattering roar.

"I crown you the Green Man—the Summer King, the eternal King of all seasons," the May Queen declared. Placing a new crown of apple blossoms upon the king's head, she cradled Ambrosius' face in her delicate hands and ever so gently kissed his lips.

"Let summer officially begin," Uther shouted to his men, as they thrust their flaming spears into the waiting timbers of the bonfires. Everyone watched in wonder as the sparks danced into the evening sky.

"It's him!" Dodinel shouted as he pulled on Lot's sleeve.

Lot turned just in time to see one of the Red Men lunge toward him, the silver luster of the dagger dulled from the dried, red clay.

Without thinking, Lionel jumped between the madman and Lot, catching the full force of the dagger's blade in his right shoulder. Dodinel and Nentres tackled the assailant, holding him down as Lot dealt several quick and heavy jabs into the man's chin, knocking him unconscious.

"Guard the High King and ladies," Uther demanded as he surveyed the crowd, pushing past his brother.

"Lionel, you will be alright, I will take care of you," Merlin cradled the young prince in his arms, blood oozing onto the white Druid gown.

"If I knew this was what was needed to get your attention, I would have stuck myself with a dagger earlier today," Lionel mused before falling into darkness.

"I can help," the red-headed girl spoke softly as she knelt in a pool of crimson next to Merlin.

"Thank you, my lady." Merlin enlisted the help of a nearby page to assist him in lifting Lionel's limp body, placing the wounded prince in the back of an empty wagon.

"Who is this man?" Uther demanded towering over the intruder.

Lot gave a quick glance to Dodinel before answering, "My liege, it is hard to be sure with the body paint, but I believe he was one of Vortigern's men."

"Do any of the others resemble the former king's followers?" Uther pointed to the remaining gathering of Red Men.

"No, my liege, we are sure he was acting alone," Lot looked to Nentres and Dodinel to back him up.

Dodinel remained quiet. Folding his arms, he simply nodded in agreement, as he stared at the ground, kicking the dirt.

"I can assure you, my lord, that the man at our feet acted alone," Nentres' voice was shaky, yet sincere.

"There is something more behind this then you are letting on," Uther stepped in front of Lot, staring deeply into his eyes. "Do I have your word that you are certain that he acted alone?"

"Yes, my liege, I swear upon the goddess of Beltane, that this man acted alone, and there poses no further threat to this evening's celebration," Lot looked squarely back into Uther's eyes.

"I trust your judgment Lot, and the word of your men. For now, secure the intruder within the fort; I will deal with this matter in the morning. I will not let this incident ruin my brother's celebration."

"Yes, my liege." Lot took a step back as Dodinel and Nentres dragged the comatose body, depositing him into the back of another empty wagon and quickly departed the arena.

Uther had the remaining Red Men line up in front of him. When he was confident that they posed no danger, he motioned for the music to commence.

"Is it safe to continue?" Ambrosius inquired as he took hold of the May Queen's arm, pulling her tightly into him.

"My guardsmen are all in agreement that the madman acted alone," he reassured his brother as he offered his arm to another of the remaining veiled ladies-in-waiting. "The night is young brother. If tonight is an indication of things to come, let us enjoy this evening while we can." As they proceeded to saunter sunwise around the blazing fires

Uther gave a backwards glance toward the retreating wagons. Logically, he knew with Merlin attending Lionel, that his wounded knight would be in the best of care. Yet, he still felt guilt in leaving an injured man, especially while he continued his brother's celebration. He felt even more trepidation towards the Young Royal Guard and the attacker. His blood ran cold, and his heart and soul were no longer into the charade of merrymaking.

21

"What do we tell Sir Uther?" Dodinel muttered as he paced the room.

"Keep your voice down," Lot reprimanded.

"Who is going to hear me?" Dodinel screamed. "Everyone in the city is in a drunken stupor, including Sir Uther and the High King. They dance under the full moon, while we are stuck in this dank rancid hole, playing nursemaid to a ghost." Spittle spewed and his face turned scarlet as he slammed his fist upon the table causing goblets to tumble.

"Be still, Boar," Nentres put his arm around his friend's shoulder as he spoke, "we will work this out. We just need time."

"Time?" Dodinel violently pushed Nentres' arm aside and resumed pacing. "We have until sunrise. Will that be enough *time* to make him disappear—again!" He walked to Faustus' body strewn unconscious on the floor and gave the wall a swift kick.

"I need some air." Lot's stomach was churning and he felt cornered. He knew Dodinel was right—time was running out. "Dodinel, you watch the prisoner. Nentres, you come with me."

"I'll be back soon," Nentres promised as he walked outside.

"Good. Go! Leave Me Be!" Dodinel bellowed after them, his words soaking into the wooden door as it slammed shut.

"We only have two options," Lot advised Nentres as they walked the deserted pathways between the army barracks. Above them the full blue moon hung large and bright giving witness to their dilemma.

Although Nentres knew they were alone, he still remained quiet, nervously glancing about.

"We can either kill him, or let him escape," Lot stated bluntly.

"You are as mad as Meleagant," Nentres laughed softly, waiting for Lot to come up with a third and viable option.

"There are no other options," Lot replied, as if reading Nentres' mind. He stopped short and wearily leaned against the barracks' wall.

"So, it is either death to him, or death to us if we let him go." Nentres stood beside Lot, pressing hard against the stone structure. "There must be a third way out of this?"

"There is no way that we can allow Faustus to be interrogated by Uther," Lot sighed. "Faustus seeks vengeance for his brother, and there is no certainty as to what he will say, truth or lie—we will be sentenced to death alongside him, or at the very least be banished from our beloved Britain."

"And your plan is?" Nentres folded his arms and bowed his head, waiting for Lot's reply.

"The plan is already in motion." Lot gently nudged Nentres' in the ribs.

"What?" Opening his eyes, Nentres was about to speak as Lot placed a hand over his mouth, pointing toward the building they had just left.

Both Lot and Nentres hugged the wall as the door creaked open. Dodinel poked his head out searching for his companions. Feeling confident that no one was near, he exited the building with Faustus slung over his shoulder.

Confused, Nentres' eyes searched Lot's for an explanation. Lot just gave him a wicked grin, and nodded his head as they watched Dodinel plop the limp body upon Lot's stallion. Looking around once more, Dodinel tied Faustus to the saddle, covering the body with a black cloak. When he was sure the body was secure, Dodinel mounted his own horse.

Reaching up to remove Lot's hand, Nentres whispered, "What in the goddesses' name does he think he is doing, and how did you know he would do it?"

"You know as well as I do, that Dodinel is not a complex man," Lot softly chuckled, "but he is a man of determination and pagan beliefs."

"Did he kill him?" Nentres asked wide-eyed.

"No, he is helping him escape—as atonement for my sins."

"You *have* all gone mad!" Nentres slid down the wall, clutching his legs to his chest as he hit the ground. "If we were not going to hang before, we will all surely hang now."

They watched as Dodinel trotted out of the Fort's main gate, turning to his right.

"At least he has the foresight to take the long way out of the city, instead of riding past the amphitheatre," Lot laughed as he gave Nentres a helping hand up.

Brushing off his leathers, Nentres gave Lot a quizzical stare.

"I suspect Dodinel will come riding back at dawn, with some cock and bull story about how he was jumped by the prisoner after we left," Lot paused, "and, how he raced after him until dawn, only to have the mystery assailant, *and my horse*, vanish into the woods."

"You had this planned from the very beginning, didn't you?" Nentres looked to Lot with both contempt and admiration.

"Let's just say that I planted a seed in Dodinel's fertile imagination on our ride from the amphitheatre to the fort." Lot led Nentres back to their sleeping quarters, "However, a plan is only as good as its executers. I am sure going to miss that stallion," Lot sighed and added, "now hit me as hard as you can on the face."

"With pleasure," retorted Nentres as he balled up his fist.

***

"Stop the wagon and listen," the handmaiden whispered. Sitting in the back of the wagon with Lionel, she reached up, tugging on the back of Merlin's cloak.

Merlin pulled hard on the reins, bringing the big white draft horses to a sudden stop. They had walked the horses up until now, not wanting to jar the young prince. Merlin also felt the fear of impending danger, coupled with a nagging urgency to get Lionel to safety as soon as possible. The last thing he wanted to do was cease to move.

"I heard horses. I sense we are being followed, "she clambered to her knees searching for the noise.

"Your intuition is running wild," Merlin cocked his head and listened intently. Although they were a great distance from the amphitheatre the sound of the revelers filtered through the streets and over the rooftops. "It is just the echo of the celebration."

"No," she insisted, "there is something evil nearby."

"In that case, we should hurry, instead of sitting here like wounded prey." He remembered the last ride with his foster parents and used the same clicking noise to quicken the horses' pace to their remote destination. Although the Druid's temple was located outside the city walls, he knew it was the only place in Londinium that harbored the potions to hasten Lionel's healing. The horses' giant hooves clumped on the wooden planks as Merlin frantically urged the steeds across the bridge.

"Please, stop," she cried out again as the horses set foot on land.

Merlin let out a sigh, but reined in the chargers once more, stopping under the shelter of a giant oak.

"Do you hear it now?" She begged him for confirmation.

"Yes," Merlin whispered as they watched the silhouettes of two horses race across the bridge. The rider was a large man wrapped in a black hooded cloak, yet, even in the bright moonlight it was impossible to make out the features. Tethered behind was a matching black horse with a pack on its back. Merlin recognized the steeds—Uther's cavalry—but then, Uther's stables were filled with hundreds of the black beauties.

"Do you know who that was?" The girl's words fell out in a tremble.

"No, but, I would be curious to find out," Merlin looked down at Lionel as he spoke. The young prince had lost a lot of blood, and his face was the color of a freshly washed Druid's gown. "We cannot delay a moment more," he slapped the reins and they galloped down the old dirt road, only slowing as they entered the temple's courtyard.

"Merlin, what brings you to us on this night of celebration?" The livery boy grabbed the reins, as he glanced at the lady sitting in the back of the wagon. "Oh, I understand now, you brought your own May Queen," he lowered his voice as he walked to Merlin's side. "No disrespect to you, my lord, but I am not sure that bringing a lady to the temple is the wisest road to travel, even on the eve of Beltane."

"It is not what you think, Elivri." Merlin frowned as he climbed into the back of the wagon. "We have an injured man, a prince, who is in need of all the healing powers we can give, including the magic of a Fae. This is the Lady…" Merlin looked to the maiden, realizing that they had not been properly introduced.

"My name is Nimue," she smiled.

Nimue, Merlin mouthed silently. He knew that name from somewhere in the future.

"I am so sorry, Merlin, I did not know." Elivri helped Merlin carry Lionel from the wagon. "He does not look good. Will he live?"

"We shall do all that we can," Merlin's words flowed softly. "His fate has already been written."

22

Uther absentmindedly plucked at a long blade of grass and placed it between his teeth. Leaning back on the misty meadow overlooking the Walbrook stream he sighed deeply. From the nearby amphitheatre the noises of celebration had ceased as morning grew near. The full moon hung low in the western sky behind them. He felt the power of Beltane's *nether time*, when the curtain between the human world and that of the fairy realm were the thinnest.

"Brother, this is the first time since we set foot on our birth land that you appear to be totally at peace." Ambrosius turned on his side scrutinizing Uther.

"I believe the fairy priestesses dancing in the waters have laid an enchantment upon us." Uther sat up slightly, leaning on his elbows, gazing at the two beauties playfully splashing in the stream below.

"Remember our boyhood lessons Uther?" Ambrosius pointed low in the northeast to a cluster of stars that still cleaved to the pre-dawn heavens, as a hungry child would cleave to the last suckle of her mother's breast.

"Some of my fondest childhood memories were spending nights under the darkened heavens, learning to question, and listen to, the stars."

"And what do the Seven Sisters say to you?" Ambrosius quizzed.

"The daughters of Atlas smile upon us Ambros. They sing of great victories, in both war and love." Uther gave his brother a mischievous smile. From the water's edge laughter rang out, bringing Uther's thoughts from heavenly delights to earthly ones.

"They are lovely creatures." Ambrosius eyed the ladies lustfully.

"Brother, I do believe that you have indulged in far too much drink for one evening." Uther grabbed the wineskin from Ambrosius and took a long swig.

"Uther, it is not the wine I am drunk on, but the intoxicating woman who bathes in the waters below us." Ambrosius tried to rise to his feet in an attempt to join the daughters of Avalon, but his body would not obey his heart, and he fell unto the ground in a state of boyish laughter.

"Stay your ground, Ambros. Never forget that you are now the supreme ruler of Britain. Let them come to you, always let them come to you..." Uther's voice trailed off, and his thoughts turned from celebration, to battles past and future.

"I know it has been hard for you, Uther. It is not in your nature to succumb to frivolity." Ambrosius did his best to change his voice to a gruff and commanding tone, "By day's light we raise our arms to fight again!" He attempted to reach over his brother for the wineskin, failing miserably.

"Yes, brother, when the sun rises upon this day, releasing winter from its bondage, so shall we rise to release Britain from the bondage of foreign invaders. Both sun and sons shall rule the days of summer." Maneuvering the wineskin just beyond his brother's reach he added, "You have had enough."

"There is never enough. There is never enough to drink, never enough women to love, never enough men to fight *and kill*, never enough wrongs to right..." he sighed, his merry mood quickly turning dark. "Your appetite for warfare can never be satisfied," he spit in anger.

"As hard as it may be for you to believe, I abhor the gifts that the gods of war have bestowed upon me. No man truly wishes to see his men wrapped in the bloody arms of combat. Wishes to hear his men cry out in agony, or see their dismembered bodies strew on a field—as fodder for the hungry men and birds of prey who feast on the battle's lost souls." Falling back on the grass Uther stretched his arms, folding them behind his head. "I do look forward to peace, and we both know that without war there can be no peace."

"Talk of war and battles is forbidden, at least until the moon fully sets," Merlin's mother was kneeling next to Ambrosius, her wet hair dripping upon his face. Looking up, she smiled to her cousin, also from Avalon, who was standing over Uther.

"Come brothers, we have gathered the sacred first dewdrops of Beltane, and need to bathe you in them before the dawning of this new day." The other fairy priestess reached out her hand to Uther as she spoke, pulling him to his feet.

"It amuses me greatly brother, that one who is always in command can so easily become the commanded, when a beautiful woman is the one giving orders," Ambrosius laughed as he too staggered to his feet.

Both men surrendered control unconditionally to the Ladies of the Lake, as they stripped the royal brothers of their clothing from the waist up—in turn, stripping them of their ranks. In the fading moon's glow, the fairy priestesses chanted as they bathed the brothers with the cool first drops of the morning's dew.

Uther shivered, not from the cold, but from the burning gaze of the maiden before him. She, like her cousin, had Merlin's hawk eyes, with their ever-changing flecks of golden hues—eyes that looked into his soul and into his future. He was mesmerized by her sensuality, tenderness, and compassion—unlike her cousin, the High Priestess of Avalon, who was elegant beyond words, yet distant and intimidating; to everyone but his brother.

As the morning sky became a blaze of color, Uther ran his hand across the lady's cheek. Instantly he drew away, ashamed of his coarse skin, afraid that it would mar her silken features. With equal tenderness the maiden halted his retreat, lifting his hand to her lips she placed a gentle kiss upon the palm, her lips burning into his flesh.

"Keep me in your thoughts," she whispered as she leaned in and kissed Uther's lips, merging her soul with his. Stepping back she looked to her cousin and nodded.

"It is time for us to take our leave," Merlin's mother's voice sang softly, as she spontaneously placed a lingering kiss upon Ambrosius' lips.

"When will we see you again?" both brothers chimed.

"When the fire dragon plunges from the heavens and tears fill the earth, we shall return to complete the prophecy," the May Queen proclaimed.

To immortalize one—enthrone the other, her cousin silently agonized.

Uther bent down to pick up their clothing. Turning back the ladies had vanished in a sudden early morning mist. Looking to his right, his brother stood trance-like, eyes glazed and arms stretched, reaching for something just beyond his grasp.

"I will see her no more," Ambrosius murmured with an ache in his voice.

"Get over it brother. Did you not hear their promise to return?" Uther tossed the damp clothing to Ambrosius. "Get dressed, we have the king's business to attend."

"Of course, brother." Ambrosius shook his head and felt the last of the dewdrops sizzle upon his skin as the first rays of sun warmed his body. Becoming fully sober, he felt more alive than he had in months. Along with the burning desire to be the keeper of Britain's soul, he now inwardly pledged with equal passion to be the keeper of the Lady of Avalon's heart.

"So, man of wisdom, guardian of Britain, what was your lady's name, and while you are at it, what was the name of her cousin?" Uther casually asked as he pulled the dew soaked tunic over his head.

"I have no idea," Ambrosius answered, looking to Uther with a perplexed gaze. "Merlin will know."

"But, of course—Merlin knows everything," Uther grumbled, as they made their way back to the fort to interrogate the prisoner.

***

Burning rays of sunshine filtered through the buildings and unto the dusty streets as Ambrosius and Uther entered the fort's main entrance. Uther's squire, tucking in his shirt and finger combing his hair as he ran, greeted the brothers, taking immediate charge of the horses. Uther opened the door to the barracks designated as a detention area, expecting to see his guards overseeing the mystery rogue. Instead, he discovered an empty room. Furious, he ran outside slamming the door with such force it nearly fell from its hinges.

"Who goes there?" Uther shouted in the direction of the main gate as he viewed a rider charging down the dirt road. Instinctively, he unsheathed his sword and took a battle stance.

The rider pulled his horse up just short of running into a bewildered Ambrosius. Quickly dismounting, he dropped to his knee, bowing his head to the ground.

"Dodinel?" Ambrosius questioned.

"Yes, Your Majesty." Dodinel fought to catch his breath, which also gave him time to capture the correct words to use for his alibi.

"Dodinel, you are back." Lot rushed to help his fellow knight to his feet.

"Where is the man who attacked Lionel?" Uther grabbed Dodinel by the collar. The hairs on the back of Uther's neck stood at attention and his face turned hot with rage.

Dodinel stood silently, giving a sideways pleading glance to Lot.

"It is my fault, not Dodinel's." Lot moved between Uther and Ambrosius, attempting to plead his case to both brothers at once.

"Continue," Ambrosius urged as he scrutinized Lot's face. The young knight's left cheek was swollen and sported a fresh bruise that was still in the process of turning various hues of red, purple and blue.

"Thank you, Your Majesty." Lot easily slipped into the tale behind the disappearance. "Shortly after we arrived to the fort, I sent Nentres to his quarters so that he could get some sleep, and be fresh for the next watch. I then sent Dodinel to find us some food as neither of us had eaten all day." He let the first part of his story sink into Ambrosius, his words acting like quicksand. "I underestimated the prisoner, thinking he was out cold, and would remain so for sometime."

With his hands still tight upon Dodinel, Uther glared to Lot and then to Ambrosius. Both brothers knew that Lot had never underestimated any man, with the exception of perhaps Merlin. With a silent understanding they also knew that there was a first time for everything. Although Lot was experienced for his age, he was still young, still learning.

"Shortly after Dodinel had left I was hit from the side, knocking me out." Wincing, Lot absentmindedly raised the back of his hand to his face, letting it linger a moment before continuing to speak. "When I regained consciousness, I found Dodinel knocked senseless just outside the building, and my favorite stallion gone." He looked to Dodinel for confirmation.

Avoiding eye contact with either the king or his brother, Dodinel merely nodded in agreement.

"Like the true hero that he is, Dodinel, still dazed, jumped on his horse, vowing to catch the villain. I was staggering about as I watched him race from the fort in swift pursuit." Lot turned his attention once more to Dodinel, slapped him on the back and inquired, "Was your quest successful?"

Dodinel sucked in a deep breath and bit his lower lip before proceeding to tell his side of the fabrication. "Like Lot said, I was hit from behind, but I have a very hard head, so I was not out long, nor hurt badly." A *lie*, but he was sure Lot would take care of that detail as soon as they were alone. "I rode hard and fast throughout the night, and at times it even felt like the escapee was riding close *behind* me—him chasing me, instead of me chasing him. On several occasions I actually thought I saw him upright on Lot's stallion, breathing down my back. Once we hit the woods he disappeared, like a spirit returning to the Underworld." *All true statements* he thought. Abruptly, he looked about perplexed. "Do you think it was a Beltane spirit?"

"I am sure Lionel does not think so," Ambrosius responded softly, eyeing Lot intently.

"Walk with me, brother," Uther urged as he forcibly released Dodinel and turned, boots scuffing in the dirt as he made his way toward the officer's quarters. Ambrosius following close behind.

***

"Do you think they believed us?" Dodinel eagerly asked Lot as soon as the brothers disappeared into the building.

"We are under Uther's command. Even if he does not believe us, he will not admit it to his brother." Lot kicked at a small stone half-buried in the road. "It is the king who will question our story. He has never trusted me from the first day of our meeting."

"Are we doomed?" Dodinel pushed closely into Lot.

"Never give up hope. We have been in worse situations and come out clean." He moved his face away from Dodinel, not wishing to inhale his foul breath. "Do not deviate from the story. Do not add to, or take away from the story. Do not deviate from it in any way. Do you understand?"

"Yes, I understand!" As he spoke, Dodinel spat a combination of dust and morning phlegm next to Lot's boots, muffling the sound of his answer.

"Good! Now, go get cleaned up and we can talk later." Lot looked toward the officer's quarters as he walked away, catching a glance of Ambrosius studying him from the window. Looking to the heavens he just sighed, it seemed fruitless to ask *why me* anymore.

***

"Do you believe their story?" Ambrosius stood near the window, fingers tapping gently on the open window's frame as he watched the young knights leave the field of inquisition.

"Lot wore his proof on his face. Do you think he hit himself?" Uther spoke as a page busily pulled off Uther's tunic, and another page tugged at his boots.

"You put too much trust in him." Ambrosius turned folding his arms tightly across his chest he glared at Uther.

"Time and time again Lot has proven a valuable asset both on and off the battlefield. Why should I not trust him?" Uther stood as a page helped him out of one pair of britches and into another.

"Their story smelled like three-day-old dead fish washed upon the shores of the Tamesis," Ambrosius stated flatly.

"Ambros, you need less wine and more sleep." Uther scrutinized his brother and did not like what he saw. Dark rings encircled Ambrosius' bloodshot eyes and his complexion was abnormally pale. "Eat and get some rest, I swear that I will look closer into these matters."

"They are your men," Ambrosius relented as he took a seat next to Uther at the table.

"But, it is our kingdom that they protect, and as the High King, you do have a right to question their motives."

Ambrosius nodded silently. Although he still wore the Beltane crown, it sat heavy upon his head. *The weight of our world*, he muttered as he removed the ring of apple blossoms.

23

"My brother has been away two months." Ambrosius paced about his office in the basilica. "Although I can understand your concern for Lionel's welfare..." he stopped short in front of Merlin, "...I feel that your presence on the battlefield, at Uther's side, is urgently needed."

"My lord?" Merlin answered, looking up from his reading.

"Why do I even bother talking of late, no one appears to be listening," Ambrosius' words flowed with exasperation as he plopped himself in a chair at the far corner of the room.

"I am sorry, sire," Merlin rose and walked to the king, kneeling in front of him. "I was lost in the world of gods and heroes. I am here for you now."

"Are you really? Are you really here?" Ambrosius reached out and touched Merlin's hair, not unlike a master would stroke his devoted hound. "I fear for the day that you enter the world of yesteryears and no longer wish to return to the here and now."

"My lord, I am always *here* for you," Merlin looked up to Ambrosius with reassuring eyes. "Do you truly feel that now is the best time for me to join your brother?"

"It is past time," Ambrosius sighed. "I have consulted with the Lady Nimue. She has pledged to stay here in Londinium until Prince Lionel is fully recovered."

"You consulted with Nimue, instead of with me?" Feeling a deep sense of betrayal Merlin pulled away. Standing, he turned and faced Ambrosius, "I shall ready myself, and leave by the break of tomorrow's dawn," the resentment in his voice did little to conceal his feelings. Although he did his best to show respect for the king's request, inwardly he was aching.

"Come now, Merlin, do not leave this way," Ambrosius reached out for Merlin, catching the edge of his tunic as he turned to leave.

"I respect your wisdom, my king. If you feel it is time for me to leave, I concur with your decision," Merlin paused a moment longer, allowing Ambrosius to have the final words.

"It is not that I want you to leave, but that my brother needs *your* insight into the future more than I do at the moment," again Ambrosius sighed. "I am not sending you away from me, but sending you *to* my brother. Britain needs you at his side."

Merlin felt his face flush at the king's words. "Of course, Britain's desires supersede all others; be they king or prophet."

"Thank you for understanding." Ambrosius smiled weakly, as he sipped on a goblet of wine. His hands shook ever so slightly and his skin appeared even more pale than normal.

Merlin turned and left without another word. On reflection, a part of him was actually anticipating a private conversation with Uther, to confer about Ambrosius' failing health.

***

It was a long walk to the palace. Lately Merlin enjoyed the time to himself that walking provided. The time to reflect on current events, to reflect on his relationships: with Lionel, Ambrosius, and especially of his feelings toward Nimue. Shortly after Lionel had been knifed, Nimue and the injured prince had moved from the Druid's temple to the king's palace quarters. This time the request to have Merlin within the walled city came directly from Uther. Concerned for Lionel's safety, Uther placed the order for the prince and his healers to be moved to the palace and kept safe under the watchful eyes of the palace guard. For once, Merlin and Uther were in agreement.

Merlin hesitated entering the palace, not knowing which he dreaded more, telling Lionel that he was leaving, or the actual act of leaving. Taking a deep breath, he mustered his courage and walked down the long hallway to the open garden area.

Lionel sat on the edge of the fountain, arm in sling, pants rolled up, bare feet in the water, his eyes transfixed on Nimue. The lovely lady was standing nearby, palm extended, baby songbirds dancing in her outstretched hand.

Leaning on a pillar, Merlin watched silently. How could he have thought that she would have gone behind his back to the king? Not Nimue, not this exquisite enchantress with the captivating laughter. No, it was just his insecurities, emotions snaking into his reasoning. He trusted her with Lionel's life and, perhaps, his own. Other than his love for Britain, and his love for his king, he had never experienced anything like his feelings toward the young priestess-in-training. He ached when he was around her, and he ached even more when they were apart. Was this the love that the bards sung about? He hoped not, there was no room in his life right now for physical love—but perhaps another day, another time.

"Merlin!" shouted Lionel and Nimue, as they ran to his side, acting as if they had not seen him for days, instead of mere hours.

"I am glad to see you outside and enjoying the sunshine," Merlin laughed. The mixture of floral and herb scents from the garden caused his nose to twitch and eyes to water ever so slightly as he let out a soft sneeze.

"My lord, I hope you are not coming down with an illness," Nimue inquired with mocking concern as she rubbed the petals of a daisy under his chin.

"Yes, that would be dreadful punishment for you to be forced to bunk next to me, while this old hag nursed us both back to health." Lionel jumped just out of Nimue's grasp as she reached to tweak his ear. Falling on the grass, he feigned injury to his good arm.

"Get up you lazy toad before I really cause you harm," giggling she reached for Lionel's hand, pulling him to a standing position and brushing the grass and dust from his backside.

A twinge of jealousy coursed through Merlin, and for a split second he wished that Lionel's prediction would come true. He wished that he had the luxury to laze around all day with this beautiful creature taking care of his every want and need. As she brushed past him, her touch caused an electric charge to race throughout his body, and his heart quickened with each whiff of her scent. For an instant, her emerald eyes connected, searching deep into his soul, plucking his heartstrings …what a pleasurable tune she played. For a brief moment in time, there was no Britain, no High King, no one, but…Nimue.

"Your visits to the king usually last until dusk, why home so early?" Although jovial in nature, Lionel's words were pinned with an underlining of serious curiosity.

"The king just received word that the fighting in the North Country has not gone as planned and that my services are needed. I regret to inform you both, that with the setting of this evening's moon I shall be leaving your company, and joining Uther's army at Hadrian's Wall." As hard as he tried, Merlin could not produce even the slightest smile. Instead he cupped his eyes, peering into the heavens for any sign of his hawk.

"Cheer up, friend, you will not travel alone." Lionel jested as he lifted his injured arm, wiggling his fingers. Searching the ground he found a fallen branch and began brandishing it about. "See, I can wield a sword with the best of them."

Nimue lightly touched the young prince's shoulder, smiling softly as she shook her head. "Lionel, do not rush the healing process, there will be many opportunities for the two of you to share battle stories."

"What do you know about sharing?" Lionel whined as he brushed away her delicate fingers, "or of battle, or friendship for that matter?" He tossed the stick on the ground, causing the songbirds to scatter into the treetops. As swiftly, he turned his anger on Merlin, "What do either of you know about anything worldly? You both live in a nether world of fairy and Druid magic. Go, run away, Merlin. That is what you do best. I will stay here, protecting the High King!" Without waiting for a response, he stormed out of the courtyard.

"Oh, Merlin, I am so sorry. I did not mean for my words to upset him so," Nimue's voice reflected her sincere concern for Lionel's welfare.

"It is not your fault, dear lady." Merlin continued to search the sky, as he spoke. "Lionel and I share a childhood history of me departing and him being left behind. His anger will calm, it always does." Turning his attention back to earth, he smiled awkwardly and shrugged his shoulders. "I am Britain's willing paramour, where she commands, I go with speed; without regret, nor remorse. Yet, when called, I go alone."

"One day, someone you love dearly will speak those words to you." She stood up straight, her playful spirit vanquished. "When those words are spoken, you too shall know the breaking of Lionel's heart."

"I long for that day, dear lady." Merlin's lust morphed into apathy. "In fact, I live for the day those words will be spoken." From far above a hawk's cry rang out. Merlin bowed to Nimue, and turned away, leaving her standing alone and bewildered in the courtyard.

24

"It feels like the goddess Coventina has been pouring pails of water on us for weeks," Pellinore grumbled as he removed his cloak tossing it to a nearby page.

"Pellly, in all the years I have known you, I have never heard you complain this much," Uther sat in his Roman folding chair, laughing as his squire pulled off his soggy boots.

"This weather can make the best-natured man a malevolent beast," Pellinore winked at Merlin, who was standing with arms folded, near the corner of the tent. "The rains have come early. I have never known the Northern Country to be so drenched for so long, especially this time of year." Pellinore looked to Uther, "Coupled with the heat, it is not a fit climate to live in, let alone go to battle. We should fight nearly nude, like the Picts."

"At least they can fight and bathe at the same time," Uther smirked. "So, prophet," he turned his attentions to Merlin, "what does the goddess tell you? What word of when the rains will stop, so the fighting can commence?"

Merlin just shrugged, and lowered his head. It had rained nonstop from the day he arrived at Hadrian's Wall. They had fought for over three months in these sultry conditions, in mud up to the warhorses' knees. They had fought in torrential rains that cut through the men's leathers, against an unrelenting enemy. It was not until the soldiers became ill that Uther reluctantly ceased the advancements of his troops. Although Merlin detested the conditions and wearing damp clothing, he was overjoyed to be out of the fighting.

"Merlin, do you not have an answer for your king's brother?" Lot taunted, as he peered over Uther's shoulder, standing casually behind his commander's chair.

All eyes went to Merlin, who remained silent as he scowled at Lot. He was not certain which he disliked the most; the weather, or the Young Royal Guard. It had been miserable to fight alongside Lot's men, and now, with the fighting delayed, he felt even more ostracized than before.

"Come now, Prince Lot, do not harass the boy. When he has an answer he will give it to Uther," Pellinore gave Merlin a supportive glance, and continued to shed his wet outer garments. As he toweled his face he inquired of Uther, "Have you heard from your brother?"

"No, Pelly, not since the last full moon, and that message was delayed due to the rains. Between the god-made and manmade cursed conditions, I am surprised that we have contact with my brother at all." Uther sighed as he leaned back in his chair, scratching his unkempt beard he longed for a warm bath. He cringed as he felt himself slowly morphing from Roman soldier to Celtic barbarian, as he brushed away long strands of wet hair from his face. "While we sit bogged down in this muck and mire, the last correspondence from Ambros, was that he had been teaching the Saxon dogs lessons in obedience."

"Do we join him in battle, my lord?" Nentres inquired as he ripped the corner from a loaf of bread, offering a piece to Dodinel, who sat next to him on a horse blanket tossed on one of the few dry areas of the dirt floor.

Even the fresh baked bread gave off an odor of mildew, which turned Merlin's stomach. He could not remember the last full meal he had enjoyed. The prospect of going back home to Londinium, and to fight alongside Ambrosius, was a bright light in his gloomy existence. His hopeful eyes sought Uther's.

"No, we will sit and wait for the outcome. If Ambros needs us, he will send word. I only hope that he will send it by a swifter rider." Nonchalantly, Uther stretched his arms behind his head.

Lot quickly maneuvered out of Uther's way, just barely avoiding being hit in the head by his commander's massive hands. Sneering to Merlin, who was smiling, Lot joined his fellow knights on the floor, near Uther's feet.

A commotion arose just outside of the tent as a guard lifted the flap allowing a courier to enter. "My lord," the young man's hair hung in stringy mats, clothes caked in dirt and grime, boots shuffled heavy from several layers of mud. "I have ridden day and night to bring urgent news concerning the High King."

"Bring this man some dry clothing and something to eat and drink," Pellinore shouted. The pages scurried from the tent as Uther's squire carefully removed the dispatcher's cloak. Immediately everyone stood, gathering closer to Uther in anticipation of the messenger's words.

"Is the message from my brother, or about my brother?" Uther did his best to keep the timbre of his voice low and calm.

"The message is from Sir Lionel. The king has fallen ill, and was unable to join the royal envoy to the Saxon peace talks," the words fell from his mouth even and well-rehearsed.

"Saxon peace talks?" Pellinore pondered the absurd notion aloud.

"What is this about my brother's health?" Uther began pacing. "Why was I not informed about that until now, and what of this ridiculous notion of peace talks with the enemy?" He stopped short, grabbing the messenger by the shirt front and pulled him close. Uther's nostrils flared and his breath fell hot upon the now quivering young man.

"Rein in your temper," Pellinore whispered into Uther's ear. "The lad is only the messenger."

"Why no word until now?" through gritted teeth Uther hissed, unclenching his fingers.

"On my journey here, I came upon the rider who was sent out a fortnight before me." Although the courier was clearly frightened, he gathered his courage to answer Uther's questions the best he could. "His body had been left for the birds of prey, his horse gone, and in his back an arrow with this note." He handed a vellum scroll, not to Uther, but to Lot. "Sir Lot's name was burned into the hide of the sealed outer covering."

"What of the message that *he* carried *from* my brother?" Uther scowled at first to the courier and then to Lot; who stood frozen with frightened and surprised eyes.

"Little was left of the body, but, I did take the time to search for the scroll and it was gone. Be it by his murderer, or from the scavengers I know not which," he sighed. "I do know that the previous message gave word of the High King's intent to meet with the Saxons near Stonehenge."

"And? Where is the current message from Sir Lionel?" Uther inquired with increasing exasperation.

"I am both the message and the messenger." The courier swallowed deeply before he continued. "Sir Lionel was concerned when the king had not heard back from you. Fearful that the previous correspondences may have been compromised, he sent me to recite the message, rather then risk it not getting to you, or falling into the hands of the enemy."

"What was the full message, lad?" Pellinore urged, as he wiped the boy down, layers of mud dropping to the floor.

"There are two messages; one concerning the king's health, the other concerning the upcoming Saxon peace talks." He looked to Uther for recognition of which was the most urgent, and without a word passing between them, he began with the news of Ambrosius. "The king was injured in a recent battle. His leg infected from the pierce of a lance. His majesty came down with a high fever and he falls in and out of consciousness. The physicians have leeched him daily, yet no improvement to his condition."

"What of the Druids, or the Lady Nimue?" Merlin pressed forward as he spoke. "Do they not offer a cure?"

"Sir Lionel anticipated that you would ask that question," he eyed Uther for permission to speak directly to Merlin, and when Uther nodded, the courier continued. "Lady Nimue returned to Avalon a month after you left, my lord. Sir Lionel wanted me to assure you that he did his best to convince the king to at least listen to the recommendations of the Druid Priest. But the king refused, saying that the only Druid that he trusted was you."

"With your permission," Merlin addressed Uther, "I will ready my horse for travel and leave at once."

"What kind of prophet are you?" Uther bellowed, "You should have seen this happen, should have known before it happened, you are useless to me. I only hope that you are of more help to my brother. If not, I shall personally send you back from whence you came."

"Uther, the boy has directed all his concentrations on our battles with the Picts," Pellinore put his hand gently on Uther's shoulder as he spoke. "You know how deeply Merlin feels about your brother. If he had knowledge of any of this, I assure you that you would have been the first to know."

"I pledge to you, that the visions *I have had* of the High King reassures me that although his majesty has fallen ill, he will survive. Grant me permission or not, it is imperative that I go to his side immediately." Without waiting for a reply, Merlin turned and stormed from the tent.

"Cursed boy," Uther growled. "We have had nothing but misery from the day he joined us," pausing, he looked to Lot, but spoke instead to his companions, "Nentres, you and Dodinel ready the troops, we will deal with the Picts in the spring, we leave for Londinium this morning."

A disgruntled Lot was about to follow his men as Uther grabbed him by the arm. Lot froze. No one ever touched him, let alone his commander. His first impulse was to brush off Uther's hand, yet he knew by doing so that he would put his command of the Young Royal Guard, and possibly his life, in jeopardy. So, he stood silent and waited.

"When I am finished with the courier, we will discuss your part in all of this," Uther glared at Lot, releasing his hold as he watched the young prince retreat to the corner of the tent. "What of the second message?"

"My liege," the courier continued, giving Lot a sideways glance, "before his majesty fell ill, he arranged a meeting with Hengist and his men, to talk of peace. Both sides agreed to come unarmed to the council."

"Oh my, that is not good news," Pellinore chirped, wringing his hands, "not good news at all!"

"With such a brilliant mind, why does Ambros always see the good in even the most evil of men?" Uther began to pace about, picking up his chair he tossed it into a corner post, nearly toppling the tent. "My brother's plan reeks of disaster. How can he not remember my predictions Pelly? We both know that the only thing on Hengist's mind is seeking revenge for his daughter's death."

"Many children died that day," Pellinore's tone mellowed, "I am sure that your brother reasoned that not all fathers seek revenge, especially when their children are a casualty of war."

"My brother is no innocent! He knows the difference between men. You, Pelly, are a man *of reason*. Hengist is a man *in need of a reason*."

"Do you send word back to the High King?" The courier hesitated to break into the conversation, but felt the urgency to do so. "If I can be supplied with a fresh horse, I can be back to Londinium straight away."

"There is no need. Merlin, with all his faults, is a swift, apt, and reliable messenger."

"Uther, do you wish me to stay with the sick and injured until they are ready to ride?" Pellinore had long fought beside Uther and he knew his commands before they were shared aloud.

"Yes, Pelly," Uther nodded in agreement to the plan. "Take this man with you and find out what is delaying the pages with the food and dry clothing."

"Dry clothing may be hard to come by…" Pellinore slapped the courier on the back as they exited the tent, "…but, we can surely find something to warm your belly."

Lot felt like an eternity had passed as he stood alone in the tent with Uther. The only sounds were that of the driving rain pounding upon the canvas overhead. Mist rose heavy from the under edges of the tent until he could no longer see the tops of his boots. He knew that the gods of sun and storm were fighting to gain control of the day. Beads of sweat trickled from his brow, matching the drizzle that fell inside the tent's poles.

"Hand it over!" Uther demanded.

Clutching the scroll in a death grip, Lot hesitated. He had no idea what was written upon the vellum, but he was certain who had written it. There were no viable options, so with great courage he looked Uther in the eyes and handed him the scroll, willing his fate to the gods.

Tossing the outer protective cover to the ground, Uther untied the leather thong around the vellum, his eyes narrowed as he searched the riddle for meaning. When he was finished he shoved the message in front of Lot's face and demanded him to read aloud and decipher the words.

Mustering every ounce of confidence, Lot casually straightened the scroll and began to read in a strong and even tone:

> *Greetings Commander,*
> *My enemies are now my friends,*
> *The Saxon savages saved me from Hades.*
> *My brother, dead before they found me.*
> *You, my once trusted friend, are now my enemy.*
> *Peace your new valiant High King may try,*
> *But all who venture to the council will die.*
> *A High King ~ for a Hight King! A brother ~ for a brother!*
> *One man is destined to pay the price, as part of the plan.*
> *Beloved Brother of Brydw*

Without doubt, Lot was certain that the ink's source was Faustus' own blood. He steadied his hands from shaking. Yet, he knew that he could not conceal the fear within his eyes. Silently, he cursed his lack of judgment at allowing Faustus to escape death a second time. Refusing to look at Uther, he instead concentrated on the words for their thinly clad deeper meaning. Lot's mind raced to concoct a believable story, as always something with a semblance of truth, yet not the whole truth.

"I am waiting!" Uther invaded Lot's space by stepping even closer, towering over the now shrinking man before him.

"My liege, this is nothing more than the nattering of a madman," as he spoke, Lot began to nonchalantly crumble the note in his hand, realizing what he had done, he hastened the action and offhandedly relinquished the scroll to Uther.

"You greatly disappoint me," Uther began pacing again. "Have I not always treated you with respect and trust?"

Lot lowered his head and softly spoke, "More so than any man, more so than even my father."

"So, why do you play these games with me?" Uther righted his chair and fell into it. "The lives of many good brave men, men you have fought alongside, men you have commanded, they all depend on your truthfulness." Uther put his hands to his head and bemoaned, "More important, my brother's life could depend on your being straightforward with me. You do know how to be fully honest?"

Lot's voice broke as he knelt in front of Uther, "I swear to you that I do not know the full meaning behind the message." He looked upward with pleading eyes. "I beseech you to continue to believe in me. I would never put you, our High King, nor Britain in jeopardy. Everything I have ever done has been for the better of Britain and her people. Every command I have been given I have fulfilled, without question."

Uther scrutinized the young man before him. He had never seen Lot in a state of submission, never known him to beg, never heard words of reverence. His first instinct was to reach out and stroke the boy's hair, as he had seen his brother do with Merlin. Yet, like himself, Lot was a man of action not emotion, not a domestic creature, but a beast of battle. He knew that a warrior was only as good as his word, and for reasons he was not certain, he believed in Lot. Or perhaps, he merely needed someone to believe in besides his brother; and Lot, by default, was the chosen one.

"My lord," Uther's squire opened the tent flap as he spoke, watching as Lot quickly rose to his feet. "Your horse awaits you." The young squire's concentration turned solely to his commander.

"Prepare Sir Lot's swiftest horse," Uther rose as he addressed his squire, "he will ride with me." Donning his hooded cloak, without a backward glance, he exited into a storm ridden morning.

25

Soaked to the skin, and dripping mud onto the tile floor, Uther entered Ambrosius' private quarters within the palace. Although disappointed, he was not surprised to see Merlin seated on the side of Ambrosius' bed. Dark circles encompassed his brother's bloodshot eyes, which stared blankly from a sunken and pale face. He was babbling incoherently, his legs flailed about sporadically. Ambrosius' hand clutched Merlin's tightly, preventing Merlin to leave his side, let alone stand when Uther approached.

"Ambros, I am here," Uther wrenched his brother's hand from Merlin's, pushing the boy prophet off the bed as he took his place next to the king.

"Uther," Ambrosius tried to sit up, but was too weak to raise his head, let alone his body. "I have done a grave thing brother, made a dishonorable decision, a deadly choice." Tears raced down his face and he gulped out the words in a mixture of whisper and whine, "I have sent hundreds of men directly to be slaughtered."

Uther looked to Merlin for an explanation.

"I arrived in time to oversee the healing of the injury sustained by your brother, and I promise that he will fully recover *physically*." Merlin paused before he continued, "I was, however, too late to save the lives of over three hundred of his bravest men, mostly royals. All died through the deceit of that snake Saxon ruler, Hengist."

Uther squeezed his brother's hand tightly, yet could not look in his direction. "I don't understand."

"The peace talks took place the night before I arrived. Ambrosius had sent over three hundred of his best fighting men, noblemen of varying ranks, their sons, and experienced knights, to parley with an equal number of Saxons. The Saxons erected a giant tent, near the Dancing Stones on the Salisbury Plain." He waited for the words to filter into Uther's military soul. "Perhaps we should call the lone survivor to finish the story."

"Get him. Now!" Uther commanded as he listened with closed eyes and gritted teeth to his brother's moaning.

"Do you wish to hear the rest outside of his majesty's bedchambers?" Merlin spoke in hushed concerned tones.

"No, bring the man here." Uther's free hand formed a fist and he struck it hard upon the bedcovers.

Within moments, Edol, Earl of Gloucester, entered the room. On his neck, just under his chin, a newly created scar pulsed in the early stages of scabbing-over. As he bowed to Uther, he put a shaky hand to his throat, causing him to flinch.

"Bring this man a chair," Uther ordered, as he motioned Edol to sit.

"My lord, Merlin has advised me that you wish to have a report of the evening of the Long Knives." Edol refused the chair, and instead stood at attention as he related the events. "When we first got notice that Hengist wished for the peace talks, Ambrosius assembled his men, asking and weighing each man's opinion. Although many of us were skeptical of any Saxon keeping his word, we knew that Hengist was, in his own right, a great leader of his people."

"So the talks were not solely my brother's idea," Uther stated.

"All who went, openly agreed to the meeting," Edol kept his gaze directly on Uther as he spoke. "Ambrosius put off the talks as long as he could, and each day that we waited the expectations of peace grew distant. When no return word arrived from your camp, the High King, even in his weakened state, had his squire dress his stallion in finery. It was his intentions to ride with us and lead the British representatives to the Stonehenge, Saxon meeting place."

Uther nodded, indicating for Edol to continue.

"As you can see, my lord, the High King in no way could ride, and although he wished for us to wait for your return, each of us agreed that time was of the essence. We all, from king to squire, insisted that he stay behind, while we completed the quest for peace. We arrived with the best intentions, and were greeted with friendship, food, and drink. As sworn to ahead of time, by both sides, we left our weapons outside the tent, as did the Saxons."

Fools, Uther thought, but did not dare state aloud.

As if reading Uther's thoughts, Edol's face reddened, yet he continued. "Hengist also insisted, for the sake of peace, that we be seated Saxon next to Briton around the table. All went well until Hengist stood to make an announcement. We all raised our tankards, thinking he was going to drink to our health," Edol smirked, "instead it was a signal for his men to recover the long knives hidden within each of his men's fur boots."

Uther somberly glared at the Earl.

"I was standing next to Hengist." Edol spit out the name, as he choked out the rest of his words. "The Saxon leader dropped his drink and put his blade to my neck," he slowly touched the scar, "dragging it just deep enough to draw blood but not so deep as to kill." Again he swallowed and continued, "He forced me to watch as his men slaughtered all at the table—my fellow companions' blood flowing into the food and drink."

Uther sat, without uttering a word, still gripping his brother's hand.

"Uther, you know me. I have killed, and seen men killed; all in the name of peace, all on the battlefield. Yet, to see hundreds of men nearly beheaded by savages posing as peacemakers was unbearable to watch." He closed his eyes tightly, and swallowed hard unable to hold back the tears that seeped from the corners of his eyes. "Hengist forced me to watch. Watch my fellow knights, my friends, my kinsmen—murdered. He stood there holding my life in his hands as he unassembled the table and tent, tossing the bodies of the fallen onto the ground. All the while, I begged him to kill me too. He refused. I can still smell his foul breath, as he whispered, hot and heavy, a message for me to bring back to my High King."

"And that message was?" Instinctively, Uther knew the jest of the upcoming message, yet he forced himself to ask anyway. Looking down he suddenly realized how wet and dirty he was. The white bed cover was now caked with mud, and steam rose from his feet as the puddle of dark brown rainwater escaped from his clothing unto the heated floor tiles. As if in duel worlds, Uther's thoughts bounced from listening to the bloody slaughter to wishing he could take a bath. Wishing he could wash the day's dirt and grime from both his body and soul. "The message?" he repeated.

"Hengist said that the only day you and your brother will find peace on British soil, will be the day that you join your peace council in their talks."

"I have heard enough. At least when we depart this world, we *will* go in peace. Let our armies know that the dead will be avenged. Before the next full moon, Hengist's body will be the main course for Poseidon's dinner feast." Uther bellowed, "Now—leave us!"

Edol obeyed, leaving Uther, Ambrosius, and Merlin alone in the king's bedchamber.

"What actions do you take?" Merlin quizzed Uther.

"What do you think?" Uther released Ambrosius hand, standing he walked toward the door, turning he said, "I assemble every man that can fight and we destroy every Saxon that we encounter; man, woman, or child, no exception." Uther glared at Merlin, daring him to utter a word against his plan. "My main objective is to kill Hengist, and all of his spawn, at any cost. Your main objective will be to bring Britain's High King back to health, at any cost. You make sure he can sit on Britain's throne, and I shall be sure that he continues to do so."

"As I told you earlier, your brother's physical health will be restored," Merlin retorted, "do you not wish me to join you on the battlefield?"

"Merlin, for once in your life—obey me without question." Uther quickly inhaled, and slowly exhaled his words. "At this moment, I am as concerned with my brother's mental, as well as his physical health. It is imperative that a king be of sound mind to rule a kingdom." Uther pushed on the bedchamber's door, and turned around once more, "I am commanding you to restore our king to health, not just for my selfish reasons as a brother, but most importantly for Britain, and for her peoples. Do you understand?"

"As you wish. I will do as you ask, for Britain." For the first time since he had laid eyes on Uther, Merlin saw a spark of greatness in Ambrosius' younger brother, a vision of power and glory, a name that would outshine even the current High King. "I shall also do this *for you*," he added in a whisper, that he knew Uther heard.

26

Salt had been steadily filtering into Merlin's nostrils miles before reaching the chalky shores of Dubris, on Britain's southeastern coast. As they approached the cliffs, the mid-morning mist lingered thick and sodden, causing his hair to fall in long encrusted tangles. His clothing was uncomfortably damp. His white cloak blackened from the soot that rained down from the funeral pyres that littered the bloody path from Londinium. With all the misery, an unexpected peace fell upon him as he heard the squawking of seabirds. His newly entered meditative state was abruptly disturbed by the sounds of Lionel dry heaving.

"Merlin," Ambrosius' shouting was stifled due to the scented scarf that covered his nose and mouth. "Do you not have a remedy that will stop Lionel's constant retching?"

"We are almost to our destination. The samphire plant grows in abundance on the cliffs of Dubris. I am certain it will help," Merlin assured the king as he maneuvered his gray next to Lionel.

"I will be fine," through muffled tones Lionel tried to reassure his companions. "It is just the constant stench of burning human flesh that has unsettled my innards." The words barely left his lips when he bent over his mare and began heaving again. This had gone on for the past day and a half, and he had nothing left in his stomach to release onto the ground.

"Put your face into your mare's mane," Ambrosius encouraged, "wet horse hair will outwit your queasiness."

With an unintentional moan, Lionel leaned over and buried his head deep within the dampness of his mare's mane. At this point, he would try anything to settle the need to release the nonexistent contents of his empty stomach.

"Halt!" Even though it was just the three travelers, instinctively Ambrosius' hand shot up as he looked back half expecting to see a legion of cavalry.

As the riders came to an abrupt stop and dismounted, the sun began to burn the morning mist. Beyond the white chalk cliffs they could now easily view British soldiers dragging the bodies of Saxon warriors; piling them onto a heap of drifted wood and dried sea-grasses. On the horizon four large wooden boats burned in various stages of destruction, the smoke turning the steel blue sky into a hazy slate gray.

"Take my horse." Ambrosius tossed his reins to Merlin and quickly descended the steep narrow pathway to the beach.

Merlin and Lionel watched as Ambrosius embraced a man dressed in black, who was supervising the removal of clothing from one of the larger, less bloated bodies.

"Is that Uther?" Lionel quizzed Merlin. His hand shaded squinting eyes.

"Of course, why do you even ask?" Merlin's words escaped more sarcastic than he intended.

Lionel just shrugged, covering his nose and mouth with his hand as he stood on wobbly legs between the horses.

"Leave the horses. The sea air will do you good." Dropping his mare's reins, Merlin gathered a handful of yellow blossomed plants as he scrambled down the path leading to the shore.

Reluctantly, Lionel followed, more crawling than walking.

"Chew on this." When they reached the path's end Merlin handed a mixture of the crushed umbels of tiny, buttery-green blossoms with fleshy, emerald, shining leaflets to Lionel. Slowly they walked into the wind along the coastline away from the troops and the still unlit Saxon funeral pyres.

"Will they know where we are?" Lionel asked, taking the concoction without question, he popped it in his mouth, and with a content expression began to chew.

"They found each other, they will easily find us." Reaching a small cove surrounded by water-logged driftwood, Merlin sat, looking back toward the king and his brother.

"What are they doing?" Lionel inquired as he plopped his body on a log next to Merlin. The wind caused the salt air to bite into his skin and his eyes to water. As always Merlin was right, the sea air, along with the herb, did help settle his nausea.

"They do what they must," Merlin replied softly, as he focused his hawk-eyes down the beach where Ambrosius knelt over the now nude corpse sprawled on its back.

Uther reached into the dead man's clothing piled on the beach, and pulled out a long knife, handing it to his brother. Methodically, Ambrosius plunged the weapon into the man's sternum. Thrusting downward to the groin, he splayed the carcass open. The sea rapidly became a beastly shade of crimson and indigo. Her waves wrapped, pounding and hungry, upon the legs of the brothers and the corpse; the only men brave enough to enter her ruthless outgoing tides. She suckled relentlessly upon their limbs, wishing to keep them near her for eternity, not satisfied to only be fed the soul of the dead.

Anticipating seagulls squawked in the skies, fighting for a better position, suddenly scattering landward as Merlin's hawk gracefully spiraled downward landing next to Ambrosius' blade. The raptor danced about, first looking to Uther and then to Ambrosius for their blessings. When both brothers nodded, she reached into the stomach cavity, opening her beak wide, tugging at the contents. Shaking her head violently, she dislodged a section of the small intestine and soared skyward, much to the delight of the awaiting seabirds. Obliged to keep his brother's promise, Ambrosius swiftly cut the contents of the man's belly as it unraveled, saving some delicacies as an offering to Poseidon.

Although a distance away, Lionel turned pale and averted his eyes. Even if he felt it well deserved, he was still unaccustomed to such brutalities, especially from Ambrosius.

Merlin continued to watch, transfixed on the ritual as Ambrosius tossed the knife into the pebbled sand and rose to join his brother. Each man grabbed a handful of the Saxon's hair, dragging the once regal figure into the ocean.

"Who was that man?" Lionel asked with his eyes still tightly closed.

"Who else, but Hengist." Looking skyward as his hawk dropped the entrails into the flock of scrapping rats with wings, Merlin absentmindedly ran his fingers along the cliff's wall, grasping a handful of chalk. Opening his hand, he methodically allowed the white powder to drift out to sea.

In the distance, a lean figure ran to the edge of the shore, where the king stood knee deep in salty brine. He then jogged up the beach.

From his lanky gate, Merlin recognized him immediately as Uther's squire. His mind flashed back to the day that they had left the tranquility of Londinium, and how disappointed Ambrosius' squire was when ordered to guard the city instead of riding with his king.

"My lord, Merlin," the boy's words came in short spurts when he finally reached his destination. "His majesty wishes you, and Sir Lionel, to join him after you have had a chance to clean up. I will guide you to your quarters." The squire pointed to the shore fort just barely visible at the top of the cliff and restlessly awaited a response.

Merlin acknowledged the request, wiping the chalk from his palms he stood. Giving Lionel a helping hand up, they both slowly rejoined the world of battle.

***

As he walked with Lionel from the old Roman Fort's bathhouse to the commander's quarters, Merlin mused to himself how good it felt to get two days of grit and grime washed from his body. Although the sea fortress walls were thick, the air was still frigid, and more than ever he regretted that his Druid's cloak was ruined. He was however, thankful for the clean and dry clothing that Uther had provided. As they rounded the final passageway, Merlin collided with one of Uther's men. The moment their bodies touched Merlin felt a premonition of events soon to come, which sent him immediately to his knees, hands pressing hard upon his temples.

"What's wrong with you boy?" the giant of a man dressed in a brilliant blue cloak asked as he reached down to help Merlin to his feet.

"Do not waste your time with him," Ulfius mocked, "that is just Ambrosius' puppet."

"The High King's prophet, you mean." Lionel shot back as he grabbed Merlin's arm to steady his companion, who now stood on wobbly legs.

"Wash your ears out boy, that is what I said," Ulfius snarled back as he and his fellow knights pushed past Lionel and continued down the hallway.

With a concerned stare, the mysterious knight reluctantly released the boy into the supporting hands of Lionel, joining the others in their exit.

Merlin took notice that all the commanders who had followed Uther from the recent fighting at Hadrian's Wall were there: Arrok, Uriens, Carados, Brastias, and of course Ulfius. All that is with the exception of Pellinore, who he knew was currently traveling back to Londinium with the battle weary. Most notably absent from the parade of royal knights were Lot, Nentres and Dodinel. He cringed again as the flash of future events scurried rodent-like within his mind's eye.

"Do you wish me to tell the king that you need to rest and will meet with him later? I am certain that he will understand." Lionel knew how draining the visions were on his friend. Without doubt, he felt more of an allegiance to Merlin, than to the royal brother's, who awaited them just beyond the closed and guarded door.

"No, I will be fine, just give me a moment to compose myself," Merlin's words, although subdued, were still assertive.

"What did you see?" Lionel knew better than to ask, but as always the words fell from his mouth.

"I will discuss it with you later," Merlin steadied himself as he spoke, "when we are alone."

As they approached the door the guard immediately granted them access to the king's new chambers. The room was filled with a mixture of makeshift seating arrangements of chairs and benches; scattered haphazardly around the interior. Absentmindedly, Merlin ran his fingers across one of the benches as he passed, shivering as he felt the warmth from its recent occupant.

At the head of the room Ambrosius lounged on a fleece covered lectus, while Uther sat next to him casually sprawled in an ornately carved wooden chair. Both men were in dry clothing, jovial moods, and slightly inebriated. Pages hurried about filling vessels with the finest wine that one of Uther's men had discovered deep within a hidden cellar.

"Come in and join us," Ambrosius motioned to two chairs, strategically placed in front of him.

"Your Majesty," Merlin and Lionel spoke in unison. Without hesitation, Merlin took his usual place in front of the king, while Lionel sat in front of Uther.

"Merlin, I must commend you on your new found mystical powers," as he spoke, Uther motioned the page to bring more wine and food. "It appears that your curative enchantments have accelerated my brother's healing. He showed me the wound. Even the scar has vanished."

"I have pledged my life to the protection of Britain's High King," Merlin bowed his head humbly as he spoke, giving Lionel a hidden sideways glance and concealed smile.

"I see Merlin's remedy has worked his magic on you as well Lionel," Ambrosius' words were followed by a smile of sincerity.

"He most certainly did. The herb not only cured my queasy stomach, it was also rather pleasant tasting," Lionel replied as he raised his eyebrows and sported a silly boyish grin.

"My liege," Merlin turned toward Uther as he spoke, "as we approached your quarters, we ran into your men. I recognized all but one. Who was the new knight? The big man with curly hair, sporting the unkempt beard, dressed in the bright blue cloak?"

"Ah yes, that would be Sir Gorlois, the Duke of Cornwall," Uther responded after a bit of pondering. He looked to his brother, who nodded in agreement. "When the duke heard of the Saxons massacring British royalties, he was the first to join us in Dubris to aide in overthrowing Hengist and his barbarian followers."

"Where do they hurry off to, my liege?" Lionel inquired as he grabbed for a small loaf of freshly baked bread offered by one of the pages, handing a piece to Merlin.

"Did the Young Royal Guard go with them?" Merlin added nonchalantly as he put the warm bread to his nose, whiffing in the delicious aroma.

"Sir Lot and a troop of cavalry, set off to Stonehenge four days ago," Uther touched his brother with a reassuring gesture as he spoke. "They have gone ahead of us to bury the dead and begin the process of erecting a funeral mound to honor the slaughtered. The remaining of the royals will be traveling with us at tomorrow's first light. We will gather there to pay tribute on the first day of the full moon."

"Are you alright?" Ambrosius leaned forward as he scrutinized Merlin's face.

"He had one of his visions when he collided with the duke in the hallway," Lionel jumped in merrily.

"Lionel," Merlin hissed under his breath.

"What is this of a vision?" Uther's curiosity aroused. He stood in the pretense of forging for food from a nearby table.

"It was nothing, my lord," Merlin did his best to mellow his tone as he spoke. "It was more of a headache than an apparition. The ride to Dubris was long, and my mind had been weakened by recent events." As he spoke he sipped upon his wine, trying his best to avert his eyes from the brothers, yet feeling their stares dig deep within him.

"Come, Merlin," Uther queried, as he walked about leaning casually upon the arm of his brother's chaise. "When has the pain in your head ever been caused by anything less than visionary?"

"Today, my liege." Merlin raised his head, staring defiantly into Uther's eyes, "Today."

"Easy, brother," Ambrosius kept his eyes on Merlin as he spoke to Uther, "if Merlin had anything to disclose of significance to our cause, he would. It is not in his nature to conceal facts of vital importance from his king."

Needles spiked down Merlin's spine as Ambrosius spoke. The king had changed. There was an unfamiliar harshness about him, a bite to his words, antagonism in his eyes. Reflecting on the situation, Merlin chalked it up to all parties being overtired. Emotions were peaked; surely it was just his imagination. Surely the man who sat before him was the same beloved king, friend, protector that he had come to admire, even love like a father. *A man's intrinsic character does not change instantaneously. No, it must be his imagination.*

"Ambros wishes for you to oversee the burial proceedings at Stonehenge," Uther nonchalantly walked back to his chair, scrutinizing Merlin. "If the weather holds, we should reach Salisbury Plain on the eve of Samhain, or perhaps the day of. What better time to celebrate the lives of the slain and usher the brave and seasoned warriors into the Otherworld."

27

"Enough! I have heard enough complaining from you today to last a lifetime," Lot bitterly spit the words at Dodinel. It had been an excruciating seven day ride to Stonehenge from Dubris, and today, their first day of burying the dead, was proving to be even more laborious than their travels.

"Lot, you are pushing your men too hard," Nentres spoke softly as he edged closer to his commander.

"Never," Lot hissed, "never question my motives." *Why could they not understand the urgency of what they were doing?* They had already lost a day in travel due to the rains and the wagons. He was accustomed to traveling with a swift unit of cavalry. He was not going to fail this mission due to the lack of motivation in his troops.

Nentres stepped back and continued to methodically shovel dirt over the nameless king whose charred remains lay strewn at his feet.

The ground was muddy from the continual downpour. Exhausted, Lot sank to his knees. Did the gods and goddesses that protected this land not realize that he could use their help? Where was that bastard Merlin when they needed him? Even though the boy prophet had not been able to control the weather while they had fought along Hadrian's Wall; Lot was certain that if Merlin were here, he could make a truce with the heavens to at least stop the rain until after the funeral barrow was completed.

"At least let us stop to eat." Consistent to his nature, Dodinel ignored Lot's previous warning. "My stomach is growling so loud that I thought one of the fallen nobles had risen from the dead."

Lot's only response was an antagonistic glare in Dodinel's direction. How could his men make light of this situation? When they had arrived late yesterday afternoon, the site of the deathtrap was visible from a distance. The death marker, reminded Lot of a giant horse's hoof-print upon the landscape, left by some mystical beast racing across the Salisbury Plain. It was not until they came in full view of the abandoned "peace council" site that the devastation of the events became a reality.

***

Lowering his head, he recalled the long ride from Londinium to Dubris. Uther had relayed Sir Edol's tale of the Night of the Long Knives. Now that Lot was upon the incongruous site, he could see for himself that each word that the Earl had spoken rang true. As were their customs, the ever-prudent Saxons, never wishing to waste good resources, had taken down the colossal tent before setting torches to the dead. He was surprised that Hengist had left behind the lumber, the benches and tables that would become the slaughtered royals' coffins. Lot deduced that the conniving Saxon leader must have known that his traitorous deeds would anger the spirits of this mystical place. *Who truly knew the thought process of a tyrant?*

Removing his fists from rubbing his eyes, Lot glanced at one of his men, so many new faces, so many inexperienced boys. He smirked inwardly at the thought of how young, innocent, and untried the new recruits were, even though half were years older than he was. None had been to a real battle. You could not call what happened between Londinium and Dubris a real battle. It was a massacre.

Uther had insisted that every Saxon they encountered be slain: old and young, men, women and children. From a military standpoint Lot understood Uther's logic. Anyone left in their wake would grow into an enemy. Death of all Saxons would prevent the potential deaths of hundreds, perhaps thousands of Britons in the future. Yet, he could no longer stomach the killing of women and children, no matter what the ultimate outcome.

When, for the first time in his life, Lot had voiced his objections, Uther had assigned him an army of four hundred to clean-up the trail of carnage. The days became never ending as Lot and his men followed Uther, and his army of thousands, into each Saxon village that dotted the countryside on the path to Dubris. It was Lot's job to oversee the gathering of the innocent lifeless souls, whose only crime was heritage of birth. Within each ransacked community, his men created giant funeral pyres, setting fire to the bodies and burning the villages to the ground.

***

Covertly, Lot continued to watch the young recruit, who had squatted next to one of the bodies, nonchalantly the boy slipped a gold ring from the boney fragments of a dead king's hand. Enraged, Lot pounced. Driving his knees into the young man's chest, Lot struck one solid blow after another until the boy's face was swollen and bloody beyond recognition.

"What are you doing?" Nentres screamed as he and Dodinel attempted to pull Lot away and disengage him from the insanity.

"This is what I am doing!" Lot shouted back, as he wrenched the ring from the boy's clutched hand. "I will not tolerate a thief within my troops," gulping his words as he stood on shaky legs. "Does everyone understand?" Twirling around, his voice broke as he screeched the command to his troops.

"Calm down," Nentres whispered reaching out to Lot, who brushed off his hand and tramped to the center of the horseshoe burial site.

"He is going as mad as Meleagant," Dodinel murmured as he shook his head and kicked at the clumps of mud.

"Gather round. Everyone gather round!" Regaining his confidence Lot knew that he did not need to shout to command an audience, as everyone was watching, waiting in silence. "These men before us," he pointed downward as he walked the inner perimeters of the fallen kings' eternal resting place. "These men," he continued, "died for a noble cause. They were," he paused, "no, they *are* brave warriors, with honorable intentions. Lower, but not lesser, kings and princes, royals from all corners of Britain who came in peace. Betrayed by the Saxon pig, who by now I am certain, has become fodder for the fish and seabirds."

A loud roar rose from the men, extending from the edges of the funeral mound to the nearby newly erected tents in the makeshift stronghold. The noise spooked the draft horses, and their grooms held tightly to the reins as the steeds pranced about, nostrils flaring and eyes wide. Forty horses harnessed to twenty wagons, overfilled with dirt gathered on their long journey from Dubris to Stonehenge—dirt that would soon provide a protective blanket over the fallen heroes.

"I will give this order but one time, so listen well," Lot spoke slowly and projected each word. "Any man who dares desecrate any part of this sacred land or these holy bodies, I shall personally behead, then pluck out his eyes," once more he paused to let his words sink in, "and feed them to Merlin's hawk." Lot smirked outwardly this time at his last remark, certain that if his reputation had not preceded him, that at least Merlin's had.

"Long Live the High King!" the chant arose deep within the crowd, one voice soon turned into hundreds.

Confident that his message had gotten through to everyone, Lot pushed past Nentres and Dodinel. When he reached the beaten boy, Lot kicked him aside with his muddy boot and knelt before the deceased mystery king's body. Gently, he lifted the royal's rotting hand and tenderly slipped the ring back on his finger. "Long live Britain's High King, and long live *Uther*, her true protector," he whispered under his breath as he rose and reverently tossed a shovel full of earth over the royal's corpse.

28

The leaves of amber, ruby and amethyst hues, crunched under Merlin's horse's hooves, as he and his companions made their way through the forest. Dusk was fast approaching, and the brisk air bit his nose and cheeks. As the procession neared the edge of the glen, the knotted beech tree branches grabbed at Merlin's leggings, begging him to go no further. Across the open meadow, directly before him stood the stone monolith circle; although Merlin had only visited Stonehenge in his visions, he knew it well. Still, even at a distance his first *actual* glimpse of the Dancing Stones, sucked the breath from his very soul. His hands quivered as he reined in his mare, stopping next to Ambrosius who also stood in awe.

"It truly is *the* temple of divine beauty," as Ambrosius spoke the blue heavens began to turn ablaze of fiery autumn colors.

"Its beauty supersedes that of Avalon," without thinking, Merlin's words flowed from his lips. Smiling awkwardly he quickly glanced to the young king and then back to Stonehenge.

Ambrosius did not press Merlin for the meaning to his statement, nor did Merlin offer an explanation. Both men stood frozen in time as they drank in the wonder, magic, and splendor before them.

"Brother, I hate to interrupt your lyrical waxing with your pretty boy poet," as he spoke, Uther wedged his stallion between Merlin and Ambrosius, "however, you did mention that you wished to pay tribute to the fallen royals before entering the henge." All eyes followed Uther's hand as he pointed to a large, freshly created barrow situated just northeast of Stonehenge's heel stone entrance.

From behind the brothers, Merlin watched Ambrosius nod and gently turn his horse in the direction of the tumulus, with Uther and the small assembly of royals following close behind.

"Are you going to join them?" Lionel quizzed as he brought his black alongside Merlin's gray.

"No, not just yet." Merlin breathed in the crisp air as he gave his friend a weary smile.

"Good, I have something for you." Lionel reached into a pouch hanging from the side of his saddle, pulling out two neatly wrapped parcels. "Happy…" looking about to make sure no ears were near by, with a mischievous grin he continued, "…happy sixth birthday. May I add that you look very mature for your age."

Joining Lionel in a loud burst of laughter, Merlin reached for the gifts.

"Not so quickly," Lionel teased as he pulled his hand out of reach. "Open this one first. It's from me." He flung Merlin a tiny sheepskin covered bag.

Grinning, Merlin accepted the gift, with the same childlike enthusiasm as he had done each of his previous five years on earth. Untying the small pouch a moment of sadness crept upon him as his mind wandered to the events of his last birthday. He shook his head hard in an attempt to vanquish the memories, causing his hair to tumble loose and fall around his shoulders. Merlin tossed Lionel an impish grin as he eagerly tore into his present.

Choking back his emotions, Lionel forced himself to smile. As he watched Merlin open his gift, for an instant, instead of a young man with the weight of the world on his shoulders, Lionel recalled a feather-haired innocent boy. Enthusiastically tearing apart the cloth from a sword twice his height, and begging Lionel to teach him the fine art of swordsmanship.

"Oh, it is beautiful," Merlin smiled with boyish glee as he slipped the silver bracelet onto his wrist. "The workmanship is amazing. Where did you find it?"

"I did not find it anywhere. I made it." Lionel grinned.

"*You* made it? Are you certain?" Merlin teased.

"Why you ungrateful spawn of a tree trunk," Lionel pulled his horse next to Merlin, feigning to take back his gift.

"Arden always said that you could not keep a secret," Merlin mocked. Unexpectedly, he grabbed Lionel's hand, pulling him closer and giving him a quick hug. "Thank you Lionel, I shall treasure it always, as I cherish your friendship."

"As I do yours," Lionel smiled as his fingers fondled the second package. "This one next, it is from the Lady Nimue." He placed the bundle of beautifully embroidered cloth into Merlin's outstretched hand. "Her strict instructions were that it was not to be opened until Samhain, on your birthday."

Frowning, Merlin looked at the gift, then turned in his saddle and looked about, "How did she know today was my birthday, and when did you see her last?"

"She is not here. At least, if she is here, I am not privy to her arriving," as he spoke, Lionel also looked over his shoulder, just to make sure his words rang true. "When Nimue was aiding in my healing, just before leaving she gave me this package to give to you."

Putting the cloth to his nose, Merlin inhaled deeply. Even after all those month's, Nimue's scent permeated his senses, and he did his best to draw in her magic, devour her essence.

"Go on, open it," Lionel whined impatiently.

Still intoxicated from her memory, Merlin's fingers fumbled with the thin leather strap tied in an intricate weave of knots around the package. After a few moments of intense struggle the thin band yielded to his persistence. As the leather fell, a gust of warm wind blew the cloth open revealing an oval shaped object that filled his palm. Even cradled within his hand it glistened in the lingering light of the setting sun. Lifting the deep, brilliant, blue translucent stone by its delicate silver chain, he marveled at its radiance. Upon further inspection, he noticed tiny etched scrolls of infinite lines encompassing the outer surface.

"She said it was a Druid Egg; a talisman of great mystical powers," Lionel voiced with authority.

"Yes, I know," Merlin whispered.

"She said she found the stone on the shores of Avalon, and engraved it with her own hands."

Nodding in acknowledgement Merlin continued to examine the moonstone and the complexity of the work.

"Now comes the best part," Lionel paused, and waited for Merlin to look in his direction. "I never told her about your birthday."

Furrowing his brow, Merlin gave Lionel an inquisitive stare.

"She created this for you on the date of your birth," smiling broadly, he paused again for dramatic effect before adding, "six years ago!"

Mother, Merlin thought as he hesitated. *Mother must have told Nimue.* With a shrug, he placed the silver chain over his head, letting the Druid Egg hang low against his chest, hidden from view. He could feel it pulse just over his heart, and he knew that as long as he wore the stone, part of Avalon would always be with him. Absentmindedly, he gathered his hair and tied it back with the leather strap that had graced Nimue's gift.

"If you ladies are done chatting, Ambrosius bids you join him."

Merlin knew the tone of the voice well and was surprised when he looked up, expecting to see Uther, instead saw Sir Lot. At first glance Merlin was taken-back, and hardly recognized him. It had only been a little over a month since they had last spoken, yet Lot had aged years. Dark circles and tiny wrinkles surrounded his once brilliant eyes, which were now dull and lifeless. Although he retained his northern accent, his voice mimicked Uther's, and had deepened to an unsettling sinister bass. Merlin wondered if it was the same with all mortal men, as they teetered on the brink of puberty and manhood.

"Sir Lot, it is good to see you." Lionel chirped in his usual boyish manner.

"You are keeping the king waiting," Lot growled at Merlin. Without giving Lionel even a nod, Lot turned his horse and proceeded to walk casually toward the burial mound.

Stretching her neck, Merlin's mare opened her mouth and took a hungry bite out of Lot's black stallion's hindquarters, causing the horse to kick, nicker and prance about.

"Control your beast," Lot shouted, his voice rising several octaves as he did his best to steady his stallion.

"Control yours," Merlin's voice was even, yet forceful, as he squeezed his mare's sides and dashed past Lot in a gallop, with Lionel close behind.

As they neared the burial mound, Merlin slowed the pace. Admiring the Celtic knot work in the silver bracelet he looked to Lionel and asked, "So, when did you become a silversmith?"

"Do you remember the Druid's stable boy, Elivri?"

Merlin nodded.

"After Nimue left me to finish my healing on my own, I struck up a friendship with him. He is a very friendly fellow and an amazing artisan. Have you seen any of his works?"

Merlin shook his head, no. Sadly, he regretted being so wrapped up in his own ambitions that he had not taken the time to get to know those around him better.

"Well, of course you know him best from his work with the horses. Yet even at his young age he has an intrinsic knowledge of crafting jewelry. He is also a patient teacher." Lionel smiled at the thought of becoming Elivri's apprentice. "His talent did not go unnoticed by the king. During my recovery, Ambrosius insisted that Elivri move from the Druid's temple, assigning him head of the royal livery."

"With Elivri gone, who was left to watch over the Druid's steeds?" Merlin knew how Ambrosius detested the Druids, but he was surprised at the announcement of the removal of their groom.

"If it was up to Ambrosius, the days of Druids would be numbered. Did you know that he has banned them from tonight's ceremony? No Druids are allowed inside Stonehenge's inner circle," Lionel sighed, "with the exception of you of course. But, then the king does not consider you a true Druid. I do believe that the king looks upon you as the son he shall never have."

The son he shall never have… Lionel's words pierced. *Could it be that Ambrosius would not play a part in the creation of Britain's savior after all?* In an attempt to give Lionel the impression that he did not hear his last comment, Merlin pushed his mare forward, just out of hearing range. *Not allowing the Druids within Stonehenge was not a good omen for the Druids, nor for the young High King.*

Not wishing to be ignored, Lionel pulled his horse next to Merlin's, blurting out his thoughts. "There are times that I do not understand the High King's motives. Why would he allow the Druids to proceed over his coronation, yet deny them access to the inner ring of stones, to oversee the royals' burial? On a Druid holy day no less."

"You, of all people, should know of the brothers' upbringing. Were you not also raised as a Christian in Brittany?"

"As *you* of all people should know, religious beliefs can be a complicated matter. It is true that we, the current royals of Brittany, were brought up in the Christian faith. Yet, we, like our Celtic ancestors, also revel in the celebration of pagan holidays."

"We both know that Ambrosius has never had faith in Druid ways. For the coronation he felt obligated, as Britain's new High King, to go along with ancient tradition." Merlin pulled back on the reins, slowing his mare. "Recent events have shaken Ambrosius. He is grasping to hold on to what little faith he does have. Who truly knows the inner workings of a man's heart and soul?"

"The only man I know of who possesses such knowledge—*is you.*"

"I fear that you put too much faith in me."

"You, Merlin, are the only person I have never lost faith in. I suspect the High King feels the same." Lionel gave Merlin a weary smile. In silence, they continued to ride to the ceremonial burial mound, with Lot trailing closely.

Arriving at the freshly created barrow, the three dismounted just as Ambrosius and Uther reached the apex of the mound. Their boots were muddy from climbing the newly turned soil.

Merlin glanced to Lot and noticed his boots wore the same mud. For a flashing moment he understood, and empathized with, the weariness of his rival.

Surrounding the foot of the barrow were kings, princes, knights, squires and pages, from every corner of Britain. Mourners came to worship the honorable men now buried beneath the feet of the High King and his brother. Silence prevailed as Ambrosius' words flowed from the top of the royal's burial mound, drifting down and penetrating the ears, hearts, and souls of the fathers, sons, brothers, and comrades of the slaughtered royals who had gathered at the base. As the High King spoke, Merlin's thoughts drifted. Even though his attention strayed, he knew every word that Ambrosius uttered.

"Merlin," Lionel shouted. In reaction to the king's speech, the roar of the crowd made it difficult, if not near impossible to be heard. "The sun is setting; it is time for you to join the king in the blessing within Stonehenge."

Pushing past Lionel, the Arch Druid offered a silver chalice; grimacing, Merlin drank the bittersweet mixture of warm wine and woodworm. Within moments Merlin felt lightheaded. Trancelike, he allowed the surrounding Druids to remove his clothing, exposing the Druid Egg.

Trembling, withered fingers reached out to touch the shimmering transparent blue stone. Jolts of tiny electrical impulses coursed through the Arch Druid, causing him to rapidly retract his hand as the etched scrolls began to move in an eternal path within the stone.

The Druid's questioning eyes locked with Merlin's expressionless eyes. Eyes no longer human, lost eyes, dilated into an ebony abyss. Quickly regaining composure, the Arch Druid instructed his fellow priests to strip Merlin of his remaining clothes, redressing him in a long white ceremonial gown.

The strong menthol-like scent of woodworm mingled with the sweet scent of mint assaulted Merlin's senses. The smoke seeped into the woolen cloth that draped loosely about his body, as the pagan priests continued to bless his person with incense.

Standing near the heel stone entrance, Ambrosius and Uther watched the ritual. Periodically the Arch Druid glanced in their direction, daring the brother's to interfere. Daring them to prematurely call the boy prophet away, to defy the gods and goddess anymore than they had already. Ambrosius and Uther stood silent and patient as the sun continued to descend.

Holding a second chalice, the Arch Druid chanted as he dipped his long bony fingers deeply into a mixture of water scented with the essence of vervain. Walking around Merlin, he flicked the mixture in a slow and deliberate manner. When the circle was complete, he poured the remaining water upon Merlin's bare feet. Exchanging the empty vessel with the wine chalice, the old priest waited and watched as Merlin consumed the last of the red hallucinogenic liquid.

"It is time," were the only words the aged Druid spoke, as he defiantly guided Merlin toward the High King.

Rigid as the ancient stones before him, Merlin paused for a moment before stepping upon the most sacred of grounds within Stonehenge. Although the cold autumn winds tugged at his clothing, and swirled about his bare feet, a warm inner glow consumed him. He watched the golden sun withdraw into the earth, and the blood red full moon rise regally. He swallowed hard as both orbs passed one another from opposite portals within the stone structure—a changing of the celestial guard.

The heavens lit, ablaze of jewel-toned colors as the procession began. Ambrosius in the middle, flanked by Uther on his right and Merlin on his left, they slowly walked sunwise within the inner circle. A select four dozen relatives of the men slaughtered on the Night of the Long Knives, were also allowed within the inner sphere and circled behind at a respectful pace.

As the trio walked in the moon-shadow of the sarsen circle, Merlin extended his hand allowing his fingers and palm to gently caress each stone; the chill of the stones soothing his flesh. He smiled as the earth's energy raced through his fingertips, swiftly flowing into his heart, into his brain, into every artery, vein and capillary of his body. Each stone exposed hidden secrets, shared experiences from time beginning. All becoming memories now permanently etched within Merlin's knowledge base.

Upon completing the outer circle of the Dancing Giants, the three led the procession along the outer side of the smaller blue stone circle. As Merlin passed the eastern most point, he paused, placing both hands upon a blue-green sandstone. Looking upward Ambrosius watched in wonder as a wind-spout funneled down from the heavens begging Merlin to join in a turbulent dance of the elements

"Blessed be the air. Grant us peace in the East," Merlin spoke in the same mysterious dramatic baritone timbre he had voiced on his first encounter with Vortigern.

Stopping at the southern most stone, he once again pressed both hands upon the stone. At the base of the boulder, flames ignited. Ambrosius stood helpless yet mesmerized as he watched the fire engulf Merlin in a flickering blaze of reds and oranges, only to recede into the soil as quickly as they had inflamed, leaving the young prophet and his garment neither burnt nor singed.

"Blessed be the fire. Grant us peace in the South," spoken with force, Merlin's words echoed in the impending darkness.

Approaching the western most stone, as he placed his hands upon the stone, from a cloudless sky, rain began to fall. It came first in a trickle and then in a torrent. So heavy was the downpour that for moments it curtained Merlin, causing Ambrosius to fear that his mystic companion had been sucked into a dimension of invisibility. The king breathed a sigh of relief as Merlin re-appeared.

"Blessed be the water. Grant us peace in the West," as Merlin spoke, the water drained from his body and clothes, leaving a small puddle at the stone's base.

Nearing the northern most point, Merlin's pace slowed. Leisurely, with passion, he leaned forward, wrapping his arms around the stone in a tender embrace and placed a gentle kiss upon the sandstone surface.

Ambrosius' heart raced as he observed the small standing stone turn from granite, to woman, and back to stone. Without question, he recognized her immediately. It was the face and figure of the Lady of Avalon. He attempted to reach over Merlin's shoulder to bring the lady back to life, but was restrained by Uther's firm grip.

"Blessed be Mother Earth, may she grant us peace in the North," Merlin's voice softened as he spoke, his fingertips tenderly touching the stone before departing.

The moon hung large and fiery within the heavens as Merlin, Ambrosius, and Uther made their way past the five trilithon stone guardians, stopping at each, they paid homage to the monolithic structures. Finally they stood in front of the massive alter stone, where the young High King and his younger brother knelt in reverence, placing their foreheads on the stone, with arms stretched, palms facing down.

Lingering slightly behind the royal pair, Merlin folded his arms and remained standing. From beyond the Giant's Dance, a large group of Druids gathered, they had come from the four corners of Britain in their annual celebration of this auspicious feasting holiday. Although, per Ambrosius decree, the Druids were barred from entering the inner circle, they defiantly formed a ring around the outer circumference of the standing stones.

Between the stones wafted the faint sound of Druid's chanting, drums softly beating, harps sweetly singing, and the peaceful lilt of Celtic flutes. Straining his senses Merlin closed his eyes and saw the hundreds of others who had also come from every corner of Britain to celebrate, and pay tribute to, the memory of their fallen fathers, sons, brothers, and comrades. Within the inner circle the chosen few began to dance, and sing, as laughter filtered into the heavens. *Oh yes*, Merlin smiled, *Samhain is indeed the best holiday of the year.*

With his eyes still closed, Merlin smiled as he became one with the elements. He felt the blades of grass growing between his toes. He felt a warm breeze embracing him, plastering the Druid gown about his legs and chest. He felt the soft mist of a creeping evening fog settle upon his feet, hands, and face.

Focusing on his inner journey, Merlin soon became oblivious to his surroundings…until he felt a heavy tremor underfoot. The rhythmic thumping throbbed within his body, and in his drug induced state, emotions superseded rationality. He imagined the giant stones coming to life and joining the celebration. Fantasy gave way to logic as the air turned frigid, the pounding increased, and the gentle ground tremor transformed into a rolling earthquake. Fear overcame utopia, and he struggled for the courage to open his eyes.

Unfolding his arms, he clutched his fist to his side and willed himself the courage to view his surroundings. Slowly he felt his eyelids obey. A thick fog hung heavy about his legs. He strained to see the ground, see his feet, yet, everything below his knees had vanished into a gray haze. In front of him the brothers remained motionless kneeling in front of the alter stone; heads still down, arms still outstretched. The music had ceased. With the exception of his rapid heartbeat, sound had vanished. Terrified that he had gone deaf, he attempted to speak, to scream for help, but no words emerged.

Lifting his left hand in front of his face, an irrational peace fell upon him as he watched his flesh-tone skin slowly dissolved into hues of black, whites, and grays. All color encompassing his world had dissipated, with the exception of the full moon, which despite the fog, hung ominously close and brilliant overhead. Although it still clung to its blood red blush, the moon cast an achromatic shadow upon the Stonehenge inhabitants.

With cautious wonder, Merlin surveyed his surroundings. Where only moments before the revelers had been dancing and singing, they now stood suspended in time. All were statuesque, perfectly balanced in motionless movement; mouths poised in song, bodies contorted in mid-dance, eyes-wide open, facial expressions frozen.

In the distance, near the newly blessed king's barrow, an otherworldly melody floated through the standing stones, fracturing the silence. The soothing notes saturated Merlin's senses, instantly lulling him into a state of peaceful surrender. Unable to move his feet, his hawk-eyes watched in calm fascination as a distant mist emerged from the dead kings' burial mound.

One by one, the ghostly images of the slaughtered royals rose from the ground and walked with pride toward Stonehenge. Single file they floated between the giant stones of the sarsen circle. Reaching the alter stone, each of the phantom kings in a show of respect for Uther's military prowess, bowed deeply in front of their former leader. Proceeding to the High King, each of the royal souls bowed once more, reverently kissing Ambrosius' ruby ring. Advancing to Merlin, each regal spirit touched the Druid Egg, causing the eternal lifeline etched into the moonstone to quiver as it absorbed the human skills and memories of each apparition. Even in death the royals displayed their devotion, pledging their everlasting dedication—their very souls—to Britain and her protectors.

Nonchalantly Merlin glanced about, curious as to the nobility's next destination. To his surprise and amusement, he watched as each of the transparent figures searched for their kinsmen among the human statues. Upon finding a relative, joyous dancing abounded followed by a cloudlike embrace and long conversation. Although the visitations appeared to be one-sided, in his heart, Merlin knew that although clear recollection of this night would be hidden, the events would be recalled in silent mysterious moments of remembrance by the living.

Before the last of the men slaughtered on the Night of the Long Knives paid their respects, a new procession of ceremonial ghostly-men entered the circle and proceeded to perform the identical ritual. These men were known to Merlin only from the drawings within the ancient scrolls stowed away within Ambrosius' library. Even in this gray monotone world, Merlin recognized the deceased nobility from their archaic clothing, the crowns and jewelry handed down from antiquity. Like their newly deceased counterparts, these men came from the numerous burial mounds that dotted the landscape surrounding Stonehenge; the ancient kings, knights, and warriors, who now called this sacred place home. With immense reverence, Merlin accepted each valiant spirit's gifts of knowledge, silently he pledged to pass their words and heroic deeds along to Britain's yet unborn savior.

***

So it went throughout the night until every space, within and surrounding, Stonehenge was overflowing with transparent otherworldly beings. Slowly the moon waned, with its departure each apparition vaporized into a heavy mist. Once more Merlin found himself standing knee-deep in a dense fog. The thin veil, that had so graciously granted passage from the Otherworld to humanity, descended velvet thick. Merlin watched in awe as the tide of sound and color rushed wavelike upon the world. Mortals began to stir, and as Merlin suspected, they were oblivious to the evening's mythical moments.

With the first rays of warmth filtering through the hallowed space, Merlin experienced a debilitating pain racing across his forehead, causing his knees to buckle and his vision to fade. He felt hands reaching out to catch him, but it was too late. His body stiffened, falling forward, his head hit the alter stone. His last recollection was watching a river of blood flow around the base of the stone. *An appropriate gift* he thought, *the sacrifice of my ancient blood in exchange for the gift of knowledge from the ancient royals*. High above the stone circle sanctuary, Merlin's hawk cried out in panic.

29

"How are you feeling today?" the maiden asked as she wrapped the bandage around Merlin's head.

"Do you have to do that in here, now?" Uther grumbled.

Merlin sighed as he felt the young girl secure his bandage with trembling fingers. He touched her hand reassuringly as she gathered the soiled bandages, turned and scrambled from the Library. Slumping back into the pillows Merlin pondered at how things had changed in Londinium since he first traveled through its gates. With the growing army, had come supporting businesses. New shops sprang up everyday, until vacant streets now overflowed with shopkeepers and their families. The once all male military staff that ran the old Roman Governor's Palace, was now overseen by servants, cooks, and maidens.

"Uther, be glad the boy is mending," Pellinore chortled, as he eyed the pretty figure, smiling after her as she rushed from his view.

"I'll be *glad* when winter has ended," Uther sighed as he paced about the room, sitting down abruptly on the lectus that Merlin occupied. Causing Merlin to maneuver his position quickly to avoid getting his feet crushed.

"How are you feeling these days Merlin?" With the maiden out of sight, Pellinore turned his attentions to the healing boy.

"He's regaining his strength every day," merrily Lionel announced, smiling first to Pellinore, then to Uther, and finally to Merlin. "The physician is concerned that the wound has not healed. Yet, he is content with our patient's progress," as he spoke Lionel reached over and ruffled Merlin's hair.

Seething, Merlin was unsure which was worse; being treated as an invalid, or as a pet. Looking upward Merlin's perturbed stare came in direct contact with Uther's twinkling eyes. Under the sheepskin that covered his legs, Merlin felt Uther grab his foot, giving a reassuring squeeze. Even adversaries, it appeared, could find common ground in Lionel's well-meaning, yet somewhat irritating nattering.

"How long before they retaliate?" Ambrosius queried, as he leaned toward the wall, devouring the mural of Alexander fighting his greatest victory, "…before spring?"

"No." Uther rose, standing next to his brother's side as he spoke. "A hard winter is fast approaching. The open waters are treacherous enough in the springtime. The Saxons will bide their time. Rest easy brother, Saxon sails will not be seen upon the horizon of Britain's eastern shores until the approach of Beltane."

"We must be prepared for their arrival," Ambrosius announced with urgency, as he turned from the wall, his sullen expression matched his words. "Allowing just one Saxon to touch foot upon our shores could bring destruction to us all," as he spoke, Ambrosius searched the room, his eyes peering into each man.

"Britain has a long eastern coastline, dear boy," Pellinore quipped offhandedly. "To keep all invaders from ever landing upon her shores is an ambitious undertaking. I fear it may prove to be a near impossible feat." The old king grimaced, as he sank decaying teeth into a firm juicy apple.

"What do you know of impossible deeds old man?" Ambrosius sputtered, unable to move, trapped within his brother's grip.

Pellinore glared open mouthed at Ambrosius. No response escaped his lips, none could. He had known the brothers from childhood; never had he heard a disparaging word from Ambrosius directed toward him. Shocked he let the apple drop from his hand as he stood and slowly walked from the room.

"Pelly!" Uther shouted. Trudging after Pellinore, he gave Ambrosius a backwards, questioning glare.

Falling into the chair behind his writing table, Ambrosius cradled his face with his hands as he slumped over mounds of paperwork.

As he made his way to the High King's side, Merlin motioned for a stunned Lionel to leave. Reaching the king, he did his best to be supportive, "It will be alright, Your Majesty." Merlin placed his hands upon Ambrosius, giving the king's shoulders a reassuring squeeze. Bending over Merlin whispered, "Pellinore knows in his heart that you meant no disrespect."

"I am tired Merlin," Ambrosius words fell in tenacious tones. "It has not even been a full year, and I am tired. Tired of the killing, tired of our brave men being killed. Most of all, I am tired of being High King." Reaching upward, he seized Merlin's hand and clutched it tightly.

"I understand. I too have grown weary of battle, the taste of blood, and the stench of the dying." Nonchalantly, Merlin slipped free from the king's hold, and maneuvered his way to the other side of the table. "Our destiny is written before we enter this world as mortal men."

"You speak as if you personally knew my thoughts and feelings. You, Merlin, the boy prophet, the time traveler, the healer—what could you possibly know of me, of those around you, of us—mere mortals." Looking upward he did his best to hold back his emotions, and like Merlin—stop time.

"Every living soul will experience fleeting moments of beauty, but, life is not beautiful. It matters not if you are of noble birth or born into servitude, of mortal or fairy blood—life is never fair, and there is no escaping the fact that life is always deadly. Some deaths are more peaceful than others, but death is eminent to all of us." Staring deeply into Ambrosius' eyes, Merlin continued, "Do not let life's recent events fuel your anger. Peace or discontentment comes from within. Man may not rule his destiny, but he does rule his soul. Your reaction to life comes from within you, not from the world around you. The reality—life is drenched in agony. The conscious decisions, how you live *within* your preordained life, will diminish your suffering and the suffering of those yet to come."

Ambrosius nodded in quiet understanding. His shoulders relaxed. A calm that he had not felt in months spread throughout his body.

"I know you Ambrosius, perhaps better than you know yourself," Merlin paused, allowing time for Ambrosius to interject. When he remained silent, Merlin continued, "If you could return to your mother's womb, you would not elect to change your life's path. Even if you had not been born of royal blood, you would still be a noble man. One day your devotion to Britain will be immortalized. The scrolls of your chivalrous deeds will fill a library twice this size." Tossing his arms in the air, Merlin twirled about the room bringing laughter from the High King and loud clapping from the doorway.

"Bravo Merlin, that was quite a speech," Uther stood in the library's entrance, with Lot and the Young Royal Guard. "Remind me to have you address my troops before our next battle." Pushing past Merlin, Uther sauntered into the room, stopping in front of his brother. "Ambrosius, while searching for Pelly, I ran across Sir Lot and his men. They have come to bid you farewell for the winter."

"I thought you had masses of Britain's best and bravest arriving to Londinium hourly, not leaving her," Ambrosius voice deepened, tapping his fingertips lightly together, he easily slipped into a stern royal posture.

"Your Majesty," Lot fell to his knee as he addressed Ambrosius, "forgive me. We have been occupied this past month training the new recruits."

"Stand up," Uther tugged at Lot's tunic, straightening him from a kneeling position. "The boys are taking a troop of men to North Cornwall. Recent raids by the Irish have led Duke Gorlois to request our aide in stopping a minor insurgence before it becomes a major threat—wise man, the duke."

Elated with the prospect of spending a winter without the Young Royal Guard's company, Merlin quietly removed himself from the center of attention. Melting into the stacks of scrolls he stood silently, drinking in the news of Gorlois, Cornwall, and the duke's Tintagel stronghold.

"Ah, so it is not on a festive retreat that you venture, but on a peacekeeping quest." Ambrosius words trailed off and he busied himself with paperwork to dislodge old memories. With a contemptuous smirk, he quickly looked in Lot's direction as he spoke, "Beware of enemies offering their hands in friendship. They will chew your fingers off like starving dogs."

"We shall take your words to heart, Your Majesty," Lot laughed uneasily, bumping into Uther as he attempted a graceful retreat.

Nentres poked Dodinel in the ribs, to make sure his friend's laughter remained stifled. *That was all that was needed, to get Lot upset at them before a long hard ride through unknown territory.*

"With your permission, we are prepared to start our journey." Lot ignored his companions as he addressed Uther. "Our horses are ready, and our cavalry await us outside the palace. With the harsh winter weather rapidly approaching, we felt it best to depart now, and ride with as much daylight to our west as possible."

"May God ride with you and your men," Ambrosius' words vibrated with a genuineness not affected by pretense. Although he often found it hard to hide his disdain for Lot, the boys were still his men. Granted it was Uther's army, but he had learned from recent events that the fate of the army's men—and boys—ultimately weighed heavy upon the shoulders of their High King.

"Thank you, Your Majesty," all three spoke in unison.

"Use your messengers," Uther urged as he pulled Lot aside. "Do not use inclement weather as an excuse. Keep me informed. Do you understand?"

"Yes, my liege," Lot averted his eyes, but nodded emphatically. "I pledge that you will know everything that I know in regards to the perceived invasion."

"If all goes well, bring the troops home for the Beltane celebration," Uther quipped as he slapped Lot on the back. "We will need your wisdom and valor in the spring, when a new breed of Saxons attempt to dock upon our shores."

"I pledge my life and loyalty to you." This time Lot stared into Uther's eyes, and even Merlin, standing in the shadows, knew the young prince spoke true.

30

"Once more, I wish that I was joining you on this campaign," Lionel sighed as he pulled on the saddle's girth, tightening the cinch, causing the gray to swat her tail across his face.

"It is important that you keep watch over the king," Merlin reassured his friend as he secured a bundle to the back of his saddle. "As absurd as it sounds, Uther and I are in agreement on this matter. Especially, since Pellinore has not yet returned from his visit to his kingdom and the overseeing of the birth of yet another son. You, and you alone, are the one person who can be trusted to guard Ambrosius in Uther's absence. Thus, you should feel honored, not disparaged, to be left in charge of the High King's protection."

"I am still puzzled that the king did not insist on going with you and Uther to battle the Saxons. Are not the new insurgents even more of a threat to the eastern coast as their predecessors? Are they not now fueled with the fury of revenge?" Lionel held the throatlatch of the mare's bridle as Merlin grabbed a handful of the gray's mane, swinging easily onto the saddle.

"A High King has many duties," Merlin adjusted his seat in the saddle and his hold on the reins as he spoke. "Granted, enemy invasions are a prime concern. At the same time, he also has to deal with the internal politics of the British people. He is, in spite of everything else, the ruler of *all* of Britain, not a mere overseer of one of her many cities or kingdoms. Ambrosius is the supreme lawmaker and law enforcer. He is the builder of cities, the accountant of land and taxes to maintain the cities and her peoples."

"Even so, does Ambrosius not have accountants, architects, peace keepers to contend with the everyday running of Britain?"

"The simple answer is, yes. But, nothing in life is ever a simple yes or no. Over the past year, I know you have also observed that Ambrosius has gained the support of the majority of lower kings from nearly every region. Yet, increased threat of invasion brings forth increased responsibility to keep Britain and Britons safe."

Lionel nodded in agreement, keeping his thoughts mute. Standing in silence, he scratched behind the mare's ear as he patiently waited for Merlin to inevitably drive his point home.

"Instead of sitting upon the saddle of a warhorse, Ambrosius has been saddled with an overabundance of royal paperwork," Merlin spoke with a far off, knowing look in his eyes. Nonchalantly, he waved a hand toward Londinium's main roadway overcrowded with men clad in various stages of battle attire. "Hundreds of new troops enter the king's army each day. Not only do they need training, but also food, clothing, and wages. Uther may be in charge of the new troops preparation for battle, but all else falls heavy upon his brother's shoulders. Today, I am sure, that Ambrosius feels a hunger to be near Uther's side, and a twinge of guilt at staying behind. I am equally confident that he knows without a doubt, that Uther can handle the new enemy insurgence without his presence, and that the building of a new government is equally important to Britain's future. It is no easy job to be accountable for the safety and well being of all who call Britain home."

"Ironically, for a short while, the Saxons also called this land their home," Lionel nuzzled his head against the mare as he spoke.

"Many lives would have been spared and alliances made, if not for greed and dishonor." Sitting upright, Merlin pulled sharply on the reins, causing his mare's head to jerk away from Lionel. "We can only live in the present, and learn from, the consequences of the past." Lowering his voice he added, "*Our quest* will bring peace to the future."

"Our quest," Lionel shook his head slowly and maneuvered closer to Merlin as he spoke. "I thought we had abandoned the treasure quest. Are not Ambrosius and Uther the keeper of Britain's heart and soul?"

"At one time I was confident that Ambrosius was the first phase in our journey to complete the quest. Now, I am tentative to voice that fact as a certainty." Merlin searched Lionel's face for understanding and smiled wearily, finding his words had only rooted further confusion. Exhaling deeply, Merlin pondered aloud, "In reality, it could be either brother, but I assure you, within this year the seed will be planted, and either Ambrosius or Uther will be the crucial contributor to the creation."

"You bewilder me with your riddles." Lionel walked away, kicked at the dirt, and sighed, "But, I am honored that you believe in me enough to share your enigma. I will guard the king with my life, and perhaps the life of the future ruler of Britain."

"Thus, the reason we once more must be separated. I go to protect one brother, while you stay behind to watch over the other." Merlin walked the gray to Lionel's side, reaching down he slapped his friend on the shoulder.

"Sir Uther is departing," with a quivering voice, Uther's youngest squire announced—his horse prancing nervously next to Merlin. "If you are not ready to join him immediately, he will leave without you," gathering his courage he reluctantly blurted out the rest of the message, "and banish you forever from the kingdom."

"Some things never change," Merlin laughed as he nodded to the messenger. Mouthing a silent farewell to Lionel, Merlin pressed his legs into the mare, and galloped toward the fort.

***

"Why do you always keep me waiting?" Uther was in his usual pre-battle foul mood. He motioned for his troops to mount and begin their long journey to Dubris. "It is bad enough that I have to contend with the Irish, Picts, and once more the Saxons, invading from all sides, weakening and dividing our armies. I do not, and should not, have to worry of your whereabouts. Stay by my side, or by my brother's, but whichever it is, do not make me come looking for you again. Do you understand?"

"Yes, I understand fully," Merlin humbled himself before the raging bull of a man. "I will heed your words. As per the king's request, my place is by your side. Rest assured I shall do my very best to not keep you waiting in the future."

"Good," Uther spat, as he scowled at Merlin. Expecting a confrontation, Uther was both elated and frustrated at Merlin's new respectful attitude. Although he would never admit it, Uther rather enjoyed their verbal battles. He had always felt that fighting with words was nearly as invigorating as swordplay, and over the past year, he found Merlin an apt opponent.

"Has Lot returned with his army?" Merlin knew the answer, but he couldn't resist asking the question.

"No!" Uther glared at Merlin as they led the armies through the streets.

Merlin mercifully dropped the subject. As soon as winter had set in, Lot's messengers had ceased to come. When Uther had sent his own messengers, none had returned. It had been over two months since any word had arrived from Cornwall. Although Merlin did not understand why, he knew that Uther tolerated more from Lot than from any of his other men. Merlin knew that the young prince's perceived defiant act of disobedience irritated and worried Uther. Merlin also knew that if not for the current Saxon invasion they would be headed west instead of east.

Crowds gathered along the route. Endless rows of cavalry turned the corner near the forum. Women and children cheered, waving brightly colored ribbons from the open windows of the variety of shops that had sprung up all over the once decaying city of Londinium. The aroma of bakery goods drifted through the air, causing Merlin's mouth to water and his empty stomach to grumble.

"Sir Merlin, I have something for you," the good natured woman smiled upward as she hurried from her shop to Merlin's side, doing her best to keep stride with his mare. "It was baked with the loving hands of my daughter, Clarisant. She bids you a safe journey and a speedy return."

"Thank you dear lady, and be sure to thank your daughter for me." Eagerly he accepted a freshly baked scone from the chubby hand of the baker's wife. Turning in his saddle, he smiled and waved to both mother and daughter. Merlin then broke the pastry in two equal parts, offering Uther one of the halves as a token of peace.

"Both mother and daughter, Merlin? I had no idea you were such a ladies' man," Uther chuckled as he grabbed the offering, shoving it into his mouth. He was still wiping the crumbs from his beard as they reached the entrance to the forum.

"Well, brother, I see you have at least broken your evening fast," Ambrosius chuckled as he spied a few stray morsels that Uther had missed.

"Blame it on the boy." Uther grinned as be removed his glove, running fingers slowly through his neatly trimmed beard and mustache. "I am glad that you could pull yourself away from paperwork long enough to bid us farewell."

"You know that I would be at your side if at all possible," Ambrosius worked his way around Uther's stallion, positioning himself between his brother and Merlin. "Take good care of each other. I shall miss you both greatly and look forward to your triumphant return."

"I do not like leaving you so close to the Ides of March," Uther whispered as he bent forward leaning his lips near his brother's ear. "It is a day of despair and foreboding."

"It is merely a day of superstition, brother." Ambrosius grabbed Uther's hand and squeezed tightly. "I will be safer within the city walls surrounded by guards than you will be upon the chalky shores of Dubris."

"Yes, but I have the mighty Merlin to protect me, brother." Uther playfully kicked Merlin in the shin as he taunted, "Are you sure you do not wish to keep the boy prophet by your side?"

"I am certain." Ambrosius reached for Merlin's hand grasping it gently. With reassurance, he added, "Merlin will provide you and your men with much needed guidance and protection."

"It is time to take our leave," Uther grunted as he pushed his horse slightly forward, causing Ambrosius to loosen his grip, and step out of the way.

"May God ride with you," Ambrosius shouted.

"May the gods and goddesses protect you in my absence as well." Uther lifted his arm, signaling his troops to move out.

Echoing in the shadows of a nearby building, Merlin thought he recognized a familiar voice. Memories squirmed within his brain, the voice belonged to someone drenched in evil, yet he could not bring the vision to full recall. He peered into the dark recesses of the building. The silhouette of the large yet ambiguous figure was unloading a cart filled with barrels of wine. As they rode past, Merlin blinked and when he looked again, the man had vanished. Omen or imagination, he was uncertain. The scar on his forehead began to throb. Blinking, his long lashes prevented a slow trickle of blood from flowing into his left eye from the still unhealed lesion.

"Is everything alright?" Uther untied the scarf from his neck and handed it to Merlin.

Merlin smiled meekly as he tied the scarf around his head. "It is nothing, just old wounds festering."

31

"Your Majesty," Lionel shouted as he walked briskly down the basilica's corridor leading to the king's council room. "Your Majesty, I have word from Sir Uther." Even in his excitement Lionel took note of the absence of guards near the doorway.

Of late, there were too many new recruits, too many new household staff to keep track of. He was glad that Pellinore had finally returned. Later, at the midday meal, he would ask Pellinore to reprimand the master of arms. Uther had taken all the well-trained disciplined men on his campaign against the Saxons. Only the new recruits and those too feeble or infirmed were left behind to protect the walled city. At the moment there were more important issues at hand. Waving the scroll he entered the king's council chambers standing breathless in front of Ambrosius.

"Good news?" Dropping his pen, Ambrosius rose with excitement as he reached for the vellum. Methodically, the king ran his fingers over the royal seal. It had been less than a month since Uther's departure, but even the waxy impression of the dragon created from his brother's signet ring soothed his nerves.

"The messenger indicated so." *Open it*, Lionel wanted to scream, but with respect to the king he held his tongue.

Nimbly Ambrosius slid his delicate fingers under the wax, breaking the seal. Pausing for a moment, he watched the oval dragon float gracefully to his feet, before eagerly unrolling and reading his brother's message.

"Wine, my lord?" A large man entered humbly, head down and wine vessel extended.

Ambrosius nodded in the direction of a cup sitting on the writing table. He paid little attention to the servant, who leisurely filled the silver goblet to the brim.

The servant's presence made the tiny hairs dance on the back of Lionel's neck. There was something uncomfortably familiar in the man's deep voice. He became even more suspect as the mysterious figure continued to maneuver his body to prevent Lionel from viewing his face. The size of the man; tall, broad shouldered with hands of a warrior not a household attendant piqued Lionel's curiosity.

"Good news indeed, Lionel. My brother and his men have pushed the Saxons out to sea, and, at least for now, have once more secured our eastern coast." Ambrosius reached for his wine, sipping on the sweet concoction as he continued to read. "He is sending additional troops along the coast, and hopes to return to us within the next two days."

"More wine, my lord?" The servant refilled the goblet, this time without waiting for the king's nod.

"Join me, Lionel. Let us drink to another of my brother's successful campaigns." The words barely emerged from Ambrosius' lips as he clutched his throat and with frantic gulps cried out, "I can't breathe." The half-read correspondence drifted to the floor, followed by the loud clang of the goblet, wine spilling bloodlike over Uther's cursive. In a feeble attempt to reach for Lionel, Ambrosius toppled across the writing table.

Lionel watched in frozen disbelief as the king fell—the royal documents scattered about the room. Gathering his wits, he ran to Ambrosius' side, grabbing the king in his arms causing both himself and Ambrosius to crumble to the floor. With great effort Lionel leaned his head close to hear the king's last words.

"Swear to tell Merlin, watch over Uther," Ambrosius gasped as his hand attempted to reach again for the young prince. Pupils dilated, his body began to shake violently, as several short bursts of a death rattle emerged from deep within Ambrosius' chest—then his body went limp.

"I swear," Lionel whispered close to the king's ear. Dreamlike he wiped the spittle from Ambrosius lips, brushing away a strand of bronze hair, and gently closing the lids over the young king's sea-green eyes.

"A High King for a High King, a brother for a brother! Let Lot know that my family's death-debt has been paid," the servant expounded with a toothy grin as he towered over Lionel.

"Guards!" Lionel screamed, as the recognition of both the voice and the man flooded his mind and jerked his emotions back to reality. Springing to his feet, he instinctively retrieved his dagger. "Sir Faustus, you murdering coward," he growled. With superhuman strength he plunged the dagger deep within his former companion's ribcage, thrusting the blade upward into his heart.

Blood poured from the wound and spurted from Faustus' mouth, as the startled man looked wide-eyed with disbelief at Lionel.

"Guards!" Lionel bellowed once more, as he pushed the bleeding man away. Watching as the traitor staggered to his knees, hands pressing hard to his chest.

"You do not even ask why?" Faustus moaned, defiant to the end. "It was after all, just part of *The Plan*—Lot's Plan."

"Liar!" Lionel shrieked as he too dropped to the floor, crawling back to the fallen king, he cradled Ambrosius. Across the room, he watched Faustus dispassionately, as the assassin's blood pooled onto the mosaic tiles.

"Lionel, what goes on here?" Pellinore quizzed as he entered followed by two guards. All three simultaneously drew their swords as they surveyed the room in bewilderment.

"Strip the conspirator and drag him naked through the streets," Lionel wailed. "He has murdered our king!"

"I am not the traitor," Faustus words gurgled as he tried to shout, blood gushing, "Lot is the instigator. He plotted to kill my father. He murdered my brother, leaving me for dead at his side. I may have killed that old woman," he continued his confession, "but her death and the death of her husband was on Lot's orders." Clutching his chest he managed to weakly kick at the guards as they circled him.

"May your soul rot in the bowels of Hades for all eternity." Lionel held the king tighter as he rocked. The curse bounced off the walls and echoed down the corridor.

"Lionel, get control! What has happened here?" Pellinore knelt next to Ambrosius, putting fingers to the king's throat to feel for a pulse. Looking up to the guards he shook his head and sighed deeply.

"What has happened here? That treacherous bastard has poisoned our king." Eyes glaring, Lionel howled, "The gods be damned, what are you waiting for? Obey my orders, strip him and drag his body through the streets for all of Londinium's citizens to view."

Pellinore's bones creaked loudly as he slowly rose, and made his way to the half-dead man sprawled on the floor in a dark pool of blood. Whispering to the guards, he watched as they grabbed Faustus dragging him from the room. Walking back to Lionel he stroked the prince's head.

"Do not patronize me," Lionel clung to the king's body as he spoke. "I know that it is my fault. I should have recognized him. I alone could have prevented this tragedy. Faustus may have provided the poison, but I am to blame for allowing the madman to conduct murder upon our High King. Uther will never forgive me, nor will Merlin. Nor can I ever forgive myself."

"There was nothing you could have done to prevent this from happening. Ambrosius fate was written in the stars long before he exited his mother's womb. Uther and Merlin will not blame you, but more important, you *must not* blame yourself," Pellinore knew that his words fell upon deaf ears. He could only hope that Lionel would absorb some of his long years of battle-weary wisdom.

"Move aside, grant me entrance," the royal physician barked, pushing through the large crowd forming outside the council room and past the guards blocking the entrance.

"Let me help you carry the king to the waiting litter," Pellinore spoke tenderly as he reached down in an attempt to untangle Lionel's arms from the royal body.

"No," Lionel snarled, "the king was left in my care. No one touches him but me. Does everyone understand? No one touches him but me." Methodically, with an animalistic vigor, Lionel rose to a standing position with Ambrosius' frail frame in his arms. "Let the people see what has befallen their beloved ruler."

"This is absurd," the physician huffed, arms waving in all direction as he looked to Pellinore for support. "He cannot physically carry the king through the streets. There is protocol to be followed."

"He can do as he pleases," Pellinore commanded. "Sir Lionel was appointed the High King's guardian by the king's brother and the king's advisor." The old knight posed a regal figure as he ceremoniously raised his sword in a salute to Britain's fallen sovereign.

"Send word to Uther," Lionel petitioned Pellinore, as he adjusted his hold on Ambrosius. The prince, still dry-eyed, started his long walk from the council room at the basilica to the king's palace quarters. As he approached the entrance to the forum, cries of despair and anguish rang out from the courtyard.

"Word has already been sent," Pellinore whispered.

32

"Take care of my stallion, Elivri. I fear he has been pushed beyond his limits," Uther commanded as he dismounted, tossing the reins in the groom's direction. Late yesterday afternoon their leisurely travel back to Londinium had turned frantic after being intervened by a king's messenger with the news of Ambrosius' death. Both Merlin and Uther had remained mute, riding their horses at a deadly pace racing to the city.

Merlin leaned over and stroked his mare's withers before reluctantly slipping from the saddle. Nearby, Uther's stallion wobbled. Pushing past the riderless mount, Merlin casually ran his fingers through the thick, white lather covering the black's coat. Nonchalantly he rubbed his hands together in an attempt to remove the sticky foam. Refusing to make eye contact, even with Elivri, he pushed past the onlookers.

Lingering for as long as he dared, solemnly Merlin followed the clumping of Uther's boots as he raced down the palace's corridors. Turning the final corner, Merlin paused once more. Illogically, he yearned for the guards to not recognize him, not allow him entrance to the king's resting place. The hopes of shrouding himself in an illusion of invisibility evaporated at the guards instant recognition. Reluctantly, Merlin entered Ambrosius' bedchamber, inwardly shivering as the door creaked shut behind him.

"It is good to see you, my boy," Pellinore grabbed Merlin, embracing him tightly.

Merlin stood limp within the old man's arms, peering over Pellinore's shoulder at the High King's body. Even in death, Ambrosius was as handsome as the first day he had laid eyes on him. Cascading over the pillows, the golden streaks within the king's long lion's mane danced in the candle's glow. Merlin longed to touch Ambrosius' face, the familiar face now masked in a ghostly transparent marble hue. One last time, he yearned to absorb the knowledge, now lost forever, from the king's blue-green eyes. As much as he tried to form comforting words, none would pass through his mind nor lips. His body became deflated, his heart ached as if shattered, and his breath came to him in short gasps.

Uther leaned over his brother, whispering something inaudible to even Merlin. Rising from Ambrosius' side, the new king walked deliberately to Lionel, who stood frozen in the dark recesses of the furthest corner. With his warrior's bear-like hand, Uther cuffed the boy across the face, sending the young prince cowering in a fetal position on the floor.

"Uther, it is not Lionel's fault," Pellinore pleaded as he grabbed hold of Uther's arm.

"He was commissioned to protect the High King," Uther screamed, his voice littered with guttural tones, causing Lionel to cover his ears in fear and remorse.

"If not for Lionel's bravery and quick thinking, Ambrosius' murderer would have gotten away with the crime," Pellinore argued as he wedged his body between Uther and Lionel.

"As always, you are right," Uther dropped his voice an octave as he turned, thrusting a pointing finger in Merlin's direction. "My brother's death lies entirely on him!" Uther seethed as he took four quick giant strides, slapping his palms against the stone wall on either side of Merlin's head.

Standing as a man before his executioner, Merlin lifted his head, dispassionately staring into his accuser's eyes.

"What good is your foresight, boy prophet?" Uther hissed as he pounded a fist against the stone, causing his skin to break and blood to trickle down the wall. "My brother trusted you, he trusted your visions." He pressed his face close to Merlin, "He believed in you."

Merlin shut his eyes tightly. Sounds became muted as the world around him began to fade. He allowed himself to slowly slip to the floor, only to be jerked back to reality as Uther slammed him against the wall.

"Not this time," Uther snarled, his fingers clutching Merlin's tunic, pinning him to the wall, "*I* am your king *now*! I forbid you to take the coward's way out."

"Enough!" Pellinore shouted in an attempt to bring order. His gnarled fingers tugged on Uther's shoulder. "Britain hovers on the brink of turmoil. Time is of the essence. There are pressing decisions to be made; or all that we have fought for, struggled for, all our loved ones died for, will have been for not."

"It is his fault, he needs to pay for my brother's death," Uther released Merlin, turned and unleashed his anger upon Pellinore. "Someone *must* pay!"

"The assassin has paid with his life, and his soul pledged for all eternity to Hades." Pellinore gently placed his hands upon Uther's broad shoulders. "We cannot bring your brother back from the Otherworld, but we can honor his spirit. We can keep his legacy alive. By birthright, you are Britain's new leader. You must gather your wits and your courage. The British people, your people, are counting on you."

"I am lost without him," Uther sighed. Regaining his composure, he walked to the far corner of the room, reached down to Lionel and pulled him upright. "Pelly, you and Lionel make ready the wagon and three fresh swift horses. Have Elivri saddle and blacken my brother's white stallion." Turning to a clearly shaken Merlin he commanded, "Prepare Ambros for travel. We leave for Stonehenge within the hour." Walking to the dead king's bedside, Uther regally bent over and kissed his brother's forehead. "Long live the king," he whispered. Rising, he exited the room with a warning to its occupants, "Let no one know of our destination."

"Can you handle the preparations by yourself?" With fatherly concern, Pellinore asked Merlin. "If you need help, I can send for the physician or the Arch Druid."

"The Arch Druid has already attended the king," gathering his courage to speak, Lionel stood next to Merlin. Waiting for words of reassurance, words of forgiveness, just words. None came, only silence.

With his back still pressed to the wall, Merlin acknowledged both men with a single nod. Turning his head toward a table near the bed he eyed a bundle of cloth, and a washbasin. He knew that the Druids had already prepared Ambrosius: washed his body, clothed him in regal attire, and wrapped all but his head in the finest of linens. The only thing left for him to do was complete the ritual. Flinching as the door shut, Merlin realized he was alone with his beloved king, his mentor, his friend.

Tentatively, sitting on the bed, he slowly lifted Ambrosius' head, gently pulling back the thick mane of hair, taking note that rigor mortis had come and gone. With trembling hands he selected a strip of the meticulously cut linen from the nearby table. Leisurely his fingers played with the cloth's soft, sensuous flax fibers, stately and pure, like the man who would soon be bound to it for all eternity. Trancelike, yet with great care, he began encasing the king's head, working diligently until only the vaguest outline of features remained.

Pulling back the bedding, Merlin gathered the limp, mummified body in his arms. Rocking gently he began humming a long forgotten melody of a comforting Celtic lullaby, sung to him by Enid. Although his eyes watered, his tears, like his words, remained captive. Footsteps near the door caused him to terminate the song and release the king from his arms.

As the door opened, Lionel and Elivri waited just outside. Each on opposite ends of a cowhide stretched litter. Entering the room Pellinore and Uther found Merlin standing where they had left him.

"Have you obeyed my command?" Uther snarled. Walking to the bed, Uther was relieved to see his brother's body swaddled in linens and ready for the long journey to the final resting place. With little physical effort coupled with great emotional strength, Uther lifted Ambrosius onto the waiting litter. With Lionel lifting one end and Elivri lifting the other, Uther followed them, as they carried Ambrosius' body down the dimly lit hallway.

"Come, boy. You have done well," Pellinore assured Merlin as he draped his arm around the boy's shoulder guiding him out of the room to the waiting horses in the courtyard below. "Gather your strength, we will be riding long and hard for the final farewell."

Slumped over and obviously heartbroken, Merlin shuffled behind the kings as they made their way to the awaiting funeral procession.

Outside the palace, the horses stood in respectful attention as Uther watched Elivri and Lionel gently place Ambrosius litter within the hay covered wagon. Next to the king's body nestled several of Ambrosius' personal belongings, including his father's sword reclaimed from the murderous tyrant Vortigern's ashes, and several favorite scrolls from the coveted library of ancient writings.

"Did you execute the order to clear the roads?" Uther queried to one of his commanders, as he hastily covered his brother's body and its belongings with white deerskin hides.

With reassurance that all villagers were secured within their homes, the party mounted and made their way through the deserted streets. At the Londinium side of the great bridge Uther had posted guards, preventing any stray mourners from following the funeral procession.

It was well past the witching hour as the four riders and royal laden wagon slowly traversed the bridge exiting the city. Uther and Pellinore took the lead, while Lionel and Merlin followed closely behind the wagon. Halfway across, the procession halted. Elivri reached into a bag next to him and retrieved five long black hooded capes. In turn, each of the men took a garment. When all were cloaked in darkness they proceeded on their clandestine journey.

***

"I swear every star in the heavens has come out of hiding to watch over our passing." Pellinore observed as they reached the old Roman road stretching to the west. Although the moon hung half full, the stars shown in abundance, giving both Pellinore and Uther guidance to their destination.

"May the goddess Arianrhod safeguard our journey," Uther asked of the heavens. As he spoke, an owl hooted from the nearby forest, its silhouette winging skyward, causing the soot-covered stallion to dance sideways.

"It appears your goddess has spoken." Pellinore watched the white owl circle the riders twice and disappear into the tree tops.

"If I recall correctly from my boyhood studies, the goddess Arianrhod took the form of an owl when leading the dead to the Otherworld," Uther choked out the words and retreated into silence.

"I remember the first day Ambrosius set eyes on his stallion," Pellinore reminisced, wishing to turn the conversation to happier times. "He was just nine, or was it ten?"

"He was ten." Uther smiled wearily, deep in recall.

"Ah, yes, and you were just barely nine." Pellinore tapped his temple with his index finger, doing his best to jiggle long past recollections about in his brain.

"Nearly fifteen years ago," Uther responded, his voice lost in another world.

"The gray colt was a birthday gift from Lionel's father, wasn't he?" Pellinore leaned forward in his saddled as he quizzed Uther for affirmation.

"King Bors promised Ambros that the colt was magical—An Iberian—beloved by many, including my brother's favorite author, Homer." Uther could not help but smile at the memory. "He told him that within a year the gray colt would turn to a white stallion. That following spring, my brother insisted that we take turns staying awake for weeks on end, so as not to miss the magical moment. Alas, we both fell ill with the fever, and months later, when we had fully recovered, we had missed the transformation."

"I was there that day too," Pellinore prodded with a twinkle in his eyes, "If I recall correctly, you taunted your brother, telling him that someone had stolen his horse and replaced it with another."

"Yet, as always, Ambros had unconditional faith in things that could not be easily explained." Uther reached back and patted the stallion's hindquarters as he spoke. "To prove that he was not duped, Ambros opened the yearling's mouth, displaying the star shaped birthmark on its upper gum—a sign only known by my brother and myself."

"Wasn't it around that time that he taught the young stallion to roll in the dirt on command?" Pellinore chuckled as he spoke.

"Yes," Uther reflected, "even at that young age, Ambros was strategizing against the inevitable. He reasoned that one day the shimmer of his stallion's coat could possibly expose our position when doing night reconnaissance, thus, he taught him to roll in the foulest muck to *magically* turn from light to dark."

"Much to the delight of your cousin Budic, and the revulsion of his mother," Pellinore chortled, "he was always planning, always thinking ahead. Did not Bors gift you a stallion two years later? What became of that colt?"

"He grew into a beautiful beast, and died defending me against the Saxons on Brittany's shores. It was my first Saxon battle, which I learned many great lessons." Turning to Pellinore he gave the old knight a toothy grin, "Of which the most important was—never become emotionally involved with human nor beast, for the destiny of both is a far too early death." Without warning, Uther pressed his legs into Ambrosius' stallion, racing off through the twisting road canopied by an overhang of newly budded branches. The scents of early spring wafted in the air as he galloped out of sight.

***

Once more the moon hung high in the heavens as the ceremonial wagon pulled near their destination. They had traveled from midnight to midnight for two days, with short infrequent stops to rest the horses and consume nourishment for both man and beast. Due to the waxing moon, the journey had been slow and tedious during the evening hours, and fast paced with a sense of urgency during the daylight.

Sworn to secrecy, Elivri had been elected to drive the wagon. On the seat next to him nodded a weary Pellinore, who had earlier that evening abandoned his saddle for a chance to rest his weary bones from his horse's constant plodding. The old man had hitched his steed to the back of the wagon and now sat snorting and muttering in his sleep with his head slumped on Elivri's shoulder. Lionel rode close by, his surefooted horse carefully picking his way in the dark.

"Why Uther decided to travel unescorted, under the cloak of darkness, is still a mystery to me," Elivri whispered to Lionel as he searched the night for Uther's silhouette. During the excruciatingly long ride, the fear of Uther's wrath had made conversation sparse between the two friends. Now that Uther and Merlin had ridden ahead, Elivri felt more at ease to engage in an exchange of questions.

"Although our new king is young, and at times may appear rash, Uther is a man of wisdom. He understands his enemies, he knows how they think and their hunger for vengeance," Lionel sighed. "He fears that his brother's body will be desecrated if found by the Saxons—hence the reason for swift and secretive travel. To make matters worse, Londinium is growing at such a rapid pace that Uther no longer recognizes, nor trusts the townspeople housed within her walls."

"Does his distrust extend to his friends, his knights, his soldiers?" Elivri quizzed as he repositioned Pellinore. Chuckling as he mopped the old man's drool with the corner of his cloak.

"His only trusted and true friend," Lionel choked back the tears as he spoke, "lies in eternal slumber behind you. As to his men, I believe his faith has been shattered—hopefully not beyond repair. A king needs to trust those around him."

"He is wise to be guarded. Men, like horses, can turn on their masters, often for seemingly no reason," Elivri quoted Ambrosius. "I fear that our days of peace have yet to materialize."

"May the days of upcoming battles hasten our days of peace, my friend," nestled between yawns Pellinore voiced his words of wisdom. "Are we near?" Arms stretching to the heavens he righted himself, trying his best to focus battle-worn eyes and orientate himself to his surroundings.

"We are closer than near, Sir Pellinore, we have arrived," Elivri stated. With a gentle tug on the reins the horses halted. Even by moon glow and starlight the giant pillars guarding the mystical circle stood visible and overwhelming. In the distance, near the heel stone entrance, two ghostly figures rode side by side, as a slow mist began to creep upon the Salisbury Plain.

***

"This will do." Walking the stallion to the center of the Dancing Stones' circle, Uther pointed to an area in front of the alter stone. "Anoint the ground. I shall get the men and shovels. Do you understand what you are to do?" Uther quizzed Merlin.

Still mute, Merlin reassured Uther with a slow nod. Before dismounting, he gently reached to his shoulder and nudged the underbelly of his hawk. Even through his cloak and leathers he could feel her claws extend and retreat as she danced from deep slumber to instant alertness. Bumping her head into Merlin's temple she rubbed her beak and gently pecked at his ear before taking flight.

"Can you do this?" anxiously Uther pressed Merlin further, hesitating to dismount until he received affirmation.

This time Merlin let out a growling sigh as he once more nodded his head, tossing Uther a concealed, cutting stare as he turned and slipped from the saddle. Dropping the reins; his steed instantly began to feed on the delicate grass sprouts freshly dotting the grounds surrounding the henge. *How the horse would react to being allowed to roam free was Uther's responsibility now.* Logically, Merlin understood Uther's reasoning for insisting that his mare be left behind to rest. Yet, he was unaccustomed to riding any horse other than his gray. He missed her, and each passing day was growing more discontent with Uther's rationality.

Somewhat satisfied with Merlin's silent response, Uther too dismounted, leading Ambrosius' stallion past the guard stones to Stonehenge's outer circle. Earlier that evening he had swam the charger in a nearby pond, restoring coat, mane, and tail to its original white luster.

Tying his brother's horse to the heel stone near the entrance, Uther walked with deliberation to the wagon, where the three companions and his brother waited.

When he was certain that Uther was out of sight, Merlin bent down and ran his hands methodically over the alter stone. Tiny mica specks glittered in the moonlight as his fingers danced across the cool, light green sandstone. Pressing his palms downward he leaped effortlessly onto the stone. Standing erect, Merlin closed his eyes and extended his arms toward the surrounding countryside in a welcoming gesture. Within a mist, one by one, the spirit bodies of the recently buried slain royals materialized. Encircling the boy prophet, the royal funeral guests effortlessly pushed and pulled the massive alter stone. When movement stopped, Merlin opened his eyes. With a knowing smile he gazed downward, into a freshly dug hollow.

***

"I can feel Ambrosius' spirit," as Uther spoke a thick fog emerged from the nearby kings' burial barrow, creeping across the plains and oozing through the stone circle pillars.

"I too can feel his presence, Uther. It is a good omen. A very good omen, indeed." Even as chills raced down his spine, Pellinore did his best to make his words sound convincing.

All four men reached into the wagon, carefully lifting the litter that cradled Ambrosius. Nestled alongside the king's shrouded body were his prized possessions. The most valued rested across Ambrosius' chest, his father's sword—the ancient Sword of Kings. Stepping with great care, the mourners made their way through the thick and growing mist. Pellinore led the procession, carrying the shovels, as Lionel and Elivri reverently carried the king's litter through Stonehenge's entrance. Uther followed closely, stopping at the heel stone long enough to untie Ambrosius' stallion.

As they entered the circle's center, Ambrosius' horse became frantic. With eyes wide and nostrils flared, the horse flung back his head, tugging relentlessly on the reins. Uther did his best to settle the stallion, but it was obvious to Merlin that the beast was winning the battle of wills. Instinctively, Merlin jumped from his perch atop the alter stone, taking control of the mighty charger. Looking into Uther's face, he saw the first glimpse of confusion as the mist began to dissipate.

"Uther, if you would have told us that the hole was already dug, I would have left the shovels in the wagon," Pellinore chuckled as he dropped the shovels—becoming instantly somber after searching Uther's face; pale within the glow of the moon's light.

"It matters not how Mother Earth opened her arms to my brother. It only matters that her arms are eagerly waiting to take Ambros to his eternal resting place." Uther glared at Pellinore, Lionel, and Elivri, daring them to question or protest. He refused to even glance in Merlin's direction. With a solemn tone he commanded, "Place my brother's body upon the alter stone."

Without uttering another word, Lionel and Elivri lifted the litter gently upon the massive slab of sandstone. In silence, everyone but Uther stepped behind the horseshoe of dolerite sentries. The short blue guardian stones came to life, radiating a brilliant blue aura, giving the inner circle a mystic glow.

Walking to Ambrosius' side, Uther knelt, placing a tender kiss upon the veiled lips and whispered his final farewells. Rising, he motioned for Merlin to bring Ambrosius' stallion into the inner circle. Confused, Merlin obeyed the command, walking toward Uther with trepidation. As the horse neared the gravesite Uther unsheathed his sword causing the stallion to rear majestically, ripping the reins from Merlin's hands. This time, instead of showing fear, the horse stood brave and steadfast on its hind legs, exposing its underbelly in sacrifice to his master's spirit. Swiftly, Uther plunged his sword into the heart of the regal beast.

"May you serve my brother in death, as well as you served him in life," Uther shouted as he retrieved the blade from the fatal wound. He watched with reverence as the horse's life force drained, spurting blood, which soon flooded the burial chamber. Slowly, the now crimson animal's body crumbled, disappearing into darkness. From deep within the grave a thud reverberated, followed by bridle and saddle clatter, and then—silence.

"Noooo!" Merlin's screams of anguish broke the calm and hung thick within the once more increasing mist.

"Hush now, it will be alright," Pellinore assured. At the same time he rushed forward, as did Lionel, both men grabbing Merlin's arms and holding tightly.

"What have you done?" Merlin's uncontrolled scorn was directed to all present, and he struggled fiercely to free himself from Lionel and Pellinore's death grip.

"It is tradition. When a High King passes, his steed travels with him to the Otherworld," Pellinore's words flowed softly, as he cautiously eased his hold on Merlin's arm.

"There was no talk of butchering the stallion!" Merlin howled, turning his wrath upon Elivri. "How could you? Especially you, Elivri; are you not the keeper of horses, their sworn protector? May the goddess Epona curse you all!" The Druid Egg glowed around his neck as Merlin flung the incantation in the groom's direction. A psychotic twitch formed on Merlin's lips as he watched Elivri's eyes beg forgiveness.

"Ignore the fool's tirade," Uther snapped. Grabbing Elivri by the shoulder, he shoved him toward the stone. "We have a High King to bury." Defiantly Uther glared in Merlin's direction. As the groom helped lower Ambrosius' litter into the grave, a thick fog also crept into the burial chamber.

"There is someone down there," Elivri cried out in fear as both men scrambled from the grave. By the expression on Uther's face, Elivri knew that the new king had also felt the invisible hands reach up, gently taking Ambrosius' body from their possession.

Digging his fingernails deeply into Lionel's forearm, Merlin escaped his captors, darting past the stone; he vanished into the murky mist blanketing the open grave. As quickly as he entered the pit, he re-emerged with the king's ancient sword, thrusting it heavenward. Within moments he was once more perched upon the alter stone. Holding the sword's hilt with both hands, he inwardly called upon the Mother Goddess for strength, as he turned the sword toward earth, driving the blade firmly into the stone.

"Bear witness..." Merlin hissed, dancing like a madman around the sword, pointing to everyone, yet to no one in particular, "... Ambrosius will be resurrected in the form of a boy king. He alone will have the wisdom, courage, and strength to pull this ancient sword from the stone of antiquity—Uther's successor, Uther's son, the true savior of Britain!"

Tossing his head back in manic laughter he rode atop the stone, as it magically inched its way home, covering the burial opening.

Gazing into the star filled night, Merlin alone saw a falling star streak across the heavens, morphing into the form of a fiery dragon.

To know Merlin was to experience the unexpected, but this was beyond logic, beyond enchantment. Stunned, Pellinore, Lionel and Elivri focused on Merlin. With his diatribe complete, all eyes fearfully drifted to Uther; standing knee deep in mist.

"A son," the glassy-eyed new High King repeated Merlin's prophecy softly. Jabbing his fist into the air, Uther roared, "I am to be succeeded by a son!"

33

Lionel took his time walking to the fort. The three weeks following Ambrosius' funeral had been filled with rain and fog. Today the sun shone bright, its warmth invigorated his soul and temperament with each footstep. Even at this early hour of the morning, Londinium was beginning to come alive with the bustle of travelers mixed with townspeople and military. For the first time in weeks, a sense of joy and excitement filled the air.

"Good day, Lionel," a young girl shouted as she pushed the door of her parent's bakery open. Her arms overflowed with streamers of multicolored ribbons. Awkwardly, she kicked and scooted a small empty wooden bucket with her foot.

"Good morning, Claire. You look like you could use a helping hand." Lionel moved toward the maiden. Holding the door open for her, at the same time he reached down and picked up the bucket.

"Thank you so much, Lionel. With the High King's coronation tomorrow, and so many people flooding into the city, there is just too much to do." Although her words were filled with frustration, her voice could not conceal her merriment.

"The crowds will be good for business," as he spoke, Lionel set the bucket upside down in front of the big showcase window. Even with the shutters closed, the aroma of freshly baked breads and cakes made his mouth water and his stomach growl.

"Sounds like you could use something to quiet your inner beast," Clarisant laughed. Handing the ribbons to Lionel, she accepted his help. Gingerly, she stepped on top of the bucket, placing a delicate hand on Lionel's shoulder for support. "It has been far too long since we saw you last. Where have you been keeping yourself?"

Although at her present height, the maiden was breast to eyelevel with Lionel, he did his best to keep his focus on the wooden rod situated over the window. Handing her ribbons of various colors, he also did his best to ignore her question.

"The red one next." Reaching for the ribbon, she looked into Lionel's eyes and asked again, "Where have you been? We have missed your daily visits."

"My friend has been ill, and I have been in charge of his recovery." His words emerged terse and he quickly searched his brain for some interesting triviality that would change the topic of conversation. "Will you be attending the coronation tomorrow?"

"No, we have not been invited. My father said it will only be a small gathering of royals and military." Tying the last ribbon on the pole, she teetered, giggling as she felt Lionel's strong hands instantly around her waist.

"Clarisant, what are you doing out there?" Deep within the bakery, her mother's voice echoed out the door and into the busy street.

"I am almost finished, Mother," Clarisant cried back. Placing her hands on Lionel's shoulders, she quivered inwardly as he easily picked her up by the waist and set her on the ground. "Will you take a pastry as reward for helping a maiden in distress?"

"Make it two, and we will call it even," Lionel joked. "I was on my way to meet Elivri, and I am sure he would enjoy something fresh from the baker's daughter."

"It is a deal." Smiling she hurried into the shop.

Impatiently, Lionel waited outside, knowing that he would be there all day if the baker's wife had her way. Clarisant's mother was a kind soul with a hunger for court gossip. Clarisant was just the opposite. Although she might, on occasion, pry into his personal life, he was certain it was solely because she truly cared about him.

"Here you are," Clarisant's voice sang sweetly, as she dashed from the shop, handing Lionel a warm bundle neatly wrapped in linen, tied with a yellow ribbon. "Mother made these especially for today's pre-celebration."

"I hope you didn't get into trouble," reluctantly he tried to give the package back.

"Oh my, no," Clarisant giggled. "When I told mother that the cakes were for the valiant Sir Lionel, she made sure I took several—fresh from the ovens."

"My reward far surpasses my knightly deed." Lionel clicked his heels together and bowed deeply. "I really must be going. I will do my best to stop by later, on my way back through town."

"Farewell, Lionel. Be sure to say hello to Elivri for me," she added with a tinge of wickedness to her words.

"I promise," Lionel smirked offhandedly over his shoulder as he continued his walk to the fort.

***

On soft footsteps, Lionel walked through the fort's stables, stopping just behind Elivri. The groom was deep in thought detangling Uther's stallion's mane.

"I cannot believe how many burs are embedded within your mane," Elivri complained loudly as he raked the comb through the stallion's coarse hair. Breaking several of the comb's teeth, exasperated, he tossed the comb across the stall.

"So, you have taken up conversing with horses?"

Startled, Elivri turned around hastily, nearly hitting Lionel. "You know better than to sneak up on a man when he is struggling with his personal demons," Elivri laughed nervously, relieved to see his old friend.

"I come in peace," as he spoke, Lionel held up the package of cakes to Elivri's nose.

"I really shouldn't. There is far too much to do."

"They were sent to you by way of the baker's daughter," Lionel teased. "If you sit a moment with me, I will pass along her private message to you."

"Well, maybe for just a moment," Elivri blushed, turning away quickly, refusing to make eye contact. He motioned for Lionel to sit on a nearby bench, while he searched the hay strewn stall for the broken comb. "I fear Merlin's curse has stuck," he said with sorrow as he found the comb, tossing it into a bucket of horse brushes. He cleaned his hands in a nearby water trough, drying them on his tunic as he joined Lionel.

"You know that Merlin was not in a sound mind when he uttered those words."

"Sound mind or not, I am sure he meant every word," Elivri's voice quivered with remorse. "How is Merlin feeling? Has his mood brightened since our return from the Salisbury Plain?"

"I have stayed with him night and day for the past three weeks. The madness passed quickly, yet the melancholy lasted far too long."

"Has Merlin talked to Uther?"

"Yes, if you call angry, earsplitting arguments talk."

"What did they argue about?"

"I was not included in their conversations—from behind closed doors, only voices filled with boisterous bellowing emerged. All I know for certain is that Uther visited Merlin at the Druid's temple on several occasions, as did Pellinore."

"So, Uther does not have the same disliking for the Druids as did his brother?" Elivri asked with curiosity.

"The High King is ambivalent when it comes to the Druids. He neither likes nor dislikes their ways. I believe that he feels they are just another worldly order. Although raised a Christian, he holds more to earthly ways than heavenly ones."

"Will Merlin and the Druids attend Uther tomorrow?"

Lionel just shrugged. Scooting to the edge of the bench, he left enough room for Elivri, and for the unveiling of their morning snack. The aroma of the delicate cakes drifted upward, as Lionel unwrapped the linen. He was going to keep the yellow ribbon, but at the last moment, handed it to Elivri.

"The baker's daughter has a delicate touch with pastries." Elivri eagerly took the ribbon, tying it around his neck. He then snatched one of the cakes, nibbling on it lustfully.

"Claire, sends her regards," Lionel grinned, speaking with his mouth full; keeping secret the fact that the cakes were made by the mother, not the daughter—that they were intended for him, not Elivri.

"Is that all she said?"

"Pretty much," Lionel gave a sideways glance to his friend as he spoke. "Do you not speak to her yourself each day?"

"We did, when her parents first set up shop, but that was just before Uther left for the spring Saxon invasion—before, his brother's demise."

"And now?" Lionel asked, wishing he had never started the conversation.

"Claire's parents have better aspirations for their only daughter than being betrothed to a mere stable boy. The mother, especially, wishes her daughter to marry a nobleman; perhaps a prince," he paused, "or even a boy prophet." He gave Lionel a sad smile before stuffing the remainder of the cake into his mouth.

"You are not a mere stable boy. You are the High King's groom," the words bellowed from a shadow of a man who stood in the stable entrance.

"Merlin, is that really you?" Elivri asked, straining his eyes.

"It is none other." Stepping into the stables, dressed in non-druid garb, Merlin strolled in, plopping himself cross-legged in the clean hay in front of Elivri and Lionel.

"It is good to see you." Elivri leaned forward offering Merlin the last cake.

"Thank you Elivri. It is good to be seen."

"You should have told me you were coming into the city. I would have waited for you," Lionel scolded lightheartedly.

"I received word after you had left that Uther requested a meeting with me concerning tomorrow's coronation." Merlin picked at the cake as he spoke, putting small pieces in his mouth, savoring each bite. "The cake tastes like it was made with love. Is Clarisant the baker?"

His companions laughed giddily at the absurdity of the question. Merlin guessed that they had both been caught in Clarisant's web of beauty. He barely recalled the girl. Yet, during his recent recovery, Lionel had filled his waking hours with never ending, but well-meaning prattle. He had droned on and on about the baker's daughter. She had the appearance and spirit of the Northern people, he had told him. Her long hair shined like ravens' feathers, her lips pink as the rose, her eyes dark and mysterious—and on and on—and oh how she could bake. Merlin could see now that Elivri was also smitten with the young maiden. His thoughts went to Nimue, and the last time he saw her in the palace's garden. Both elation and sadness filled his heart and soul. He missed her, he missed Ambrosius—he missed so much and so many.

Seeing the sudden change in Merlin's disposition, Lionel pushed the discussion to what he hoped would be happier matters. "Do you think the weather will hold for tomorrow's coronation?"

"I have it on the best authority that Apollo will smile upon us."

"Well, Merlin, if anyone has a direct line to the gods, I am sure it would be you," Elivri's words flowed with sincerity.

"Will you both walk with me to the officer's quarters?" Merlin asked as he stood up, brushing the hay from his backside.

"I wish I could," Elivri moaned, as he pointed to the horses. "Just stopping for a short bite and conversation has left me behind in my duties."

"I understand." Merlin smiled and looked to Lionel.

"I will meet you outside. It is too nice of a day to be stuck indoors smelling of horse dung." Lionel laughed as he gave Elivri a gentle shove.

"Are we alright?" Elivri asked of Merlin, when he was certain that Lionel was out of earshot.

"I beg your forgiveness for my insanity. The loss was too sudden, too great and my grief too deep."

"Please know that nothing of that night was my doing?" Elivri begged.

"I know," Merlin smiled as he sighed. "At times, destiny has a way of making madmen of us all."

"I must get back to work now. Besides the horses, I still have some final touches to apply to Uther's chest armor. Will I see you later?"

"Yes, we will stop by on our way back."

"Have you seen Sir Merlin?" Uther's squire shouted to Lionel just outside the stable doors.

"It looks like I am also being called back to duty," Merlin smiled again to his friend, giving Elivri's shoulder a reassuring squeeze, before turning and re-entering the reality of kings and kings' devotions.

34

With the coronation complete, Merlin had slipped away unnoticed from Uther and the cheering masses, taking refuge in the palace library. He smiled with warm memories, as his fingers glided across the mural, resting on the figure of Alexander bravely riding his stallion to battle. How simple life had been the first day he had entered the great library. How peaceful it had been to be in the presence of the great man. He yearned for those days—the days of Ambrosius.

Turning, Merlin gazed across the room, the wall with the floor-to-ceiling shelves; once overflowing with neatly tied scrolls, was now dark, dusty, and half-empty. The ancient tales important to Ambrosius were buried with the king. Yet, those precious to Merlin, he had persuaded Pellinore to smuggle from the library, one-by-one over the past three weeks; stowing them away in the Druid's temple across the Tamesis. If Uther had noticed the missing parchments, he gave no inclination. The only scrolls the king had been vaguely interested in were those of military matters.

Closing his eyes Merlin breathed in deeply, trying to recall the fragrance of incense burning and the delicate scent of the silks that Ambrosius had draped from the walls and over the chaises. Yet, as hard as he tried, those past memories were lost forever. The cushioned lounges of beautifully carved wood had been replaced with rustic benches and chairs from the fort's officers' quarters. Any resemblance of luxury, of civility, of Ambrosius, had been stripped. All except for Ambrosius' exquisite writing table and chair.

"Merlin," Uther shouted as he entered the room, "where are you hiding now?" The chain mail jingled under his decorative breast plate as he stomped about the room.

As Merlin silently studied Uther, he lingered in admiration on Elivri's craftsmanship. The groom had worked day and night since their return from Stonehenge on the ceremonial cuirass. The highly polished silver metal of the breast plate glimmered. A golden embossed dragon slithered up the armor's back panel, coming to rest furiously upon the right front shoulder. Over the king's left breast, close to Uther's heart, Elivri had etched a likeness of Ambrosius upon his mighty steed—the stallion rearing, the former king wielding an ancient sword.

"The gods be dammed, Merlin, where are you?" Although his hand gripped tightly to the hilt, Uther's sword swung leisurely in its new sheath brushing against his black leathers, his red cloak swirling.

"I am here, Your Majesty." For a fleeting moment, Merlin lingered once more on the mural, imagining Ambrosius as Alexander. "I am always here for you…" turning to face his new king, Merlin willed his words to drift into the past.

"You are never here!" Uther grumbled as he stormed behind his brother's scroll laden table, tossing the cape onto the floor and throwing himself into his brother's chair.

Merlin cringed as Uther's metal clad body scraped against Ambrosius' chair. His skin crawled as he imagined the decorative dragon's tail and legs, of the body armor, gouging deep chunks from the wood. Biting his lip, Merlin watched quietly as Uther reached for a parchment, hastily dipping a nearby writing reed into the waiting inkwell. Without so much as reading what he signed, he tossed the document onto the pile with the others.

"How did he ever manage to sign his name to all these documents and never once get a drop of ink on his fingers?" Uther smiled as he rubbed blackened fingertips together, and for a fleeting moment, he too was swept away to happier days. Suddenly, as a snake ready to strike, Uther repeated, "You are never here!"

"How can you say that I am never here? Yesterday, I came to your side the instant you commanded, to help you finalize the preparations for today's ceremony. Was I not by your side this morning for your coronation? Did I not march with you through the streets afterwards to show your people my support?" Merlin still feared Uther's temper and clung to the shadows in dread of fueling his wrath.

"Oh, you are here in body." Uther's fist came down swift and heavy into a pile of haphazardly stacked opened scrolls. "But, your mind and spirit are always soaring with the hawks, swimming with the dolphins, or running with the deer. You are never truly here, with me, nor for me. Not like you were for my brother." With a swift movement he cleared the table, sending scrolls flying throughout the room. The crystal inkwell clattered several times on the mosaic tiles and miraculously came to rest un-spilled at Merlin's feet.

"Have I not treated you with the respect bestowed upon a High King?" Bending over, Merlin picked up the small inkpot. It had been created in Avalon: a gift from his mother on the day of Ambrosius' coronation. Holding it up to the candlelight, Merlin watched in mesmerized wonder as tiny rainbows shimmered upon the walls.

"Respect? How can you even imply that you have given me the same respect as my brother?" Enraged, Uther rapidly stood, causing the chair to propel backwards, slamming with an unnerving crash against the wall. "My brother ordered you to stay within Londinium's walls, forbidding you to sleep at the Druid's temple. How is that bestowing respect? You dishonor my brother's wishes." Uther's voice quivered, "Some might consider that treason." Pressing hard against the table's marble surface, he did his best to conceal trembling hands.

"Not once did Ambrosius order nor forbid me to do anything," the words poured as Merlin clung tightly to the wall, gaining strength from the mural. "Your brother requested, never demanded, and I honored every request, even his dying words. I am here with you now. Although ill, I have still been within your reach for counsel, every day since we buried him." With every ounce of strength he had left, Merlin willed logic to replace emotion, lowering his voice to a soothing tone.

Letting out a primal scream, Uther tossed his body into his chair, slumping over the table. Ripping the thin golden crown from his head, he flung it violently at the door.

"What is all the commotion?" Pellinore inquired, nearly tripping over the crown as he opened the door to the library. "Is this anyway to start your official first day as Britain's High King, throwing a temper-tantrum?" Picking up the royal circlet he casually placed it on the table.

"How did he do it, Pelly? How does any king do it?" Uther ran his fingers through his now long neatly pulled back hair, causing the leather strip of cording to come undone and his hair to fall disheveled about his shoulders. His days of morphing from a coarse Roman commander to civilized Celtic overlord were outwardly complete. Yet, he still lacked the *inward* journey to his final destination. He looked to Pellinore with mournful pleading eyes.

"How does a king do what, my boy?" Pellinore asked, his bones creaking as he bent down, picking up several scrolls strewn about the room.

"How does a king contend with all this busywork?" As he spoke Uther's arms stretched over the scrolls Pellinore had placed on the table. "I cannot fight battles like this. It is no wonder my brother died so young. Toward the end, the only weapons allotted to him were pen and ink. How does one defeat the enemy trapped behind a writing table?"

"Your brother was a beloved king," Pellinore sighed as he sat wearily into a nearby chair. "Ruling a country is a complicated matter. A High King must balance protection of Britain's shores with the unification and caring of her peoples. Ambrosius yearned for peace. He longed for the day when words of reason would replace the clash of swords."

"Yes," Uther spit out the words, "see where that logic got him. Hundreds of brave, noble men—slaughtered—all in the guise of peace!"

"See where the logic of fighting got you?" Speaking, not caring of the consequence of his words, Merlin broke in. "If you had not gone to battle to kill Vortigern, his son would not have killed your brother. War or peace—both have dire consequences."

"Merlin, leave now," Pellinore shouted. He jumped in front of Uther, preventing the red-faced and wild-eyed king from crawling over the table and attacking. From behind him, Pellinore heard the door shut quietly and knew that Merlin had heeded his warning.

"Why does he stay near?" Uther bemoaned, "Even a better question, why do I allow him to stay?" Drenched in sweat, emotionally drained, he once more collapsed into his brother's chair.

"Even a blind man can answer that question, Uther." Pellinore picked up the crown and walked behind the table. With fatherly hands, he combed the new king's hair with gnarled fingers. Retrieving the fallen leather cord, Pellinore tamed the tousled mane, replacing the crown gently upon Uther's head. "By keeping each other close, you keep your brother closer. For as much as you hate to admit it, Ambrosius loved you both. As long as you are near each other, his spirit remains alive."

"That is foolish talk, old man," Uther did his best to give harshness to his words, but failed miserably. Reaching up, he grasped Pellinore's hand, squeezing it tightly.

"I bring good news; a message from Sir Lot." Slapping Uther on the shoulder, Pellinore succeeded in changing the course of conversation. "Lot, and his entourage, will be arriving in time for this evening's festivities, along with the Duke of Cornwall. Lot begs your forgiveness for not making it in time for the coronation. Unfortunately, they are journeying with the duke's wife and two young daughters. Poor Lot and the boys, they must he beside themselves to be forced to travel at a snail's pace."

"Good news indeed, Pelly." Uther's voice measured his first signs of joy since discovery of his brother's passing. His euphoria was swiftly broken by loud pounding on the door, immediately followed by anxious voices, scuffling of boots, unsheathing of swords, and the frantic barking of a lone dog.

"My liege," a familiar voice cried out, "please, tell your guards that we have come to honor your majesty, not to do him harm!"

"Meleagant?" Uther sang out in delight. As the doors flung open, a giant deerhound bounded in. Circling the room twice, he picked up a tied scroll tossing it about, finally coming to a stop with feet firmly planted on Uther's breastplate.

"He remembers you, my liege." Meleagant laughed nervously as he, three guards, and two of Uther's pages, did their best to pull the giant of a dog from the king. Yet, the hound stayed his ground, merrily wagging his tale. Dropping the scroll, he eagerly began licking Uther's face.

"Leave him be. It is good to see a grown version of a life I have saved." Grabbing the beast by the scruff of his wiry gray neck, Uther gently pushed the hound down. "You have grown into a regal beauty." Squatting he joined the dog on the floor. "What's his name?" Uther inquired, as the gangly hound flopped across his lap.

"Phoenix."

"Rather odd to name a British hound after an Egyptian legend. Was his naming influenced from Nentres' tales?" Uther smiled to himself as he scratched behind Phoenix's ear, causing the dog to thump his right leg in rapid succession. The last time he had seen Meleagant, the boy barely knew his own name. Uther knew that the young prince worshiped the ground Lot walked on, but he also knew that Lot had no need for fairy lore. And, the fables Dodinel told were strictly of Celtic origin. Thus, an ancient legend of the dead rising from ashes could only be passed on from the only articulate one in the bunch—Nentres.

"Yes, you know Nentres. His mind is always wrapped around something of intellect." As if on queue, Meleagant's fingers began to twitch. Nonchalantly he slid them within the long fur of his dog's coat, gathering tranquility from the animal's inner calm.

Kneeling behind Uther, two of his pages busied themselves undoing the straps attached to the hinges of the cuirass. Attempting to wipe paw prints from the silver breast plate, one of the pages scowled guardedly at Meleagant. His frown deepened when he noticed the claw marks within the precious metal. Retrieving the armor and mail, both boys left the library hastily, leaving the door ajar.

Glancing up as the boys retreated, Uther motioned for one of the servants to bring ale and fruit. He had not eaten all day and, although the banquet was fast approaching, his stomach was starting to rumble. Oh, how he longed for the simple days of only squires and pages. Now the palace was overflowing with a houseful of guards, townspeople, and servants that he neither knew nor trusted. *Perhaps a dog was a good idea; a dog would have saved my brother's life.* As he thought the words, Phoenix's tail thumped upon the tiles.

"Your Majesty, I have a gift for you. Not just for your coronation, but," he paused, as he reached into a large satchel attached to his shoulder by a thick strap, "but for saving both Phoenix and my life." From deep inside the leather pouch he pulled out a gray ball of fur. "For you, King Uther, she is the only bitch from Phoenix's first sired litter."

Pellinore leaned back in his chair, smiling contently. He sent a silent prayer heavenward that this moment would linger. He could not remember the last time he had seen Uther smile, had seen Uther truly happy. With a twinkle in his eyes, Pellinore took great delight in watching not a king in negotiations, but instead a boy content playing with a puppy.

"What shall I name you?" Uther asked holding the wiggling pup in the air. Opening sleepy eyes she eagerly licked his nose.

"Do, you like her?" Meleagant inquired with childlike curiosity and a slight stutter to his speech.

"I can tell by her bright, alert eyes that she will be a fine hunter, and an even finer bitch. Rest assured that Phoenix's royal lineage will continue. Her home shall be next to my bed. When she is old enough, I swear wherever I shall go, she shall be by my side."

"I am pleased beyond words, Your Majesty," without warning Meleagant reached out and kissed Uther's ruby ring, Ambrosius' ring, in a silent allegiance to the king and his brother's spirit. Just as quickly he went back to playing with the puppy.

Uther glanced momentarily in Pellinore's direction and then back to the master of the hounds. For the first time he really took notice of Meleagant, how different he was from Lot's companions. The others had all grown into strong handsome young men, even Dodinel; yet, Meleagant was different. He had not aged like the others, nor had he grown but slightly taller than when they had last fought together. *A man forever imprisoned within a boy's body and mind. Perhaps, not such a bad way to live life.*

"What news to share?" Pellinore quizzed as he ripped off a hunk of bread, shoving it and a slice of cheese into his mouth.

"Rumor has it that Sir Lot has stayed in Tintagel longer than needed for reasons other than peacekeeping." As Meleagant rolled on his back, the puppy crawled onto the boy's belly, causing him to giggle as he talked.

"Go on." Rising from the floor, Uther sank into a chair and glared at Pellinore.

If Meleagant noticed a change in Uther's attitude, he gave no indication. "It is said that Lot is *in love*," his words came out in a syrupy mocking tone, "with Gorlois' eldest daughter. The girl is just thirteen, and Lot, although he thinks of himself an old man, is in reality merely a boy. He *just* turned seventeen, a month younger than me. I suppose among royals, the union is not *that* ridiculous."

"Does not Gorlois have two girls?" Pellinore inquired, always interested in gossip when it came to war or courtly romance. He had always been well informed of the royals in Brittany, as well as those in the southeast and north of Britain. Yet, Cornwall, with its rugged southwestern shores, remained a mystery to many Britons, including himself.

"Yessss," a sudden freakishly high-pitched hissing laughter emerged from Meleagant. The sound caused both Phoenix and the puppy to scurry under Uther's legs, begging for protection. Due to his size, Phoenix was only able to get his head under the chair, and his hindquarters quivered as he scratched at the stone floor. "We heard, even as far away as my father's kingdom, that when the old duke first married, that his beautiful bride had just turned twelve. She had not yet turned thirteen when their first daughter was born."

Crawling on his belly, Meleagant coaxed the reluctant Phoenix from his hiding place with a wedge of apple. "Old Gorlois was furious with his young bride. He wanted a son, an heir to his kingdom. Rumor, from a good source, said the duke had the newborn snatched from her mother immediately, handing over the baby to be raised by a wet nurse. Locking his wife in a tower, he forcibly bedded her every day after, until he was certain she was again with child. Ten months after giving birth to her first baby, she gave birth to another daughter."

Uther reached under the chair and picked up the frightened puppy, protecting her as he knew he would have protected the duke's wife. He felt the frightened creature immediately relax, although his own heart continued to race with the details of the deranged man's tales.

"When Gorlois was told the baby was once again a girl, he went berserk. He called a formal council declaring no claim to either child," laughing again, this time in the mellow tones of a boy being licked by his dog, Meleagant rolled around with Phoenix before commencing with his story. "This time Gorlois' wife was furious. She insisted that the duke name the girls his legal children and rightful heirs. Upon doing so, she barred him from her room, and from ever laying hands upon her again."

"I too have heard that portion of the myth. One must wonder why, if the old boy wanted a son so badly, he just didn't banish his wife from his kingdom. Find himself a new wife with fertile male ground to plant his seed." Pellinore reached over and scratched the now sleeping puppy as he spoke.

"Oh, I am sure he would have, if she was an ordinary girl, or even a girl of royal heritage, but his child bride was not ordinary." Meleagant pushed his dog away. Sitting up, he hugged his knees tightly to his chest as he stared intently into Uther's eyes, "It is whispered that her birthright is of mystery; a daughter of Avalon, a Lady of the Lake, second cousin to your majesty's prophet, Merlin."

35

Pausing for a moment at the entrance to the great hall, Merlin was awed by its vastness and splendor. He had never explored the room before, never had a need to. During Ambrosius' reign, the young king had never finished the restoration of this once magnificent part of the old Roman Governor's Palace. Sadly, many things had never been restored, so many things left unfinished.

Scurrying by, the servants ignored him as they darted about long empty tables in silence: lighting candles, setting dinner plates, and pouring goblets with wine. The walls, covered in long flowing yards of jewel-toned fabric billowed softly as they passed. Walking into the room, Merlin lifted a panel of cloth, sadly viewing a once beautiful fresco hidden beneath. Age and water damage had caused stains to creep upward from the floor and down from the ceiling, leaving only flaked paint and a hint of its former splendor.

"It is a shame to hide beauty, even when in a decayed state."

"Welcome, Mother." Merlin could sense her presence even with his back to her, "How thoughtful of you to come on this day of celebration." Slowly he turned to face his creator, his eyes blank and dispassionate.

"We have come to celebrate the past life of one brother and the new life of another," her words were filled with a mixture of remorse and joy.

"We?" Merlin looked about the room, other than the servants, no guests had yet arrived in the hall.

"I have traveled with my cousin, Igraine and her family." She gently brushed her son's cheek, lingering only for a moment until Merlin pulled away as if struck by an asp. "You remember, Igraine?"

"Barely." Merlin's lips formed an impish smile as his eyes softened in memory of Ambrosius' coronation and the ladies of Avalon, the thieves of hearts. "Uther will be pleased to see her again."

"I must go and finish my preparations. We shall save you a place with us at the king's table."

"My place is already saved." Merlin softened his harsh comment with, "It will be my pleasure to join both you and my cousin for drink and conversation."

Without further words, she smiled softly, turned, and strolled from the room. Gathering his strength, Merlin leaned into the wall, fingers clutching the fabric. Her presence always unnerved him, yet, he could not keep his eyes from her as she appeared to float down the long hallway. Instinctively, he knew her attendance at tonight's feast would be a prelude to disaster. Closing his eyes tightly, he stood pondering; wondering what part would his mother have him play in her plans now.

"Not wearing your Druid garb?"

Startled, Merlin opened his eyes to see Lot emerging from the shadows. Although dressed in his usual black attire, there was something curiously different about him. Perhaps it was the neatly trimmed beard, or a renewed intensity in his eyes. He had put on weight in the form of muscle, and it was clear, even at a distance that he had grown in height. With certainty, the months spent in Cornwall had changed him, any lingering signs of boyishness had vanished, Lot now wore the mantle of full manhood.

"Have you no greeting for a returned warrior to the new king's court?"

"The Cornish coast has agreed with you." Regaining his composure, Merlin steadied his voice as he unclenched his fingers. Releasing the rumpled fabric, he walked toward the dark knight. "You missed the coronation." Fumbling with a plate upon the table he continued, "Have you spoken to Uther since your return?"

"I have newly arrived with my men and Duke Gorlois' family. Once I had them settled and myself presentable, I came straight to the hall." Lot smiled with a slight hint of guilt. "I was sorry to hear of Ambrosius' passing. He was a good man, a good king."

Looking up, Merlin caught a flicker of remorseful authenticity in Lot's eyes. With growing curiosity, he weighed the man standing before him. Prior to the campaign on the southwestern shores, Merlin knew that, without hesitation, upon arriving to Londinium, that Lot would have reported directly to Uther. Something, or someone, had vied for Lot's allegiance—and won. Merlin was about to press for further information, when feminine laughter filled the room. Without excusing himself, Lot spun around and sauntered off in the direction of two attractive young maidens.

Stepping back into the protection of the cloth covered walls Merlin watched as the parade of royals filtered in: lords and ladies from all regions of Britain dressed in their finest attire. How different he thought, from Ambrosius' Beltane celebration, where the older brother had invited all of Britain. Uther had limited the guest list to royals and a select number of knights. From lack of space or lack of trust, Merlin was not privy to the final decision making. Uther's court was filled with suspicion and perceived betrayal. The old ways were quickly vanishing.

No longer seated at the king's side, instead, Merlin had been assigned to blend into the crowd, to search the minds of men, to seek out and squelch treachery before it could manifest into treason. It had been a short journey from being Ambrosius' advisor to Uther's spy. Smiling inwardly, he amused himself with his new found skill, invading the hopes, dreams, and ambitions of the mere mortals surrounding him. Each man's mind was a learning experience, and he gathered their battle strategies along with their life's lessons. All information he would tuck away, eventually passing along to Britain's true savior.

"I nearly lost you in this sea of people."

The pressure of Lionel leaning into him, along with the comforting tones of his friend's voice, momentarily released Merlin from his vision quest. "You are my rock among the waves; the tides always pull us together."

Laughing at the unexpected remark, Lionel responded with pride, "It has been a long time since so many have gathered together under one roof." To be heard over the din of the crowd he pressed into Merlin; lips touching earlobe, "Yet, there are many men of importance absent."

"Will you be the only member of Brittany's court?" Merlin asked, arms folded, his eyes continued to search the room.

"Due to the constant threat of invasion, my father and family sent word that I would be my country's sole representative," Lionel shrugged. "Perhaps it is the same reason that so many of the other nobles did not attend tonight's gathering?"

"Perhaps."

"I do not envy Uther, taking over the role of king so soon after Ambrosius' death. He has not had time to properly mourn the loss of his brother. Nor has Britain time to mourn the loss of her king."

"Uther is a strong man, a leader of men and a master of battle. He will do all he can to carry on the legacy of his brother. As Uther loves Britain, so do his men love him, as will the peoples of Britain grow trust and respect for their new leader."

Horns trumpeted, followed by the entrance of the king's herald. "His Majesty—Our New High King—Uther Pendragon!"

A blanket of silence fell upon the room as all heads turned to the main doorway. A low gasp rumbled through the crowd, as Uther entered, stepping onto a makeshift platform. Even Merlin was taken by surprise. There, before them, stood Uther, dressed in his brother's white coronation clothing. His face, normally bearded, was now clean shaven. His hair, always pulled back, hung loosely about his shoulders, upon his head, a thin gold crown. With the exception of his dark features, in the dimly lit room, Uther, had been transformed into his brother—Ambrosius resurrected.

"I, Uther Pendragon, son of Constantine, brother to Ambrosius Aurelius, welcome you to this night of celebration." Unsheathing his sword, Uther raised it high, candle light danced upon the blade. "As your new High King, I pledge fidelity to Britain and you, her children." Thrusting the sword even higher, he continued, "Upon this sword, I swear an oath to serve and protect my homeland, our land, from *all* enemies."

A roar rose from the crowd as Uther sheathed the sword and casually stepped from the dais. His stern expression suddenly morphed to amused excitement as he spied Lot standing next to a cluster of ladies.

"Your Majesty," Lot bowed, "I apologize for arriving late."

"I am content that the inclement weather, and the Irish, retreated long enough to allow you to attend at all," Uther grasped Lot firmly by the shoulders and squeezed tightly as he spoke. Looking over his shoulder Uther came into eye contact with the lady from his brother's coronation, *his* Lady of Avalon.

"My liege," noticing Uther's path of distraction, Lot's lip curled into a smug half-smile, "may I introduce you to…"

"No need for introduction," Uther added under his breath, "I remember the lady well." Uther released Lot from his grip, gently pushing him aside to gain access to the lady, only to have his passage suddenly blocked by a burly older man.

"Your Majesty, it would be an honor for me to present my family to you," Duke Gorlois said as he motioned to the ladies surrounding him.

With mischief in his eyes, Lot lingered nearby, looking on with anticipated fascination.

"Of course, Duke Gorlois," Uther gave the Lady of Avalon a wanting glance before turning his attentions to the Duke of Cornwall. Not wishing to offend his guest, Uther convinced himself that kingly duties must come before pleasure. The night was young. There would be time enough to speak to his estranged love interest.

"This is Morgause, and her sister Morgan," Gorlois proudly stepped aside as he introduced his daughters. Both girls smiled shyly and curtsied.

Uther looked from Gorlois to the girls, searching for a resemblance. He recalled Meleagant's tale from earlier that day, and was surprised that although nearly the same age, the girls appeared years apart in appearance. Morgause, obviously the eldest, teetered on the cusp of womanhood; her figure giving way to feminine curves. He remembered Meleagant stating her age to be barely thirteen, yet she wore an aura of maturity. Within her facial features he saw the subtle glimpse of a child prematurely aged, her lips formed a sensual smile, within her gray eyes a haunting emptiness, projecting a quiet reserved nature.

In contrast, her sister Morgan was bubbly and full of life. Although both girls were lean, the baby fat still clung to the younger girl's face, giving her an angelic appearance. Her laughter was infectious, and her golden eyes glowed with pure delight. *Merlin's eyes*, Uther froze, only to be brought back to reality by Gorlois as he introduced his wife.

"And, this is the crown jewel of Tintagel, my beloved wife, the Duchess Igraine."

Uther's eyes darted from Gorlois to Igraine; swiftly scanning the duke's face for any hint of recognition to the lust that he, the High King of Britain, held for the duke's wife. With the startled look of a wild animal caught in a hunter's trap, Uther did his best to regain his dignity. Extending his hand to Igraine—the lady he had spent the past year yearning, dreaming, aching for. Bowing, he brought her hand to his lips, placing a lingering kiss upon her soft skin, instantly he melted into a myopic dream world. He sensed others speaking, moving, laughing, but he heard and saw only her.

Fully aware of the dangers the king's actions could impose, Merlin rushed to Uther's side. "Cousin, it is good to set eyes on you." Unexpectedly Merlin embraced Igraine. "Mother requested that I join you at the king's table." Without a backward glance to Uther, Merlin nonchalantly led Igraine and her family to their seats. His mother was already seated near the head of the table. Merlin took his place next to her, with Igraine on his side. Morgan nestled next to her mother. Gorlois reluctantly took the empty seat next to his youngest daughter, leaving Morgause sitting across from him next to Lot.

With Pellinore's guidance, Uther walked trancelike to the head of the table. His eyes devoured Igraine once more before coming to rest upon the king's chair, invoking the night's feast. While the servants brought trays of succulent pork, wild game, and platters of fruits and vegetables, Uther continued his scrutiny of the duke's wife.

"In the early morning hours after my brother's coronation, you should have told me she was married," Uther lamented to Merlin's mother, his teeth ripping into a hunk of venison.

"Would it have mattered?"

"Would it have mattered?" Pondering her question, Uther drank with great thirst from his wine goblet. "No, it would not have mattered." He could do nothing but answer her with honesty.

"She is your destiny."

"I knew that, the first moment I laid eyes on her. I knew she was destined to become a part of me; and I of her."

When dinner was consumed, the musicians took their places upon the dais. As they began tuning their instruments, the crowded room clamored in anticipation of the evening's dance. As the first chords played, Uther rose from his place at the head of the table and walked behind Gorlois. Merlin held his breath as Uther addressed the duke.

"My lord, will you grant me your permission to have the first dance of the evening with your lovely lady?"

"But, of course," Gorlois responded. Taking a long gulp from his goblet, his stomach filled with ale, as his voice filled with pride.

Walking to Igraine's side, Uther helped her rise, offering his arm they walked onto the dance floor. One by one, the others joined the king in the revelry of the evening. Covert tittering and concealed stares followed the new High King and his dancing partner. Even to the most casual observer the passion exchanged between Uther and Igraine was blindingly obvious. To all it would seem except for the Duke of Cornwall, who sat happy in deep lustful conversation with a flirtatious serving wench.

Merlin casually chatted with his mother and Lionel as he vigilantly watched his cousin with the king, feeling both powerless and passionate as the evening unfolded into early morning. Exhausted and thirsty, the dancers regained their places at the tables, as Lionel called upon Merlin for a song.

"My harp is safely tucked away across the river, within the Druid's temple."

"Look again." Lionel raised an eyebrow with drunken impish delight as he pointed to Merlin's harp leaning against the wall.

"Your king demands a ballad from his bard," Uther declared, taking a deep drink from his wine goblet.

"As you wish, Your Majesty," reluctantly, Merlin replied as he walked to his instrument. The crowd hushed as he took up the harp. Sitting on the platform, he sensually stroked the strings and began to sing a tale of Ambrosius the Great, brother to Uther Pendragon. He told the tale of a fire dragon streaking across the heavens on the night of Ambrosius' burial. How, soon after the sighting, Uther had been given the title of head dragon, the Pendragon of Britain. As he sang, forward visions rushed into his memories causing his head to ache. Before he could finish the song, the pain became uncontrollable, causing him to cease playing and press his palms to his temples. The world began to spin. His mother vanished from sight, as if her presence had been mere hallucination. Trying to speak, to stand, he found himself spiraling into darkness.

With a speed unbeknownst to himself, Uther rushed the stage. He gathered Merlin in his arms before the boy prophet could touch the floor. Igraine hovered nearby as Uther picked up Merlin's limp body.

"Where will you take him?" whispered Igraine.

"To my chambers," Uther replied without hesitation. Searching her eyes he pleaded, "Can you heal him?"

"I will try," Igraine laid her hand gently upon Merlin's neck, searching for a pulse.

Chairs pushed aside as Gorlois marched in a drunken stagger to his wife's side, screaming his protest. "It is not proper."

"Hush, husband," Igraine reprimanded. "The boy is my cousin and in need of my healing powers. The girls are tired, take them to our quarters. I shall join you as soon as possible."

"Mother," Morgause implored, "let me assist you."

"No," her mother answered flatly, "your place is with your sister."

Near the doorway, Uther stood, cradling Merlin within his arms; waiting patiently for Igraine to follow.

36

Perched on the palace's outer ledge, Merlin's hawk pecked franticly at the leather ties holding the cowhide taunt against the window. With vigorous persistence she managed to loosen one corner of the hide, allowing the first rays of sunlight to stream into the king's bedchamber. As the hawk was about to maneuver her head through the tiny gap, the corner of the window flung open.

"I thought it might be you." Amused, Igraine rested her hand on the window's ledge in a gesture of invitation. Without hesitation the hawk sidestepped up the lady's arm, resting upon her shoulder.

"You have nothing to worry about." Igraine assured the hawk as she walked next to the bed where Merlin lay. "See, he is not hurt, only sleeping."

Nudging the lady gently, the hawk gave out a low guttural sound. As if on command, Igraine lowered her arm allowing the raptor to hop down. The hawk crossed Merlin's chest, coming to rest near his face. With inquisitive eyes the hawk slowly tilted her head in a rhythmic side to side motion. She then placed her beak next to Merlin's lips searching for a sign of breath, an utterance of sound. Assured that her ward was indeed alive, she took flight to the window's ledge. Pausing for a moment she glanced back, gave out a shriek, and took flight.

At the sound of the hawk's cry, Merlin's eyelids flickered. Slowly he ascended from his vision induced coma. On the brink of consciousness his head throbbed with excruciating pain, and for one fleeting moment he wanted only to fall back into the comfort of a sleepless slumber. Upon his head delicate fingers rested, beckoning him to open his eyes. Unable to resist her cool healing touch, he slowly obeyed.

"Welcome back, dear cousin," said Igraine with soothing calmness.

"How long have I been gone?" Merlin grimaced, feeling the headache grab him as he tried to sit.

"The visions overtook you last night."

"Where am I?" Sinking back into the bed he tried to recall the previous night's events, tried to summon the prophecy that had abducted him into the agonizing shadows of obscurity.

"The king was gravely concerned for your welfare; so much so that he carried you immediately to his bedchambers."

"You stayed with me throughout the night?" he sighed deeply. "What of the king?" Trying once more to raise his head, failing, he fell back exhausted.

"The king?" Puzzled, Igraine tilted her head, her eyes giving way to ponder. "I am not sure. He was here. He brought you here." Thinking hard, she remembered him standing next to her, and then he was gone, vanishing into the night. "Kingly duties must have beckoned him away. The day is just breaking, I am sure he shall be here to check on you soon." Bending over, Igraine grasped Merlin's hand as she placed a tender kiss upon his forehead.

The moment Igraine's lips touched his skin, a surge of energy sparked. All pain rushed from his head, down his arm, dissolving from his fingertips into hers.

"Better?" she whispered.

"Yes." Merlin blinked his eyes in disbelief.

"Henceforth, your visions will cease to induce pain." Squeezing his hand she added, "A gift from Avalon." Smiling she released her hold on him. "I must go. The Duke, my daughters, and your mother await my return."

"Wait!" He was about to ask why his mother had not attended him, but a flash of the previous night's vision flickered. "There is a message to pass along." Squinting to bring the vision into fruition his words flowed, "By winter's solstice you shall bare a child. The rightful heir to the throne of Britain; a man legends are made of—a son of Avalon."

"If you envision it," her voice quivered, "it must be so." Face flushing, her trembling fingers brushed a stray hair from his face, tucking it behind his ear. Lingering she gazed into his eyes, searching the full meaning of his prophecy. With a sad smile, she bowed, turned, and exited the room, leaving behind a deadly silence.

"You can come out now." Merlin directed his words to the far corner of the room.

Ghostlike, Uther emerged from the dark recesses. Still dressed in his coronation attire, he made his way to the foot of the bed.

"You have been there all night," Merlin uttered more as a statement than a question.

Leaning momentarily upon the massive bedpost, Uther paused, and then made his way to one of the two chairs positioned in front of the fireplace. Unsheathing his sword, he poked the embers with the tip of the blade, causing the dying fire to come alive with a renewed vigor.

From the bed Merlin leaned on his side and watched in silent wonder. Unsure of how much Uther had overheard, how much he suspected, how much he fully understood.

"She is an amazing woman." Uther flung himself into the chair. He leaned forward until his forehead pressed against the pommel of his sword. Both hands wrapped around the sword tightly.

"Yes, my liege, she is." Gathering the bed sheets around his naked frame, Merlin joined Uther by the fire. Sitting in the chair opposite Uther, Merlin pulled his legs to his chest.

"I have finally been conquered—defeated by love."

"Not defeated. You have surrendered. Fate can be an overwhelming mistress. It takes a wise man to acknowledge her and succumb to her desires."

"What do you know of love, Merlin?" Uther turned his head, lip slightly snarled, eyes glaring, "Have you ever loved a woman?"

"Have you?" Merlin pulled the bed clothing closer to his body, feeling a sudden chill.

"Must you always answer a question with a question?" The sleepless night and long preceding day was quickly wearing on Uther's last nerve.

"I am sorry, but this day is about you, not me."

Uther threw back his head, his deep unrestrained laughter echoed within the room. "Merlin, from the day my brother first set eyes upon you, *everything* has been about you!"

Merlin hated that laugh, and curled his legs even closer to his body, arms hugging his knees tighter.

"Do I know of love?" Uther laughed again, but this time softer. Leaning back into the chair his thoughts drifted to the night of his brother's coronation. To the night he unknowingly first set eyes on Igraine; the wife of another. To the night spent with the Ladies of Avalon. "I have lusted after many women, yet, until the Lady Igraine came into my life, I have never felt the ache of love." He allowed his grip on the sword to loosen, casually resting it at his side.

"I understand."

"Do You? Do you really understand? Love drains a man of his power to reason. A king cannot afford to love." His fist suddenly clinched as tightly as his jaw.

"How can a king afford not to love?" Merlin cooed, relaxing his body, doing his best to radiate calm. "The future is written, and Igraine plays a pivotal role. You must follow your destiny, follow your heart, you have no choice."

"Man always has choice. That is what separates man from beast." Their heated discussion was suddenly interrupted by a pounding on the door. "Enter!" Uther barked, secretly relieved for the break in conversation.

"Your Majesty, a messenger..." before the guard could fully announce the purpose of the intrusion, a young girl brushed by.

"I bring a message from my mother to Merlin." Morgause's monotone voice was accented by her steel-gray eyes, which shot daggers into Uther as she passed. With a royal curtsey, she handed the scroll to Merlin. "Mother wishes that her words be read promptly. No reply is requested."

"Is there a message for me?" Uther inquired, reaching out in an effort to touch the young maiden's arm as she attempted to exit.

"Stay away from our family, stay away from my mother," Morgause hissed as she recoiled from his touch and ran from the room, the heavy door slamming behind her.

"Read it," Uther urged, his eyes burned with a mixture of urgency and confusion.

Nervously, Merlin broke the seal binding the secrets of the vellum's contents. Reading quickly he gazed up from her words, staring into Uther's eager eyes.

"Aloud!" Uther growled.

Inhaling deeply, Merlin slowly delivered the declaration.

Dear Cousin,

I fear I have caused a terrible wrath to be brought upon the king, and the kingdom. My husband awoke this morning with a head still full of ale. He has accused me of spending the night in the king's chamber, which I cannot deny. Yet, he believes that I spent the night in the arms of the king. In his rage he refuses to listen to reason and has declared vengeance upon Uther. We leave for Tintagel immediately. ~ Igraine

"You know that I must have her," clutching his sword once more, Uther plunged the blade into the fire, furiously attacking an unknown adversary.

"Yes, I know," Merlin sighed. "Destiny cannot be denied."

"Man is not ruled by destiny, but by rational decisions." Uther continued his swordplay with the flames. "This is insanity! What manner of king am I? Even my dear departed brother, with his passionate heart, would not wage war for the mere love of another man's wife."

"What kind of king? You shall be remembered as a king of historical magnitude."

"This is all your doing!" Uther screamed. Fragmented thoughts seized his reasoning. Visions of Ambrosius' library mural and the fall of Troy; the devastation that followed the battle flooded forth. *There was no rational justification for the demise of a kingdom, for thousands of brave innocent men to die, for crucial alliances to be broken—all for the love of a woman. No, not even love. He truly knew nothing of love—all for the illusion of love.* Twisting in his chair, he drew the sword from the flame, piercing the blade's tip to Merlin's throat.

Merlin's eyes grew large with fear. The smell of burning flesh, his flesh, invaded his nostrils. He felt a trickle of blood slide down his chest causing the Druid Egg, which hung around his neck, to hiss and glow brightly. He tried to move backwards, tried to escape, yet he was pinned to the chair, his fate within the hands of a madman.

"Once this blade was stained with the blood of Britain's enemies." Uther's eyes burned into Merlin, matching the sword's heat. "Now, it is blackened by the soot of burning passion, a plague you have placed upon my weakened heart."

As swiftly as Uther attacked, Merlin countered. Bringing his hands to the sword he pressed palms tightly upon either side of the blade. Pushing with superhuman strength he propelled Uther, sword, and chair across the room, causing them to hit the stone wall with a thunderous crash.

Releasing his bed clothing, Merlin's naked body flew upon Uther, as a hawk would attack his prey. He captured the king's hands, clutching them tightly to the arms of the chair. Bending over, he pressed his face dangerously close to his quarry. For a fleeting moment he hesitated, contemplating the reflection within Uther's dilated pupils. Within the king's eyes, he was not sure which vision disturbed him the most: the undeniable fright radiating within Uther, a man unaccustomed to the taste of fear—or the reflection of a crazed version of himself.

"From this day until you take your dying breath," as he spoke, Merlin's voice fell into the ominous rhythmic tone of *the ancients*. "You will reign as the High King of Britain. But, your true purpose as Britain's High King is twofold: to defend and protect the land, and to produce Britain's next heir. It is from this second purpose, this necessity, this importance, that your alliance with the Lady Igraine be consummated with urgency!"

With great restraint, Merlin released both his physical and psychological grip on the king. Gathering the bed sheets about him, slowly he moved to the window, fully ripping off the hide, allowing the new day to flood the gloom. From behind him, he heard the rustled of boots and the clang of steel.

"So it begins!" Rising from the chair, Uther gathered his sword, driving the blade into the sheath.

Merlin listened as the words emerged from Uther, echoing in a calm and confident tone. Words he had heard from the king so many times on the eve of battle. Without turning and without question, Merlin knew that Uther had also gathered his composure.

"Get dressed and meet me at the fort. We have a battle strategy to plan," hesitating in the doorway he added with a guttural laughter, "and our destiny to fulfill."

As he listened to Uther's boots disappear down the long hallway, Merlin continued to gaze into the heavens. From above, white feathers floated like newly fallen snowflakes as his hawk took her morning meal—*so it begins!*

37

With the prospect of civil war looming, within hours of the duke's departure, chaos abounded in the streets of Londinium. The crowds made travel across the bridge from the Druid Temple to the fort slow and arduous. Merlin had grown to hate crowds. Upon entering the city's inner walls he made haste, traversing his horse through the backstreets, he followed the Walbrook stream, riding close to its bank.

A mixture of apprehension and excitement filled the air as he neared the eastern gate. The sentries allowed him to pass without question as he urged his mare into a rocking-horse lope toward the council building. Reaching his destination, he hastily dismounted. Neither words nor glances were exchanged as he removed a package tied to the saddle, and tossed the mare's reins to Elivri, who stood ready near the doorway.

"Are you alright?" Rushing to his friend, Lionel stopped short of grabbing Merlin in a frantic embrace. "I was so worried last night. Uther's guards blocked me from attending you. This, is all my fault." Lionel waved his hands toward the council room doors.

"How is *this,* your fault?" Exasperated, Merlin stopped and stared into the heavens for an answer.

"I should have attended you last night. If I would have been there instead of the Lady Igraine, none of this would have happened."

"None of this bedlam is your fault, nor is it your concern."

Startled, Lionel stepped back shaking his head. He knew both the look and the tone, and he understood without doubt what Merlin was about to command.

"You are to leave Londinium at once." Pausing, pacing about, waiting for inspiration to strike, Merlin's words suddenly flowed, "You must make haste to the Forest Sauvage. Alert Sir Ector and his wife— for the treasure we have been seeking will soon be created. You are the treasure's guardian. As such, you must be exempt from this upcoming battle. You must be kept safe, to make ready the sacred place of the treasure's safekeeping."

"But my place is with you and Uther," Lionel vehemently objected.

"Your place is where I send you!"

Opening his mouth, Lionel's words refused to find passage. He knew it was useless to lodge further complaint, so he stared silently at the ground.

"In nine months and nine days, just after midnight, on the eve of the winter solstice we shall meet again in Camelford. I will send a messenger to you before that date with additional details. Do you understand the importance of the task I have set before you?"

"You are not my ruler, nor the ruler of Britain!" Lionel spat, immediately wishing he could retract the words.

"True, I am not Britain's High King, nor have I official power over you. Yet, by my birth's oath, I am Britain's protector, and I have assigned you the honorary role of collaborator. If you no longer have belief in me, nor the faith to proceed..." pausing, Merlin gave a sideways glance in Elivri's direction, "...perhaps I can find another who will not question my wisdom."

"My faith holds true!" Lionel hissed. His face burned, and he knew that his anger could no longer be concealed nor contained. "You dishonor me by doubting my loyalty."

"Lionel," Merlin's tone softened, "I honor you with the opportunity to help. You are the faithful holder of my secrets, how could I doubt your loyalty?" Lingering a moment he put a reassuring, firm hand on Lionel's shoulder. "Our frequent partings have never been easy for either of us. Yet, for now we must, but briefly, once again part ways."

"For the good of Britain, then, I will do your bidding, without further question." Bowing formally, he turned to Elivri and shouted, "Ready my steed, I leave Londinium immediately."

"When will you return? What shall I tell Claire?" Elivri asked, confused at overhearing bits and pieces of Lionel's conversation with Merlin.

"If Claire asks, tell her I have been sent on a quest of utmost importance." Lionel glared back at Merlin as he spoke, "I know not when I shall be *allowed* to return." With those last words, he stormed ahead of Elivri toward the stables.

"For the good of Britain," Merlin sighed under his breath as he wearily watched Lionel vanish into an oncoming sea of marching infantry.

***

When Uther had first set up camp in Londinium's fort, he had converted a portion of one of the larger stables into headquarters for battle strategy. As Merlin entered the building, the pungent odor of sweat, from both men and horses, caused his nostrils to flare. Clutching the package that he had retrieved from his saddle, Merlin lingered in the doorway. Slowly his eyes adjusted to the torch lit room. Now, dressed in earth-toned clothing, Merlin casually leaned into the archway. His body blended into the mossy aged stone in hopes of giving him the advantage, at least for a moment, of seeing without being seen.

Twenty-plus of Uther's high commanders formed a horseshoe around a large sandy pit in the middle of the room. Some squatted. Some stood. Some leaned into the pit. All spoke at once; asking questions, giving advice, shouting solutions to the upcoming battle. The noise was deafening and it assaulted Merlin's ears, grating upon his nerves.

Standing near the far end of the pit, the Roman mapmaker Cassius stood. His young son, Marcus, hovered by his side, taking in the fine details of his father's work. With stick in hand, Cassius finished outlining the last markings of the territories surrounding Bodmin Moor within the sand. A tension breaking laughter filled the room as one of Uther's junior commanders reached to move a strategically placed stone; causing the old mapmaker to swiftly crack his stick upon the young man's knuckles. At the same moment, Uther's new puppy grabbed one of the map markers and romped playfully about the room with young Marcus in urgent pursuit.

Uther sat shirtless on a bench across from his men, surrounded by several pages. So engrossed was he in the ensuing battle strategy, that he was oblivious to the boys who were in various states of undressing and dressing him. On a nearby barrel, the remnants of his coronation clothing were neatly folded. In front of him a boy tugged at Uther's white deerskin boots, while another stood by patiently holding the king's traditional black attire. Merlin watched in silent amusement. The warlord allowing others to dress him, gave proof of Uther's heritage; princely ways, long ingrained and taken for granted.

At the same time, the familiar sight of the young king on the eve of battle still held Merlin captivated. For, even with all of Uther's faults, he proved time and time again that he was a natural leader. Merlin smiled as he watched the interaction between the king and his men. He marveled at Uther, hanging on each man's word, even when several men spoke in unison. Uther's eyes moved from one man to the next soaking in the counsel of each, as he weighted and evaluated each man's battle strategy for merit.

"Where is Lot?" Pellinore inquired suddenly, his eyes searching the room for a glimpse of the dark prince and his cronies.

"He has taken sides with the duke," a voice yelled out among the pack, with several others expressing similar concerns.

"Enough!" Uther's temples visibly throbbed, an outward sign of his growing annoyance with the mass dissension voiced toward his favorite commander. "I sent orders for Lot and his men to escort the Lady Igraine and her court to Tintagel."

"Your men, you mean," the venom in Sir Dornar's words sliced through the uproar of those surrounding him. "Lot has no respect for anyone, but Lot! Nor has he any allegiance to anyone but himself."

Uther glared at Pellinore with a look that was easy to read within his silent stare—*curb your son.*

"Let us get back to matters at hand," Pellinore pleaded as he reached for Dornar's arm, squeezing it tightly.

At that same moment, the page holding Uther's clothing leaned forward, whispering into the High King's ear. His words caused Uther's head to snap toward the doorway. With a sinister smile, Uther motioned Merlin to enter, as he mouthed the words *welcome to our future.*

With a sigh, Merlin pulled away from the wall knowing that Uther was the one person whom he could never hide from. A moment of quiet fell within the room as Merlin leisurely walked next to Uther's side. The sound of Cassius' stick dragging a line from Londinium to Tintagel drew the men's attention back to the matters at hand.

"Welcome, Merlin. What do you think of our campaign so far?"

"Your Majesty, as always, you and your men have the situation under control." Surveying the map, Merlin knew in an instant Uther's plans.

Draw Gorlois' men away from the southern path of the fortress by the sea. He nodded with silent agreement.

Easing the tension, Uther let out a throaty laugh. Within moments the room was once more filled with the deafening sound of men's minds in verbal motion.

"Do we travel tonight?" Pellinore asked.

"No, tomorrow will be soon enough, perhaps the day after," Uther leaned back allowing a black tunic to be pulled over his head.

"That is insane! If we wish a speedy victory we must strike now, before their numbers have a chance to grow." With a quick glance into Pellinore's direction, Dornar knew he had overstepped his bounds once again. He regretted his rashness, having already been reprimanded for speaking without first considering the consequences of his words.

"Excuse my son, Uther." Pellinore smacked Dornar on the back of his head in a lighthearted manner. "His youthful exuberance betrays his courtly manners."

"No harm in speaking the truth Pelly," Uther reassured. Turning, he directed his words to Pellinore's young son. "Every man knows deep within his heart that the mere act of war is steeped in insanity. It is the strategy of battle that keeps men lucid. You do understand, more is at stake here than mere victory? There are several ladies who ride within the company of the duke. Their safety, above all else, must be considered first and foremost."

"Forgive me, Your Majesty, I spoke without consideration."

"A great leader thinks, before he acts." Pellinore patted his son on the back. "A lesson you will do well to remember."

As Uther's commanders returned to talk of strategic maneuvers, Merlin scrutinized the sand pit once more. His body began to tremble as the stone and stick markers slowly morphed into men. He visualized the battleground—blood red. Looking up into the men's faces that surrounded him, he winced as a ghostly aura appeared upon those who would not survive the battle. The realization of death and destruction his plan had set in motion knotted his stomach.

"My lord. My lord," The strained voice, of the page standing closest to Merlin, sharpened to a high pitch as his hand frantically pulled on Merlin's fingers.

Perplexed, Merlin looked down at the blood trickling under his fingertips, staining the shoulder of the page's white shirt. Trancelike he relaxed his hawk-like grip, causing the boy to scurry out of reach.

Uther dismissed the page with a wave of his hand as he stared intently into Merlin's eyes. Over the past year, deciphering the boy prophet's visions had become a standard prelude to battle. As much as he loathed Merlin's presence, he eagerly looked forward to hearing his prophetic sightings. After all, knowing a battle's outcome had its advantages.

"Many will die." Merlin broke the silence.

"Many always die. Why would this differ from battles past?" Uther shrugged.

"The only reason that this battle differs from those in the past, is the cause for which we fight." Walking behind Uther, Pellinore could not help but voice his opinion in hushed tones.

"Always the man of reason," Uther laughed wearily. "The ludicrous cause for which blood will flow. Isn't that what you truly mean?"

"Lust has a way of corrupting a man's logic," Pellinore whispered.

"This is more than a battle over lust, Pelly." Uther bristled at the old man's comment and looked to Merlin for reassurance of the truth to his words.

"It is the ultimate battle for Britain's future son," Merlin added in muted monotones, his cryptic prophecy being heard by only those nearest the king.

***

So it went, throughout the morning into late evening they deliberated, until at last the final plans were set forth. One by one, the men departed leaving only Merlin, Uther, and a sleeping puppy, alone in awkward silence.

"What do you have concealed within your clutches?" Uther indicated to the sheepskin wrapped bundle tucked under Merlin's arm.

"Due to the manner of their departure, the duke insisted that the ladies leave behind all but the barest of essentials. As, I am the Lady Igraine's cousin, she had her belongings brought to my quarters at the Druid Temple."

"I am overtired and have no patience for riddles." Uther grabbed the package, ripping open the leather straps that bind it. Puzzled, he looked to Merlin for an explanation of its contents.

"A cloak, my lord."

"I know what it is," Uther growled as he thoughtfully ran his fingers across the fine gold threads embroidered on either side of the ornate clasp. "Is this not the insignia of Duke Gorlois?"

"The very same," Merlin confirmed the king's suspicions and smiled as he continued the story of the cloak's discovery. "I found it upon opening Igraine's trunk, in hopes of gaining something of value we could use on our campaign. It was strewn haphazardly on the top of her garments. I thought it may be of interest to you."

With a sudden flurry, the sleeping puppy began sniffing the air. In an instant she was fully awake and running joyously to a man standing quietly in the doorway.

"Lot?"

"Yes, Your Majesty." Lot bent down and ran a hand through the coarse hair of the young deerhound.

"How did you get by the guards without being announced?"

"I still have friends within the court, my liege."

"Friends?" Merlin mocked.

Lot scowled in Merlin's direction.

"Rumors have flourished," Merlin taunted.

"Rumors?" Lot nonchalantly stroked the puppy's backside.

"That you have *once more* changed allegiance."

Lot crossed the room and knelt before Uther. The puppy followed, sitting quietly by Lot's side. "Your Majesty, I assure you that the rumors are but that, mere rumors. I assure you that my loyalties lie with you, this court, and to the safekeeping of Britain."

"Sir Lot, I may at times doubt your motives, but I have never doubted your loyalties. Now, get off your knee and give me a full report."

"As you suspected, my months spent with Gorlois gained me trust with the duke. He was overeager to have myself, and my men, escort Lady Igraine and her entourage to Tintagel. Giving him the speed to push forward and gather his army. He eagerly awaits defending his honor on the field of battle."

"Does anyone know that you have returned to Londinium?"

"Only Nentres, Dodinel and the Lady Igraine know that I have left camp—no one else—especially no one from Gorlois' court."

Uther was about to ask why Lady Igraine was among those knowledgeable of Lot's departure, but he bided his time, letting Lot finish his report.

"Upon leaving Londinium this morning, we traveled hard throughout the day, by early evening the ladies were ready to retire. We will ride again at first dawn." Feeling more confident, Lot sat cross-legged at Uther's feet. He paused a moment as the puppy crawled onto his lap. "As soon as all was quiet within the camp I set off through the back roads for the city. Elivri has a fresh, swift mount, identical to the one I rode in on, waiting at the western gate to take me back."

"As usual, a well calculated plan," Uther commended.

"There is one more matter of urgency. The Lady Igraine was anxious and concerned about an article of clothing left behind in her personal belongings. She was afraid if it got into the wrong hands it could lead to deadly consequences." Noticing the open package next to Uther, Lot glanced to Merlin and grinned. "Well done, Merlin. I see you have already rummaged through the lady's garments and come up with the prize." He knew his words had hit their mark by the blush upon Merlin's cheeks.

"I can guess the meaning behind this," Uther held up the cloak as he spoke. "Indulge me just the same."

"The duke is known by his covering." Standing, Lot reached for the cloak and asked, "May I?" In a sweeping gesture, he wrapped the garment around his shoulders.

"It is unique." Uther observed. The cloak was meticulously dyed: variegating from a rich, dark ocean aqua at the bottom, to a soft sky blue at the top. Near the clasps embroidered in fine gold threads two sea serpents faced one another, their mouths wide, ready to strike at the wearer's throat.

"There is only one other like it. Gorlois wears its mate now." Undoing the clasp Lot folded the cloak and handed it to Uther. "The cloak is the key to his identity."

"More than cloak cover will be needed to persuade the duke's guards," Merlin grumbled.

"Have your army keep Gorlois and his troops busy on the moors," Lot turned his attention to Uther, "and I pledge that you, and your doubting prophet, will have easy access across Tintagel's bridge when the time comes."

"What is your price?" Merlin grabbed Lot by the shoulder, abruptly turning him around.

"Do not ever touch me again," Lot snapped, easily removing himself from Merlin's grip. His actions caused the puppy to run whimpering under the bench, her head timidly peeking out from between Uther's boots.

"I do this for the good of Britain." Ignoring Merlin, Lot turned once more to Uther. "I do have one request."

"I knew it. A commander in the royal army should never request favors for doing his duty," Merlin shouted in bitter accusation.

"By The Gods!" Uther bellowed. "Stop your childish bickering. Lot, if you can pull off this deed I will bequest whatever is within my power."

"I wish to take the Lady Morgause as my bride."

"What?" Merlin mused. "She is but an innocent child."

"Just this past winter, she has passed into womanhood." Lot hesitated, an unexpected flush covering his neck and face. "We are passionate for one another."

"It is one thing for a High King to seek a queen in hopes of producing an heir. But, quite another matter for a man with military aspirations to take a wife," Uther pondered aloud.

"Allow me to continue if I may, Your Majesty. Upon completion of this undertaking; I formally petition that my men be allowed to return to their homelands. Furthermore, I have had word that my father has fallen gravely ill. As his sole heir, I shall take up the title of King of the Orkney Isles. The Lady Morgause will serve as my queen, and mother of *my* sons."

"As young boys, you have all been trained in the ways of war under the rule of three High Kings." Uther smiled wearily. "I agree, it is time as men, that you take your knowledge home and train your kinsmen. However, I impose a caveat to your release of service. When time comes again to gather forces against an overwhelming enemy; that you will keep your pledge of allegiance to me, and to any kinsman of mine that may follow me to the throne."

Merlin stepped forward, about to voice additional stipulations, and was silenced by the stern sincerity upon Uther's face.

"On behalf of my men, we agree to your terms."

"Until we meet again, on the road to Tintagel." Uther got to his feet and uncharacteristically pulled Lot into him. "You shall be sorely missed," he whispered.

"I pledge that I shall not let you down," Lot murmured, returning the hold, and for one fleeting moment, he felt remorse for the deed he was about to do.

38

The ride to Cornwall was exhausting. Lot and his retinue stopped infrequently along the way, only long enough to feed and water the horses, and allow the ladies to rest. Reaching their destination late last night, Lot and his men had little time for sleep before rising in the predawn darkness. Gathering on the banks of the outer mainland courtyard of Tintagel, Lot's men appeared as ghost riders in the thick fog. Directly across from them, the castle, surrounded by sea, gave little protection from the elements.

Persistent winds tore at Lot's cloak. Tiny ice daggers of sea spray cut into his body, saturating his clothing. Stray strands of damp hair fell upon his face, trickling down his cheeks, stinging his chapped lips. His arms ached from containing the nervous energy of his mount, as the black stallion relentlessly pulled on the reins. Yet, for all his discomfort, he hesitated to seek shelter, hesitated to leave.

"Do you have to go?" Morgause tightened her grasp on Lot's sleeve, balancing herself from the winds that whipped at her hair and gown.

"Your father is expecting me." Bending down from atop his charger, Lot wrapped his gloved hand around Morgause's small, delicate one. Freeing her hold from his clothing, he brought her hand to his lips, placing a soft kiss upon her palm. Closing his eyes, he lingered a moment. With each pulse of her wrist, her fragrance filled his nostrils. A mixture of lavender and sandalwood invaded his senses and he breathed her essence in deeply, committing her scent to memory. In his young life he had experienced a variety of maidens, but none made his heart race like the duke's daughter.

Without further conversation he released her. Pressing his knees into the stallion's barrel chest, he cantered down the stone path en route to the north-western edge of Bodmin Moor. Following closely, were the three remaining members of the Young Royal Guard: Nentres, Dodinel, and Meleagant. Behind them in perfect formation, now under Lot's command, were one hundred of Uther's youngest cavalry; eager, innocent, and hungry for battle.

***

"Halt! Who goes there?" A lone guard on horseback emerged from the fog that covered the moors, causing Lot's horse to nicker and sidestep.

"The duke is expecting us," Lot's tone exuded authority with a hint of exasperation. "I come from Tintagel with reinforcements."

"Sir Lot," the guard's voice held an apologetic tremor. "I did not recognize you in the cover of misty darkness. Duke Gorlois is at the crest of the hill. His orders were to have you join him upon your arrival."

After briefly conferring with his men, Lot preceded up the grassy slope alone. Nentres and Meleagant kept watch halfway up the embankment, while Dodinel escorted the cavalry to the rear of the duke's troops.

"It is good to have a man I can count on," Gorlois shouted as he lifted the visor to his helmet.

"You can count on me to be at your side when you take your last breath," Lot assured the duke.

"Let us hope that will not be today," Gorlois chuckled. Turning in the saddle, his blue cloak waving like an ocean in the misty air. Without warning, the duke's attitude quickly changed from jovial to serious. "Do your men understand our battle strategy?"

"At the first rays of daylight, they will follow your army into battle." Lot walked his horse to the crest of the hill, straining in the mist to get even the slightest glimpse of the open field below. He knew the land well, and had walked its parameters many times prior to this day. He knew exactly where Uther's troops would be gathering. He knew the precise formation of Gorlois' foot soldiers. He knew where Dodinel would lead his cavalry.

There was something eerily comforting to be in control of all sides of the battle. Knowing that he held the power! With a single action he could change the tide of victory for either king or duke. He pondered and weighed the outcome of both scenarios. He weighed the advantages, and his loyalties to each man. More important, he weighed what would be best for Lot. As he rode back to Gorlois' side, without a doubt, he knew what *must* be done.

"We still have some time before the sun graces us with her light." Dismounting, Gorlois walked to the lone beech tree on the knoll; slowly he removed his gloves, neatly tucking them into his sword belt. Next he unclasped his helmet tossing it gently by his feet. "We have the advantage—we know the land," Gorlois said with reassurance, confidently folding his arms, leaning his massive frame into the bark. Breathing deeply, he took in the sweet smells of early spring that drifted through the air. An unnatural silence surrounded the land, broken only by the occasional horse's whinny.

Lot slipped from his stallion, joining the duke. The time had come. Nervously, he tossed back his cloak to give his arms easy access. Standing dangerously close, he leaned into the duke and whispered in his ear, "I pledge to give your daughter many sons."

The cold taste of steel mixed with blood rushed into Gorlois' mouth and choked his thoughts before they could become words. In an instant he was dead.

Lot sidestepped the river of blood. It was a messy business plunging a blade into a man's throat, but a swift and painless way to die, Lot rationalized as he retracted the dagger from Gorlois' neck. As the duke slumped to the ground, Lot snatched the gloves from the dead man's sword belt. Casually, he tucked them into his own belt. He then cleaned the blood from his dagger on the brilliant blue cloak. When he was confident that the blade was clean, he sheathed the weapon. Kicking aside the duke's boot, he picked up the old warrior's helmet, tying it to the saddle of Gorlois' roan warhorse.

Lot groped in the mist for the duke's left hand. Even in the dark he could feel the scarred, gnarled knuckles; hands abused from years of swordplay. Spitting on the fingers, Lot wrenched the insignia ring from Gorlois' possession. Holding the band of silver close to his eyes, he marveled at the deep, brilliant blue hues of the perfectly cut star sapphire. He could feel his pulse race as he pocketed the jewel, hiding it away in the coin pouch concealed within his breeches—the perfect dowery!

Now, to execute the final and most thought out deed. This maneuver would take precision from both himself and his stallion. He had gone over the movement many times on his ride from Londinium to Tintagel. Late at night, with the help of Dodinel as a stand in for the duke, he had practiced lifting Dodinel's limp form onto the saddle of his stallion. Smirking, he recalled his conversation with Dodinel from the previous evening.

***

"Why not just kill him astride his mount?" Dodinel had asked.
"We must be prepared for all eventualities," Lot had grumbled.
"Why then not just leave him on the knoll?" Dodinel's verbal torment continued.
"We must give the illusion that the duke died in combat," Lot snarled back.
"But..."
"Play dead," Lot had finally advised. Mercifully, Dodinel had obeyed.

***

Looking back on those nights there were times Lot had wished to practice his dagger's death plunge into Dodinel's incisive questioning mouth. Yet, deep down he was thankful that his companion had offered his body as the duke's double. Lot was especially glad he had taken the time to work through each possible scenario.

Without further thought, Lot reached for his stallion, grabbing the reins he pulled the horse to its knees, and then on its side. With the horse's saddle nudging close to Gorlois' side, Lot rolled the giant of a man onto the stallion's back. Undoing a long delicate strip of linen he had hidden under his tunic, Lot tied one end loosely around the duke's left wrist. He then snaked the strip under his stallion's neck, tying the other end to the duke's right wrist. Taking great care not to bloody himself—Lot coaxed the charger to its feet—steadying the duke until the horse regained its footing. Pulling the hood to the blue cloak over the duke's head, Lot let out four sharp owl hoots and waited patiently for the battle horn to blow.

At the first hint of daybreak, Lot heard the sound he had been waiting for. A single blast from Dodinel's horn, coupled with a loud roar of men and the thunder of a thousand horses hooves. Holding tightly to the duke's roan, Lot slapped the backside of his stallion, sending horse and rider into the raging battle below. He knew in the confusion of the early morning combat that the flimsy strips of linen would shred, causing the duke to plummet from the saddle, die a hero, a casualty of war. *Oh, how I am going to miss that stallion.*

When he was certain the duke had made his way onto the killing field, Lot mounted the roan and leisurely rode down the opposite hillside. He felt no regrets for his actions. Remorse was reserved for lesser men. He was of royal birth; in his mind a justification of un-noble deeds performed for the preservation and betterment of the nobility.

"Nentres, ride to Dodinel. Have him join us."

"Did all go as planned?" Meleagant queried.

"Yes, my friend, we have given our support to the High King." Lot leaned forward in his saddle, casually wiping his hands on his mount's mane, eliminating any residual remnants of blood. Pulling on his gloves of the finest black leather, he concealed what could not be removed.

"Come," Meleagant commanded of Phoenix, as the dog licked at the bloody sole of Lot's boot.

"He has a good nose. He will be an asset to you on both battle and hunting fields."

Lot's nonchalant, cynical manner caused Meleagant's hands to shake, and trickles of sweat to drip from his brow. A sudden flash of hidden memories caused him to involuntarily pull back on the reins, causing his horse's head to flail. Panic flooded his mind and body, followed by a strong impulse to flee—an irrational notion that he could escape the past by escaping the present. Beneath him the ground began to tremor as another haunting long blast from the battle horn echoed. He relaxed—relinquishing himself once again into the psychological hold of the dark prince before him.

"It is done," Nentres shouted, as he pulled his mount short.

"While Uther's troops are advancing upon Gorlois' men from the front, our cavalry are pressing in from the back...taking his men by surprise. It will be a bloody, yet swift victory for the High King," Dodinel added, as he reined in his horse next to Nentres.

"Well done, men," Lot commended. "We still have one more task at hand before this day ends. May the gods favor us with continued inclement weather." Into the mist the four men galloped past the guard, the skin on his neck torn and grisly. Romping after the group in joyous abandonment, the deerhound followed, licking blood from his muzzle.

***

"What is keeping them?" Uther scowled as he searched the road for movement.

"They will be here as soon as possible." Merlin had dismounted and was tightening his saddle's girth.

"Not soon enough." Uther growled, as he adjusted the clasp to the sea blue cape. His irritation growing with each advancing hour spent waiting. "Something has gone wrong."

"I assure you, I would have known if something had gone wrong." Above him the hawk soared. Lifting his arm, she glided onto his outstretched hand. "See, we have advanced notice, they are in sight." As Merlin's words fell, the sound of rapid horse hooves thundered toward them. Phoenix bounded about, causing Merlin to scramble onto his gray. Their actions caused the hawk to take flight, finding refuge within nearby tree branches.

"Your Majesty, we bring good news," Lot shouted. "Gorlois is no longer a threat to the kingdom, nor is his army. The ruler of the sea, rules no more." As he spoke the midmorning fog began to clear and the sun shone bright through the treetops.

"Good news indeed." Uther laughed nervously, looking up into the heavens. Turning his attention from Lot, he added, "Merlin, my men have done all they can do. Now it is up to you. Call upon your father to grant us help in completing our quest."

Merlin bristled at the implication of his parentage. Yet, he knew that Uther was aware of the growing powers he held over the elements, which increased with each visit to Stonehenge. With a sigh, Merlin closed his eyes and lifted his arms skyward. A string of chants flowed from his lips, first softly, then with a powerful rhythm. From the east, dark clouds rolled overhead gaining momentum as they headed in a northwesterly manner. Over the sea castle bright strikes of lightning danced, followed by cracks of thunder.

"Your Majesty," Lot called out as he trotted the roan to Uther's side, untying the helmet from the horse's saddle. "Do not forget your guise."

Tossing the reins to Lot, Uther dismounted his black stallion. He paused for a moment before putting the helmet upon his head.

The lingering scent of Gorlois momentarily unsettled his nerves, and he felt his stomach turn as he pulled the visor shut. Upon mounting the roan, Lot relinquished Gorlois' gloves to him. The stretched and worn leather made them an awkward fit, causing Uther to curl his fingers tightly in an attempt to keep them from slipping off.

"Not exactly what you are used to wearing, Your Majesty." Lot did his best to keep the moment light. "Even in close proximity the glamour of the duke has settled upon you. Gorlois' Tintagel guards will be easily fooled."

"The ring? Where is the duke's ring?" Even muffled, Uther's voice rang out with authority.

"When I left the duke, there was no ring upon his hand." Lot looked directly into Uther's eyes as he spoke.

"Dressed in Gorlois' hooded cloak, helmet, gloves and astride his warhorse, you shall have no need for the duke's ring for passage into Tintagel's inner chambers," Merlin said with equal authority.

The sky grew black as the group rode within the castle's mainland passageway. A sudden strike of lightning illuminated the massive stone citadel sitting upon the equally massive stone jetting upward from the sea. With only slight persuasion, the first guard granted them access to the long narrow walkway that bridged land to stone. In single file they carefully rode. Far below, the waves crashed hungry upon the rocks; spraying a salty mist upward, beckoning the travelers to misstep.

When they reached the island entrance to the castle, Merlin eyed Uther carefully for any flaws in the deception. How easily Uther had slipped into Gorlois' skin. Merlin smiled inwardly, taking note how well the High King played his part: slouching over the roan's withers, grasping the reins tightly exposing the duke's gloved hands, teetering ever so slightly in the saddle. The distinctive cloak and the helmet's shut visor, only added to the illusion. Coupled with a sudden downpour, Merlin was confident in the mastery of their betrayal.

"Halt! Who goes there?" The inner castle guard was proving Merlin's predictions erroneous.

"Move out of the way, Gurcant, before I run you through." Pointing to the slumped-over rider behind him, Lot added, "Are you blind man? Can't you see the duke is seriously injured?" Lot, who had taken the lead, stared into the face of the guard. He knew a moment like this would come, it always did, and he was prepared. During his recent spring campaign to the southwestern shores, Lot had made it a point to get to know each of the duke's men on a first name basis.

"My lord commanded that none should pass without positive identity, including his lordship. I repeat…" Gurcant pressed on, "…who rides with you?"

"My men and a physician," Lot snapped, as he reached for the hilt of his sword, daring the guard to give him a reason to use it.

Without further discussion, Gurcant took several steps back, bowed, and allowed the riders room to pass.

Drenched, cold and exasperated, Lot pressed his knees hard into Uther's stallion's side, pulling back on the reins. The horse reared, the front hooves barely grazing the guard's head.

Taking up the rear, Merlin peered from under the hood of his cloak, and was surprised to view only a handful of guards left behind to protect the castles precious contents. As the party reached the keep's entrance, two men rushed out: one old and barely able to traverse the steps, the other in his early twenties—who flew to the duke's side.

"My lord, are you alright?" the younger man was visibly shaken, his words filled with concern.

"Leave him be," Lot commanded as he dismounted, pushing the man aside. "The duke wishes to be taken directly to Lady Igraine's room."

"Take care of our horses," Merlin addressed the young man, in a firm but gentle tone.

Lot nodded to Dodinel and Nentres, who rushed to his aide; supporting the ghost of Gorlois on either side, they half-pulled, half-carried the despondent figure into the castle. Lot led his men up the long stairwell and through the dark, dank hallways. Merlin followed the makeshift parade. Meleagant and his monster of a dog stood vigil below in the great hall.

Reaching their destination, Merlin casually leaned into the stone wall of the hallway, doing what he always did best, concealing his presence. In curious anticipation, he watched as Lot knocked on Lady Igraine's door. Within moments it flew open. Igraine stood in a thin white shift; her long hair cascading down her shoulders: face pale, eyes red from tears.

"My lady, the duke has been seriously injured," pushing the door fully open, Lot motioned for Nentres and Dodinel to bring the false duke into her chambers. Laying Uther upon her bed, Lot bent down and removed the helmet. He expected Igraine to react in horror at the site of the High King masquerading as her husband, and was at first confused and then amused at her casual response. Logically, he knew she had left behind the duke's cloak, but for reasons he could not understand, he did not believe that she was part of the conspiracy to murder her husband. Then the reality struck—*by the gods—she truly was part of the plan all along.*

"You may take your leave, and your payment," her words were cold and commanding as she guided the young men out of her chamber. The door slammed shut behind them; the latch locking their entrance back into her sanctuary.

"What kind of mother willingly gives her children away?" Dodinel asked, shaking his head, addressing his question to no one in particular.

"The kind of woman who will bear a king," Merlin's words flowed sweet and gentle from his hiding place across the hallway.

"It is a poor excuse for a mother to exchange two good children in hopes for a better one," Dodinel continued, ignoring Lot's irritated stare.

"Nentres, take Dodinel downstairs. Remember, no witnesses," Lot smirked and looked to Merlin as he spoke.

Merlin's face burned. He took a step toward Lot to challenge him in a final confrontation. Before he could reach his intended target, gleeful girlish laughter rang out. Suddenly, Merlin's path was blocked by a dashing figure, her black hair flowing wildly.

"Sir Lot, you have returned to me unharmed." Morgause ran past Merlin, jumping into Lot's open arms. Pressing her body close to his, she covered his blushing face with tiny kisses.

"I see you are dressed for travel." Embarrassed, Lot disengaged Morgause, holding her at arms length. "Did you do as I asked?"

"But of course." Morgause stared into Lot's ebony eyes. Her expression betrayed the annoyance she felt at the very thought of him questioning her obedience. "All our belongings have been secretively taken aboard your ship that awaits us in the inlet. The ship carrying the flag of the Orkney Isles," she added proudly.

"Have you said your farewells?" Lot inquired as he removed his glove, running his fingers across the silken skin of her cheek.

"You are injured," Morgause's eyes grew wide as she examined his hand, unaware that the dried flakes of blood belonged to her father.

"It is nothing," Lot insisted as he pulled his hand away, quickly gloving the evidence of his deceit. "Get your sister; we need to depart with haste." Turning her around, he playfully slapped her on the bottom as she dashed toward her sister's chambers.

"How can you live with yourself?"

"Merlin, I forgot you were there." Lot gave out a deep throaty laugh. "To answer your question, I live very well within this skin. Can you say the same for yourself?"

"I have never committed murder."

"We are not that different." Lot suddenly grew serious. "We are both motivated by our own greed, our lust for power, the creation of our own moral code."

"I am nothing like you."

"Is this beautiful day not all your doing?" As Lot spoke, a bolt of lightning struck, illuminating the hallway through the arrow slits. A sudden gust of wind caused a sheet of rain to pour onto the floor. Nearby thunder cracked loud and deadly. "I dare you to deny that you are not the mastermind behind the killing of the duke, the father of my beloved. Try to escape the knowledge that you are directly responsible for the slaughter of hundreds of innocent men; British men, our kinsmen."

Merlin, a loss for words, turned pale as he once more pressed against the wall for support.

"All for what?" Lot sneered, "So that you can take from the High King something that you shall never have of your own—*a son*!" Lot laughed as he continued to drive his point home. "Morgause has told me of your plot to turn their mother against them. Giving Uther hope that by killing their father and marrying their mother, he will gain an heir. When in reality, it is you who hopes to gain everything."

"You are an ignorant fool," Merlin bemoaned, closing his eyes tightly, doing his best to block Lot's words. In agony he screamed, "We are nothing alike."

"But, of course, you are right." This time Lot stepped into the shadows. "We *are* nothing alike. I only obey orders to kill. You, on the other hand, are the creator of the orders that *I obey*."

"No, I don't want to go," Morgan's protests drowned the storm that raged between the two men, and the one that raged outside the castle. Her high-pitched whine radiated along the stone wall as Morgause dragged her younger sister down the hallway.

"Morgan, it is time for you to grow up." Morgause hugged her sister tightly. "Our father is dead." She glared accusingly at Merlin, "Our mother has abandoned us. We are no longer welcome in our father's castle, our home. We have worn out our usefulness."

"But, what shall become of us?"

"I will be married to the future King of the Orkney Isles." Morgause smiled lovingly to Lot. "I shall become Queen of the Isles, and bare my husband many children—all boys!"

Merlin opened his eyes and shut them as quickly when he realized that it was true, Morgause had also inherited an insight into the future.

"What of me?" Morgan licked the tears as they flowed down her cheeks.

"Our dear cousin, the Lady of the Lake, shall take you to live with her in Avalon." Morgause wiped her sister's nose on the sleeve of her gown. "You remember Avalon? You will be trained to become a great Lady of the Lake."

"Like our mother?"

"No, nothing like our mother," Morgause smirked.

Meleagant's hysterical laughter preceded his words as he ran up the stairs. "We have done it again, Lot. No, witnesses! No, witnesses!"

Morgan's tears began to flow once more, this time accompanied by frantic screams. Morgause pulled her sister into her, covering Morgan's eyes to shelter her from the gruesome sight.

Meleagant, drenched in blood, bounced off the walls, collapsing in a heap on the floor, his eyes wide and wild. Rushing after him—Dodinel, Nentres, and an elated Phoenix. The dog's muzzle was once more red from a fresh kill. The massive paws, from the sanguinary act, left blood-spattered prints on the stone walkway as the deerhound playfully romped about his master.

"What is going on here?"

Merlin came fully alert to his surroundings at the aura of his mother as she emerged from the girls' room.

"Get that crazed boy and beast out of here. Clean them up and get them aboard the ship." She turned to Lot. "What are your intentions toward those two?"

"I plan to leave them at the port in South Wales," a bewildered Lot answered. "Dodinel will escort Meleagant, and his hound, home from Caerdydd."

"Not those two, you fool," she sighed with exasperation. "Have your intentions changed toward the duke's girls?"

"They have stayed the same, my lady," Lot stammered. "I shall marry Morgause on our journey to my homeland. The ship's captain has already agreed to the ceremony." Pausing for a reply that did not come, he swallowed hard and continued, "As per our previous conversation, I have made arrangements for you and Morgan to be left off at a port of your choosing. Nentres will accompany you until you reach your desired destination." He held his breath, waiting for her approval.

"I can see that Ingraine's daughters will be in good hands. Take the girls and leave me alone with Merlin—we have matters of importance to discuss."

With a sweeping bow, Lot picked up a sniffling Morgan, cradling her in his arms. A pouting Morgause clutched his arm, shuffling close to his side. The sound of their footsteps lingered in the hallway long after they had departed.

"Are you prepared?"

"As prepared as any man can be." Merlin was both drawn to and repelled by his mother.

"I have provided you with the knowledge of the ancients. It is up to you to use it wisely." She stood closely, taking his hand into hers.

"Mother, you gave me life. For that I am in your debt." His tone was cold, void of emotions, and he stood frozen, refusing to respond to her affections.

"Pay no heed to Lot's ranting."

"His words, although cutting, were true. I am not like him, I am worse than him." Merlin blinked back the tears. "Lot's hands wear the dried blood of an innocent man. Yes, Gorlois was prone to atrocities, yet his crimes were never so great that he be condemned to be murdered. Yet, it is the blood of the innocent multitudes that invisibly stain mine." Pulling away from his mother, Merlin splayed his hands under her face.

"No man is immortal. For those who died on this day, it was merely their time." She took his hands once more into her own, placing a kiss upon each palm.

"How can you be so callous?" Merlin's remorse turned to anger, as he once more pulled away from his mother's clutches. "Is one unborn man's soul worth the death and destruction of so many? How can this day be justified?"

"Only the future writers of history can fully answer that question." Refusing to give up, she placed a gentle kiss upon his forehead. Standing back slightly, she opened her arms, offering him an embrace.

"Fighting in the name of freedom has too high a price." Merlin sighed as he leaned into the comfort of his mother's arms.

"The cost of not fighting is even higher. Remember, you have taken an oath for all eternity, an unbreakable oath as Britain's guardian."

"Can I be held accountable for an oath I took as a child?" His eyes pleaded for an answer as he gazed into her face.

"You have proven your accountability time and time again." She cradled Merlin gently in her arms. "Through your actions, this night, in that room," she said, as her eyes wandered to Igraine's bedchamber, "Britain's greatest treasure will be created. His life will be in your hands. You are the kingmaker; his mind, body and spirit are yours to mold. His name shall be Arthur. Like you, a son of Avalon. The stories of his life deeds will be legendary. *That*, my son, is your noble purpose for this grand day!"

***

Outside, the earth rumbled, as a lightning bolt dashed through the nearby arrow slot, dancing across the stone floor. An eerie silence followed—broken by a hawk's cry.

LORDS, LADIES AND BEASTS

The Lords and Ladies

Aglovale: Knight and eldest son of King Pellinore.

Ambrosius: High King of Britain. Son of High King Constantine. Middle brother of Constans and Uther. At the age of five, Ambrosius and his younger brother, Uther, were raised, in Brittany, by their cousin, King Budic I. When they reached their early twenties, they regained their rightful place on the throne of Britain. Merlin was Ambrosius' prophet, advisor, and protégé.

Arden: Merlin's foster father. Married to Enid. In his prime, he was a great knight in the service of King Bors. In his twilight years, he left the king's court in Gannes to work as an apple farmer in Caerfyrddin, Wales.

Arrok: Uthur's knight who fought at the Danebury hill fort battle.

Ban: King of Banoic, Brittany. Brother to King Bors, and uncle to Lionel. Father to Lancelot and Hector de Maris. Married to Helen.

Bedivere: Young knight fostered at Sir Ector's villa in the Forest Sauvage, Cornwall. He is the future companion of Arthur.

Bors the Elder: King of Gannes. He is also brother to King Ban of Banoic, Brittany. He fathered two sons, Bors the Younger and Lionel.

Bors the Younger: Eldest son of King Bors the Elder of Gannes. Older brother to Lionel.

Brastias: Knight, Warden of Trisantona. Fought alongside Uther.

Brydw: Illegitimate son of the High King, Vortigern. Member of the Young Royal Guard. Half brother to Faustus.

Budic I: King of Brittany. Nephew to Britain's High King, Constantine. Raised Constantine's young sons, Ambrosius and Uther. He had two sons, Meliau (who succeeded him as Brittany's king) and Riwal.

Carados: King of Estrangorre. Fought alongside Uther and Ambrosius.

Clariance: King of Northumberland. Fought alongside Uther.

Clarisant: Daughter of a Londinium baker.

Constans: High King of Britain. Eldest son of Constantine. Brother to Ambrosius Aurelius, and Uther. Murdered by his advisor, Vortigern.

Constantine: High King of Britain. Fathered three sons: Constans, Ambrosius and Uther. Constans, his eldest son preceded him as Britain's High King. Uncle to King Budic of Brittany.

Dodinel: Son of King Belinant of Sugales. Also known as The Boar. Friend of Lot and Nentres. Member of the Young Royal Guard.

Dornar: Prince and knight of Uther's court. Second eldest son of King Pellinore. Fought in battle against Duke Gorlois.

Ector: Knight and nobleman who rules within the Forest Sauvage, Cornwall. Cai's father. Future foster parent to young Arthur.

Edol: Earl of Gloucester. Lone survivor of the Night of the Long Knives, where over three hundred British Royals were slaughtered by the Saxon warlord, Hengist.

Elivri: Ambrosius and Uther's head groom and silversmith. Close friend to Lionel.

Enid: Merlin's foster mother. Arden's wife. She discovered Merlin as a newborn in a charred oak tree near their orchard in Caerfyrddin, Wales.

Faustus: Illegitimate son of the High King, Vortigern. Eldest member of the Young Royal Guard. Half brother to Brydw.

Gorlois: Duke of Cornwall. Resides in Tintagel. Husband to Igraine. Father to Morgause and Morgan. Declared war upon Uther.

Hengist: Saxon warlord. Led Saxon invasion of Britain. Collaborated with High King Vortigern, including betrothing his youngest daughter, Rowena, in wedlock to the Britain's aging High King. Initiated the infamous slaughter of British Royalty on the Night of the Long Knives.

Igraine: Wife of Gorlois, the Duke of Cornwall. Mother to Morgause and Morgan. First cousin to the Lady of the Lake. Second cousin to Merlin. Resides in Tintagel. Love interest of Uther. Mother of Arthur.

Lady of the Lake: Fairy High Priestess of Avalon. Merlin's mother. First cousin to Igraine of Tintagel. Love interest to High King Ambrosius. May Queen at Ambrosius' coronation.

Leodegrance: King of Cameliard. Father to Guinevere. One of the Royal witnesses at Ambrosius' coronation.

Lionel: Prince and knight. Son of King Bors the Elder of Gannes. Merlin's trusted friend and closet companion. Member of the Young Royal Guard.

Nimue: Young priestess of Avalon. Love interest of Merlin.

Mark: King of Cornwall. Resides in Castle Dore, in Fowey.

Meleagant: Son of King Bagdemagus of Gorre. One of the youngest members of the Young Royal Guard. Close friend of Lot. Slowly driven insane by results relating to *The Plan*!

Merlin: Mystical son of the Lady of the Lake. Arden and Enid were his foster parents. Advisor and boy prophet to three High Kings: Vortigern, Ambrosius, and Uther. Sworn protector of Britain. Close friend to Lionel. Infatuated with Nimue. Possesses forward memories. Doomsday forecaster to Vortigern, boy prophet to Ambrosius, and battle advisor to Uther.

Nentres: Prince of the kingdom of Garlot in Alba. Also known as The Dove. Friend of Lot and Nentres. Member of the Young Royal Guard.

Pellinore: King of the Listinoise Isles. Pellinore is a father figure to Ambrosius and Uther. He is the father of eight sons and one daughter: Sir Aglovale, Sir Dornar, Sir Tor, Sir Lamorak, Sir Percival, Driant, Alan, Melodiam, and daughter Elaine. Of the Royal line of Joseph of Arimathea.

Lot: Prince of the Isles of Orkney. Leader of the Young Royal Guard. Ally to Uther, and adversary to Merlin. Served under three High Kings: Vortigern, Ambrosius, and Uther.

Morgan: Youngest daughter of Gorlois, the Duke of Cornwall and his wife, Igraine.

Morgause: Oldest daughter of Gorlois, the Duke of Cornwall and his wife, Igraine. Love interest of Sir Lot.

Rowena: Youngest daughter of the Saxon leader Hengist. She was Vortigern's second wife, and was forced into marriage as a military tactical maneuver by her father.

Ulfius: Knight, who fought alongside Uther and Ambrosius.

Uriens: King of Rheged. Fought alongside Uther and Ambrosius. Future husband to Arthur's half-sister Morgan.

Uther: High King of Britain. Son of High King Constantine. Youngest brother of Constans and Ambrosius. At the age of four, he and his brother, Ambrosius, were raised, in Brittany by their cousin, King Budic I, until they reached their early twenties and regained their rightful place on the throne of Britain. Succeeded his brother, Ambrosius, as Britain's High King. Merlin was his prophet of war and rival for his brother's attentions. Uther was infatuated with Igraine, the wife of Duke Gorlois.

Vortigern: High King of Britain. Was instrumental in the death of Britain's High King Constantine. Upon the king's demise, Vortigern became advisor to the High King's eldest son and heir, Constans. He conspired to have the young king murdered, and seized Britain's crown as the new High King. Vortigern trained many young knights, and created the Young Royal Guard. He had one legitimate son, Vortimer, and two known illegitimate sons: Faustus and Brydw. Just before his death, he married Rowena, the Saxon leader, Hengist, youngest daughter.

Vortimer: Vortigern's eldest and only legitimate son.

Young Royal Guard: Established by High King Vortigern. Consisted of Lot (the group's leader), Nentres, Dodinel, Faustus, Brydw, and later Lionel.

The Beasts

Black Horses: Renown for their size and endurance. Uther bred the infamous black warhorses for Ambrosius' cavalry.

Phoenix: Puppy found in the ashes of the Danebury hill fort after the battle. Given to Meleagant by Uther.

Merlin's Hawk: The Lady of the Lake's mystical hawk and Merlin's guardian.

Merlin's Mare: Merlin's gray, mystical pony with fairy blood.

PLACES

Alba: (Scotland) Land above Hadrian's Wall.

Avalon: Island of mystical properties with various unknown locations.

Banoic: (Brittany) Northwestern peninsula of France. Kingdom of King Ban.

Bodmin Moor: Located southeast of Tintagel, in northern Cornwall.

Caerfyrddin: (Carmarthen) Wales. Merlin's birthplace. Home of Merlin's foster parents, Enid and Arden.

Cameliard: Kingdom of King Leodegrance, Guinevere's father.

Cornwall: Region of southwestern Britain. King Mark's kingdom. Location of Tintagel, Castle Dore, Bodmin Moor, and the Forest Sauvage.

Danebury: Hill fort near Nether Wallop, where High King Vortigern married his young Saxon bride, Rowena.

Dore: Castle in Fowey. Residence of King Mark.

Dubris: (Dover) Southeastern point of Britain, and site of the Saxon invasion.

Estrangorre: (Norfolk) Kingdom of King Carados

Forest Sauvage: Protective forest surrounding Sir Ector's villa. Safe haven where young Arthur will be raised.

Gannes:(Northern France) Also known as Gaul. Kingdom of King Bors the Elder, and sons Bors the Younger, and Lionel.

Garlot: (Lothian) Alba. Kingdom of Prince Nentres.

Gorre: (Area surrounding Bath) Kingdom of King Bagdemagus of Gorre, and Prince Meleagant.

Hadrian's Wall: Stone and turf fortification wall constructed in the 2nd century by Roman Emperor Hadrian. Dividing Britain and Alba (Scotland), the wall was built to prevent raids by the Picts.

Listinoise: (Anglesey) Northwest Wales. King Pellinore's kingdom.

Londinium: (London) Main quarters of Ambrosius and Uther.

> **Amphitheatre**: Site of Ambrosius coronation in Londinium.
>
> **Basilica**: Ambrosius' working headquarters in Londinium.
>
> **Fort**: Training area of Uther's armies in Londinium.
>
> **Druid Temple**: Druid's temple. Across the river from Londinium.
>
> **Forum**: Marketplace in Londinium. Attached to the basilica.
>
> **Governor's Palace**: Ambrosius living quarters in Londinium.
>
> **Roman Baths**: Main bathhouse in Londinium.

Mount Erith: (Beddgelert) Wales. Vortigern's northern stronghold.

Northumberland: Northeastern region of Britain. Kingdom of King Clariance.

Orkney Islands: Group of small islands north of Alba (Scotland). Kingdom of Prince Lot.

Rheged: Kingdom of Uriens, in northeast Britain.

Sugales: (Dyfed) Wales. Kingdom of King Belinant, and his son Prince Dodinel.

Stonehenge: Ancient stone megalithic ruins, also known as the Dancing Stones. Located on the Salisbury Plain. Sacred place with mystical powers. Surrounded by prehistoric burial barrows of royals.

Tintagel: Castle atop a jutting slate peninsula located on the northwestern Cornwall coast. Residence of Duke Gorlois of Cornwall, and his wife Igraine. Future birthplace of Arthur.

Trisantona: (Trent) Kingdom that Sir Brastias was appointed Warden.

ABOUT AUTHOR

Dee Marie is an award-winning author, photographer and artist. She has a vast knowledge of Arthurian Legends, with a reference library that is overflowing with British, Celtic, and Druid history.

Research for her *Sons of Avalon* series also included a visit to Britain, where she was privileged to walk within the inner circle of Stonehenge, embracing the Dancing Stones on the Salısbury Plain. While in Cornwall, she explored the moors surrounding Bodmin, and ambled upon the ancient ruins of Tintagel.

Former Managing Editor, and later Editor-in-Chief, of an internationally published computer graphic magazine, when not writing novels, she supplements her time working as a freelance journalist. Dee Marie currently lives in Upstate New York, and is completing her second novel in the *Sons of Avalon* series.

***

The author invites you to continue your journey—visit the *Sons of Avalon* website: www.sonsofavalon.com